Antoine

The Falsifiers

Translated by Howard Curtis

ISBN-13: 9781549800986

For Laure, my little princess

PART ONE

Reykjavík

"Congratulations, my boy," Gunnar Eriksson said, watching me sign my contract. "Now you're one of us."

I put my copy of the contract away in my bag, pleased once again with the turn that events had taken lately. Two weeks earlier, I had been on the verge of accepting an offer to become the assistant export manager of a canning factory in Siglufjördhur (population: 1,815, not including bears). The recruitment officer had boasted about how dynamic the industry was and how it was likely to develop in the future, while stressing that I should not be put off by the wretched salary, given that the opportunities to spend it were practically non-existent.

Both my mother and the careers officer at the University of Reykjavík, from which I had recently graduated, had urged me to accept: such an offer, they said, might not come around again in a hurry. It was true that at that time—September 1991—the job market wasn't exactly encouraging to a twenty-three-year-old geography graduate. The first Gulf War had plunged the world economy into recession, and companies were more likely to be hiring restructuring experts than geologists or cartographers.

Fortunately, the morning of the day I had set myself as a deadline for my decision, I had come across an ad that could have been written for me. "Environmental consultancy seeks project manager. Degree required in geography, economics or biology. Can be first or second job. Based in Reykjavík, but travel involved. Competitive salary. Please apply to Gunnar Eriksson, Director of Operations, Baldur, Furuset & Thorberg."

Determined to seize the opportunity, I went in person to the address indicated, taking my resume with me. Much to my surprise, the receptionist sent for Gunnar Eriksson, who agreed to see me immediately. I gladly accepted, although I had to apologize for the way I was dressed, which was hardly appropriate for a job interview.

"Pah," Eriksson retorted, gesturing to me to follow him. "I don't care about your clothes any more than I care about my first aurora borealis."

It was a surprising remark from someone who clearly paid as much attention to his clothes as he did. I've never seen someone so well dressed and at the same time so consistently sloppy. If ever I were to wear monogrammed shirts, I thought, I'd make sure they didn't hang out of my pants.

Eriksson led me to his office. To judge by the view of Reykjavík harbor from its window, it was clear that the post of Director of Operations was more than merely honorary. Oak paneling, restful lighting, thick carpets, even a fireplace: this was luxury, Icelandic style. Eriksson sat down in an elegant brown armchair of artfully worn leather and motioned to me to do the same.

"You may be wondering what we actually do here," he began. "Do you want the plain version or the flowery one?"

"Both, I suppose," I replied, somewhat thrown by this introduction.

"Let's start with the official version, the one you'll find in our brochure. Every new infrastructure project is backed up by one or more environmental studies. Before anyone can build a dam, lay a road or divert a river, the possible impact on the ecosystem has to be considered. The developer has to be able to guarantee to the community that the work will respect the flora and fauna and even sometimes the local demographic balance. Are you following me?"

"So far, one hundred percent."

"Of course, the studies we produce are not an end in themselves," he went on. "Usually they're just the starting point for full and fruitful discussions between the developers, the governments and the environmental associations." He broke off and gave me a crafty look. "Wonderful, isn't it? Let's see if you can fill in the rest of the picture."

I thought for a few moments, pulling at my lower lip with my fingers. Eriksson's introduction seemed to allow for only one possible conclusion.

"Well," I said, "I assume that if the report flags up any risks to the environment, the developer will either have to pay to adapt his project, or else quite simply abandon it."

"You see, you got it. We didn't need the flowery version. If the promoter wants his construction permit, he'll have to fork out. The exact nature of what he has to do takes different forms every time and never ceases to surprise me: sometimes he has to make a commitment to reintroduce brown bears into the mountains, sometimes he's asked to provide financial support to redevelop farms that were quite likely to fail in the not too distant future anyway. I've even heard it said that some elected representatives ask him to transfer large sums of money to numbered Swiss bank accounts, but I find that hard to believe." Eriksson was keeping an eye open for my reaction as he said this.

"And does your consultancy support practices like that?" I asked, cursing myself inwardly for sounding so priggish.

"Oh, no!" Eriksson exclaimed comically, his hand on his heart. "Our competitors, yes, but not Baldur, Furuset & Thorberg. No, seriously, we obey very strict ethical rules. The profession has even adopted a code, so you see, we have clean hands. And don't worry, the little game I've described is always conducted in an eminently respectable manner. You'd be surprised, for example, at the number of people who take an interest in our work. Elected representatives, industrialists, town planners: they all want to know our opinion, if possible before we put it down in writing. It's their way of trying to influence us to shift the balance in their favor. Generally speaking, it's always those who have the most to gain or to lose who talk the loudest. We listen to what they have to say—after all, it's our job to gather facts and opinions—but we never tell them what we're really thinking. I hope you can keep a secret?"

"Yes, I think so," I replied.

"You're not the kind of person to gossip, are you?" Eriksson insisted.

"Definitely not." I might have added that having only one sister, six years older than me, and having lost my father when I was very young, I'd been spared the temptation to indulge in idle chatter.

"Good for you. Now, what did you learn at the University of Reykjavík? It's a good school, isn't it? One of our partners, Furuset, obtained his doctorate there. You probably weren't even born yet."

For a few minutes, I did all I could to make my course appear more impressive than it really had been. To be honest, the specialization I had chosen in my fourth year—territorial conflicts— was not much of a preparation for working on environmental studies, but that didn't seem to bother Eriksson. He soon shifted away from academia and started bombarding me with questions about current events, eliciting my opinion on subjects as varied as the Palestinian conflict, the breakup of the Soviet Union, or what advantage Iceland might gain in joining the European Community.

Then we talked about myself, my hobbies, my love of travel, my country roots (I come originally from Húsavík, a small fishing village in the north of Iceland where my mother raises sheep). Eriksson never took my first answers at face value, but kept spurring me on to reveal more, regularly making incisive, almost brutal comments. At first a little shaken by this unusual treatment, I decided to give as good as I got and tell the truth—not the flowery version.

After two hours, Eriksson dismissed me, making me promise that I would return the following day for a second interview. I was so excited that I couldn't even wait until I got home: I called the canning factory in Siglufjördhur from a phone booth and turned down its wonderful offer.

The second interview was followed by a third with the Human Resources Officer, then by a fourth with Furuset, who came across as almost excessively friendly, and finally by an endless session of psychological tests. Eriksson then made me a firm offer, including a salary that exceeded my expectations by a good third. In the meantime, I had made inquiries and had been able to verify that the consultancy was considered one of the best in Europe and had clients throughout the world.

And now I was entering officially into active life as a project manager with Baldur, Furuset & Thorberg. I was as happy as a king.

"Well," Eriksson said, "now that everything's sorted, what would you say to a little tour of the offices?"

"I'd like that," I said following him. This time, it was not his shirt that was badly adjusted, but his belt, with one loop out of two neglected.

"The firm occupies two floors," Eriksson declaimed as if addressing a lecture theater. "We're on the fourth floor here, the fifth is given over to research and records. On the left, the offices of the partners. They aren't here at the moment. Furuset is in Germany, Baldur in Denmark. As for Thorberg, you won't see him around here very often: he's retiring next year and spends every afternoon on the golf course. On the right, accounts and administration. Seven people in all, I'll introduce you later."

At the end of a corridor, we came to a vast open-plan office.

"This is where the marketing people hang out. There are four of them."

Three heads turned in our direction. The fourth belonged to a pretty blonde who raised her hand in greeting even though she was in the middle of a phone call.

"Only four?" I said in surprise. "That doesn't seem much for a firm employing a hundred people."

"Ninety-four to be precise. But you're right, our sales force isn't very large. That said, we're not selling ballpoint pens. The smallest contract involves hundreds of thousands of dollars. Plus, as you'll soon realize, the marketing people are not the only ones involved in selling: the project managers also have a role to play. If the client is pleased with their work, they need to press home their advantage, lay it on thick if need be."

"I don't know if I'd be able to do that."

"Of course you will," Eriksson replied, tucking his shirt back in his pants (his explanation had been accompanied by some wild gestures that had once again spoiled his appearance). "You'll see, you'll just have to get used to it. It soon becomes second nature. Now, let's go back to my office. I already have something for you."

I was pleased to see those brown leather armchairs again. Eriksson grabbed a blue folder that was lying on a coffee table and sat down beside me.

"We won this contract last week," he began. "It's the perfect job to cut your teeth on."

"What is it?"

"A new water purification plant that the state of Greenland is planning to build at Sisimiut."

"I thought the population of Greenland had been stagnant for years," I said. "Why do they need a new plant?"

Gunnar Eriksson raised his head from the folder and stared at me.

"A good comment," he said. "Clearly, I was right about you. To answer your question, they already have a plant at Nuuk, a little further south, but a breakdown last summer paralyzed the island for several weeks and put the wind up the government. Just think: all it takes is for a seal to get trapped in a pipe and the country's whole water supply system is blocked. For reasons that are as much political as sanitary—the electorate of Sisimiut is traditionally left-leaning and building a plant will provide many new jobs—the Parliament has just voted in favor of doubling the country's treatment capacity. Nobody's going to complain, and especially not Baldur, Furuset & Thorberg, which is being paid 130,000 dollars for a report detailing the environmental requirements, which will then be submitted to the companies responsible for the construction."

"It sounds interesting," I said, unable to think of a more intelligent comment than that.

From the way he looked at me, I realized that Gunnar was wondering if I was serious. My studious air seemed to reassure him.

"Don't get carried away. It's only a modest assignment, which will involve just three people for two months. I'll be supervising it personally. In practical terms, our role consists of defining the parameters of the environmental study, selecting the appropriate experts, a hydrologist and a landscape architect, and finally, of course, writing the report. Olaf Elangir, who's been with us for five years, will work with the hydrologist, and you'll assist the landscape architect, who's a German named Wolfensohn, in searching for a site that best respects the environment. We've used him before, he has exactly the right qualifications for this kind of assignment. You leave on Wednesday. The client has authorized only one-way plane tickets, so you'll be stuck in Greenland for two months. Is that a problem?"

"Not at all," I said.

"Are you sure?" Eriksson insisted. "No girlfriend who'll cut her wrists out of despair or come to my office and make a scene?"

"Nobody who can't survive my absence for two months," I said, pretending to forget that my mother had made me promise to visit her in Húsavík soon.

"Perfect. Between now and Wednesday, Olaf will have prepared for you a bit of literature about Greenland, along with a few files from records that deal with similar projects. Any questions?"

"No, it's all very clear. I can't wait to get down to work."

"And I can't wait to see you at work. We have great expectations for you, Sliv."

As I extracted myself with some difficulty from my armchair, Gunnar called his assistant Margrét and asked her to escort me to my office.

Any illusions I might have had after hearing the word "office" were soon lost when I discovered, behind a frosted glass door, a cubbyhole with a single tiny window, which did somehow, miraculously, look out on the harbor. Even though I had imagined better, especially after Gunnar's welcome, I realized that it would have been unseemly of me to complain about my work conditions.

The janitor who came to open up for me greeted me with a nod of the head, then, in a self-important tone, told me that this had been Lena Thorsen's office. I turned this name over in my mind for a few seconds. Should I have known who Lena Thorsen was? Had she been responsible for some definitive treatise on the relationship between Reykjavík and its hinterland? Luckily Margrét came to my rescue.

"Lena came from the same university as you. She was an excellent recruit, perhaps the best we've ever had. I wish you the same success."

"What became of her?" I asked. I didn't really like the air of nostalgia with which the two of them were recalling her.

"She left us last month for another, much better paid job in Germany."

Meanwhile, the janitor was trying every key in his bunch, one by one. I remember thinking that he was pretending not to find the right one, in order to postpone as long as possible the moment when I would finally violate the sanctuary of Lena Thorsen.

2

Airlines aren't exactly falling over each other to serve Greenland. At the time, only three airports (Kangerlussuaq, Thule and Narsarsuaq) had runways long enough to accommodate jet planes. That's a comparatively minor problem, though, given the even greater rarity of another resource: passengers actually wanting to go to Greenland.

It had been arranged that Hans-Peter Wolfensohn, the German landscape architect, would join us in Reykjavík. There, we would board a fragile two-engine plane, chartered by the Parliament of Greenland to take us as far as Sisimiut. During the approximately three hours of the flight, I had plenty of time to get to know Wolfensohn. He was a well-built man, with a bit of a pot belly and a thick blond beard, who reacted with great kindness when he discovered that I was only just starting in the profession.

"A beginner!" he exclaimed. "Wonderful! And you're starting with an easy assignment, that's lucky."

"What makes you say it'll be easy?"

"Just think about it. We have to make sure the new plant won't have any negative effects on the environment. By environment, we traditionally mean the flora and fauna and the population. The former first of all: do you really think Sisimiut is known for its extraordinary biodiversity? Apart from a few bears and some reindeer, there's not much that's likely to be disturbed. The flora? I don't think anything green grows on the ice field. As for the population..."

I completed the sentence for him. "You could build one plant per inhabitant and still have space."

"You said it. No, really, I'm not worried for you." With this, he grabbed a bottle of whiskey and spent a while examining the label. He must have found what he was looking for, because he filled his glass three-quarters full, leaving just enough room to add two huge ice cubes. He raised the glass as if proposing a toast.

"You should do what I do and drink while there's still time. Who knows if the Lapps are even aware of the existence of alcohol?"

I accepted his offer, omitting to point out that the Lapps live in the north of Scandinavia and have never set foot in Greenland. There was no point in alienating the sympathy of the person with whom I was going to spend twelve hours out of every twenty-four for the next two months. Wolfensohn was in fact to prove an excellent traveling companion. He spent the rest of the flight telling me about his most colorful assignments. By the time we arrived, I was convinced of two things: first, Gunnar Eriksson had put me in good hands, and second, money made the world go round in the environmental field just as it did pretty much everywhere else.

There isn't much to say about Sisimiut. If the pilot hadn't announced that we were nearing our destination, I'd never have imagined that those few shacks scattered across the ice field were the second largest town in Greenland. To my great surprise, it wasn't too cold (zero Celsius on September 10), and the pilot told us it seldom snows before September 15. "Afterwards," he said with a laugh, "it's another matter. It doesn't usually stop snowing until June 15."

We were treated to an almost official welcome. After solemnly shaking our hands, the mayor of Sisimiut ushered us into his old Volvo, which was parked at the side of the runway. Within four minutes, we were shown into our hotel rooms (welcoming, if a touch Spartan), and barely half an hour after landing, we were already going into a meeting with the municipal council. Business in Greenland is conducted briskly, so briskly, in fact, that by the end of the meeting we already knew where we stood. Nobody was really waiting to hear our conclusions. The site had been chosen a long time ago.

Over the beer that we had that evening in town (alcohol had indeed reached Greenland), Hans-Peter went so far as to say, with a touch of bitterness, that the decision had probably been made even before the vote in Parliament. Actually, we were to learn some time later that the land in question was owned by the mayor's son. The fact that it was situated right in the heart of Sisimiut, even though the plant would have been perfect for the industrial zone of Novgatir, was a matter of complete indifference to the people we were dealing with, whose main concern was how much compensation they would have to pay to expropriate the land. The leader of the council made no bones about what exactly was at stake in our report: the more we boosted the merits of locating the plant in the town, the more likely it was that Parliament would release significant funds.

I confess that all this was quite a blow to me. Even at that time, I wasn't completely stupid, and Gunnar had taken care to stress that our intervention had financial implications that it was not up to us to judge. But, even without judging, there was something shocking about the crassness and obviousness of the councilors of Sisimiut, and it stuck in my throat. In addition, the prospect of spending those two months in the land of the Eskimos suddenly seemed beyond human endurance.

Fortunately, Wolfensohn, who had seen it all before, made an effort to cheer me up. He began by pointing out the irony of the very idea of a compensation fee for the expropriation of land in a country two thirds the size of India and with a population of barely 50,000, then added: "Nobody will read our report, and we'll be paid anyway. Let's take advantage and have a good time. It isn't every day we have the opportunity to crisscross Greenland at the expense of the Princess of Denmark."

And crisscross it we did. In less than a week, we had confirmed what Hans-Peter had predicted, i.e. that the location chosen for the new plant, although it may not have been perfect, represented no danger to the environment. If there was a negative impact, the only people to feel it would be the Danish taxpayers (Greenland is officially an administrative province of Denmark), and they weren't our clients, as Gunnar remarked on the telephone when I called him to inform him of our findings.

As this important phase of our assignment was over (five weeks earlier than planned), we used a need to evaluate other locations as an excuse to do a bit of tourism. The mayor, panicking at the thought that we might discover a site with greater virtues than the center of Sisimiut, tried to dissuade us, but Hans-Peter silenced him with barely veiled threats to ask the Prime Minister to arbitrate. The mayor beat a prudent retreat and even offered to organize our trip.

We went all the way along the West Coast, a coast whose most unusual characteristic is that it expands in winter, when the Baffin Sea ices over, and shrinks in spring, when whole areas of ice break off and drift toward the coast of Canada. Aasiaat, Ilulissat, Uummannaq, Upernavik: names I had no difficulty remembering, but which Hans-Peter could never get his head around, let alone spell. We visited several canning factories, including one that did business with the company in Siglufjördhur where I had almost ended up. Even today, I sometimes think about the turn my life might have taken if I had become part of the fish canning industry.

Everywhere we went, we were treated like kings. There are few non-Inuit beyond the Arctic Circle, and even fewer who agree to share their indigenous lives for a few days (or rather, a few nights, because even at that time of the year the sun never appears for more than three or four hours at a time).

I noted with slight disappointment that the Inuit no longer live in igloos, which were hardly ever used except as temporary dwellings during their long hunting expeditions. These days they lived in small wooden houses built by the government. The men of a village situated on the Arctic Circle invited us to go with them on a seal hunt that lasted three days. I have to confess that I was naively expecting to chase seals across the ice. What I discovered was that they actually did more fishing than chasing, placing nets under the ice field, although the purists continued to cut holes in the ice and harpoon their prey through them.

I knew the North, now I was discovering the Far North. I thought I was hardened to the rigors of the winter, but now I saw laughing women confront a blizzard at -25 degrees Celsius and their children, hands and ears exposed to the air, leading herds of reindeer across the ice sheet.

The further north we went, the sparser the population. The northern half of the island is pretty much deserted, with the notable exception of the air base in Thule, built in the fifties, which houses three thousand American military personnel — 6 % of the population of Greenland.

Hearing the commanding officer boast of the contribution of his base to world climate science, one might almost forget that Thule has the most sophisticated anti-missile detection systems in the world or that the fighter planes that take off from it can reach Russia in less than two hours.

Needless to say, we were refused permission to visit the base. By way of consolation, we went on a sleigh ride through the Northeast Greenland National Park, where the ice is more than a mile thick and the last authentically Inuit villages can be found.

Even the best things come to an end. After three weeks, we had to go to Nuuk, where Gunnar Eriksson was waiting for us for the second, more official part of our assignment. We met with him at the Hans Egede Hotel, the best (the only?) hotel in town, where he had been given the finest room. He seemed horrified at the sight of our greasy hair, unkempt beards and filthy cardigans, and without further ado sent us off to take a shower and a sauna (the Icelanders almost outdo the Finns in their love of saunas). I wouldn't describe myself as a hedonist, but I must admit I enjoyed my hot shower that evening.

Nuuk has just over 13,000 inhabitants. That makes it a major metropolis by Greenlandic standards, although I would never have thought I'd one day discover a capital eight times smaller than Reykjavík. Nuuk is basically an administrative town, which houses all the official buildings of the island. Gunnar asked me to accompany him wherever he went, while Hans-Peter stayed at the hotel and wrote his report. By this stage, our meetings had only two aims: to make a final decision on the location of the purification plant and to position Baldur, Furuset & Thorberg for future lucrative assignments, or what Gunnar had once called "laying it on thick."

In the space of a week, we visited the purification plant at Nuuk, the very one whose breakdown the previous year was responsible for our being here in the first place; we met with the most important dignitary on the island, Lars Emil Johansen, who questioned me at length about my journey to Inuit country; and, last but not least, the Danish high commissioner to Greenland told us in the course of a conversation that the county of Bornholm in Denmark might well call on our services soon to decide on the route of a major new road.

Gunnar made a note of this and called the office in Reykjavík to inform the marketing manager. "They'll pay 300,000 dollars for a study," I heard him say on the telephone, "or my name isn't Gunnar Eriksson."

It was then that the first incident occurred in a long series that were to turn my life upside down. I was lying on my bed, rereading the interim report that Gunnar had passed on to me for my information and which he was preparing to submit to Parliament. I was skimming through the first pages, which dealt with the general environment, when my gaze came to rest on a particular paragraph. In it, Gunnar wrote that the inhabitants of Skjoldungen had recently abandoned cod fishing to concentrate on a far more lucrative activity: the extraction of thorium ore.

Skjoldungen is a village in the south-east of the country, just below the Gyldenloves Fjord. I had spent a night there during my sleigh ride, and I specifically remembered eating dried cod, which my host boasted of having caught the previous summer. I had in addition talked at length with his son, who spoke good English, and never once had he mentioned thorium. I called Gunnar on the hotel's internal line and commented on this. He replied that they must have provided him with the wrong information, adding that, on such a short assignment, there wasn't always time to check one's sources. He promised me that he would correct the error and told me to continue reading and inform him if I discovered any other anomalies.

A few pages later, I spotted another inaccuracy: the plant at Nuuk had been opened on March 23, 1982, and not on February 19 of the same year. I had noticed the date on the commemorative plaque at the entrance to the building, and I remembered it because it was my sister Mathilde's birthday. Gunnar took note of this second correction and that was where the matter appeared to end. Obviously, at the time, I didn't think anymore about such small errors.

A week later, Olaf Elangir and I swapped notes. Although no longer harboring any illusion as to the influence our report would have, I had made it a point of honor to qualify Wolfensohn's conclusions. Good old Hans-Peter, being the kind of expert who would never dream of biting the hand that feeds him, had spent thirty pages detailing the reasons that led him to favor locating the plant in the center of Sisimiut. Going over his work, I had been unable to stop myself from pointing out the disadvantages of such a solution. Anyone taking the trouble to read my report carefully would understand that our conclusions were dictated by considerations that had nothing to do with the environment. That was at least a modest sop to my conscience.

Olaf's hydrological report was less polemical. Admittedly, on a purely technical level, there was no great difference between building the plant at Sisimiut or at Novgatir. Either way, construction costs were so high in Greenland that any attempt to skimp on the technical aspects would have been absurd. The new plant would incorporate all the latest advances in the fields of ventilation and sewage treatment.

The only real difficulty lay in the ice, which for several months a year prevented the discharge of water treated in the traditional way. The planners had had the idea of laying pipes a long way offshore and sixty-five feet below sea level, an idea that Olaf and his hydrological expert had approved.

One detail in the report drew my attention, though. Olaf had written that the following February 19 would mark the tenth anniversary of the opening of the Nuuk plant. When I asked him what he based this on, he replied that he had found it in the general information provided by Gunnar Eriksson. My first thought was that I had made a mistake. My memory must have been playing me tricks. After our conversation, Gunnar would surely have checked the date in question. But returning to the plant at Nuuk the next day, I was able to verify that my senses had not betrayed me. There was the plaque, hanging above the reception desk, and on it were the words "On March 23, 1982, the mayor of Godthaab [the Danish name for Nuuk], Poul Effelman, opened this water purification plant in the presence of the Prime Minister of Denmark, Anker Jorgensen." I pointed out the error to Olaf, and he replied that he would make a note of it. Our assignment was coming to an end, and none of this was of any great importance.

We spent our last evening in Gunnar's suite (he had managed to have his things moved into the only suite in the hotel as soon as it had fallen vacant) finalizing our report and munching our way through sandwiches brought up by room service. As the youngest on the team, I was sitting at the computer—an ancient IBM ThinkPad—on which I was entering the final changes dictated to me by Gunnar and Olaf. Coming across the passage dealing with the plant at Nuuk, I took it upon myself to correct the mistaken date, without informing my colleagues. Toward midnight, I printed the final report and we all went off to our respective beds, Gunnar's fit for a Roman emperor, Olaf's and mine considerably more Spartan.

The presentation went off without a hitch. Everybody pretended to be surprised by our report and to drink in our words. The Prime Minister congratulated us on the significance of our work and wished us a safe journey home. The work would begin the following summer, once the construction company given the task of applying our findings had been appointed. The same two-engine plane took us back to Reykjavík that very evening. Hans-Peter Wolfensohn flew on to Bonn, making me promise that we would stay in touch. I saw him slip a bottle of whiskey in his bag, no doubt for fear of discovering that Germany had banned the import of alcohol during his absence.

3

Thinking back over my two-month assignment on the bus taking me to the office that Monday morning, my overall conclusion was positive. I hadn't really felt that I had been working, I had seen a bit of the country, and most of the people I'd met had been pleasant. The pay was good, even excellent when you considered that the firm had paid all my expenses.

The secretaries seemed genuinely delighted to see me again. It was only just 8:30 and everybody was already hard at work, as if the survival of the planet depended on our environmental studies. I remember thinking, as I opened the door to my cubbyhole, that I had made the right choice and that I was going to stay with Baldur, Furuset & Thorberg for quite a while.

My euphoria was short-lived. On my desk lay a copy of the report we had submitted to Parliament. In it, Gunnar had slipped a card bearing the words: "I hope that this first assignment has left you with good memories. This report owes a great deal to you." He didn't know how right he was. There beneath the business card, which I knew immediately had been deliberately placed in that very spot, lay the first sentence of the report: "Almost ten years after the opening of the plant at Nuuk on February 19, 1982, the time seems right for Greenland to have a second purification plant." I'll never know what possessed me at that moment, but I let out a volley of curses that must have been heard all the way to the reception.

I think Gunnar was waiting for me. At any rate, he didn't seem surprised to see me burst into his office, my face contorted with anger, brandishing the report in my hand. He had already taken off his jacket, and greeted me in a positively cordial manner.

"I hope you had a good weekend, Sliv. Did you watch the hockey yesterday?"

"Do you think I'm an idiot, Gunnar? What's the meaning of all this?"

"Calm down, my boy. What are you talking about? Don't you like hockey?"

He was obviously making fun of me. "You know perfectly well what I'm talking about!" I exploded. "That error in the date of the opening of the plant at Nuuk. I took the trouble to correct it three times: in your interim report, in Olaf's report, and last Thursday night at the hotel. It certainly wasn't in the document I printed at midnight. And now here it is again in the final report. Are you doing this on purpose or what?"

"Obviously I'm doing it on purpose. You surely don't think I'm stupid or malicious enough to go behind your back three times even though I know you're right."

I stood there open-mouthed: my immediate boss, one of the most important people in the firm, had just confessed that he had been deliberately undermining my work.

"Sliv," he resumed, looking me straight in the eyes, "I owe you an explanation. But before anything else, I want you to know that the report you have in your hands is not the one I gave Parliament on Friday. It's a copy I had made especially for you. I know that means a lot to you, because I know how conscientious you are professionally."

"Clearly more conscientious than you."

I knew, as soon as these words had left my lips, that I had gone too far. There was no way Gunnar was going to take a remark like that from a twenty-three-year-old. And yet he showed no sign of annoyance. Rather, he was looking at me like a lenient priest regarding a young lout who's just blasphemed in church. He took a silver box from his shirt pocket, extracted a cigarette and lit it unhurriedly, looking at me all the while. Then he sat down in one of his brown armchairs and motioned to me to do the same. I did so mechanically, mesmerized despite myself by his affability.

"Is that what you really think, Sliv? You saw me at work for two months. Do you really think I do a bad job? Given the time and the means at our disposal, could we really have produced a better study? Honestly, I don't think so."

"It would have been even better without those errors I pointed out to you and which you seem determined to retain."

I was cut off in full flow by the whistling of a kettle. Calmly, as if I had left the office, Gunnar unplugged it, picked up a fine blue porcelain cup and made himself a blackberry tea. He sipped it, and must have found it too hot, because he put the cup down in front of him.

"Honestly, Sliv, what does it matter whether the plant was opened on February 19 or March 23?"

"I think it matters."

"Why?"

"Because one of those statements is the truth and the other is a lie." As I uttered the words, I couldn't help finding them pompous.

"That sounds very grand. You're in possession of the truth, aren't you?"

"Let's just say that I can read. The plaque in the entrance hall is categorical."

"Is that your only evidence? A plaque like one a funeral director could produce for you in an hour?"

"What are you getting at? Are you questioning the date the plant was opened?"

"Oh, forget about the damned plant!" he said angrily, extricating himself from his armchair. The immediate consequence of this movement was to uncover his hairy navel. A sip of tea helped him regain his composure.

"Let me put this another way," he resumed. "Supposing that the purification plant at Nuuk really was opened on February 19, 1982— I say supposing—and you sought to convince somebody that it was opened on March 23, how would you go about it?"

"What a question!"

"A rhetorical one, I admit. Never mind that, just answer."

"Well, I'd obviously start by changing the plaque."

"But how? Don't tell me you'd just show up at the reception with a new plaque under your arm and ask to replace the old one..."

"Of course not. I suppose I'd find an excuse. I'd claim that I'd been called by maintenance to check that the plaque was fixed properly. I'd take it off the wall to examine it and as I was doing that I'd replace it with one I had in my bag."

"All right, go on," Gunnar urged me. His tea must have been the right temperature by now, for he drank it in sips, looking at me out of the corner of his eye.

"But what's the point of all this?"

"Don't think about the why. For the moment I'm only interested in the how."

"We couldn't just stop with the plaque. The local newspaper must have reported the opening. We'd have to find that day's edition in the archives of the municipal library."

"Ah, yes!" Gunnar cried. "That's always the first thing people mention, the newspapers! As if it was difficult to steal a newspaper from the library in Nuuk and replace it with an almost identical edition. It's child's play! Especially in Greenland, one of the few countries in the world with only one library. Although, come to think of it, they may send a copy of their rag to Copenhagen. In fact, they almost certainly do. We'd have to check that."

For a moment, he was totally lost in thought. "No, Sliv," he resumed at last, "that's not where the difficulty lies. It lies in the multitude of details over which we have no control: the memories of the locals, the letter in which the director of the plant proudly tells his mother that he shook the hand of the Prime Minister, the pay slip from February 1982 that the night watchman keeps to prove his right to a pension, the detailed telephone invoices that the head of maintenance requested to confound a dishonest employee. Believe me, I wouldn't launch into such an operation unless I had a six-figure budget and the active co-operation of at least three centers."

"What are you talking about?" I suddenly had the impression that I had stumbled into a parallel universe. And yet I could still see the skiffs dancing in the good old harbor of Reykjavík on the other side of the window.

"I'm talking about the fact that, if I'd wanted to change the date that stupid plant opened, I could have done it. It would have taken time, cost quite a bit of money, but I'd have gotten there in the end. An interesting challenge, isn't it?"

"If you like," I conceded, not sure if he was talking seriously. "Gunnar, where are you going with this?"

He poured himself some more tea and, this time, offered me a cup, which I refused with a gesture.

"What I'm trying to say, Sliv, is that we could have a lot of fun, you and I. Of course, we wouldn't limit ourselves to paltry stories about opening dates. Do you remember Skjoldungen? It wasn't a bad idea, my story about thorium. It's a radioactive metal that can be used to produce nuclear energy. I checked, and most of the world's thorium comes from India and Australia. Given the price of a ton of the stuff on the raw materials market, I suspect your cod fisherman is soon going to swap his nets for a pickax and a sieve. It's only a matter of years, months perhaps. Sometimes all we do is bring reality forward."

"We? Are there several of you playing this little game?"

"Oh yes, you'd be surprised how many of your colleagues share this hobby."

"Who, for example?"

"Who is it you know? Well, look no further than Elangir..."

"Olaf Elangir? Come on, Gunnar, you must be joking."

"Amazing, isn't it?" Gunnar said, pensively. "Who would have thought that in the space of five years Olaf would become a master in the art of falsification? But then, you can never be sure of anything with him. So, Sliv, would you like to join us? I'm sure you'll make a wonderful recruit..." I was now scrutinizing Gunnar's facial expression as if my life depended on it. Could he possibly be serious? He had the kind of gleam in his eye that can usually be found in madmen or preachers.

"But I have no idea what you do. Tell me a bit more about it."

I knew immediately that I had fallen into his trap, speaking the very words he'd been expecting me to, because he immediately replied:

"Ah, it seems I've aroused your curiosity. But that's enough for today. Go home, I don't have anything interesting for you this week. We'll talk again next Monday."

"But I have to work," I protested. "There must be files I—"

"No, really, I have nothing for you. And besides, you've worked hard these past two months. A week's vacation will do you a world of good."

Gunnar had stood up: the conversation was over. It was 8:45 A.M. and I had not even had time to take off my coat. Gunnar walked me to the landing and pressed the elevator button, as if to make sure that I was really leaving. As the doors of the elevator closed in front of me, the thought crossed my mind that I had left my newspaper on my desk and hadn't read the sports pages.

Gunnar had said it: I had a week to think. But think about what?

4

The day after our conversation, returning from a trip to the supermarket, I was surprised to find a wet umbrella lying open in the corridor of my building, beside my doormat. No sooner had I turned the key in the lock and opened the door than I heard a voice coming from the couch in the living room.

"Oh, Sliv, hello!" Gunnar Eriksson cried, as if surprised to see me cross the threshold of my own home.

I was somewhat relieved to see things speed up like this. For twenty-four hours, I had been literally consumed with curiosity. The whole of the previous day, I had fought the temptation to burst into Gunnar's office and drag his story out of him. And, unusually, I had slept badly. That was a sign I'd learned to trust more than any other over the years.

Gunnar was reading the newspaper I had left lying on the kitchen table. He never did anything that wasn't calculated. He wanted me to know that he could get into my home at any time and that, although he had told me we would meet a week later, he alone decided the timing of our conversations. But I made up my mind to ignore his blatant act of breaking and entering and, as I put my shopping away in the refrigerator, asked him if he'd like something to drink.

"I wouldn't say no to a cup of tea. With all this rain, and the cold weather starting, I'm afraid I might be coming down with something."

So Gunnar had come to talk about his health. If that was the case, I wouldn't be the first to change the subject. "Yes," I said, "I think we're in for a tough winter."

"I'm sure you'll be pleased to learn that yesterday afternoon the architectural commission of the Parliament of Greenland approved our proposals. It's a superb conclusion to our assignment."

"Obviously I'm delighted," I replied in a tone that implied the exact opposite.

"But you suspect I'm not here to make small talk."

"Oh, really?" I said, raising one eyebrow. "Why are you here then? What do you wish to talk about?"

"About you, Sliv," he replied, pretending to ignore my insolent tone. He carefully folded the newspaper and put it on the table. I waited for what was to follow, leaning back against the wall of the living room, but he signaled me to sit down.

"Sliv," he began when I had done so, "I'm about to tell you a number of things that may well change your life. I know you're angry, but unless I'm mistaken about you, you'll listen carefully and without any preconceived ideas. Above all, I ask you, in your own interest, to stop me if at any moment you feel you don't want to hear anymore."

His tone was grave enough for me to refrain from interrupting him.

"Can I count on you to do that, Sliv?" he said, looking me straight in the eyes.

"Yes, Gunnar. I'm curious to hear what you have to say."

"All right. What you need to know is that within Baldur, Furuset & Thorberg there is a handful of men and women for whom environmental studies are merely a cover. Olaf Elangir, I and a few others whose names you don't need to know for the moment actually work for a secret international organization. The CFR—that's its name—operates on all five continents and in more than a hundred countries. What we have in Reykjavík is classed as a branch. Above the branches are the bureaus, which in turn report to the centers. Oh, isn't that the water boiling?"

I ran and turned off the gas under the kettle. It must have been boiling for a while, because I burned myself when I grabbed the handle. I poured two cups and quickly returned to my seat.

"What does the CFR do?" I asked.

"The agents of the CFR," he replied, leaving his tea bag to brew, "construct perfectly plausible scenarios, to which they then give substance by altering existing sources or even creating new ones. In other words, they change reality. I don't suppose you have any honey? Honey in tea does wonders for a sore throat."

"No, Gunnar, I don't have any honey," I replied, making no attempt to hide my annoyance, "and I don't give a damn about your throat. Give me an example of how you change reality."

"That's a pity, if it gets any worse I might lose my voice," Gunnar said, as if that prospect were likely to remind me where I kept my stocks of honey.

"Let's say the assignment might have been to falsify the date the purification plant at Nuuk opened. As I told you yesterday, it wouldn't have been difficult: a plaque to be changed, a few issues of the local rag to be reprinted, and you'd be done."

"But what would be the point?"

"In this particular case, there wouldn't be any. This is only an example to show you how we work. The Plan would never have authorized such a pointless assignment."

"The Plan? What Plan?"

"The Plan is the body within the CFR that determines our overall strategy. Its priorities change over time. This year, it's encouraging the creation of new schools of painting, last year it asked us to tone down primitive African myths. Sometimes, there's a more obvious connection with what's going on in the world. In the late fifties, for example, our predecessors worked on the conquest of space: how could we cause the great powers to spend more on something in which nobody had been at all interested ten years earlier?"

"I'm sorry," I cut in, "but are you trying to tell me the CFR was responsible for Neil Armstrong walking on the moon in 1969?"

"No, of course not, things are never that simple. The idea was already in the air, and the Americans would have gotten there sooner or later. But if we go any further with this, you and I, I can prove to you, with documents to back me up, that thanks to a few exceptional agents, what might have taken twenty years was accomplished in ten."

"This Plan you talk about, what are its objectives? Between African myths and the conquest of space, I admit I find it hard to see any common thread."

"Sorry to disappoint you, Sliv, but you don't have access to that level of information."

"Hold on a second, Gunnar, you're trying to recruit me into an organization, but you won't disclose its aims?"

"Yes, that's precisely what I'm trying to do. I might as well tell you immediately, I'm not authorized to reveal much more to you today. For example, I'm not going to tell you who's in charge of the CFR or when it was founded."

"What do the initials CFR stand for? Can you at least tell me that?"

"The generally accepted explanation is that they stand for Consortium de Falsification du Réel, which is French for Consortium for the Falsification of Reality, but to be honest no one knows for sure."

"So it's a French organization?"

"Or Belgian, or Swiss, or Canadian, or African. Honestly, I have no idea."

"But, Gunnar, how can you agree to work for an enterprise you know so little about?"

"That's a valid question, one I've frequently had occasion to ponder. But ask yourself what you knew about Baldur, Furuset & Thorberg when you accepted my offer. You'd read the company brochure, so you knew the names of the partners, but surely not much more than that. And yet, on the basis of those few elements, you decided you wouldn't be taking a big risk in joining us and that there was a strong possibility that you'd find the work fulfilling. It's the same for me and for most members of the CFR. I don't know everything about the CFR, in any case surely less than you'll end up learning about Baldur, Furuset & Thorberg. But I'm happy, I like my daily work, I like my colleagues, and I share most of the values of the organization, to the point where today I couldn't imagine working anywhere else."

"I'm sorry, but I have to insist. This daily work you talk about, what is its purpose? Taking me as an example again, I know why I'm working and whom I'm working for. I slave away for you and for three old men, in the hope that you'll notice me, give me increasing responsibilities, and eventually promote me to partner. I also know the world isn't ruled by philanthropy and that the reason the shareholders of the company pay me is because they pass on the costs of my time and pocket the profits in the process. At the same time, I'm working to learn things, to satisfy my curiosity, and to acquire skills that should prove useful to me one day, in this job or elsewhere."

"Your arguments could just as easily apply to the CFR, apart from that bit about profits. To the best of my knowledge, the CFR isn't motivated by financial gain, just as it isn't trying to seize power or to help mankind to achieve a state of cosmic bliss. The aims of the CFR, if there are any, are quite different."

"If there are any?" I echoed, somewhat taken aback. "Please reassure me, Gunnar. You do know the purpose of the CFR, don't you? At your age, you do at least know if you're working for mercenaries, criminals or cranks?"

"What I know or what I believe is of little importance. We aren't talking about my recruitment but yours." He must have sensed that this last remark was a bit curt, because he quickly added with a smile, "And please don't mention my age again."

"How many agents do you recruit in a year?"

"You mean in total? Several hundred, a thousand perhaps."

"No, you in particular, Gunnar," I stipulated, determined to get as much information from him as possible.

"You would be the twelfth in nineteen years."

"That's not many," I said.

"Unlike some of my colleagues, who can live with a high failure rate, I don't like taking risks. I derive a certain pride from never having made a mistake so far."

"Why me? You hardly know me."

"More than you think. I've put together a fairly complete file on you. The psychological analysis alone cost me $1,500."

"So those damned tests you made me take helped you to establish a psychological profile?" I asked, making an effort to appear shocked, although in fact I was dying to get my hands on that document. "And am I allowed to know what they revealed?"

"That you're highly imaginative but also have your feet planted firmly on the ground. The psychologist thinks you acquired your pragmatism from having been brought up in the country. A combination like that is quite rare and generally produces excellent agents. You also speak four languages, three of them fluently, which is nothing to be sniffed at, either."

He stood up, took a few steps and looked through the window for nearly a full minute. I was searching in vain for more questions to ask him when he turned and went on:

"Tests can be mistaken, but my intuition has never betrayed me. I kept a close eye on you during our assignment in Greenland and I predict a great future for you, whatever the path you choose. You can continue doing environmental studies. Baldur, Furuset & Thorberg is a real company, which can offer fine prospects to a project manager as motivated and competent as you."

"I'm sorry, Gunnar, but if I decline your offer, I can't see myself staying with Baldur, Furuset & Thorberg. Can you imagine me at internal meetings, staring at my colleagues one by one and wondering how many of them belong to your little brotherhood?"

"Or you can join the CFR," Gunnar continued. "In other words, you can choose to work undercover. In many ways, the CFR is like any other organization. If you prove yourself, you'll rise through the ranks, received increasingly interesting assignments, and enjoy regular pay rises."

"Just for my information, what is the salary of an agent at the end of his career?" I asked with heavy irony.

"Spare me your sarcasm, Sliv. The CFR treats its workers well. And we both know you're not motivated by money, so don't try to make me believe you're going to base your decision on whether or not we pay travel expenses or issue luncheon vouchers. Whatever you decide, you'll be making a commitment to keep the activities of the CFR secret. The first infringement of this rule would automatically mean dismissal from both the firm and the organization. We take a very hard line on that."

"As I would have expected. When do you want my answer?"

"When you're ready. You have two important questions to ask yourself. What do you want to do with your life? And will you be able to live with the burden of secrecy? Take time to think it over. I don't expect you back in the office until next Monday."

He put on his coat and looked for his gloves, which he had left on the console table in the entrance. Then, as if suddenly remembering something, he opened his leather case and took out a green folder secured by two elastic bands.

"I'd like you to read this dossier. It was put together three years ago by a young recruit as an initial assignment. It's far from perfect but it will give you a good idea of our daily work. Traditionally, the author presents his scenario in the first part: what is it I seek to make people believe? In the second part, he lists the measures to be taken to give the scenario credibility.

"A word of advice: if reading this doesn't arouse any kind of intellectual excitement in you, then stop immediately. If you get to the second paragraph and start to wonder if it could have been improved on, and what you would have done differently, then you're on the right track."

He put on his gloves, opened the door and picked up his umbrella, which was now quite dry. He held out his hand and cleared his throat.

"Of course, this folder doesn't leave your apartment."

"That goes without saying," I said. "Sorry about the honey."

He raised his hand as if to absolve me of a shameful sin. As he walked to the elevator, I noticed that both his shoelaces were untied. Decidedly, Gunnar Eriksson was nothing like my image of a master spy.

5

SKITOS, NEBRASKA, CAPITAL OF THESSALY

SCENARIO

On May 28, 1854, just a few days after Franco-British forces landed in Pireaus, Spyros Tadelitis, a young shepherd from the Greek province of Thessaly, embarked as a ship's boy on the *Tarmata*. It was his way of paying his passage to Genoa, where he planned to use the same stratagem to reach the New World.

It had been a heartbreaking decision on the part of Spyros, who was barely seventeen, to leave his family and his village of Actinonia. And yet, after the humiliation he had recently suffered, the young man knew it was his only option. However hard he tried to think of other things, his mind kept returning to that painful day a month earlier when he had seen his life collapse around him.

People had come from Stavros, Sofadhes and even Velestinon, to attend the wedding of Spyros and Dimitra Kallistinos, the loveliest, haughtiest girl in Thessaly. The two young people had known each other all their lives. Constantin Tadelitis and Phaedon Kallistinos led their sheep to the same pastures to graze; Lea Tadelitis and Andrea Kallistinos often exchanged gossip in the wash house; Spyros and Dimitra were united by a bond such as is usually only seen in those related by blood. The two families had pooled their meager resources to give their children a wedding to remember.

Unfortunately, the day after the wedding, Dimitra announced to the whole village that she was withdrawing from the world to devote herself to meditation and prayer. Phaedon and Andrea Kallistinos tried to reason with their daughter, but to no avail. As for Spyros, he was not even granted the opportunity to speak to her. That very evening, Dimitra entered the convent of Margarition.

The days that followed had been the most difficult of Spyros's life. He could not bear the loving concern shown him by his mother and his two sisters, or Phaedon Kallistinos's clumsy attempts to provide words of comfort, or the villagers' lack of understanding, or, especially, the ugly rumors spread by his sworn enemy Coubilakis, whom he had once replaced in Dimitra's heart.

Spyros had no alternative but to go into exile. He immediately knew it was something he must do and his mother's entreaties were unable to shake his determination. He would go to America, as far away as possible from Actinonia. There, he would find a job and try to forget that terrible Sunday in 1854 when his life had been turned upside down.

Spyros arrived in Genoa on June 3, 1854. A week later, he embarked on the steamer *Lorrimer* as a kitchen hand. Two months later, Ellis Island came into view. While many immigrants assume that their qualifications or their knowledge of a foreign language will prove useful, Tadelitis soon realized that he had nothing to offer but the strength of his arms. Just then, the Chicago and Rock Island Company was recruiting hard-working men to build a railroad linking Illinois and Missouri. For three years, Spyros broke boulders twelve hours a day. He learned English and euchre, a card game whose infinite combinations gradually chased from his mind the memory of Dimitra Kallistinos Tadelitis, his wife before God and man.

It was in 1858 that Spyros arrived in Nebraska. He liked it so much that he settled there and remained until he died. Nebraska covers an area twice the size of Greece. It is a state almost as flat as Thessaly is mountainous. It hardly ever rains.

Spyros asked for land. He was given seven hundred acres, which it was his responsibility to enclose. He built a cabin, vowing to enlarge it as soon as he had saved enough money. Meanwhile, he sank three years' savings into the purchase of a herd of pigs. He called the fattest one Coubilakis.

The basics of pig farming are relatively simple, and Spyros soon mastered them. Every month he would go to Omaha, sell his fattest animals, and reinvest his profits in ever fatter, ever more fertile sows. In less than five years, his herd was five hundred strong.

The years 1863-1870 were years of expansion and consolidation. Spyros bought a share in an abattoir in Omaha. In this way, he felt he was spending more time with his animals. He developed new techniques that allowed him to fatten his pigs more quickly and so get a faster return on his capital. In 1866, he at last began tilling his land. He was already growing corn, which he used as feed for the pigs. He now planted wheat and soya, which brought in significant income for very little extra cost. At Christmas 1870, the First Union Bank informed him that he had accumulated more than $100,000 in his account in its Omaha branch. The sum struck Spyros as excessive. He had never worked for the money, but because hard work seemed to him healthy and natural. Now, all at once, he realized that he had become wealthy.

It was only now that he felt justified in writing to his village. His first letter was to his mother: "Time has passed, and you must be quite old now. I want you to know that I've never forgotten you, or Papa, or Dimitra, or that pig Coubilakis." The letter caused a great stir in Actinonia. Spyros was alive! He had crossed the Atlantic and was now living on the other side of the world.
Lea replied with news of the village: old Gregorios had passed away, and his son was now mayor; the Khondylis girl had had twins, who were always driving the goats crazy; the Turks had finally finished the road to Leondari. Of Dimitra, there was no mention. By a kind of tacit agreement, mother and son never mentioned her.

Thus began a correspondence. The letters from Tadelitis were as eagerly awaited as the Delphic oracles had once been. Whenever Mikis Almendros, the postman, spotted a blue envelope in the mail, he would ride up the main street on his bicycle crying, "News from Spyros!" In no time at all, half the village would be trotting along beside him as far as the Tadelitis house, where old Lea would receive the missive from the hands of Mikis. She would have no choice but to read aloud the lines written to her by her son, who probably had no idea that his most intimate feelings were on display to all and sundry, to be commented upon and dissected. Even the unfortunate Coubilakis listened with half-closed eyes to this account of the strangeness of American life and the inevitable mention of his own infamy that appeared in every letter.

Little by little, Spyros revealed himself. Yes, he had made his fortune. His land now extended over many thousands of acres and it took him nearly a day to ride all the way around it on horseback. He had so many pigs that a dishonest employee had been able to start the second largest ranch in the state by stealing from him without his realizing it. And yet Spyros was not happy. Money meant nothing to him. He missed his family. "It isn't good," he wrote, "for a man to live away from his own people for too long." He yearned above all for his native Thessaly. "I've called my ranch Skitos, after that warm breeze that used to caress our cheeks when evening fell."

Vicariously, Actinonia experienced the great days of the conquest of the West, applauded when the two railroad lines that cut the country across the middle met at Promontory Point, debated in detail the latest irrigation techniques or the migration from the gold mines of Colorado to the more promising ones in Northern California.

In 1883, after thirteen years of correspondence, Spyros finally suggested that his parents come and join him. Lea had informed him that his father was suffering from a respiratory disease and had no more than a few months to live. The thought that his father might die without seeing him again was intolerable to Spyros, who mailed them a generous sum to cover their travel expenses.

But Constantin and Lea hesitated. Spyros's fame went so far beyond the family circle that his parents felt that the postman and the baker's wife had almost as much right to be invited as they did.

"I suppose this is going to seem foolish to you," wrote Lea at the beginning of January 1884, "but I'd feel terrible about leaving the people of Actinonia behind." "Then bring them," was Spyros's reply, and with his letter he included a money order that left no doubt as to his intentions.

So it was that the most enthusiastic and spontaneous of all the waves of migration from Greece to the United States came about. Five months and two weeks was all the time it took for the people of Actinonia to wrap up their lives and prepare their passage for the New World. The houses were closed up, the flocks sold. As the mayor, young Gregorios (as the villagers persisted in calling him even though he now had a white beard), gave an astonishing speech in which he did nothing less than dissolve the village. And they set off. Forty-two families set sail on the *Tarmata*.

The people of Actinonia crossed the Atlantic in six weeks. They were kept in quarantine on Ellis Island, after a colony of obese rats had been found on the ship. Constantin had a relapse, which almost finished him. But at the height of his illness the old man clung to the prospect of soon seeing his son again. Even as young Gregorios was frantically scouring the streets of Manhattan in search of an Orthodox priest to administer the last rites, Constantin gave the signal for departure.

After these incidents, it was child's play for the villagers to travel the twelve hundred miles from New York to Nebraska. A woman gave birth on the train between Springfield and Dayton. On October 29, 1884, the locomotive drew into the station at Omaha. Young Gregorios mustered the few words of English that he had learned on Ellis Island to hire some thirty wagons. At the end of the afternoon, the procession rode in through the gates of the ranch of Skitos.

Spyros Tadelitis was sitting in his rocking chair in the arbor when a cloud of dust on the horizon announced the arrival of the immigrants. He had borne separation with dignity; now he faced the reunion like a man. He shook his father's hand, clasped his mother to his chest, and waved to the hundred and thirty-four people from Actinonia standing by their wagons. "We're going to have to find somewhere for all of you to live," he said. "But we'll see about that tomorrow. In the meantime, let's enjoy ourselves, as we have a lot of catching up to do." He called one of his men, and asked him to kill and prepare the fattest pig on his whole ranch. The feasting lasted all night.

Spyros kept his word. He gave each family a roof over its head, a couple of acres, and work. After a few months, the little community became a village, to which it naturally gave the name Skitos. Young Gregorios was again appointed mayor. The elder of the Khondylis twins was made sheriff.

The terrible winter of 1888 at last got the better of old Constantin's fragile constitution. Lea survived him by some twelve years. As for Spyros, he lived long enough to see the first airplanes. When he died, he left an enormous inheritance, which the people of Skitos, in their great wisdom, reinvested entirely in the development of their town.

Today, Skitos is a cheerful little place with a population of about twelve thousand. Its important role in the meat industry has generally protected it from the ups and downs of the economy. Above all, it is one of the major centers of Greek culture in the United States, a place where one can eat some of the best souvlaki in North America.

POINTS OF REFERENCE

Actinonia exists. It is a hamlet in Thessaly, 1,850 meters above sea level, and located between Leondari and Karava, at latitude 39° 13' north and longitude 21° 43' east. Only two or three families live there permanently. A number of shepherds remain during the summer to tend their flocks.

Skitos is a small town in Nebraska with a population of 12,500, located halfway between Omaha and Norfolk, at latitude 41° 38' north and longitude 96° 49' west. The exact date of its founding is not certain, but it is generally thought to be about 1880.

ACTIONS TO BE TAKEN IN ORDER TO CREATE A NEW REALITY

In Skitos, Nebraska:

1) Creation of the Association for Thessalian Culture, based in Skitos but with officers scattered throughout the United States. Berlin and the branches in Richmond, Saint Paul, Thomasville and Decatur are prepared to provide four legends: Wilbur Kapis (chairman), Nikos Faraday (deputy chairman), Lynn Samarina (treasurer) and Chrissantos Galatas (secretary). Association created retroactively on March 25, 1971 (150th anniversary of the uprising against the Turks). Minutes of meetings practically up-to-date (last one delayed). Account opened in the Omaha branch of the First

Union Bank on March 30, 1971, and kept up to date through the complicity of our branch in Lincoln. 1988 Budget: $134,000. Main items: Grant of $25,000 to the Association of Greek Americans (whose chairman is traditionally a member of the Onassis family); grant of $79,185 (20 million drachmas) to the Thessalian Folk Museum in Larissa; financing to the tune of $4,400 of a Greek food stand at the county fair in Skitos; purchase for $7,000 of tickets to take a hundred young people from Skitos to see Leach Gravos (an American football player of Greek descent) play at the Super Bowl with the Dallas Cowboys, etc.

2) Opening of two Greek restaurants: Nights of Byblos on Wayne Trace and Delights of Mykonos on Stellhorn Boulevard. Funding obtained from the Dukakis Foundation for Entrepreneurial Achievement. Imminent opening of a franchise of the sandwich chain Pita Express (350 branches throughout the United States).

3) Personal grant by Wilbur Kapis of $15,000 to Rosalind High School. Mr. Kapis named an honorary citizen of Skitos. Chemistry laboratory named Tadelitis Laboratory.

4) Before 1900, plots in the cemetery at Skitos were allocated for forty years and were renewable only once. It is therefore hardly surprising that we do not find there the graves of Spyros, Lea, and Constantin Tadelitis. On the other hand, we can take advantage of the extension of the western area of the cemetery to place a number of gravestones, of which one will bear the words: "Costis Gregorios (1831-1922), Greek and American citizen, mayor of Actinonia and Skitos. May the Lord welcome him to His breast." It will be necessary to burn down the watchman's hut in order to destroy the cemetery's register (it has been confirmed that there is only one copy).

5) Erection of a monument to the memory of the Greeks of Skitos who died during World War II.

6) Insertion of articles in thirty-seven issues of the *Nebraska Observer*. In each case ten copies are to be printed and substituted for existing copies in the newspaper's archives and in the municipal libraries of Omaha and Lincoln. Examples of subjects: Spyros Tadelitis wins the top prize at the Minneapolis Agricultural Fair in

1895 with his pig Coubilakis; interview with Kosta Almendros on the occasion of his winning a bronze medal for weightlifting, heavyweight category, at the Olympic Games in Antwerp in 1920; a report on the funeral of Costis Gregorios on March 7, 1922; report that the fall in the price of meat in 1953 dealt a hard blow to the little community of Skitos, etc.

7) Publication at the author's expense in 1949 of *Memoirs of a Child of Actinonia* by Agamemnon Gregorios, the son of Costis Gregorios, who succeeded his father as mayor of Skitos. Eighty pages of anecdotes attributed to the dead Costis on life in Thessaly (First part: Greek by blood) and the move to the United States (Second part: Nebraska, land of welcome). One hundred fifty pages of memoirs and notes on American society by a man who describes himself as "a Greek shepherd thrown into the meat business" (the title of the third part). Five hundred copies printed. Four hundred sent to school and college libraries in Nebraska and Iowa with an accompanying letter from the Association for Thessalian Culture.

In Thessaly:

1) Placing of a plaque on a shepherd's house in Actinonia:
"In this house lived Constantin, Lea, Spyros, Anna and Vanina Tadelitis. They emigrated to other horizons but few Greeks loved their country as much as they did." Plaque signed by the Association for Thessalian Culture.

2) Sending *Memoirs of a child of Actinonia* by Agamemnon Gregorios to the fifty-odd municipal libraries in the province of Thessaly.

3) Falsification of the register of births in Actinonia, today preserved in Leondari. Birth of Spyros Tadelitis dated May 7, 1837.

4) Creation of a medical record for George Coubilakis, who died on July 20, 1887, less than three years after the exodus of the people of Actinonia. Coubilakis would be said to have remained alone in the village, finally settling in the Tadelitis house (even sleeping in Spyros's bed), and would eventually succumb to a complicated form of neurasthenia.

5) Creation of an ecclesiastical record for Dimitra Kallistinos, the wife of Spyros, who became Sister Appollonia on the day she entered the convent of Margarition. In 1861, Sister Appollonia left Greece for India, where all trace of her has been lost.

6) Insertion in Odysseus Gavras's standard work, *Hellenes In Exile*, of references to the massive emigration from several villages in Thessaly to the United States in the 1880s. The author, publisher, and rights holders are all dead.

7) Insertion of the *Tarmata* and the *Lorrimer* in the register of merchant ships allowed to dock in the port of Genoa.

ACTION PLAN AND CALENDAR

All the actions described above are feasible and have been approved in principle by the branches and bureaus concerned. If I obtain the consent of the bureau in charge of demographics by July 1, 1989, I think I can bring all these actions to completion by December 31, 1990.

BUDGET

I have yet to receive estimates from Decatur and Patras. Nevertheless, I estimate the total cost of the actions described above at about $280,000, in other words, slightly less than the sum of $300,000 set aside for my first assignment.

6

"Lena Thorsen had—and still has—an exceptional gift for falsifying sources."

Gunnar Eriksson was sitting on my couch, sipping a glass of whiskey. I had phoned him the morning after his previous visit, and he had asked if he could drop by that afternoon. I had a host of questions for him but, as usual, he told me only what I needed to know.

"It's extremely rare to find so many skills all combined in a young recruit. In a first dossier, the agent usually pays particular attention to the scenario, presumably because that's where he feels he can contribute the most. Unfortunately, he then makes a botched job of the second part, because he thinks it's less important and less gratifying than the first part. And even when he attaches the necessary importance to the falsification process, he lets himself down with crude measures borrowed from bad spy novels, which are nothing like the measures we use every day in the field.

What astonished me when I read Lena's project was that a novice who hadn't yet received any training could get so close to reality. Up until then, I'd have sworn that only an experienced agent could have thought of financing a couple of Greek restaurants. And what about the cemetery? The number of young people I've seen overlook that, even though it's a fundamental aspect of any attempt at falsification! I don't know any assignment that's even slightly serious that doesn't have to tackle the question of cemeteries at some point... No, quite simply, when the Approval Committee saw the dossier, the chairman phoned me to make sure I hadn't written it for her. 'Is she really only twenty-four?' he asked me at least three times.

"I should tell you that Lena also attached a number of things to the dossier that left those old fogies on the committee speechless. For example, she'd written up, as a taster, the minutes of a number of board meetings of the Association for Thessalian Culture. You'd have thought you were there! A little gem! I've heard they study extracts from it at the Academy. And she didn't stop there. When she was given the green light, she went straight ahead and wrote up the rest. The minutes of twenty years of meetings of an association that has never existed. It's all there: the electoral speeches, endless discussions about the renewal of the cleaning contract, stupid personal quarrels, even an attempted coup in 1982."

Gunnar had taken his glasses from his pocket as if getting ready to reread Thorsen's scenario. He reminded me of one of those gourmets who rub their stomachs as they recall their latest feast.

"All the same," I said, "was it really necessary to go that far?"

"You can never go too far. Lena's work may seem a little excessive in relation to the requirements of the dossier and, in fact, it is. But its significance is much wider than this particular case. One thing you can be sure of: the Association for Thessalian Culture will come in useful again in other circumstances. In ten years' time, a Taiwanese agent working on agricultural policy for the Mediterranean coast of Europe will draw elements from it to support his argument. If Lena had limited herself to planting a few gravestones or suggesting to Pita Express that they open a fast food outlet in Skitos, she wouldn't have earned her stripes so quickly. Take a character like Agamemnon Gregorios: what a name, for a start! The stuff that heroes are made of! A mayor torn between Greek culture and the smell of fresh meat! I'd bet my bottom dollar he'll turn up again quite soon in the work of one of your colleagues. And, believe me, the CFR can tell the difference between those agents who work only for themselves and those who, by creating powerful universal myths, work for the collective. There's no doubt Lena Thorsen is part of the second group. Her final report on this assignment, which she handed in to me just a few days before you arrived, is more than five thousand pages long. I'll eat my hat if she isn't quoted a hundred times in the next five years."

"I'm happy to admit that Thorsen has a certain talent for forging sources, but you must admit her scenario is a bit weak."

"Weak? It's terrible! Oh, it's not so much the subject: population movements are one of the subjects most often tackled, especially by young agents. Everybody has his own little migration story; it's almost become a stylistic exercise. Her original idea isn't especially bad, a little melodramatic, of course, but I suppose that's the price we have to pay if we want to attract and keep female members." Gunnar gave me a heavy wink. "Anyway, the story is just about acceptable. The treatment, on the other hand, is an absolute disaster, and I'm weighing my words. That thing about Skitos—'you know, the warm breeze blowing against our cheeks as evening falls'—is completely ridiculous. Mawkish, clumsy, everything we hate."

"And yet her project was accepted." I said, pleased to hear that Gunnar shared my opinion of Thorsen's scenario.

"Not in that form, believe me. If I'd submitted her work to the Dossier Committee as it was, she wouldn't be deputy head of the Stuttgart bureau as we speak. I made her revise it from top to bottom. Obviously, it's still not as good as the second part, but at least the dossier passed the hurdle of the committee."

"Which seems to suggest you don't have to excel in all departments to make your mark in the CFR."

"Absolutely not. Would you be so kind, Sliv, as to pour me another glass of whiskey?" (He seemed to have forgotten that he had brought the bottle himself.) "Become a star in one of the two fields and you'll be Class 3 before you're thirty. And besides, you'll always find someone who possesses the qualities you lack."

"And if I want to go higher?"

"That's another matter. You'll have to be an ace in both scenario and falsification, but I might as well warn you now, such people can be counted on the fingers of both hands. Anyway, your first dossier should give us a good idea of your abilities."

There was a transition in this that I couldn't let pass. "You talk as if I'd already given you my answer. I haven't made my decision. I still have several questions to ask you."

"You won't get anything more out of me. Nada. You already know enough to make up your mind. Why would I reveal more to someone who isn't even a member of the organization?"

I came back as quick as a flash: "I could join the CFR and resign a few weeks later, after gathering as much information as I can about the way you work…"

Gunnar looked me in the eyes, then very, very slowly put his glass down on a sideboard. This simple gesture was enough to put an immediate damper on the playful tone of our conversation.

"Never say that kind of thing, Sliv. You never know whom you're dealing with. Personally, I don't take offense, but some of my colleagues, who are less broad-minded, wouldn't hesitate to order immediate retaliatory measures."

Seeing the effect his words produced on me, he added:

"Please don't think I'm threatening you, Sliv, but we're talking about the possibility of your joining a secret organization. Claiming you can keep a secret is one thing; actually keeping it is another. The reason our leaders demand ruthless discipline in the ranks isn't for their own pleasure. In the twenty-six years that I've belonged to the organization, I've known three major alerts. Each in its own way endangered the very survival of the CFR. You have no idea how ingenious we had to be to deflect the unfortunate attention we were getting. We never take the slightest risk, or, to be more precise, we take only very carefully calculated risks. In the present case, the internal code of conduct I swore to uphold when I entered the CFR requires me to cut short the recruitment process immediately. We don't accept blackmail. Your candidacy is rejected."

"But I wasn't trying to blackmail you," I said, stunned.

Gunnar had stood up and was looking around for his coat. "Come now, Sliv, your words were very clear. No hard feelings, but let's not talk about it anymore. Come and see me tomorrow. I have a very interesting assignment for you: a project to build a dam in Savoie."

This was too much. "I don't give a fuck about your dam, Gunnar!" I exploded. "What is all this melodrama? Fifteen minutes ago, I was the ideal candidate, you were letting me in on top-secret information, and now, suddenly, all because of a few unfortunate words I didn't even believe myself, you're sending me back to doing environmental studies?"

All at once I understood, and I felt stupid for losing my temper. "Oh, I get it, this is one of your recruitment techniques! You begin by holding out the bait, telling your prey he's suited for the job, then you explain that you made a mistake and he has to forget everything he heard. Is that it, Gunnar?"

During my harangue, Gunnar had stopped looking for his coat, sat down again, picked up his glass, and turned it around in his hand, apparently totally absorbed in the movements of his ice cube.

"Yes, that's more or less it. If that's how you want to take it, I'm prepared to stretch the code of conduct and put your words down to an attempt at humor. But I don't want it to happen again."

He stopped moving his glass and watched as the ice cube came to a standstill. Its mad dash had reduced it to almost nothing, to a mere sliver swimming on the surface of the amber-colored liquid.

"Seriously, Sliv, if you envisage a career with us, you'll need to watch your language. We've excluded people for less than that. Now I must go. Call me tomorrow and tell me if we can count you in. If you have any doubts, please do us both a favor and decline."

When Gunnar had gone, I sat down in the place he had occupied. He hadn't finished his glass. The ice cube was now completely melted.

Now that I was about to make a decision that Gunnar himself had said would be one of the most important of my life, I found it impossible to think clearly. Was I or wasn't I cut out for this kind of life? Would I find it more fulfilling to give substance to imaginary migrations than to write environmental reports? I couldn't hide from myself how attractive a prospect it was to put together a dossier like Lena Thorsen's. It sounded like a fascinating exercise, at once so rich and so unusual. In addition — why try to deny it? — after reading her dossier several times, I had become convinced that I could do better than she had. For someone as strongly competitive as I, it was a major draw.

All the same, and however great my curiosity, how could I compare such radically different options? While I had a pretty good idea what a career with Baldur, Furuset & Thorberg would entail, I had no way of knowing if I would like working for the CFR. What would I actually be doing? What kind of relationship would I have with my colleagues? Wouldn't I tire quickly of a job that at bottom seemed very artificial? In that respect, shouldn't Gunnar's reticence worry me? He had highlighted all the advantages of the job, without saying anything about its disadvantages, and I didn't know any job that didn't have at least a few of the latter.

And what about the motives of the CFR? Gunnar was a persuasive speaker, but he never revealed anything important. After three conversations, I knew hardly more than I had the first day. Why did the CFR falsify reality? Where did its money come from? On whose behalf was it working? So many questions, and as yet not the slightest inkling of an answer. What would I do if I were to learn within a few weeks that the organization was financed by a foreign government for purposes of subversion? This whole game wouldn't seem quite so amusing then, especially as, if Gunnar were to be believed, it was neither common nor advisable to hand in one's resignation. It's a well-known fact that secret organizations don't like to see their former members go back into civilian life. Gunnar had mentioned retaliatory measures. Could things really reach that point? Was I in danger?

I knew only one representative of the CFR: Gunnar Eriksson. I felt an instinctive sympathy for my boss, who had the gift of putting people at their ease while at the same time getting to the heart of the matter. But wasn't that open, honest personality a mask? Gunnar had already demonstrated a real talent as a manipulator, and I was forced to admire the cool way he had gradually lifted the veil on what was really going on at Baldur, Furuset & Thorberg.

First, he had put my perceptiveness to the test: maybe I wouldn't have been invited to join the game if I hadn't picked up on his first hints. Then he had gradually shown his hand by giving me several opportunities to stop him, each time taking, as he himself had said of the CFR, only carefully calculated risks. He had first introduced the idea of falsification, without ever letting me think that anyone else was involved. As I hadn't flinched, he had then given me to understand that he was not working alone, even mentioning Olaf Elangir— although I was now prepared to bet that he had nothing to do with the CFR. By this stage, Gunnar still hadn't taken any risks.

Supposing I went to the police to report our conversations, he could easily have claimed that he had led me up the garden path. He might even have accused me of acute paranoia. I had no evidence. Hadn't Gunnar made a point of telling me that the report handed over to the Parliament of Greenland did not contain any errors? Yes, there was a faulty version, but I now remembered seeing him take it away with him after our conversation. As for Elangir, the genuinely befuddled way he would have reacted if he had been questioned would certainly have convinced any police officer that my superior was telling the truth.

It wasn't until our next encounter that Gunnar had started taking risks. True, he had engineered it himself by coming to my apartment. Maybe he had been afraid I might record our conversation. Speaking of which, had he used his visit as an opportunity to bug my phone? That was something I'd have liked to be able to rule out categorically.

But that day, Gunnar had given me Lena Thorsen's dossier, or, to be more precise, a dossier he had attributed to Lena Thorsen. If my memory served me well, the document was neither signed nor dated. There was no mention in it of Gunnar Eriksson, or of Baldur, Furuset & Thorberg, or of the CFR. Once again, he'd been clever.

Devoid of clues as it was, that dossier was the only tangible thing I had held in my hands. Gunnar had subsequently taken it away with him, but he had left it with me for almost twenty-four hours, in other words, more time than I would have needed to go to the post office and make a photocopy. I hadn't done that, though. I hadn't even left my apartment between Gunnar's two visits. If I had, would he have had me tailed?

With hindsight, Gunnar's ploy seemed clear. He had been following a well-prepared script, and now that it was too late, now that it served no useful purpose, I could see the mechanism of it. I had been played by someone cleverer than myself. It was a thought that was both exciting (these people were true professionals) and a bit frightening (in a certain context, the word "professional" can have disturbing connotations).

For all of these reasons, I found it hard to believe that it was still possible for me to turn back — to decline, as Gunnar had put it. I knew a lot; I probably knew too much, even if I didn't have any evidence to back up my suspicions. My curiosity was urging me to join the CFR—I was like a little boy being urged by his friends to join them in a game—but that feeling was tinged with bitterness at the thought that I didn't really have any choice. Because he had told me too much about some aspects and not enough about others, the freedom Gunnar had apparently given me was nothing but a trap. I suddenly felt terribly angry with Gunnar Eriksson, Olaf Elangir (even though he was probably entirely innocent), Lena Thorsen and all the CFR bigwigs who must be watching me struggle with my moral choices.

I wriggled out of the dilemma by telling myself that I had nothing to lose by leading a double life for a year or two. After all, I would continue to exercise the profession for which I had been hired. I had been able to verify that Baldur, Furuset & Thorberg enjoyed an excellent reputation in its field: no headhunter would ever hold it against me that I'd learned my trade there.

In writing these lines, I realize how naïve I had been. As if my choice to join the CFR were anything like the usual choice of an employer! I suppose I was too young to understand all the implications of my decision. I had just left university; I had had six job interviews in my life (how far away the bears of Siglufjördhur seemed right now!); and so far I had only asked myself the great question of existence (what do I intend to do with my life?) in terms of either educational options (economics or geography? International affairs or political science?) or professional ones (Iceland or the Continent? a small company or a multinational?). I joined the CFR just as, when I was a student, I had taken optional courses in Spanish: to see what it was like, and because it didn't cost me a lot.

I would have plenty of time, in the years to come, to ponder the consequences of my devil-may-care attitude.

7

That same day I began my two new assignments: the environmental study for the dam in Savoie, and my preliminary research toward writing my first dossier for the CFR.

Joining the CFR did not excuse me from doing my share of work for the firm, quite the contrary. By putting together certain things that Gunnar had told me, I had deduced that only one of the three partners in Baldur, Furuset & Thorberg belonged to the CFR. The other two were unaware that the organization even existed, and they saw me merely as a project manager.

Gunnar's position as Director of Operations made it possible for him to reduce my workload in the firm as much as possible, so as to free up time for me to do my second job. During the year and a half that I spent in Reykjavík, I was involved in six assignments, each time under the command of Gunnar Eriksson, who made sure he distributed the different jobs to my advantage, while taking great care that my colleagues noticed nothing. All in all, my days were well filled. The fact is, people work hard in the CFR, for all kinds of reasons: the agents are almost all leading a double life (except in the central services, and above a certain level in the hierarchy); the work is fascinating; and the competition is especially fierce, as I'll have a chance to explain later.

Gunnar had stressed the importance of the first assignment in an agent's career. In his opinion, the personality of a new recruit—both his promise and his limitations—was generally revealed in his first dossier. Every time an agent, the head of a branch, or even the director of a center was mentioned, Gunnar would give me an outline of that person's first dossier and try, usually successfully, to find in it the key to his current behavior. At first, I thought this innocent pastime was another of Gunnar's little quirks. When I later started to climb through the ranks of the CFR and heard people congratulate me on the diamonds of the Kalahari, I realized it was an extremely widespread practice.

I had given myself two weeks to decide on the subject of my first dossier. I was determined to make a splash. My great ambition was to outshine Lena Thorsen, whose name I kept hearing. Gunnar, whom I questioned endlessly, had told me that the really great dossiers had half a dozen very specific characteristics, and he agreed to list them for me.

The most important, he said, was ambition, which he also called a certain claim to universality. Provided the technical quality was equivalent, it was better to create the history of Atlantis than some umpteenth variety of orchids. The former would enter the collective imagination and influence thousands of poets and Utopians whereas the latter would delight only a handful of botanists, without having any serious repercussions.

"See the bigger picture!" Gunnar kept saying. "You can do better than some godforsaken hole in Nebraska."

Gunnar liked to link the idea of ambition to a related concept that he called "the ability to set things in motion." Some dossiers, brilliant and ambitious as they might be, never went any further.

Ten years earlier, for example, a Romanian agent had created a major Renaissance painter. All the art historians had immediately pounced on this invention, devoting books and conferences to the hitherto unknown artist. The Metropolitan Museum in New York and the Louvre in Paris had fought tooth and nail at an auction in London to acquire a large oil painting of the adoration of the Magi. All this excitement had naturally delighted those who had worked in any capacity on the project, but, basically, it had had almost no impact. "It might have been different," Gunnar said, "if that artist had become famous for a particular technique of preparing his colors, which might have influenced his followers. But without anything to really distinguish him from dozens of other old masters, our painter was destined to leave no trace."

The great dossiers, according to Gunnar, were like stones in a pond. Forming rings around themselves, they forced the experts, and even sometimes the general public, to reconsider their opinion. Above all, they gave rise to actions, not just words.

He gave me as an example a dossier by a Mexican, all about oil supposedly discovered by peasants in Chiapas. The agent had put it all together so well that within a year Texaco was digging holes everywhere. Apparently, the company had sunk $250m into the venture, which had supported a community of fifteen hundred people for two years.

Good dossiers also reused characters and situations previously created by the CFR. Gunnar sometimes compared the CFR to an ecosystem or a self-sufficient economy. "If you need to mention the opinion of a nineteenth-century French literary critic, avoid Sainte-Beuve, over whom we have no control, and quote Simonet, whose supposedly lost notebooks that we bring out periodically. If your scenario has any connection with the Midwest of the United States, try to mention Skitos, Nebraska. That way you'll kill two birds with one stone: you'll strengthen your own dossier while at the same time giving Thorsen's even more credibility. I'm not exaggerating when I say that some dossiers make several hundred references to in-house efforts.

Conversely, think of those who come after you. Create myths, experts, catalogs, bibliographies, award winners, from which they'll be able to draw at will. Don't be stingy with new sources."

The relationship with time was another important criterion. The CFR favored scenarios that took a long time to mature, that had their origins in a distant past while extending for several years, even several centuries, into the future.

In that respect, Lena Thorsen's dossier was of genuine interest. Sixty years had gone by between Spyros Tadelitis's exile and his death, a time lapse that had given Thorsen the opportunity to evoke, and if need be to invent, a whole raft of events and episodes: a great exodus of people, the conquest of the West, the building of the railroads, the industrialization of pig farming, etc. In addition, by its very construction, Thorsen's scenario had repercussions on the present-day town of Skitos, whether in its restaurants, in its traditions, or in the type of tourists it attracted.

"Let me give you another example," Gunnar said. "Let's suppose you decide to write a dossier about John F. Kennedy. Personally, I wouldn't recommend it: so many agents have tackled his life that it's become almost a myth. But if you absolutely insist, choose an angle that allows you to take in the whole of his career. Invent a nervous ailment that might explain both his indecisiveness during the Bay of Pigs invasion and his feeling of impunity when he went up against the Mafia. Or else describe how his compulsive sex drive can be traced back to the way his mother bathed him when he was a child. Above all, don't limit yourself to a single episode, a single day, a single year, because your dossier wouldn't survive much longer than that."

Gunnar also insisted that I should fabricate the majority of my sources myself. "More and more young agents," he said disapprovingly, "think that all they have to do is change a name or a figure in a database to make their scenario credible. But they're making a basic mistake. Alteration may sometimes be necessary, but it's no substitute for a good ad hoc source. That's what Lena Thorsen understood when she created the Association for Thessalian Culture and decided to write twenty years' worth of minutes. What better way to present characters, to establish a chronology? A good agent controls his sources, that's what our young recruits all too often forget. I guess they're terrified by the amount of work involved in creating something out of nothing."

Last but not least, every dossier was judged by its ratio of risk to profitability. According to Gunnar, any journalist could think up a spectacular scenario, but bringing it to life without endangering the CFR requires much rarer qualities.

"Never forget," Gunnar said in a grave tone, "that you are merely one link in the chain. The reason the CFR has survived so long is attributable to the constant efforts of men and women who have always put the safety of the organization before their personal gratification. In any case, you'll soon discover that our leaders have an infinitely smaller tolerance of risk than you do. Where you think in terms of probability, they know that it takes only one mistake to endanger the whole organization."

Gunnar could have added a final imperative: always respect the instructions of the Plan. I learned, however, that agents putting

51

together their first dossier were released from having to conform to them and could give free rein to their creative impulses.

"Take advantage of that," Gunnar advised me, "it's the first and last time you'll be able to."

During the two weeks that followed, I must have thought up a hundred scenarios. The ideas came to me without warning, while I was jogging, or in the shower, or during my endless meetings with the general council of Savoie. I would go over them carefully, without preconceived ideas, but I would generally reject them almost immediately. I worked for three days on the thorium idea suggested to me by Gunnar. Unfortunately, it turned out that the permanent ice layer in northern Greenland was too deep to allow the extraction of the precious ore in large enough quantities to make it financially viable. My dossier would be unable to set anything in motion, to borrow Gunnar's expression.

After a week, I really thought I had found my subject. I told Gunnar that I was going to create a French minimalist writer named Zu. The unusual characteristic of Zu's novels was that they were not more than a thousand words long, with each one shorter than the previous one.

Gunnar didn't try to dissuade me, but he suggested that I pay a visit to the archivist of the Grenoble bureau (French literature, 1821 to the present day), a man named Nestor Bimard. "You'll see," Gunnar said with a laugh, "he'll try to persuade you to turn Zu into a Romantic poet. That's his favorite genre, and he finds it hard to talk about anything else."

Thus forewarned, I took a train the following morning to Grenoble, carrying a letter of accreditation signed by Per Baldur. In handing me the small blue sheet of paper, Gunnar had explained to me that I had just passed from the status of novice to that of freshman. In the terminology of the CFR, those who have not yet been cleared by their recruiters are described as novices. Once they have been cleared, they become freshmen, and they stay that way until the Dossier Committee gives the green light to their first project, which confers the rank of Class one agent.

Freshmen and Class one agents do not have access to the records without the authorization of the head of their branch. That is how I learned that it was Baldur who was in charge of the Reykjavík branch. Baldur, the only one of the three partners whom I hadn't yet met...

The Grenoble bureau is located in a local government office in which Bimard was in charge of the research department. He came to fetch me from the reception and led me to his office. He was a short, tubby man, with exaggeratedly bushy eyebrows, the spitting image of my professor of international law at the university. He motioned to me to sit down, carefully examined my letter of accreditation and asked after Baldur, with whom he had collaborated fifteen years earlier on the creation of a great wine related to Chassagne-Montrachet.

"As strange as it may seem," I spluttered, "I've never met Per Baldur."

Bimard's face lit up. "New, are you? Welcome to the CFR, my boy. Have you published anything yet?"

"No, actually, I'm working on my first dossier."

"And you chose French literature? Congratulations, a wise choice. Do you already know the author, the period perhaps?"

"The author and the period, twentieth century. But that's about all."

"What's the author's name?"

"Maximilien Zu," I said, adding, almost apologetically, "He won't necessarily be a Romantic."

"No, of course not. Maximilien Zu, that's very interesting. Is it a biography you're writing?"

In less than a minute, the polite formulas had given way to a genuine professional interest. Would it be a biography? A very good question.

"Um, I haven't yet decided. What do people usually do?"

I immediately realized from the self-important air that Bimard assumed that we were now dealing with his favorite subject. He sat back in his armchair and put the tips of his fingers together.

"Obviously, biography is the most popular genre. In French literature alone, the CFR has given birth to more than twenty authors. You may know a few: Louis-René Circulaire, Paul Dussard, Alain Fagot..."

"Alain Fagot? The man who wrote about Mallarmé and Blanchot?"

"That's the man, the author of the famous *Who speaks when I fall silent*? That surprises you, doesn't it? I've heard that the University of Dijon was planning to award him a doctorate, can you imagine?"

He gave me a few seconds to digest this, then went on with increased vigor:

"The value of a biography can be measured by two criteria: the significance of the author, and the amount of documentation. If you want to try your hand at it, I advise you to begin with a Romantic, an obscure associate of Lamartine or a childhood friend of Charles Nodier. You don't run too many risks, especially as you'll be able to rely on the support of the *Cahiers du Romantisme*. It's useful, you know, to have the backing of a friendly publication. It allows us to correct our mistakes. I know, you don't intend to make any, that's what they all say. But trust the voice of experience, your first dossier will contain at least three basic errors, and when Hong Kong tries to make trouble for you, you'll be quite happy to have us. An erratum, an article on the publication of 'a thesis that at last re-establishes the truth about Zu', and everything will be back to normal."

"What about creating a successful author?"

"Don't even think about it! It'd be suicidal. Oh, of course, who hasn't dreamed of inventing a Nobel Prize winner? I wouldn't be so ambitious, but I'd happily give ten years of my life for a Prix Goncourt. A shared first prize that comes out of nowhere... But all that's just fantasy. Can you imagine the work it would take to establish credentials for a Prix Goncourt winner? Because, as I'm sure you'll have realized, the greater the fame of the writer, the more important it is to make sure the sources are impeccable. I categorically advise a beginner not to try it."

"And apart from a biography?" I asked, somewhat disconcerted.

"You have the work itself, which can encompass an infinite number of variations: an unpublished novel by Benjamin Constant found in a secret drawer in his study; an unpublished translation of an obviously imaginary German author; even the insertion of a text of our own in a great classic."

I was learning more every day. "For example?"

"Well, I personally supervised the writing of six pages of *The Three Musketeers* by Alexandre Dumas."

"How is that possible?"

"Our starting point was a letter from Dumas to one of his mistresses, in which the great man complains that his publisher hasn't included certain corrections that he sent him after the novel had been serialized. When I learned of the existence of this letter, which had been acquired by a collector at a sale at Drouot in 1967, I immediately got down to work. Six months later, I produced my manuscript, and it was authenticated by the Society of the Friends of Alexandre Dumas. Do you know why?"

"Because it was a very good forgery?"

"Partly, but also, and above all, because our version was better than old Alexandre's! I'd like you to compare them when you have the chance; it's at the beginning of the section about the captivity of Milady. Our dialogue writer performed wonders. He and I were planning to rewrite the whole of the *Musketeers*. Alas, he died before we could get down to it in the earnest."

Which of the two things had upset Bimard more, the death of his colleague or the abandonment of his project, I would have found hard to say.

"Biographies, works..." he went on. "To that we should add a few minor genres: fake critical apparatus, literary movements, schools of thought, etc. All of them have yielded good results, but all are still waiting for their masterpiece. So do you have a clearer idea now?"

"I still prefer biography."

"Perfect. One thing worries me, though. You speak French quite well, but how good is your written French?"

"Much the same, I guess. Good, but not exceptional."

"That's what I thought. You see, my boy, I fear that your linguistic level may not quite be up to an entire biographical project."

"My idea was to make Zu a minimalist writer. His books would be very short, a few pages at most."

"That's a wonderful idea, really. But, however short these novels are, they'll still have to be written. Were you planning to subcontract that part of the work? I don't know many agents who'd agree to do the work for a freshman unless they thought there was a major advantage in it for them."

"I was thinking you might help me." I ventured, quite aware that I was burning my bridges.

"And I'd do it with pleasure," Bimard replied with a big smile that revealed his lower teeth and made him look even more like my professor of international law. "Of course, I'd have to find a certain intellectual interest in your project. Don't we owe this Maximilien Zu a few sonnets about unrequited love? I think I heard you say he shared a mistress with Musset."

The deal was a clear one: Nestor Bimard would help me on condition that I make Zu a romantic writer. At that moment, I realized that Gunnar didn't like my project, but that he had preferred to have it demolished by someone else. I beat a hasty retreat:

"It was certainly kind of you to see me, but I wouldn't like to abuse your kindness. You've opened a lot of horizons for me. I'm going to think it all over and get back in touch very soon."

Without even leaving Bimard time to reply, I stood up and gathered my notes. Fortunately, my host accepted his defeat graciously.

"As you wish, Sliv," he said, also rising. "But don't take too long to make a decision. Next month I'm bringing out a special issue of the *Cahiers du Romantisme* entitled: *They lived in the shadow of geniuses.* I can't imagine a better springboard for Maximilien Zu."

"Neither can I," I said as I took my leave.

What I omitted to add was that this so-called springboard was meant to launch my own career, not that of an obscure would-be poet.

8

Having laughed heartily at my account of my interview with Bimard, Gunnar Eriksson confirmed what I had suspected: he didn't like Maximilien Zu.

"Pointless and over-clever," he declared. "Frankly, Sliv, did you really think you'd make a stir with that constipated scribbler?"

"The idea amused me. Plus, I was thinking that minimalism might find some echoes in other disciplines."

"Let me make one thing quite clear," Gunnar said, raising his eyes to heaven. "You're not here to amuse yourself. And what would I have looked like, sponsoring your hoax?"

"Frankly, I don't much appreciate your reprimands. I may not be here only to amuse myself but it's one of the reasons I'm here. And I present my ideas to you only so that you can give me your opinion, not in order for you to have the Grenoble bureau run your errands."

Gunnar looked at me for a long time. He was clearly searching for his words. I sometimes had the impression that I had to take him down a peg or two if I wanted him to take me seriously.

"You're right, Sliv," he resumed at last. "And I apologize if you feel you've been wasting your time. But in my eyes, your trip to Grenoble had an educational purpose. I wanted you to meet someone like Bimard. As God is my witness, I love Nestor dearly, but he is the prototype of the Class 3 agent who's completely lost touch with reality. He indulges himself in producing dossiers that are technically impeccable but haven't served our purposes for a long time. And when he meets a young agent, instead of opening his mind, he tries to get him interested in his own obsession, which is of no interest to us."

"But I thought the Plan forced agents to work on specific themes."

"The word 'force' is unfortunately a bit strong. Every year, the Plan publishes its priorities and, believe me, the French Romantics haven't been on that list for quite a while. But Bimard doesn't care. He always finds a way to justify his work: sometimes it's a question of prolonging an old dossier; sometimes he claims to be strengthening a weak source."

"What'll happen to him?"

"Not a lot, that's the problem. The Human Resources department has already summoned him several times, but as they can't apply any real sanctions, their warnings ring hollow. Bimard knows perfectly well that the CFR will never take the risk of sending him back to civilian life, although that would be the only threat capable of getting through to him."

"Can't the CFR reduce his salary?"

"At most they could freeze it. The collective labor convention forbids reductions in salary."

"The labor convention?" I echoed in surprise.

"Yes, Sliv," Gunnar chuckled. "That's what I'm trying to make you understand: the CFR is a big organization, it can't totally escape common practice."

"So Bimard is untouchable?"

"To all intents and purposes, yes. Fortunately he's nearly fifty-five, and Human Resources will nudge him into taking early retirement. He'll get 70 % of his salary until he reaches his official retirement age. Now I don't want this to depress you. We'll always need brilliant young agents."

Despite Gunnar's encouragement, our conversation left a bitter taste in my mouth. I had only just joined the CFR, and I was already getting an idea of how cumbersome it could be. Even though a voice inside me whispered me that such excesses were inevitable in a structure of such size, it saddened me that the CFR was not and could never be the ideal employer.

I resumed my search for a subject, although I now had less time to devote to it. My visit to Grenoble had delayed my work on the dam project and my colleagues in the firm made it clear to me that I was now going to have to take on a larger share of the work.

Inspiration came to me one morning as I was having my breakfast in the hotel restaurant and reading *Le Figaro*. An article on page 12 mentioned the death at the age of seventy-seven of the famous French ethnologist Gaston Chemineau, member of the Academy of Science, Professor at the Collège de France, and author of several works on native African tribes.

Chemineau, according to the article, had returned three months earlier from a two-year trip to Africa, in the course of which he had stayed with several tribes in the Zambezi Basin. He had died of a heart attack at his home in Ville-d'Avray, where he had lived alone while working on a new book. *Le Figaro* called him one of the last giants of the social sciences and a humanist whose work was appreciated around the world.

I immediately saw this death as a blessing. An idea had come to me in a split second: given that Chemineau had not yet sent a manuscript to his publisher, there was still time to amend his book, even perhaps to add an account of his experiences with a fictitious tribe.

By a happy coincidence, I had some knowledge of African demographics, a subject that had been part of the program for my master's degree in geography. I even recalled studying a work of Chemineau's at a seminar: a monograph on the habitat of the Kikuyu, a Bantu tribe in Kenya. That morning, sipping my coffee, I tried to remember what I could. The demographics of southern Africa were dominated by the Bantu, a collection of thousands of tribes who speak some four hundred different languages. The Bantu were settled farmers. They had learned to use iron, which had allowed them gradually to steal a lead over two rival groups who were actually older than they: the Bushmen and the Khoikhoi (a name that has been a great source of schoolboy amusement). The Bushmen and the Khoikhoi were the last peoples to speak the Khoisan languages, which were characterized by an intensive use of particular consonants called clicks. That about all I could remember at this stage. Could my imagination take over?

Unfortunately, a busy morning awaited me. In an hour I had an appointment downstream of the dam with two geologists from Lyons. Realizing it was too late to cancel the meeting, I called Gunnar in Reykjavík. Luckily, he was already at his desk. I briefly explained the situation, as well as my idea of creating a new tribe. He thought it over for a few seconds, during which I heard a teapot whistling.

"That's a pretty good idea," he said at last. "Better anyway than the previous one. Why did you call?"

"Because I have the feeling we're not going to have much time. It may already be too late. My project will only work if I can insert a chapter into Chemineau's book. You've repeated often enough that dossiers need an authoritative source."

Gunnar completed my thought: "And what better source than the posthumous work of one of the world's leading ethnologists? I'll call Paris immediately and ask them to find out what they can about Chemineau."

"And about his publisher, if possible," I added.

"Consider it done. What else do you need?"

"I'll be back tomorrow. The fieldwork is nearly over, and I'll tell Mika that you need me for another assignment. In the meantime, could you put together some literature? Anything you can find on the demographics of southern Africa, the Bantu, the Khoikhoi, the Bushmen, their rituals, their languages, and so on."

"And all Chemineau's publications. If you have to write a chapter of his book, you might as well know his style. All noted."

"Gunnar," I asked, "do you think I have something?"

Several seconds passed before he answered. By now, the kettle was whistling very loudly. "I really think so. But don't get too excited. First, Paris may well inform us that the book has already gone to press. Secondly..."

"Secondly?" I asked feverishly.

"Secondly, you have only one idea so far. Or, to be precise, an idea and the possibility of faking an authoritative source. But you still don't have a scenario, and without a scenario there's no dossier."

"I'll find it," I said, making an effort to sound self-confident. "Thanks, Gunnar, I'll see you tomorrow."

Before taking the plane to Reykjavík the following morning, I found time to drop into the municipal library in Annecy. As I had expected, the section devoted to demographics wasn't large, but I still managed to gather some valuable information. Most Bantu societies are matriarchal, revolve around clans, and are characterized by a pious respect for the old. The Bantu also like to define themselves, beyond their family or their clan, by their membership in brotherhoods of various kinds, for hunting, dancing— and even laughing. As I turned the pages of the encyclopedias and took notes, I felt a growing excitement, so obvious did it seem that Africa lent itself naturally to falsification. It seemed to be a rich, mysterious world of the imagination, filled with fabulous stories. Everyone had an idea of Africa, yet nobody really knew it. At a time when television cameras had revealed every corner of Europe and North America, Africa remained essentially virgin and unknown. It was a land of demiurges in the making.

One article fascinated me more than the others: an account of the situation of the Bushmen, a nomadic people believed to be among the oldest in the world, who had been chased from their lands, first by the Bantu, then by the Dutch and British colonists, and who seemed condemned to perpetual wandering. Thus the Bushmen were a vanishing people, of whom there were probably no more than a hundred thousand left, although no one could be sure.

Clustered into groups of a few families, the Bushmen lived in huts made of branches and subsisted on hunting and gathering. Their development seemed to have stopped a few thousand years ago; they had never learned to use iron or any chemical procedure, and obviously they could neither read nor write. When an old person became incapable of taking part in the work of the group, the Bushmen would build him a hut, fill it with food, say goodbye without any particular show of emotion, and abandon him to certain death.

The first anthropologists who had encountered the Bushmen had taken their unusual language for the cackling of hens. Linguists had subsequently established that they spoke a dialect of Khoisan, one of whose unusual characteristics was that it had no words for the spectrum of colors or for numbers higher than three: six was simply "two and two and two."

I could have spent hours reading about the Bushmen, but I didn't want to miss my plane. I made a few photocopies, thinking once again how little I knew of the world. Who would have thought that in 1991 men and women still lived as they had ten thousand years ago?

On the flights from Geneva to Paris, and from Paris to Reykjavík I let my mind wander. What to do with the Bushmen? Invent new rituals for them, rewrite their myths? Rehabilitate a people whose right to be different had been flouted by the Bantu and the European colonists? All that was necessary, but not sufficient. One question above all gnawed at me: how could I give the story of the Bushmen a universal perspective?

The plane landed just before six in the evening, but I resolved to go straight to the office, in the hope that Gunnar had left some documentation on my desk. I wasn't disappointed: he was there to greet me in person. He motioned me to my favorite armchair and closed the door of his office. His shirt was sticking out of his belt; he had pulled his sleeves up over his forearms; and I noticed that his fly was open. I had never seen him so excited.

"My boy," he began without preamble, "it seems the gods are with you. Our colleagues in Paris have done an excellent job, and the situation is looking good. Let's start with Chemineau. His wife died in 1985, knocked down by a car in Paris. That gave him the idea that he ran fewer risks in Zimbabwe than in France, and he made several trips alone to Africa, even though he was well over seventy. He left a daughter, who is a cellist in the Berlin Philharmonic. She was on tour in Asia when she heard the news of her father's death. According to Paris, she's coming back for the funeral and will leave again immediately afterwards."

"Did he have any brothers or sisters?"

"They're all dead. The only person who might be a problem for us is his cleaning lady. She had been working for Chemineau for twenty-five years. She comes three times a week, even when he's in

Africa. Now about his publishers. Our agent in Paris called them, pretending to be a journalist. To be honest, he exceeded his instructions, but I don't think you'll be too upset with him when you hear what he found out."

"The publisher hasn't seen the manuscript?" I asked anxiously.

"Not only hasn't he seen it, he wasn't expecting to see it for another three weeks!" Gunnar roared in triumph.

"And is that good news?"

Gunnar seemed astonished by my question. "It's excellent news," he explained. "It means the old fellow had almost finished his book. Imagine: if he hadn't started, you'd have had to write the whole thing, instead of which you just have to insert a chapter."

"All the same, three weeks isn't very long."

This time, Gunnar seemed at a loss. "Are you doing it on purpose, Sliv? Chemineau had promised to deliver his book in three weeks, but he's no longer there to write it. Right now, his publisher must be starting to worry about the manuscript. He's going to want to bring the book out very quickly, before the body's cold."

"But that gives me very little time," I stammered.

"From what I can see, a week, ten days at most." Seeing my crestfallen air, Gunnar added, "Of course, that may not seem very long, but actually it'll give you more time to put the rest of your dossier together. Even if he works twice as fast as usual, the publisher will still need a month or two to prepare the book for publication: he'll have to edit the text, correct the proofs, have the book printed. We'll take advantage of those weeks to work on the other sources. Even though Chemineau is our most authoritative source, he still can't be the only person to mention that tribe."

"Ten days," I echoed in a daze. "Ten days to write in French and in the style of a world-famous ethnologist a monograph on a non-existent African tribe?"

"Don't worry, my boy. When you put it like that, the task may appear daunting, but we'll get through it. I've already reallocated all your work to other people in the firm and informed the partners that you and I are supposed to be handing in an intermediate report on that blasted dam tomorrow. Nobody will be surprised to see us working all night. As you'll see, I've put together a bit of literature. I'll make us some coffee to start our brains working, especially yours: you'll need some caffeine if you hope to write a scenario by tomorrow."

"Tomorrow?" I repeated, still in shock. "No problem. And thanks for the coffee."

"Don't mention it. Let's meet here again in two hours. I have a few calls to make. Try to find out if the organization has any opinions on the Bantu tribes."

"Not Bantu," I corrected him mechanically as I opened the door. "Bushmen."

9

Two full boxes of documentation awaited me on my desk. I dropped my case on a chair and started going through them without even taking off my coat. There were Chemineau's last six books (the previous ones were out of print), brief monographs on the demographics of every country in southern Africa (South Africa, Zambia, Botswana, Swaziland, Namibia, Mozambique, Angola and Zimbabwe), several works on the Bantu, a compilation of recent press articles on geopolitical and economic developments in the region, two reports from the United Nations Economic and Social Council on the territorial eviction of indigenous African peoples, and three books on the Bushmen.

The first, entitled *The Harmless People* (which was how the Bushmen described themselves), was the work of an American woman named Elizabeth Marshall Thomas, who, back in the 1950s, had been one of the first Westerners to share the life of the Bushmen. The book I was holding was the 1989 edition, lavishly illustrated and revised by Thomas after her recent trips to Africa.

That same year, a man named Steyn, also an English speaker, had written *The Bushmen of the Kalahari* (the desert where most of the Bushmen now live).

The third book, written in 1954 by a Frenchman named Jacques Mauduit, was entitled *Kalahari, The Life of the Bushmen*.

Although I'd have liked to start with these books on the Bushmen, I decided it would be best to learn a little of the context first. My geography teachers had trained me well: in order to preserve an overall vision, one should always go from the general to the particular.

What did I get from my reading? First, that Africa was the continent that had been populated the longest. Evolving from the apes, the first men had appeared there between three and four million years before the Christian era. In such a vast territory, it was natural that not all peoples developed in a homogeneous manner.

In the north, for example, the Egyptians had acquired knowledge of astronomy and masonry, and had developed one of the most advanced civilizations of the ancient world.

In the south, the Bushmen and the Khoikhoi seemed to have stalled, remaining unaware of the benefits of metallurgy or agriculture. Then, little by little, the Bantu had asserted their superiority. Learning to use iron, and eager to expand, the Bantu had gradually colonized the whole lower part of the continent, pushing more ancient peoples like the Bushmen ever further south. Between the sixteenth and nineteenth centuries, the great European colonial powers had claimed a large slice of the territory, not to mention religious brotherhoods like the Huguenots, who settled in South Africa to escape persecution.

Without weapons or diplomacy, the Bushmen had had to make way for the intruders, until eventually they had been flung into the most inhospitable territory imaginable: the Kalahari Desert.

Several non-governmental organizations had tried to draw the attention of Western countries to this scandalous eviction (the most polemical pamphlets even used the word "genocide"), but to no avail. Nobody was any longer in doubt that within a few generations the Bushmen would disappear completely.

Even ethnologists seemed divided on the best way to help the Bushmen. Certain passages in the book by Elizabeth Marshall Thomas eloquently demonstrated the ways in which assistance from the NGOs had sometimes missed its target.

For example, in an attempt to educate the Bushmen children, mothers had been deprived of their ancestral role; projects to feed them had blunted the warrior instincts of the young men; and in trying to care for the old, who had previously been abandoned to their fate, the NGOs had confronted the families with moral dilemmas they were philosophically ill-equipped to resolve.

It must have been nine in the evening when Gunnar came into my office without knocking and found me staring at a photograph showing a mother with unusually protuberant buttocks and her daughter: such exaggerated development of the adipose cells of the backside is a characteristic of the Bushmen's women.

"They look like car fenders," Gunnar commented subtly. "Would you like a slice of pizza? It's just arrived, and it's piping hot."

"I wouldn't say 'no'," I replied. I hadn't eaten anything since a packet of wafers on board the Geneva-Paris flight.

"So, where are we? Have you got something to show me? A project? A draft?"

"Nothing like that," I sighed. I turned the photograph toward Gunnar. "I want to talk about these people, but I can't find the right angle."

"Tell me about them," Gunnar suggested, sitting down opposite me. He put his hands behind his head as if preparing for a long story. "Be objective. I don't want to know whose side you're on.

I complied, without looking at my notes. I had stood up, because I had already noticed that I could gather my thoughts more easily when I walked up and down. More than once, I had to return to my desk to look for a card or a photograph to support what I was saying. When I had told Gunnar all I knew, I turned to look at him, hoping for a miracle.

"Devilishly interesting," he commented, staring into the distance. "I can understand what attracts you, but I can also see what's missing."

"What's that?"

"Two things," Gunnar said, leaning forward as if preparing to give a lesson. "First of all, I still don't see how you're going to link Chemineau with the Bushmen. From what you've told me, the Bushmen aren't exactly unknown. I wouldn't go so far as to call them the most famous people in the world, but I don't know many African tribes that can boast of having inspired three books. There's no question of claiming that Chemineau discovered the Bushmen. He could at a pinch reveal some little-known aspects of their daily life, but your three authors, who probably spent several years studying the Bushmen, would quickly smell a rat. They'd all want to go see for themselves, and in six months they'd publish a denial that'd demolish your dossier."

"What are you trying to tell me, Gunnar? That I should abandon the Chemineau angle?

"Not at all. But you must start from the premise that Chemineau never encountered the Bushmen, unless it was a sub-tribe, or blood relatives who had fled the Kalahari. If you're going to have him make revelations, you can't run the risk that they'll immediately be denied. That's the first thing.

"The second thing that's lacking is anything that opens it to the outside world. Your dossier can't just be about the tragic fate of the Bushmen. It wouldn't make any waves outside a small circle of scholars and NGOs. We need to give it a world resonance, make it emblematic of a significant global tendency."

"Such as?"

"Such as the gradual disappearance of dialects, or perhaps the inability of indigenous peoples to hold on to their lands in the face of territorial claims by sovereign states. The reader of Chemineau's book has to feel concerned about the fate of the Bushmen, but he also has to tell himself that what's happening to them might eventually happen to him, too."

"I see," I said, although actually I didn't see anything at all.

"Have you had a look at Chemineau's previous books?"

"Not yet. I've been a bit snowed under lately." I pointed to all the documentation, in the hope that Gunnar would get the message and let me work. But he seemed to be in a talkative mood.

"Our agent in Paris told me over the phone that Chemineau was very popular in France, and that his fame extended well beyond academic circles. The wise old man with the mane of white hair, the defender of noble causes who's interviewed on New Year's Eve about the place of the human race in the cosmos, you see the kind of thing I mean?"

"Yes, I do. Another slice of pizza and I'll get back to work, I promise."

"I also called an old friend from the Plan. We don't have much when it comes to indigenous peoples. Your idea definitely excited him. He thinks having our own tribe could prove very useful in the future."

"Thanks, Gunnar. Now I really have to get back to work."

"Of course, of course, I'll get out of here," Gunnar said, and went back to his office.

I resumed my reading, underlining certain sentences and making copious notes in the margins, but without really knowing what I was looking for. Around midnight the cleaning woman knocked at my door and asked me if she could empty the garbage. She didn't seem surprised to see me still working. When the firm had to make a bid for a contract, some of my colleagues stayed in the office even later than the witching hour.

I started to see the light at the end of the tunnel just before one in the morning, as I was skimming through Chemineau's most famous book: *The Peoples of the Earth in the New World Economic Order*. In it, the great French champion of ethnic diversity expounded an especially pessimistic theory: contrary to received ideas, it wasn't states that posed the biggest threat to cultural plurality, but the multinationals. With almost nobody to challenge them, the multinationals laid down the law to the governments of small countries, especially in Africa and Asia, and forced them to agree to exorbitant conditions in order to exploit their natural resources.

In the last part of the book, Chemineau openly condemned three petroleum giants, one French—Elf Aquitaine—and two American—Chevron and Exxon—demonstrating conclusively how they had demanded from several African states that they relocate certain tribes who were hindering the exploration of petroleum deposits.

The companies had responded to Chemineau's attacks by launching PR campaigns that attempted to show how their investments in fact contributed more to the development of the African continent than any government aid. But the harm was done, and for years the NGOs used the Frenchman's work as the basis of their condemnation of the growing power of the multinationals.

Chemineau's theory reminded me of something I had read in the monograph on Botswana. The previous year, the South African company De Beers had discovered in the east of the country, near the border with Zimbabwe, a very promising diamond deposit that went by the name of Martin's Drift. The Prime Minister of Botswana said that he was counting on this new discovery to give an extra boost to the already burgeoning national mining industry. This declaration implicitly suggested that other deposits were already operational, and I was interested in where they were located.

When I read that De Beers had been mining a deposit at Orapa, in the middle of the Kalahari, since 1971, I thought I was about to faint. I finally had my angle. I scribbled a few notes, and went down the corridor to see Gunnar.

I found him standing by his desk, in the middle of a phone conversation with an Italian colleague. I had no idea he spoke Italian, but he spoke it well, rapidly in any case, and in a sharper voice than usual. When he became aware of my presence, he made a gesture to indicate that he wouldn't be long.

"Sit down," he whispered, covering the receiver.

While waiting for him to hang up, I went over my argument in search of a flaw that might have escaped me.

"I'm all yours," Gunnar said. "Sorry about that. A colleague from Milan, a real bore."

"Shouldn't he be in bed at this hour?"

"If only he were! No, Signor Mattei stays up late to make himself seem important." Gunnar didn't seem to realize that this description could just as easily apply to himself.

"This time, I think I have my link," I announced. "As you know, for centuries the Bushmen have been condemned to constant movement. The territory available to them was reduced, first by the Bantu, then by the Europeans."

"Yes, you explained all that. What of it?"

71

"They ended up in the Kalahari Desert, a land so hostile that nobody thought anyone would ever want to take it from them. Well, just listen to this, diamonds have been found in the Kalahari. De Beers has been mining a deposit there for twenty-five years."

"So what?" Gunnar repeated, stifling a yawn. "If it's been going on that long, it must mean the Bushmen and De Beers are on good terms."

"That's a moot point," I replied, determined not to be contradicted. "Thousands of Bushmen work in the open cut mine at Orapa. They've forgotten how to hunt and won't be able to hand down their ancestral traditions to their children. But that's not the main point. The recent discovery of Martin's Drift proves that De Beers hasn't given up on the idea of exploiting the resources of Botswana. Sooner or later, the Bushmen will be an embarrassment to them, and De Beers will ask the government of Botswana politely but firmly to give them a hand."

Gunnar completed my sentence— "in shifting the problem, and the Bushmen with it. Yes, I'm beginning to understand. Obviously, it gives the dossier more substance."

"It's not just about the Bushmen anymore, it's about a thirty-thousand-year-old people chased from its home at the request of a multinational by a state that's been independent since 1966. That's the fact Chemineau would have emphasized. He would have patiently gathered his information, then publicized it as widely as possible."

"Trust me, Sliv, we're going to make one hell of a stir. Good. I think you have your framework. Now for the details..."

We got back to work in his office, Gunnar walking back and forth, thinking aloud, while I sat with my legs across the arm of a chair, taking notes. Officially, Gunnar wasn't supposed to help me. It was my dossier, not his, and his contribution should have been limited to methodological support. In fact, he didn't suggest any actual ideas, even though he had his own way of framing my thoughts to bring out the main points of the scenario. Suddenly, he looked at his watch:

"All right, you're going to write all this up. Poulsson, the janitor, gets in at 6:30 on the dot. I don't want him to find us here."

I sat down at the computer to type out a first draft. One hour later, Gunnar caught the last sheet straight from the printer, held it out to me and asked me to read aloud the entire draft.

"'In 1967,'" I began, "'the South African company De Beers discovered a diamond deposit at Orapa in the region of Makgadikgadi in the northeast of the Kalahari Desert. This discovery was of vital importance to Botswana, which had gained its independence a year earlier and was searching desperately for a way to ensure its economic viability. The only inhabitants of the Kalahari Desert were the Bushmen, a collection of nomadic tribes considered one of the oldest peoples in the world, who had been forced to migrate several times over the centuries, first by the arrival of the Bantu, then by the Dutch and English colonial powers. The Bushmen, of whom there are about sixty thousand, are divided into cultural or family groups, each clan living on a territory of two or three hundred square miles. None of the clans lived at Orapa, and Botswana had no problem in authorizing De Beers to mine the new deposit, which today produces ten million karats.'"

"Very good, very clear," Gunnar commented appreciatively.

"'At the end of the 1970s, De Beers discovered a new deposit further south, at Jwaneng in the Naledi Valley. The mine, which opened in 1982, is still operating and produces about ten million karats a year.'"

"So far, everything is true."

"'In 1983, some twenty Bushmen clans met in the desert at the request of Maraqo, chief of the Morafe clan. Such meetings are extremely rare, but Maraqo had stressed that the situation was out of the ordinary. His idea was that the Bushmen needed to come together and make a stand against the government of Botswana. That country, he argued, had to stop exploring the subsoil of the Kalahari, which had belonged to the Bushmen for thousands of moons.'"

73

"You'll have to check whether they actually talk about moons," Gunnar cut in. "It seems logical, but one never knows."

"I think I read it somewhere but I'll certainly check," I replied, making a note in the margin. "'Maraqo's speech was not well received. The chiefs of the other clans were resigned to their fate. "It's in our nature to move and look for other lands," they said. "If we're chased out, we'll go somewhere else. In any case we wouldn't know who to turn to for help." Maraqo admitted that he didn't know, either. The discussions lasted two days, but none of the other chiefs would budge from their positions, and they eventually all went back to their lands.

"A year later, a South African whose name we cannot reveal but whom we shall call Jan went to see Maraqo. He had just been fired from De Beers, where he had spent his entire career. He explained, through an interpreter, that he had objected to some of his employer's methods, and that the company preferred to dismiss him rather than risk him disseminating his ideas.

"Jan, who knew his job very well, had become embittered by this experience and decided to help the Bushmen. He revealed to Maraqo that the government of Botswana had just signed decrees authorizing De Beers to prospect four further sites in the Kalahari. According to Jan, there was far too much money at stake for the government to worry about the fate of the Bushmen. Only pressure from the international community could cause it to receive a delegation of natives and grant them territorial concessions. Unfortunately, the Bushmen did not have the means to finance a public relations campaign...'"

"Delete 'unfortunately'," Gunnar cut in. "We're not here to give brownie points to one side or the other."

"You're right. 'At these words, Maraqo crouched on the dirt floor of his hut and picked up a translucent stone. Jan let out a cry and tore the stone from Maraqo's hands. Dirty as it was, he had recognized it as a raw diamond which, when cut, would be at least eight karats.'"

"There's a risk this part of the story may seem far-fetched. Chemineau will have to point out that it's quite possible. In the last century, a South African boy found a twenty-one-karat diamond on the ground."

"I'm aware of that. But don't worry, Gunnar, Chemineau will explain all that. To continue: 'Jan plied Maraqo with questions. The chief explained that a child from the clan had found the stone along with a few smaller ones and that he thought it might be possible to find more if doing so could help the Bushmen make themselves heard. Jan replied that he would be able to sell the diamond in Antwerp, where he had many contacts, but that he would have to be careful in order not to attract attention from De Beers. He estimated that he would need a million dollars to orchestrate a worldwide public relations campaign. If Maraqo was willing to trust him, he would open a bank account in which he would deposit the revenue from the sale of the stones. Maraqo told him he trusted him completely and thanked him for everything he was doing. Jan left with the stones. The question of his own fee was never mentioned.'"

Gunnar raised his hand to interrupt me: "By insisting on that last point, you suggest that Jan's intentions are not as pure as he makes out. I'm not sure that's very smart."

"On the contrary," I replied. "The ambiguity is deliberate and will serve our purpose."

"All right, carry on."

"'The following year, Jan made three round trips from Botswana to Belgium. After the third one, he told Maraqo that he had the impression he was being followed. There was now more than 700,000 dollars in the account he had opened with the Banque Bruxelles Lambert. One more trip, and the Bushmen could begin their campaign. This time, Jan left with three huge stones and promised to return the following month. That was the last the tribe heard of him.

"Maraqo could only surmise what had happened. Obviously it couldn't be ruled out that Jan was a conman. The Bushmen might not use money, but Maraqo knew the allure it had for white men.

Nevertheless, on reflection, the idea struck him as unlikely. After all, when Jan had come to see him the first time, he had had no idea that the Morafe had discovered diamonds. Could Jan have been robbed or, worse still, murdered? How to find out? Maraqo didn't know Jan's surname; as for the account in the Banque Bruxelles Lambert, he had never even seen any documents relating to it.

"Not long afterwards, a convoy of 4x4s drew up near the Morafe camp, and some twenty black men and two white men got out with measuring equipment. They spent the afternoon methodically going over a patch of about two square miles, picking up stones, apparently at random, which they slipped into numbered transparent plastic bags. Maraqo tried to establish contact with the black men, but none of them spoke any Bushmen dialect. On the cap worn by one of them, he recognized the De Beers logo, which he had seen before on signs at the entrance to the mine at Orapa. The convoy left again at nightfall.

"'The following moon, a helicopter flew over the Morafe camp, terrifying the children. Maraqo, who had never seen a plane before wondered if this event had any connection with the earlier appearance of the convoy. He started to feel afraid. What if Jan had gone to De Beers and told them the secret of the Morafe? Maraqo took the diamonds that the children of the clan continued to bring him regularly and hid them outside the camp, in a place he did not reveal to anybody.

"'It was in 1990, while he was visiting a number of tribes in the Zambezi delta, that the French ethnologist Gaston Chemineau heard about the council summoned by Maraqo some years earlier. The author of *The Peoples of the Earth in the New World Economic Order* could not help but be stirred by the story of this patriarch who had tried to unite the Bushmen in fighting the imperialistic designs of De Beers. He decided to change his schedule and made a detour through Botswana to meet the Morafe.'"

"I assume you'll be able to document all that?" asked Gunnar.

"Actually, I wanted to ask your advice. Apparently, for the past thirty years Chemineau has been in correspondence with another well-known French anthropologist, Claude Lévi-Strauss. Do you think it's possible to fabricate a letter, imitating Chemineau's style, and to send it with a postmark showing that it came from Maputo in Mozambique?"

"Absolutely. Lévi-Strauss is familiar with the postal services in Africa. He won't be surprised to receive a letter from his friend a year or two late. To do it well, we'll have to find previous letters in order to form an idea of Chemineau's letter-writing style. I guess it could be something like this: 'My dear old friend, I'm interrupting my trip up the Zambezi for a hop over to the Kalahari, where I've been told there's an incredible tribe of Bushmen, the Morafe. Apparently the chief has decided to wage war on the diamond companies. About time, I say! I'll write at greater length once I'm there.'"

"That's exactly what I had in mind," I said, impressed by the ease with which Gunnar had made up the letter. "To continue: 'Maraqo did not confide in Chemineau as easily as he had in Jan. The Frenchman had to summarize all he had done to help indigenous peoples, and to use all his wiles to tease the story out of the African chief.

"Chemineau's first thought, on hearing Maraqo's incoherent account, was that his interlocutor was paranoid. According to Maraqo, De Beers was slowly but surely tightening its grip. Everything that happened—the motorized convoys that were appearing more and more frequently, the drying up of a well—he saw as a sign that the company was gearing up to expel the Bushmen. He himself had contracted an illness and was sure that he would soon die. After he was gone, would Chemineau agree to become a spokesman for the Bushmen and thwart De Beers' devilish plans? Chemineau swore solemnly, and Maraqo told him where he had buried the diamonds.'"

"Is that all?" asked Gunnar.

"For the moment, yes."

"Very good. It's a solid scenario, because it opens up several avenues simultaneously. You understand what I mean by that, don't you?"

"I think so, yes. We have to be prepared for the reaction of De Beers. The first thing they'll do is to attempt to identify this Jan. I won't reveal much about him, just that he's South African and worked for De Beers for many years before he was dismissed. In themselves, these clues won't be enough to identify him."

"Then," Gunnar said, "they're going to try to locate the Morafe camp. And if it really is a place where you just have to bend down to pick up diamonds as big as pigeon eggs, they're going to try very, very hard to find it."

"And that's where we have them. The Morafe don't exist, but obviously they won't know that..."

"By the way," Gunnar cut in, "I think Chemineau ought to say that he invented the name Morafe to protect the clan: a totally justified precaution that'll make De Beers' task even harder."

"But above all," I resumed, "we'll have taken care not to reveal anything about the location of the Morafe. De Beers will crisscross the desert looking for them, and we'll alert the NGOs, who will go there and see for themselves that Chemineau was telling the truth."

"Of course!" Gunnar cried. "'We caught you,' they'll say. We're not taken in by your lies. We know you're looking for the Morafe in order to expel them and to steal their diamonds.' That's the whole beauty of this kind of scenario: it's self-sustaining. By scouring the Kalahari to verify the rumor, De Beers will give it substance and do your job for you!"

"The Bushmen will have the whole world on their side," I said, "and the government of Botswana will no longer dare issue a prospecting permit to De Beers."

"You're single-handedly going to turn the Kalahari Desert into a sanctuary, Sliv!"

I'll never know if it was my scenario, the late hour, or the cold pizza, but at that moment the euphoria was tangible.

"What other avenues did you have in mind?" I resumed after a moment or two.

"This Jan who plays a crucial role in your story: will you give him a real existence or condemn him to be only a ghost?"

"Which do you advise?"

"We need to start from the assumption that the De Beers staff will really be looking for him. I dread their reaction if they don't find him. Either they'll realize they've been tricked, or they'll pick on someone completely innocent. We don't want either alternative. Contact the Legends Department: they'll provide you with a list of profiles, and all you'll need to do is choose the most suitable."

"The Legends Department? We have a Legends Department?"

"Of course. Based in Berlin and in close liaison with the Plan. You'll be dealing with them a great deal."

"But what do they do?"

"Haven't you ever read any spy novels? No? That's a pity. It's really quite simple. Let's imagine, for example, that thirty years ago a South African teenager named Mark Miller died while traveling abroad. For some reason, nobody informed the South African embassy of his death. A few years later one of our agents from the Legends Department, carrying a vague letter of authorization, visited the town hall where Mark Miller was born and asked for his birth certificate. Once he had the certificate, he filled out an application for a passport and mailed it off. A conscientious civil servant checked a centralized database, and found that Mark Miller was still alive. There was no reason not to issue a passport, which the Legends Department will make sure to renew every ten years. Mark Miller is now part of our catalog."

"But that's a huge job!" I said, amazed by the fantastic resources available to the CFR to help me write my first dossier.

"One that's been made a lot easier with the latest developments in technology. To be honest, it's more boring than anything else. Now let's not forget the Bushmen. Obviously nobody will remember taking part in that council in 1983..."

"No, but that's not a serious problem. There are several hundred Bushmen clans and only twenty are supposed to have taken part. There again, Chemineau can be vague about it, on the pretext that he doesn't want to make De Beers' task any easier."

"OK. No doubt about it, you have your dossier. Get a few hours' sleep, and we'll meet here about ten o'clock. We'll draw up a list of sources to be falsified as a matter of priority, and I'll make a few phone calls to the other bureaus to make sure your dossier is put on top of the pile."

"Thank you for all your help, Gunnar," I said. "I don't know what I'd do without you."

He laughed. "Without me, you'd be moving a few commas in a report on that dam in Savoie."

"What a prospect!"

"Believe me," he replied, "within two weeks you'll be envying your colleagues in Baldur, Furuset & Thorberg."

This time, he wasn't laughing.

10

Gunnar was right. I've never worked as hard in my life as I did during the next two weeks. There was so much to do and so little time.

Entering Gunnar's office the next day, I found him deep in conversation with a short, heavy-set man in his early thirties.

"Hello, Sliv," Gunnar said. "A cup of tea? Let me introduce Stéphane Brioncet. Stéphane works for the Paris Center. He's just flown in from London."

"Pleased to meet you," Brioncet said, holding out his hand.

"Stéphane is an old accomplice. We worked together a few years ago on the awarding of the Olympics to Atlanta."

Without giving me time to grasp the implications of these words, Gunnar turned to the visitor. "Stéphane, tell Sliv what you did last night."

"With pleasure," said Brioncet. "I had a look inside Chemineau's house in Ville-d'Avray."

"Who let you in?" I asked, rather stupidly.

Brioncet smiled, pretending charitably to think I was joking. "Nobody. I happened to have a key that opened the door and I walked in. Apparently, one of our agents in Reykjavík is trying to get his hands on a specific manuscript. I searched Chemineau's desk and his bookshelves. Nothing. I finally found the text in the drawer of the night table. Seems the old man liked to work in bed."

"So you have the manuscript?" I cried.

"Here it is," said Brioncet, opening his briefcase and handing me a black folder. "I also grabbed his travel notebooks and dozens of rolls of film that haven't been developed yet."

"What about the typewriter?" Gunnar interrupted. "Did you check on the typewriter?"

"An Underwood. Standard model No. 5. Obviously I couldn't take it with me; the cleaning woman would have noticed."

"Obviously," Gunnar said. "You did a good job."

"Excuse me," I intervened. "Do you often break into people's houses?"

Gunnar did not let Brioncet reply. "Of course not. Wherever possible, we subcontract this kind of operation, but in this case we had no choice. If things had gone wrong, Stéphane would have had to pass himself off as a common burglar."

"I don't have a criminal record," Brioncet said, as if that fact were sufficiently unusual to be worth mentioning.

"The reason I asked Stéphane to hand the results of his larceny over to you personally," Gunnar resumed, "is that the two you are going to be working together. Believe it or not, Stéphane is even more gifted at imitating a style than at picking a lock. You can write in French or English as you wish, and he'll adapt your ideas to old Gaston's style."

"I glanced at his last book on the plane," Brioncet said, adding modestly, "He's easy enough to imitate."

"Another thing," Gunnar went on without giving me time to say a word. "I told Stéphane you could put him up in your apartment. If my memory serves me well, you have two bedrooms, haven't you? You can't work here; you'd be noticed."

"All right," I muttered, not sure what else to say.

"Thank you for your hospitality," Brioncet said politely, as if the invitation had come from me.

Gunnar stood up to let us know that the conversation was over. "Off you go now, gentlemen, down to work! I'll drop by to see you twice a day, in the morning and in the evening. You can give me your instructions then, Sliv, and I'll pass them on to the rest of the network."

Later, as I made Brioncet's bed, and then gave him a clean towel and washcloth, I had a chance to reflect on the incongruity of the situation. Here I was, preparing to share my roof for two weeks with a French colleague whose very existence I had been unaware of two hours earlier. Everything was being organized so quickly and smoothly, as if obstacles were non-existent...

Fortunately for me, Stéphane turned out to be both a pleasant companion and an efficient professional. Within a very short time, we had formed a formidable double act. In his hands, my laborious academic prose was transformed into a vivid, poetic narrative in which Chemineau's wisdom shone through. Every evening I would hand him what I had written that day, knowing that his version would be waiting for me when I woke up the next morning, impeccably typed.

Having the support of a plagiarist of genius did not excuse me from having to do my share of the work. I had set myself the goal of forty pages: thirty to tell the story of the Morafe and condemn the position of the government of Botswana and De Beers, and ten to broaden the viewpoint to a debate on the rights of indigenous peoples to preserve their ancestral way of life against predations from modern society.

Each of the two parts presented its fair share of difficulties: in the first, I had to weigh every word, every sentence, conscious that a single inconsistency would be enough to bring down the whole edifice; in the second, I had to formulate a few original ideas, both sufficiently provocative to give rise to debate and sufficiently predictable to be consistent with the work of a professor at the Collège de France.

As promised, Gunnar dropped by twice a day to inform us how things were developing elsewhere. An observer watching our meetings could easily have taken me for a general deploying his troops on the battlefield and conveying his orders to his aide. Gunnar noted down everything I said in a small leather notebook. One sentence from me and he would wake some agent on call in Singapore and dictate a barrage of instructions to be carried out immediately.

The Legends Department had come up with four identities, from which I chose Nigel Maertens. The minions in Berlin were now working relentlessly to document every aspect of the scenario: Maertens's inclusion in De Beers' pension fund, his journeys between the Cape and Antwerp, the account he had opened with BBL and, obviously, his disappearance in November 1984.

We had also given a name to the Bushman who had served as an interpreter for Maraqo and Maertens. Rather than wasting another legend, Berlin had suggested the name of an unmarried interpreter who had died in 1987, just real enough to please the investigators from De Beers and just dead enough not to be able to answer their questions.

Six thousand miles further east, in Madras, India, where the bureau in charge of demographic questions is based, six people were working full-time on the dossier. Their mission was to go through all the articles and publications that mentioned the Bushmen, and to systematically exaggerate the injustices that had been done to them.

The CFR's Indian agents claimed, for example, that the Bantu, who had in fact based their supremacy on their mastery of metallurgy, had also committed numerous acts of violence, raping the Bushmen's women and enslaving their children.

The English and Dutch had not acted any better: hadn't they forced the Bushmen into the Kalahari Desert, knowing they would die of thirst? And what about the Huguenots, who had given some Bushmen the nickname Hottentots, comparing their language with its clicks to the babbling of a village idiot?

The government of Botswana also was not spared, accused by Madras of distributing alcohol to the Bushmen in the hope of hastening their decline.

Sitting at my table, I would correct the texts and the modifications that had been suggested to me, knowing that Gunnar would send them back to their authors that very evening. Sometimes I would ask for a brilliant but overly sketchy idea to be accentuated, sometimes I would propose other previously unknown but plausible aspects of the sufferings of the Bushmen.

Of course, there was no question of changing every single book or article. As a matter of priority, Madras tackled the works of those authors who had since died. Being academic publications, these never had more than a few readers, anyway. Bury the author, and the risks of being discovered were virtually non-existent. Stéphane taught me another technique, which was to alter the translations without touching the original versions. If a knowledgeable multilingual reader happened to compare the two texts, he would naturally blame the translator's carelessness.

Meanwhile, an agent from the Johannesburg bureau was crisscrossing Botswana, his camera loaded with film of the type used by Chemineau. He visited several Bushmen camps and took more than three hundred photographs: portraits, scenes of daily life, views deliberately chosen not to include any distinctive landmarks, and, of course, a few close-ups of a boy he had asked to hold a number of shiny pebbles in his open palm.

Chemineau mentioned in his text the sense of delight he had felt upon discovering the raw diamonds of the Morafe, and his publisher would probably want to insert a few photographs of these at the end of the book.

In all, I calculated that about fifty people were working on my dossier. Although some of them, especially in the lower echelons, might be performing their tasks somewhat mechanically, the majority were showing enormous dedication and professionalism. To take just Stéphane as an example, he was working eighteen hours a day on a dossier that wasn't even his. What other organization could boast such devotion from its members?

To be honest, I needed all the help I could find. However clear I tried to make my instructions, I was inundated with requests for clarification that cruelly underlined my inexperience and, conversely, the skill of the agents in the field. Nobody blamed me for my blunders, except myself.

This part of the project turned out to be far more difficult than the first. At no point during those two weeks did I feel again that mixture of mastery and jubilation that I had felt when I had first conceived the scenario of the Bushmen. There were so many things to control, to anticipate. One line, one word of the scenario might necessitate hundreds of hours of work.

Gunnar had forced me to put the whole of the story down on paper, not just the account Chemineau gave of it. Who was Nigel

Maertens? Who were his contacts in Antwerp? Why had he chosen the Banque Bruxelles Lambert in preference to another bank? What kind of chief was Maraqo? What variation of the Bushmen dialect did the Morafe speak?

I had produced a document of sixty pages that Gunnar referred to as the Bible. During our meetings he would go through it line by line and never let anything pass without comment. Maertens mentioned an eight-karat diamond: had stones of that size been processed in Antwerp in 1984? Had De Beers really produced caps bearing its logo in the 1980s? And shouldn't the Banque Bruxelles Lambert have informed the authorities of the large cash sums Maertens was depositing? What was the ceiling allowed in law?

I couldn't help admiring Gunnar's meticulousness, the care he took to check every hypothesis, to tie up every loose end. But how clumsy and disorganized I felt by comparison! Deep down, I was sure I would never reach that degree of perfection. But Gunnar stuck to his original opinion of me: it was only a first dossier; as long as I genuinely wished to, I would make rapid progress, and my qualities as a falsifier would finally reach the level of my imagination. I really wanted to believe him.

Even today, I have very mixed memories of those two weeks. The time pressures (Gunnar described our performance as like being in the Olympics) made it impossible for me to step back, let alone to savor the moment. Stéphane and I, always occupied with more urgent tasks, never managed to have our meals together. I would cook huge quantities of pasta shells that would last for five or six meals, while Stéphane would make himself sandwiches with whatever he had to hand. We ate at our computers, quickly and badly, like peasants.

Once, about three in the morning (Stéphane was snoring in his room), a fleeting thought crossed my mind. "Hold on a minute. Here I am, telling the story of a completely fictitious African tribe that discovered an exceptional diamond deposit, which it has to defend from the greed of a South African multinational, and yet I've never set foot in Africa. I couldn't tell the difference between a solitaire and a piece of glass, and I don't know anything about the mining industry. Does this make any sense?"

A question of such import deserved serious consideration at the very least, but I had neither the time nor, to be honest, the inclination, preferring to congratulate myself in advance on the impact that my dossier was likely to have. I was changing the world, nothing more, nothing less. Oh, of course, I hadn't discovered a cure for cancer, but my work was going to affect, directly or indirectly, the lives of several thousand men and women. Botswana would have to look for new sources of revenue; De Beers would have to do reduce its prospecting program in the Kalahari. As for the Bushmen, I allowed myself to dream that perhaps one day they would be left in peace, free to lead their lives as they wished. Who among my friends at university could boast of having such influence?

But the dream had its downside: the kind of stress I'd never known before. My body, overexcited by the absurd quantities of caffeine I was imbibing just to stay awake, was threatening to quit on me. In the last few days, I would explode over nothing.

One morning, I threw the papers containing Stéphane's latest efforts back in his face, accusing him of having misunderstood the meaning of Chemineau's conclusion. The poor fellow got down on all fours, gathered his papers together, then carefully pointed out how my approximate French had led him into error.

Even Gunnar was getting on my nerves: every time he made one of his speeches about the catastrophic consequences the slightest mistake might have, my adrenaline level shot up. When I told him this— and I didn't mince my words— he calmly replied that he had thought I'd be able to stand the pressure, but that he had clearly been mistaken. That day, he forced me to lie down for a while before resuming work.

On the afternoon of the thirteenth day, I put the final touches to Chemineau's account. Unable to wait for Gunnar's arrival, I decided to take a bus to the office. Gunnar didn't look pleased to see me, especially as hairy and disheveled as I was. He reread my text, sipping his eternal tea, while I slumped in his armchair and at last stopped struggling against my tiredness. Gunnar would be a while, I thought, letting my eyelids droop and abandoning myself to a delicious half-sleep.

My torpid brain continued to convey to me, more and more distantly, more and more softly, Gunnar's approving murmurs, the rustle of the pages as he turned them, the screech of his pen correcting my typing errors, the Bushmen chanting around a crackling fire, the muted applause of a row of CFR executives, the sensual voice of Lena Thorsen admitting that I had outshone her, the pressure of Gunnar's hand on my arm...

"Good Lord, Sliv, you're asleep!" Gunnar cried.

"Who, me?" I said, sitting up abruptly. "No, I'm not! Daydreaming maybe. Have you finished?"

"I've just sent Stéphane the final pages. He'll be a few hours yet. He's leaving for Paris tomorrow morning, where he'll have the manuscript typed on a typewriter that's the same model as Chemineau's. Then he'll go back to the house in Ville-d'Avray to leave the text and the rolls of film."

"Stéphane..." I muttered, still half-asleep. "I must thank him. I was a bit rude to him toward the end."

"Don't worry about him, he's used to it. Tell me, Sliv, before you go home to bed, are you interested in knowing what I think about your dossier?"

I didn't feel up to discussing the shortcomings of my text before I had slept at least eighteen hours. "I didn't have much time, Gunnar, you have to take that into account. I'll do better next time..."

"I'm sure you will. All the same I wish to say that this is the best first dossier I've read in my entire career. A little weak when it comes to the sources, but all in all, remarkable, especially given the time constraints."

I rubbed my eyes and cheeks to make sure I wasn't still dreaming. "The best, really? Better than Lena Thorsen's?"

"That's hard to say; each of you has their own style. But, yes, all things considered, I think yours is superior. We can talk about that another time. For now, go home."

Before sinking into sleep, I had time to wonder what perverse motive drove me to compare myself to a Danish agent I knew only by name.

11

It didn't take me long to realize that I had achieved a great feat. Gunnar Eriksson's reaction had seemed like a good omen, but Per Baldur's surprised me even more. I passed him one morning in the corridor and greeted him with the kind of customary "Good morning, Sir" that didn't require a response. But I clearly wasn't about to escape so easily. The old fellow was more cheerful than I had ever seen him.

"Oh, you old devil, Liv" (the poor man could never remember my name: Gunnar told me one day that, toward the end, he had gone completely off his rocker), "You're a dark horse, aren't you? So that's what you write in your spare time?" I stammered a few words, but Baldur interrupted me with a laugh: "A council of Bushmen tribes in the middle of the desert in Botswana, that really takes the cake! My boy, we're going to give those stupid Mexicans a good hiding." With that, he punched me on the shoulder and walked away, talking to himself: "I wish I could have seen the look on Lévi-Strauss's face when he opened that envelope, ha, ha, ha." His laughter echoed down the corridor, making several heads turn.

In two days, the news had spread through Baldur, Furuset & Thorberg like wildfire. I still didn't know my fellow members, but I was able to identify them by the winks and broad smiles they gave me in the elevator. Events were starting to take a decidedly pleasant turn.

Gunnar confirmed the next day what I had expected. My dossier about the Bushmen had met with general approval. There was no doubt that the international community would sympathize with the terrible fate of a people at once so proud and so defenseless, or that it would have nothing but contempt for the greed of the government of Botswana. Of course — Gunnar could tell me this now — my dossier wasn't perfect. Most of my sources betrayed a certain naiveté. He considered the battery of falsifications I had suggested to be both superficial and incomplete. But I was not to worry. In this respect my work was similar to many first dossiers.

Gunnar was only sorry that the second half didn't live up to the promise of the first half.

To be sure, these remarks hurt me all the more because I knew they were well founded. Chemineau's cleaning lady had, as predicted, found the manuscript and the photographs, and had handed them over to the publisher, who had immediately issued a press release to announce that the book was almost finished and would require only a little revision to be ready for publication.

Stéphane predicted that the publisher would seek to take advantage of the media attention traditionally surrounding the Paris Book Fair. That left us just over two months to authenticate the final details. Obviously, there was no question of changing Chemineau's account, which was now *the* authoritative source, but I could still work on a host of associated sources.

With that in mind, I went back to my dossier, adding several new angles, tackling details that I had originally dismissed, but that I now realized were absolutely essential.

On rereading Lena Thorsen's dossier and a few others that Bimard had passed on to me, I realized how great was the gulf between my talents as a storyteller and my abilities as a falsifier. I could effortlessly improvise on the persecution the Bushmen had suffered over the centuries, but when it came to drawing up a list of the items that needed fabricating in order to corroborate my assertions, I hardly went any further than the traditional academic theses.

On the same subject, someone like Lena Thorsen would have spread her net much wider to encompass explorers' notebooks preserved in the museums of their home towns, the launch by a British NGO of an international petition for the creation of a legal category of indigenous people, verse epics by a Bantu poet expressing the shame of the oppressor, rock paintings scattered throughout southern Africa establishing once and for all the route of the Bushmen's exodus, etc.

As I made a final perusal of the pages of my dossier as each one emerged from the printer, I had an intuition — which was subsequently to be confirmed — that when it came to falsification I would never be anything but an amateur.

I had noticed Gunnar's reluctance when he granted me the extra week I had asked for. Officially, he hadn't wanted to see me spend too much time polishing my dossier. A few weeks later, I realized that he had been afraid I would miss the deadline for entries for the annual trophy for first dossiers. One day, as I was putting the finishing touches to a supplementary report commissioned by the general council of Savoie, Gunnar came into my office waving an envelope in his hand.

"Lucky Sliv," he said, visibly delighted with his role as a bringer of good tidings. "Something tells me that when I chose you, I bet on the right horse."

He put the envelope down on my desk. I realized that he would not leave the room until I had opened it in front of him.

"Who's this from?"

"It was Baldur who asked me to give it to you. According to the postmark, it's from Toronto."

"And what's in Toronto?"

"For heaven's sake, just open it and you'll see!"

On plain un-headed notepaper, somebody named William N. Dakin informed me that my project *The Diamonds of the Kalahari* was one of the five finalists for the first dossier trophy 1992 and invited me to the awards ceremony, which would take place in Honolulu on June 19. My travel and accommodation expenses would obviously be taken care of. I don't think Honolulu was a place I'd ever have gone on my own initiative, but if the ticket were paid for…

Gunnar almost tore the letter from my hands. "Congratulations, my boy, well done. You had me scared for a while back there! You were taking so much time, I really thought you were going to put us out of the running."

"You should have told me, I'd have hurried up!"

"And spoil your work, no thanks! Anyway, the regulations stipulate that freshmen aren't supposed to know about the trophy before they've handed in their dossiers. Anyway, now comes the hardest part. Baldur has had a look at the list of candidates. Two men, a Mexican and a Sudanese, and two women, an Indonesian and an Italian. You'll be representing the smallest country by far, but that doesn't mean anything."

"A Mexican?" I said, recalling Per Baldur's words.

"Yes," said Gunnar. "They have one or two people in the final every year. It's as if they train them just for that. Not that they always have much of a career afterwards. I met one of them in Singapore last summer. He came third in 1984, a brilliant, cultivated young man, a really nice fellow. Well, believe it or not, he's still waiting to move up to Class 2."

"And is that bad?"

From Gunnar's look of dismay, I could tell that it was.

"If after four years, let's say five at the most, you're still Class 1, you should start to get worried. Oh, you won't be thrown out — we always need pencil pushers — but you can say goodbye to the company car, the seminars in Mauritius and the rest of it."

"Tell me, Gunnar, is this the first time one of your protégés has gotten into the final?"

"You're the second."

"And the first was..."

"Lena Thorsen, yes. In 89."

"And where did she place?"

"Second. She was beaten for first place by a Mexican. That stuck in Per's throat. You'll never convince him the Mexicans didn't bribe the jury."

"And what do you think?"

"That given the weakness of her scenario, second place was the best she could have hoped for. The Mexican's dossier was better: that story about petroleum deposits I mentioned to you once."
Wow, I thought, not bad for a first dossier.

"And what about me, Gunnar? Do you think I stand a chance?"

He thought this over for a while before answering. "Yes, I think you may. You know what I think of your second part, I've already told you. But your scenario, Sliv, your scenario, you could have knocked them down with a feather."

When he said that, a thought crossed my mind. "So does that mean my dossier has been accepted?"

"You bet! As of today you're not a freshman anymore: you're now Agent Class 1 Dartunghuver. You can pick up your uniform from the steward's office later."

"A uniform? You never mentioned that before..."

Gunnar burst out laughing. "Oh, Sliv! You really are innocent! I have to tell Baldur right now."

12

"I knew Gaston Chemineau," Angoua Djibo said. "He did a lot for the peoples of Africa."

Around us, the waiters of the Hyatt Hotel in Honolulu were busy clearing the table, but I was still clinging to my glass of red wine, cupping it to keep it warm. Magawati Donogurai, the Indonesian candidate, encouraged me with her eyes to say something in reply. I think we all wanted to keep the conversation going as long as possible.

"I'm sure he did," I said, somewhat flatly. "Africa lacks really talented champions. Chemineau was probably its best advocate."

No sooner had the words left my lips than I realized how stupid they must have sounded. Angoua Djibo was born and brought up in Cameroon. He had subsequently studied in Europe and the United States, but the passion with which he had defended the Bushmen an hour earlier proved beyond any doubt that in his heart he was still an African. And having raised himself to the rank of Chairman of the Plan in the CFR, he was surely among the few people in the world who could really help the continent.

"Perhaps not the best," he corrected me gently. "But one of the best, without any doubt." He turned, hailed a waiter, and asked for the wine list. "Just because we're on American soil doesn't mean we have to restrict ourselves to Californian Cabernet Sauvignons." He put on his glasses, looked carefully at the list, and indicated a red Bordeaux to the waiter.

He was in his early fifties. His short curly hair was starting to turn gray but he was still an extremely handsome man. And his charm didn't work only on young women: even Fernando de la Peña, the Mexican candidate, who hadn't relaxed up until now despite all our efforts, was literally drinking his words. Djibo gave the impression that he had completely assimilated every culture. When we had discussed Iceland's unusual history, I'd had the impression that I was talking to a peace-loving, socially concerned Scandinavian. Then he had talked about the separatist movement among the peasants of

Chiapas with de la Peña in a totally South American Spanish that was totally unlike the Spanish I had learned at university. Youssef Khrafedine, the Sudanese candidate, whom he questioned about the *sharia* law now in force in Sudan, told me subsequently that he had been flabbergasted by the extent of Djibo's knowledge. But Djibo had primarily won us over with his kindness and curiosity. He knew our five dossiers like the back of his hand and had had a friendly word for each of us.

The restaurant was now almost empty. Our waiter must have been afraid we were taking root, because he strode back to the table, holding the bottle by the neck, and waving it about like a club. Djibo shook his head sadly, took the bottle, and waved the waiter away. I saw that it was a Château Haut-Brion 1983. I don't know much about wine, but enough to know that it must have cost several hundred dollars.

Djibo noticed my surprise. "If we can't drink a bottle like this tonight, when can we indulge ourselves?" he asked with a smile. "Did you see the waiter? A bystander would have thought he was bringing us lemonade."

"I love good wine," said Francesca Baldini, the Italian candidate, who was already quite merry and clearly not aware that the price of the bottle was higher than the monthly rent on her apartment in Bologna.

Djibo undertook to serve us. Grasping the bottle in a fist, he made that final flick of the wrist that is the mark of an experienced wine waiter.

Youssef Khrafedine covered his glass with a hand. "No, thanks, I don't drink alcohol."

"Neither do I, usually," Magawati Donogurai said with a laugh. "But something tells me I should make an exception tonight."

"I don't make any exceptions," Youssef retorted, perhaps a touch more curtly than was necessary. Magawati shrugged her shoulders.

We watched as Djibo twisted his glass, then raised it to his lips. His face lit up with happiness. "Well, now. That lout didn't ruin it completely."

For a few minutes, nobody spoke, not even Youssef, who watched us as we sipped our Haut-Brion. It was Magawati who broke the silence, asking Djibo if he saw any common themes in our dossiers.

"What strikes me," Djibo replied, "is their idealism."

"You mean their naiveté," Magawati retorted wickedly: with her mischievous air and her petite body, like a Romanian gymnast's, she was incredibly cute.

"No," replied Djibo. "Their idealism. Two of them deal with environmental issues. A third is about insects, inquiring if they can teach us anything. The fourth about a people that has been mistreated for centuries and in danger of vanishing completely if we don't tread carefully. That one strikes me as similar to the two environmental dossiers: it displays the same urgency, the same desire to sound the alarm and to act while there is still time. As for the fifth, even though it is centered on the personality of the conquistador Cortés, it can't help but make us think about the fate of those civilizations swept away by the Christian invader."

"The Catholic church has a lot of blood on its hands," Youssef Khrafedine said somewhat sententiously. Perhaps because he was six and one-half feet tall and must have weighed more than two hundred and fifty pounds, I hadn't expected him to take an interest in such things.

"All churches have demonstrated their intolerance at some time in their history," Djibo replied calmly, as if trying to avoid inflaming the debate.

"Is such idealism good or bad?" I asked.

Djibo seemed surprised by my question. "A good thing, obviously. I'd be very worried if young people had already abandoned all hope of changing the world. There are so many things on this earth that need improving."

"And is it the CFR's job to improve them?" I asked boldly.

"I see what you're getting at, Sliv," Djibo said. "Let's say it's part of our role, and that's why we need idealists. But we also need pragmatists — or realists if you prefer — to attain the other goals of our organization."

"Which are...?" Magawati asked.

"You'll find that out in due course. On Friday, Ismail Habri will lecture about the broad lines of the Plan over the next three years. That should give you a better idea. You've had free rein so far, but from now on your dossiers will have to fall within the instructions of the Plan. You may feel as if you're losing a degree of freedom, but what you do will be more consistent and with stronger foundations. Believe me, when all the members of an organization like the CFR work toward the same goals, we really can change the world, more than any of you in isolation could do or even dream of doing."

We sat talking for a while longer. As soon as one of our glasses was empty, the waiter managed to remove it. When he started laying the tables for breakfast around us, we realized it was time to leave. Djibo wished us all a good night and announced that he would be back on Saturday for the official prize-giving.

When the elevator opened on the eighth floor, where we were all staying, Francesca and de la Peña went straight to their rooms. I continued talking to Magawati and Youssef outside my door, then suggested they come in to inspect the contents of the minibar. We had no desire to sleep.

"These rooms are positively gigantic," Magawati said in awe.

"My apartment in Reykjavík could easily fit into the bathroom," I replied, barely exaggerating.

"Now, what have we here?" Magawati asked, opening the minibar. "Cognac, whiskey, vodka..."

"Cognac for me," I said.

"There are also soda and tomato juice for Youssef," Magawati continued.

"I hate you," Youssef said, smiling despite himself. "And my friends call me Kili."

"Kili?"

"Short for Kilimanjaro, the highest mountain in Africa," Youssef replied, standing on tiptoe.

"That's funny!" Magawati laughed. "And I'm Maga."

"Good," Kili said. "All right, please throw me a Coke, Maga."

"I'm pleased you didn't take the tomato juice," I said, teasing him in my turn. "Maga and I may need it later for a Bloody Mary."

Youssef skillfully caught the can tossed by Magawati and sat down in an armchair that hardly sagged under his weight. Of course, by American standards, Kili was almost a ballerina. Magawati lay down on the bed with the TV remote, while I sat down on the floor with my back against the bed.

"I don't know if we're allowed to talk about this," I said, "but how did you two come to join the CFR?"

Kili looked at me closely, as if debating with himself whether or not it was appropriate to answer. Magawati had her back to us and was hopping compulsively from one channel to another.

"Well," he said at last, "I don't think it would do any harm. Djibo even suggested the opposite, didn't he?"

To be more precise, he had said that we had a lot to learn from each other. Like Youssef, I had interpreted those words as an invitation to compare our experiences.

"Absolutely," I replied. "If you want, I'll start with my story."

And I told him in detail about my recruitment to Baldur, Furuset & Thorberg, my first assignment in Greenland and the way Gunnar Eriksson had dropped clues that had attracted my attention.

"Fascinating," Youssef said when I had finished. "I followed the same process down to the slightest detail. I answered an advertisement for the World Bank in Khartoum, I had four interviews with my future boss, a very friendly Egyptian in his early fifties, who then asked me to take a battery of psychological tests. My first job consisted of writing a report on the Sudanese government's recent agricultural reforms."

"Is that your profession?" Magawati asked behind me. I had almost forgotten she was there.

"Yes. The World Bank has lent a lot of money to Egypt and to Sudan, and our mandate authorizes us to ensure that the economic changes instituted by their governments are headed in the right direction. Anyway, I checked out several previous reports my boss had given me for reference and detected a whole lot of contradictions, some of which looked more like sabotage than carelessness. But unlike you, Sliv, I didn't talk about it with my boss: I handed in my resignation."

"That was drastic," Magawati said. "Are you always that impulsive?"

Youssef avoided answering the question directly. "Let's just say I couldn't see myself working a day longer for an organization that was so unprofessional."

"And what did your boss do?" I asked.

"He grabbed me by the sleeve and told me more or less the same things you were told. He made me read an old dossier in his presence, but wouldn't allow me to keep it, which I found really annoying."

I recalled Gunnar, who had left Lena Thorsen's dossier with me overnight. Did he trust me, or did he have people watching me, ready to intervene if I left my apartment? I rather suspected the second of those two possibilities. Youssef must have read my thoughts, because he continued:

"Anyway, they never let us keep anything compromising: no dossiers, no memos, no mail. Whenever I get my hands on anything important, I can be sure that my boss will find an excuse to ask for it back before I have time to go to the photocopier."

I recalled Gunnar personally bringing me the letter about the prize — a letter supposedly intended for me. He had asked me to read it aloud and had then taken it away. There was my answer: even now, he didn't trust me.

"My boss in Djakarta regularly has the offices searched for bugs," Magawati said. "He once joked that he used the same company as the Indonesian Secret Service."

"I don't see what's so funny about that," Youssef remarked grimly. "What about you, Maga, how did you join the CFR?"

"My case is slightly different," she replied, temporarily turning down the sound of the television. "I'm a little older than both of you. I studied management in the United States and had been working in my parents' company for five years when I was approached by someone from a recruitment firm."

"What do your parents do?" Youssef cut in.

"They have an exclusive license to import Ford cars to Indonesia. I was in charge of accounting and finance. Actually I still help them a little."

"And what did this recruitment person have in mind?" I asked.

"He offered me a job in a big public relations firm. It was a field that interested me, and the position paid very well. It didn't take me long to say 'yes.'"

"How did they choose you?" I asked.

"I asked the same question during my first interview with the recruiter. He replied that it was his client who had suggested he call me. In spite of all my efforts, I've never managed to find out who had given him my name."

"Interesting," Youssef said, pensively. "That means they sometimes directly recruit people who interest them."

So all the newcomers had more or less shared the qualms that I had assumed were unique to me. I was no longer alone, although that revelation brought a mixture of comfort and disappointment.

"It's my turn to ask a question," Magawati said. "Do you have any idea of the number of CFR members inside your particular workplace? Personally, I know only my boss."

"I'd say about ten, but I'd only be able to identify half," I replied.

"My boss, obviously," said Youssef, counting on his fingers, "the researcher in the Cairo office — which is quite practical — a credit analyst, and myself. But I suspect the World Bank of being overrun with agents, and not only in Khartoum."

"That seems logical," I said. "If I were the boss of the CFR, I'd start by infiltrating the big international organizations."

"Speaking of bosses," said Magawati, who had resumed channel-hopping, "Djibo's great, isn't he?"

"If you mean really impressive, yes, he is," I replied, although even that praise seemed wide of the mark.

"Let's say he has genuine charisma," Youssef said in a more balanced tone. "In addition, I have the impression he isn't prejudiced against Muslims."

"Given his position, don't you think that's the least we could expect of him?" Magawati asked, provisionally plumping for an old black and white film.

"At the World Bank," Youssef replied, "you'd be surprised at the number of people who raise their eyes to heaven when they hear a Muslim invoke the name of Allah, even though they find it perfectly normal to swear on the Bible."

"In your opinion," I said, "what was he referring to when he talked about the other aims of the CFR?"

"You'll find out in due course, Sliv," Magawati said, imitating — quite well — Djibo's warm voice. "How should I know? Maybe what all other organizations want. Power? Money?"

"Influence?" I suggested.

"But influence in the service of what cause?" Youssef asked. "They must have a program, a platform..."

"Is that so important to you?"

"It's fundamental," Youssef answered. "I joined the CFR to change the world, but not just in any old way."

"And in which do you want to change it?" I asked.

"Well, first of all, I believe in a certain number of basic freedoms: freedom of speech, freedom of movement, freedom of religion, the right of nations to self-determination..."

"The right to democracy?" Magawati, who was now watching a basketball match, suggested.

"Not necessarily in the way you mean it," Youssef replied: he had clearly thought about the question. "We can spend a long time debating the kind of system most likely to guarantee the basic freedoms I just enumerated. Many philosophers think that constitutional monarchies—the Scandinavian ones for example—have a better track record than democracies like the United States."

"Or Indonesia," Magawati said. "I agree with you. And what about the other principles close to your heart?"

"Let's see," Youssef said. "The assertion of the equality of cultures, the preservation of the planet and its resources, the liberating power of science and knowledge..."

Magawati again turned down the sound on the match and turned her head. "I don't hear you talking much about the equality of men and women, my dear Kili. Or maybe you think that principle contradicts the principle of religious freedom?"

Youssef was unfazed. "I assume you're referring to the fact that I'm a Muslim?" he asked calmly.

"So I am," replied Magawati. "But unlike you, that doesn't give me the right to stone my spouse if he's unfaithful to me, or even to ask him to cover himself from head to foot as soon as he goes out."

"I see," Youssef said, his tone implying: "I see I'm dealing with a first-class agitator."

"What about you, Maga, did you also join to further your personal causes?" I asked, both out of real interest and also to relax the tension.

"My list isn't as long as Youssef's," Magawati replied, a touch sardonically. "But let's just say I wouldn't be upset to see the billion women who are currently deprived of the right to vote being enfranchised someday."

"And what makes you think the CFR shares your position?"

"For the moment, nothing. But the very fact that I, a woman who has lived in the United States, was recruited, and by an Indonesian to boot, seems to me a good omen."

"All the same," I went on, "I find the two of you quite innocent. You know nothing about the CFR, except that it pays well, uses the same methods as secret agents, and is probably bugging our phones. I agree there's a chance the aim of the CFR is to save baby seals and give the vote to Muslim women, but I wouldn't bet my life on it. It's just as possible that the CFR is working hand in glove with the multinationals or trying to gain political control of the Western world."

"Yes, it's possible," Youssef said, again unfazed. "But I don't think it's very likely. Believe me, Sliv, I studied philosophy and ethics for five years and there's nobody on earth who can make me act against my beliefs. So far I've produced only one dossier, and I don't think the invention of a Finnish forest with an excess of chlorophyll can do much harm to anybody, unless we assume the CFR's main aim is to destroy the European paper industry."

"I agree with Youssef," Magawati said, turning to me. "Obviously, I'd like to know more about the goals of the CFR, but as long as I feel I'm doing useful work, I'm prepared to trust it."

"I've already resigned once," Youssef resumed. "I won't hesitate to do it again if I find out I've been lied to or manipulated."

"I don't doubt that," I said. "But will they let you? The fact that neither you nor I had ever heard of the CFR before we joined tells me that former agents are a bit thin on the ground. Do you really think your boss would permit you to return to civilian life?"

"He mentioned a drug that makes one lose his memory," Youssef said, somewhat weakly.

"I heard the same story," Magawati said.

"Rubbish!" I cried, a little louder than I'd intended. "That kind of magic potion doesn't exist."

"Then what do they do?" Magawati asked, clearly troubled.

"I have no idea, and that's what worries me. The kinds of techniques that come to mind have more to do with brainwashing than with magic cures."

I sensed that my words were casting a chill over the room. Magawati switched off the television. The sudden silence was deafening.

"And what about you, Sliv?" Youssef resumed abruptly. "You got us to talk, but we haven't heard why you joined."

It was the question I most dreaded, one I'd been asking myself for six months without coming up with a satisfactory answer.

I sighed. "Oh, I'm afraid my aspirations are much less noble than yours. The thing that most attracted me to the CFR was the game element. I never thought I could enjoy myself so much and get paid for it."

"You mean to say you aren't interested in any of the things Youssef mentioned?" Magawati asked, and her disappointment was clear in her voice.

"No, of course, I don't mean that," I replied, ill at ease. "For example, I agree with what Youssef said about the environment. I grew up in the country, in a wild, magnificent region, and I'm ready to fight for my children to have the same opportunity. But as for the right of peoples to decide their own fate, or the right of women to vote, I don't really see what impact I could have."

"But that's stupid!" Magawati cried. "You can protect the coasts of Iceland but not the women of Sudan? What's the point of having picture postcard landscapes if half the population can't admire them because it's confined to the kitchen?"

"Let's not get carried away," Youssef said, as gently as possible.

"I'll get carried away if I want to," Magawati retorted.

"Sliv," Youssef continued, "I don't believe you. I had a look at your dossier last night. I haven't yet read the others, but I don't see anyone else who could keep you from the trophy. You may have joined the CFR to enjoy yourself, but to me it's obvious that that's not the whole reason. I know how international organizations work: believe me, your dossier is going to do more for the Bushmen than all the petitions of all the NGOs put together. From time to time, Western countries look at themselves in the mirror and when they don't like what they see, they feel obliged to make a gesture, to delay the inexorable march of their so-called progress for a few years or a few generations. This time, it's the Bushmen who'll gain from that guilty conscience. Good for them, but I'll know to whom they owe their survival."

"I really don't know what to say," I stammered in embarrassment. "I can assure you I wasn't thinking about any of that when I was working on my scenario." "Once again, I don't believe you. Maybe you weren't aware of all the implications, but the fact that you were able to write such a scenario means that you understand how the world works. You spotted an injustice and thought you could remedy it."

"It's possible, I said, somewhat doubtfully. "And what's your dossier about? You mentioned a Finnish forest." I was anxious to divert attention away from me.

"It's one of the two environmental dossiers Djibo mentioned," Youssef replied. "I chose a forest in the north of Finland that really exists and gave it unusual biological properties. Thanks to the unique composition of their chlorophyll, the trees in Karigasniemi absorb about ninety cubic feet of carbon gas per square mile every year, in other words, nearly fifteen times as much as the Amazon rainforest."

"Fantastic!" Magawati cried.

"Let me guess the rest," I said. "An American multinational is getting ready to cut down the forest with no concern for the environmental consequences?"

Youssef smiled. "Not quite as crude as that. It's actually a Finnish paper company that was granted the concession three years ago. They were supposed to start cutting down the trees last month, but the Finnish government has appointed a commission of inquiry after reading a report by a Japanese professor."

"We're going to see what those famous Scandinavian democracies you love so much are really like. And what about you, Maga, what did you work on?" I asked, standing up. My legs had gone numb.

"It's funny," Magawati replied, looking at Youssef, "Listening to you, I realize our dossiers are very much alike. Mine is called: *Save the*

Gallowfish. I've invented a new kind of fish that's supposedly threatened with extinction."

"What kind of fish?" Youssef asked.

"A bony fish of the *Scombridae* family, like tuna or mackerel. The gallowfish lives in cold waters, in the North Sea and the Baltic. The survival of the species has been at risk ever since the Piper Alpha oil rig fire off the coast of Scotland in 1988..."

"I remember that," I interjected. "Two explosions occurred a few minutes apart, and the emergency services watched the platform burn without being able to intervene. There were hundreds of deaths, weren't there?"

"One hundred sixty-seven to be precise. The decrease in the number of gallowfish in the North Sea coincides almost exactly with that disaster. Thanks to the statistics produced, some brave environmental activists in Scotland have started an association which they've called Save the Gallowfish!"

"Brilliant," Youssef said soberly. "It's true that our dossiers are similar. The motivation is identical: both you and I are calling attention to an imaginary danger, in the hope that by raising people's consciousness it will be possible to prevent similar real disasters."

"That's exactly it," Magawati confirmed. "Do you think it's an Islamic way of thinking?"

"I doubt it," I said, pensively. "Unless I'm a Muslim, too, because my dossier works in almost the same way. Everyone knows the Bushmen are threatened, but rather than wait for the government of Botswana or De Beers to commit a blunder that would alienate the support of the international community, I preferred to take the initiative and write the scenario myself."

We reflected for a moment on this curious similarity. Magawati and I were drinking our cocktails, while Kili appeared lost in thought.

"All the same," he resumed after a moment, "it's disturbing, that similarity. Why do you think three young agents who don't know each other and were raised on three different continents have spontaneously written the same dossier?"

"Maybe," said Magawati very softly, "because you don't have to be a magician to realize that in this world many causes and peoples need to be defended against those better armed than they."

Not another word was uttered. There wasn't much to say in answer to that.

13

"The notion of a scenario's probability brings up this basic question: Why do we believe a story? We generally distinguish four basic criteria, but I'd prefer to hear them from you. Any volunteers?"

Ignacio Vargas, a thin nervous Colombian who had come from London, was giving the second of the five lectures that made up our academic program for the week. We were sitting around an oval table in a small conference room in the Hyatt Hotel in Honolulu. Each of us was allowed a little bottle of mineral water, but not the traditional notebook. We were forbidden to take notes.

I had found the first lecture, *General Organization of the CFR*, slightly disappointing. The talent of the lecturer, Terence Brabham, deputy chairman of the Plan, and the man in charge of relations with the various units, was not in question, but I had quickly come to realize that Gunnar had already given me a fairly clear idea of the structure of the CFR. On the other hand, Francesca Baldini, who was sitting on my left, had apparently only just discovered the concept of resource centers or even that there was someone running the Plan. Although Brabham had refused to give precise answers to a question from Youssef about the number of agents in the CFR, it was obvious there must be several thousand. His description of the specialties of the various branches and bureaus was far more eloquent than any speech about the range of the CFR: ancient civilizations in Stuttgart, independence movements in Lima, mind games in Vilnius, agriculture in Indianapolis, chamber music in Venice, chemical and non-conventional weapons in Osaka, etc. Whatever the subject — troop movements on the India-Pakistan border or the impact of genetically modified organisms on the agricultural policies of the developing countries — Brabham always pulled out of his hat a bureau or a branch that devoted most or all of its time to it.

Today's theme, *Constructing a Dossier: The Writing of the Scenario*, interested me much more. Unfortunately, the amount of alcohol I had consumed the previous evening seriously limited my mental abilities. Even though I had taken three aspirins when I woke up, Vargas's words barely penetrated the fog filling my mind.

"Anybody?" Vargas turned to my neighbor. "Magawati?"

Magawati, who had discovered a fondness for Bloody Marys the previous night, seemed even more rumpled than I. Vargas was being quite cruel to pick her out like that.

"I'm sorry?" Magawati asked. "What was the question, exactly?"

"I was asking," Vargas patiently repeated, "what determines whether or not we believe a story."

"I suppose," Magawati said bravely, "that it all depends on who is telling the story."

"That is indeed the first criterion. You will give more credit to a story if you trust the person or the institution telling it, but on one condition: that his or its neutrality and impartiality cannot be called into question.

"If, for example, a car manufacturer states that scientific studies have proved that diesel vehicles do not emit more polluting particles than those powered by gasoline, you'll assume that the manufacturer is attempting to justify its own choices.

"If, however, an Australian research laboratory that doesn't receive any financing from the car industry reaches the same conclusions, you will definitely be more inclined to accept them. Hence the importance of being able to rely on what we call authoritative sources. But I won't say more about that, because it's a subject that will be developed at some length in tomorrow's lecture about falsification and the production of ad hoc sources.

"Who can tell me the other criteria?"

"We're more likely to believe a story if it confirms an opinion we already have," Fernando de la Peña volunteered.

I saw Francesca nod vigorously. She had raised her hand, but Fernando had been called upon first.

"Absolutely," Vargas said. "That's a well-known phenomenon in human sciences, one that has been proved to favor and to accelerate the spreading of rumors. If, for example, I tell a European that Jews avoid military service twice as often as Catholics, it has unfortunately been demonstrated that he's more likely to believe me more than if I reverse the proposition."

"Not to mention Muslims," Youssef said, just low enough for me to hear him.

"We are more likely to believe a story with a happy ending?" de la Peña again suggested.

"Well, that's certainly what Hollywood screenwriters think!" Vargas joked. "But seriously, you've put your finger on something important. We are more likely to believe a story that we like. Having said that, we have to remember that not everyone has the same tastes. Some people will like a story because it makes them laugh, others because it makes them cry, or makes them think, or makes them forget their worries. Consequently, the way you tell a story depends entirely on your audience.

"If, as is often the case, you are addressing multiple audiences, tell them the same story, but in different ways. And, above all, rely as often as possible on universal narrative structures: the challenger who defies the champion and triumphs to everyone's surprise; the man without a past who has come back to avenge his family; the young woman who breaks off her engagement to a millionaire to marry her childhood sweetheart, whom she has loved in secret, etc.

"I teach a course at the Academy in which I show my students the twenty most popular films of all time. Then we pull the scripts apart to figure out what gives them their universal appeal."

Gunnar had already mentioned the Academy. I was sure it would come up again during the fifth lecture, entitled *Career Prospects in the CFR*.

"There's one more criterion," Vargas resumed. "Perhaps the most important, because it's the only one that is more about the dynamics of the scenario than the scenario itself."

Seeing that no one was ready to venture a guess, he continued: "Some stories are more than stories; they are points of departure. As soon as they are released, they escape their author. Groups take them over, change them, embellish them, and, in so doing, give them a substance that makes them credible to even the most skeptical. That's basically because the creators of these stories are not content merely to imagine a few clever twists, or to present people who are larger than life; they anticipate the consequences of the story and integrate those consequences into the scenario, of which they become the essential mechanism.

"But all this must seem quite abstract. Let me tell you a story. Who knows the name of the first animal in space?"

"A dog called Laika in 1957," Francesca Baldini said, looking, with her perfectly groomed hair and her embroidered blouse, every inch the model pupil.

"Well, that's the name everyone knows," said Vargas, getting to his feet.

This was something I had noticed: most people, not least myself, preferred to walk about while they told a story. I trusted blindly in two signs that someone was getting ready to lie to me: did he stand up? And did he begin with the word "honestly"?

"The fact is," Vargas continued, walking around the room, "two other dogs named Dezik and Tsygan had been on a suborbital flight in 1951 but, for some mysterious reason, it's the name Laika that's gone down in history.

"Now, let us put ourselves in the context of 1957. On October 4, the USSR launched Sputnik 1, the first satellite to orbit the Earth, for twenty-two days. This was a great blow to the Americans, whose space program was not nearly so advanced. Some highly placed people even blamed this embarrassment on the inadequacy of the American educational system!

"On the opposing side, Nikita Khrushchev, the chairman of the Supreme Soviet, was quite determined to push home his advantage. His next idea was to send a man into space, and he wanted to do it by November 7, the date of the fortieth anniversary of the Bolshevik Revolution.

"Sergei Korolev, the head of the space program, objected that it was impossible to be ready before December. Khrushchev called everyone every name under the sun, but eventually listened to reason: Sputnik 2 would be unmanned, but the data gathered would make it possible to prepare a manned flight for December."

Vargas stopped for a moment to gauge our reaction. We were hanging on his every word. My headache had abruptly vanished.

"This is where a young CFR agent came in. I can't tell you his real name, so for convenience sake let's call him Ivanov. This young man worked for one of the members of the Presidium of the Supreme Soviet, and, as such, he knew the details of the imminent launch of Sputnik 2. In a few hours he put together a plan that at first struck him as so hare-brained that he didn't dare submit it to his contact in the CFR, whom we shall call Poliakov. Fortunately for us, Ivanov finally made up his mind. As expected, Poliakov rejected the plan, calling it insane. But then, again fortunately, he took another look at the project, examining it from every angle, and finally concluding that it had a more than fifty percent chance of success."

"What was the plan?" Magawati asked in a dry voice.

"The plan was to wait exactly one hour after the launch of Sputnik 2, then to send a communiqué from the Tass agency to some fifteen newsrooms around the world, announcing that the satellite had on board a two-year-old dog named Laika."

"Whereas in fact the satellite was empty?" Youssef said, incredulously.

"Whereas in fact the satellite was empty," Vargas echoed. "What happened? The communiqué reached all the major newsrooms on both sides of the Iron Curtain at about the same time. Nobody imagined that it could have been sent by any other organization than Tass, the official Soviet news agency.

In fact, another communiqué, this one genuine, had arrived just half an hour earlier, announcing the success of the launch, but no one was surprised by this, since the Tass agency was in the habit of inundating journalists with triumphant communiqués. In addition, the two documents were identical in presentation and both contained quotations from Sergei Korolev and Comrade Khrushchev. No, really, nobody suspected the trick.

"Not that all the journalists immediately printed the story of Laika. Tass had the unfortunate reputation of exaggerating Soviet achievements. The Associated Press in the United States tried to obtain confirmation from the Pentagon and the White House.

"Accordingly, President Eisenhower called an extraordinary meeting in the situation room. Allen Dulles, head of the CIA, said that his agency had no information about a dog having been placed into orbit, but that he couldn't rule out the possibility, because the Russians were capable of such a technical achievement. Eisenhower called his staffers every name under the sun, then asked the White House Press Secretary, James Hagerty, to put out a statement admitting that the Soviets were temporarily ahead of the United States but announcing a spectacular American initiative in the very near future.

"Meanwhile, in Europe, a reporter from Bulgarian State Radio phoned one of his sources in the Kremlin — let's call him Orlov — for confirmation of the story. Although this reporter generally took anything that came from Tass at face value, he found it surprising that Moscow hadn't asked the television channels and radio stations in advance to make room in their programming for an announcement of this magnitude. Orlov took the call. He sounded uncomfortable, and replied that his superior, a member of the Presidium of the Supreme Soviet, had gone into a meeting a few minutes earlier with Comrade Khrushchev. The reporter agreed to wait half an hour. Orlov promised to call him back."

Vargas came to an abrupt halt. In a few minutes he had walked around the table almost as many times as Laika had orbited the Earth.

"Now," he said, perfectly well aware that we were waiting with bated breath, "What do you think was said at that meeting? Fernando?"

De la Peña muttered a few words in a guttural voice. "That's Russian," he said. "It means, 'What the bloody hell's going on?'"

We all laughed, even Francesca, whose laugh came a little late, as if she were listening to a translation of the conversation through headphones.

"In fact, that was pretty much how Khrushchev opened the meeting. His first thought was that Korolev, the head of the space program, had disobeyed him by putting an animal on board Sputnik instead of a human being. When he realized that no one had the slightest idea how the dog had ended up in the spacecraft, he asked who had written the communiqué.

"But just as the head of the KGB was assuring him that the culprit would be found and would be made to give up the name of whomever he was working for, several secretaries entered the room to hand messages to their bosses. Requests for confirmation — including the one from Orlov — were flooding in from all over, and it quickly became obvious that a decision would have to be taken first and the mystery cleared up later. All those at the meeting turned to Khrushchev, the only person authorized to involve the Presidium of the Supreme Soviet. What do you think he did?"

Nobody replied. My eyes met Magawati's and I plunged in.

"He chose not to deny it," I said, without really believing it.

"Of course," Vargas said, looking at each of us to make sure we were following his train of thought. "The reason the world is still convinced, even today, that Laika orbited the Earth two thousand five hundred times is because the USSR confirmed the Tass communiqué. But Ivanov and Poliakov weren't playing poker. How had they arrived at the conclusion that Khrushchev would validate their scenario?"

For a few seconds, we all considered the elements of the problem. I raised my hand a second time: "We have to place ourselves in the context of the time, as you say. The cold war was at its height. The United States and the Soviet Union were locked in a merciless struggle, with space merely the ultimate battlefield. The two countries hated each other, but they also feared each other. The United States knew they had fallen behind the Soviets. In 1962,

Kennedy would launch the Apollo program to send a man to the moon before the Russians."

"All that's correct," Vargas said, "but what exactly are you driving at?"

"I'm trying to say that Eisenhower's reaction was predictable. The Americans didn't know if the Russians really had sent a dog into space, but they knew they had the ability to do so, and that was the main point."

"I understand about Eisenhower," said Youssef, "but how do you explain Khrushchev's attitude?"

"If you think about it," I said, "you'll realize that it's even more predictable. Consider the alternatives. If Khrushchev denied the presence of Laika on board Sputnik, he'd make himself look doubly ridiculous: first, by admitting that the USSR wasn't yet capable of sending an animal into space, and second by acknowledging publicly that some practical jokers had managed to purloin a stock of headed notepaper from the official press agency. If, instead, he confirmed the presence of Laika, on the other hand, he would drive home Soviet supremacy in space in the most striking way possible, establishing once and for all what a visionary he was. After all, wasn't he the one who aspired to send a man into space on the day of the fortieth anniversary of the Russian Revolution?"

"When you put it like that," Magawati said, "I don't think he hesitated for very long. Heads, I win; tails, you lose. Only a fool would have denied the reports."

"And if there's one thing that Ivanov had grasped," Vargas said, "it was that Khrushchev was no fool. Congratulations, Sliv, that's exactly the way it happened."

At this point, Fernando intervened. "But surely too many people knew the truth: those who were at that meeting, the KGB, the people who worked on the space program. How could something like that be kept secret for so long?"

"That had been Poliakov's first objection. Let's see if you'd have been able to quell his fears. Sliv?"

"Khrushchev swore everyone to secrecy?" I ventured.

"Oh, no!" Vargas chuckled as if I had told a good joke. "Khrushchev couldn't be bothered with vows of secrecy from his subordinates. He believed in terror, not in promises. But he was also much more subtle than people think. That day, he set out his position in such a way as to make it appear that he himself had authorized the Laika operation. In the coded language of the Kremlin, that meant that whoever questioned that version of events would be questioning the authority of the chairman of the Supreme Soviet himself and would win a one-way ticket to Siberia.

"Korolev took it upon himself to explain to his men that he had introduced a dog into the capsule just before the launch of Sputnik. Khrushchev rewarded him with a dacha on the Black Sea."

"All the same, it seems hard to believe," Fernando said, summing up the general feeling.

"I agree with you," said Vargas, "and if Ivanov hadn't persisted, Poliakov would probably never have given his consent. But Ivanov was thinking two moves ahead and he set out to tell Poliakov what would happen over the next ten years.

"His first prediction was that the Kremlin would confirm that Laika was on board Sputnik 2. That is what happened. Orlov called back the journalist, and Bulgarian Radio was the first to broadcast the news. All the media in the Eastern bloc followed suit, and before long so did the United States, Britain and France.

"The KGB, he next predicted, wouldn't launch any investigation. Looking for the author of the communiqué would be tantamount to proclaiming that it was a fake. The facts proved him right.

"The USSR, he said, would regularly publish news of Laika, then announce that the dog had died painlessly. After ten days, in fact, the world was told that Laika had been poisoned.

"The Russians would soon be sending a real dog into space. Here Ivanov got the idea right but not the timing. It wasn't until three years later, in 1960, that the USSR sent two dogs, Strelka and Belka, into space.

"The CIA would see its budget increase: that was obviously what happened, although that agency always uses both its successes and its failures to request extra funds.

"The Pentagon would next launch its own satellite. In fact, less than two months later, with the launch of Explorer 1, the United States became the second nation in space.

"The conquest of space would become a political tool. The Sputnik program gave the impetus to a frantic race that lasted twelve years and ended with American victory and the landing on the moon of Apollo 11—perfectly real this time, and even shown on television."

Vargas had concluded his demonstration. Turning my head, I saw that I was not the only one to be struck dumb by all these revelations.

"Basically," I said, thinking aloud, "Ivanov's dossier suited everybody."

"Exactly," Vargas said, sitting down again. "And because it suited everybody, the work of falsification was reduced to its simplest expression, since both Russians and Americans took it upon themselves to cover the tracks left by Ivanov. In ten or fifteen years, everyone involved in this story will be dead. Some may well have told their children or their mistresses that they suspected a trick, but that no longer matters. Laika has entered popular mythology; man has walked on the moon; and the CFR has moved on to other things... Yes, Youssef?"

"What was the aim of the dossier?" Youssef asked, clearly even more shaken than the rest of us.

"What do you mean, exactly?" Vargas replied with a frown.

"What was Ivanov's aim? Why was it important to make the world believe that a dog was orbiting the Earth?"

As always, it was the question of the cause that was bothering him. I was still admiring the how while he was already thinking about the why.

"That's a question you should ask Ismail Habri, who'll be talking to you about the instructions of the Plan at the end of the week. But

I don't suppose he'd have any objections to my answering you. Let's say that in the early 1950s the people in charge of the Plan, worried by the turn the Cold War was taking, were looking for great causes likely to unite the nations of the world in a common purpose. They decided on the conquest of space, a theme that has in fact almost never been dropped from the Plan's list of priorities since that time.

"Ivanov's dossier had the great merit of thrusting the space race onto the political agenda. The competition between the United States and the Soviet Union did the rest, and over a period of some ten years science took great strides."

"I'm sorry to contradict you," Youssef said, "but American-Soviet rivalry was never as intense as it was in space. So much for the brotherhood between nations the Plan was hoping for."

"First, let me reassure you," Vargas replied with a smile. "I completely acknowledge the contradiction. The wise men behind the Plan anticipated that the Russians and the Americans would first tear each other apart. But they hoped that, after a few decades, reason would prevail. That's exactly what's happening now. NASA has just joined with its Russian counterpart to develop a project for an international space station. And, in 1975, fifteen European countries joined together to form the European Space Agency. The world doesn't change in a day..."

This answer appeared to satisfy Youssef, and I took advantage of the pause to ask a question that had been bothering me for a long time: "How do you evaluate a scenario?"

Vargas looked at his watch for a few seconds, as if wondering if it might not be better to reserve this subject for lunchtime. But then, he launched into an answer.

"Your immediate contacts are obviously the first filter. They're authorized to reject your dossiers if they see fit. You have a right to appeal their decision, but, unless you feel you've been the victim of a major injustice, I don't advise doing so. Your superiors have years of experience and they themselves are regularly evaluated by London."

We had learned the day before that London was where the Dossier Department was based.

"Every dossier is subject to two evaluations," Vargas went on. "The Plan first checks that it conforms to the general instructions of the CFR. Toronto sometimes accepts dossiers that don't fall within the Plan, but it doesn't encourage them. The only real exceptions are the sagas, those dossiers that are so powerful that their authors periodically renew or enrich them.

"My team in London handles the second reading. We judge both the significance and the safety of a scenario, grading each of these from one to ten. By its significance, we mean the ability of the scenario to lead to consequences that are positive, at least in our eyes. As for safety, it doesn't depend, despite what you may think, on your abilities as falsifiers. Every scenario has an intrinsic level of risk—and therefore of safety—independent of the labor of falsification that will be expended on it. This level of risk is generally linked to the subject's media visibility, the period chosen, the number of living specialists, and so on. A competent falsifier will reduce the risk, while an incompetent one will aggravate it, but the concept of safety pre-exists any action on our part. Of course, scenarios of the greatest significance are generally also the least safe. Conversely, if you're not prepared to take risks, your scenario may very well not interest anybody at all."

"For example?" Francesca asked, unable to stop herself.

"Let's take the case of a scenario that came through last month, one actually based in your country, Italy. In it, the author posits the idea that Fontana, the architect who discovered the buried city of Pompeii in 1599, deliberately neglected to exhume a number of licentious frescoes and mosaics that offended his sense of morality. Significance of the scenario: 2/10. Safety: 9/10. Combined score: 18/100. I forgot to mention that we multiply the two grades to get an overall assessment."

"How would you have graded Ivanov's scenario?" I asked.

"I could tell you that it deserved 9 and 10 respectively, but that wouldn't be honest. The safety of a dossier can only be fully appreciated only at the time it is submitted. Needless to say, neither London nor Toronto validated that particular scenario. Given the time constraints, it was his contact who gave the green light."

I tried to imagine Gunnar in the same situation. Would he have assumed such responsibility?

"If our selection committee has judged your personalities correctly," Vargas resumed, "you will spend all your lives chasing the Holy Grail of the CFR: the dossier that gets a perfect 10-10. I'm glad. But please, I beg you, be careful. Safety above all else. A 5-8 is always better than an 8-5."

And with those cryptic words, Vargas brought the meeting to a close.

14

The great moment had at last arrived. After a fantastic week, during which we had alternated fascinating lectures with recreational activities, Angoua Djibo, Chairman of the Plan, had brought us together to announce the winner of the trophy for the best first dossier.

On one side of Djibo was Ignacio Vargas; on the other, Jiro Nakamura, the CFR's head of human resources.

On a table behind them, drinks and canapés awaited us. Rather curiously, Magawati, Francesca, Fernando, Youssef, and I sat facing them, side by side, at a rectangular table. If it weren't for the differences in age, an observer might have thought that Djibo was about to take an exam, and that we comprised the examining board.

We, the contestants, pretended that we didn't care about the prizes. When Francesca had declared that morning at breakfast that it was already fantastic to be in the final five, we had all noisily agreed. Then Magawati had added that, on second thought, it would be nice all the same to carry off the trophy, and nobody had contradicted her…

We had been informed that only three prizes would be awarded. The two competitors who won nothing would have to console themselves with the fact that no one would ever know who had finished last. That was an outcome we all hoped to avoid.

Fernando de la Peña was the most nervous of all of us, or at least the one who found it hardest to conceal just how nervous he was. The day before, he had admitted to me, during our excursion in the surrounding mountains, that his office would regard any place other than first as a disgrace.

"I wanted to tell you by way of introduction," Angoua Djibo began, "how much we've enjoyed spending this week in your company. From having read and admired your dossiers, we knew we were dealing with talented professionals, but then we had the added pleasure of meeting affable, promising individuals whose collaboration I hope we will enjoy for many years to come.

"But without further ado, because I know how eager you are to learn the results, I'm going to announce the names of the prizewinners."

He took a sheet of paper from his pocket and put on his glasses.

"The Committee for the First Dossier, which I have the honor of representing this evening," he read, "has decided to award third prize to Fernando de la Peña for his dossier *The True Reasons for the Disgrace of Cortés.*"

Fernando rose to vociferous applause and attempted a clumsy bow. Although he was smiling, he could not totally conceal his disappointment. He was presumably thinking about how he would present the result when he returned to his workplace.

"As we all know," Djibo resumed, "Hernán Cortés conquered Mexico in the first half of the sixteenth century, in the process almost completely wiping out the civilization of the Aztecs. Having made his fortune, he returned to Spain in 1540 and assisted Charles V at the siege of Algiers. In spite of his feats of arms and the invaluable services he had rendered the Spanish crown, he then fell into disgrace, for reasons that are far from clear to historians, and died near Seville in 1547.

"According to your colleague Fernando, Charles V's secret police had in fact discovered in 1543 that Cortés had not been baptized, a fact of which the conquistador himself was unaware. How ironic when we recall that the Spaniards slaughtered thousands of Aztecs because they refused to embrace the Catholic faith, and that some fifty years earlier Isabel of Castile had expelled from Spain all those Jews who refused to convert to Catholicism.

We liked Fernando de la Peña's dossier, because, in plunging into one of the shadowy areas of history, it casts a bright light on the extraordinary religious intolerance shown by the great European powers.

"Who remembers that Pope Julius III had the Talmud burned in public in 1553, or that in 1609 Spain decreed the expulsion upon pain of death of all the Moors, those Arabic-speaking Muslims it had absorbed on taking Grenada in 1492?"

"Half a million deported at the time!" Youssef said to Magawati, who was sitting next to him.

"Given that we are currently witnessing a troubling rise in religious fundamentalism, especially in the Islamic world," Djibo went on, "it seemed timely to recall the kinds of abominations that narrowness of mind and restrictions of freedom of worship can breed. Congratulations, Fernando!"

Fernando bowed again, more cheerfully this time. Djibo's praise had clearly heartened him.

Magawati turned to Youssef, who had found Djibo's conclusion a little hard to take, and asked innocently, "Anything else to add, Kili?"

"The second prize goes to Magawati Donogurai for her dossier *Save the Gallowfish.*"

Magawati gave a charming little cry and applauded herself. Her gaiety was a delight to see and her eyes sparkled more intensely than ever.

Djibo immediately launched into a summary of the story of the gallowfish and praised the environmental awareness of the young recruits, but Francesca, Youssef, and I didn't really have the heart to listen to him: we were too busy evaluating our chances of capturing the trophy.

While I liked Kili's scenario, I found it a touch conventional and, in all honesty, less substantial than mine.

In contrast, I considered Francesca Baldini's dossier, *Geometry in the Anthills,* to be another matter altogether. Using the famous entomologist Professor Spader, doctor *honoris causa* of the University of Wellington, as cover, Francesca had recorded the fruit of her observations on the Polynesian ant. Like all other ants, this species divided leaves into little pieces in order to make them easier to carry. But, according to Professor Spader, only those pieces cut by the Polynesian ant invariably took the shape of regular pentagons!

Another equally surprising observation was that female ants ready to lay eggs moved in sine waves, which grew larger as the end of the gestation period approached.

Gunnar, who had read Francesca's dossier, had praised it to me. The CFR had always shown a certain predilection for zoology, and had made several important contributions to the fields.

Gunnar had warned me that several members of the jury were likely to be impressed by her dossier. So, ants against Bushmen: which would prevail?

"And I have the immense pleasure of awarding the trophy to Sliv Dartunghuver, for his wonderful first dossier, *The Diamonds of the Kalahari.*"

I was overcome with pride. My first thoughts were of Gunnar and, strangely, of my father, who had died thirteen years earlier. What would he be thinking if he could see me now? Would he approve of the unconventional path I had chosen?

I felt my sleeve being tugged. It was Magawati, telling me to stand up. Djibo seemed to be waiting to hand me some kind of glass sculpture that had, as if by magic, materialized in his hands. Walking behind Youssef and Francesca, I gave them friendly taps on the shoulders. Youssef squeezed my hand in his.

Djibo embraced me. "Sliv," he said, "I'd like you to accept this trophy, especially designed by one of our most brilliant agents, who is also a talented sculptress. It depicts a desert rose, its petals representing the manifold layers that lead to the truth. You'll notice that the artist has used ten more or less translucent pieces of glass to illustrate the relativity of knowledge and the absurdity of the notion of transparency."

I raised the sculpture aloft. The rays of the setting sun shining through the plate glass window were caught in the layers of glass, and made them glitter endlessly. It was an extraordinary sight, and I knew immediately that I would never tire of it.

"At the risk of offending Sliv's modesty," Djibo said, gesturing for me to remain by his side, "I'd like to share with you the reasons that led us to single out his dossier.

"By a remarkable coincidence, *The Diamonds of the Kalahari* perfectly embraces the objectives defined in the current Plan. Yesterday Ismail Habri had the opportunity to provide you with a broad outline of the CFR's actions for the period 1992-1994. It so happens that the defense of indigenous peoples figures prominently among our priorities and our best agents have been working hard to find the best angle with which to alert the general public and the community of nations to this important issue.

"The reason the CFR cares so much about the fate of indigenous peoples has nothing to do with nostalgia. The world changes; peoples develop; borders move: we've known all that for a long time, and yet, perhaps more than anyone, we have gone along with this organic process, and in some cases actually initiated it.

"There are many considerations that render the CFR — and the whole of mankind —duty-bound to come to the aid of indigenous peoples. The first of them stems from our notion of justice. Most of the peoples in question, whether the Bushmen or the Guarani of Brazil, can claim documented legal rights over the territories they inhabit.

"When a government dispatches its army to expel an Indian tribe, or when it passes a new law without first granting the tribe in question any representation in Parliament, it is applying the principle that might is right and demonstrating its contempt for the minority.

"Emboldened by its success, it won't stop there. Tomorrow, perhaps, it'll abolish the religions it doesn't like, or the political parties that dare to question its authority."

Djibo paused to take a sip of water. He had put his speech and his glasses back in his pocket, and was now speaking without notes.

"I'm sure you're now waiting for me to invoke the need to preserve what is normally called cultural diversity. Well, yes, I'm not afraid to say it: we have to protect the Bushmen even if they can't count beyond two and keep their reserves of water in dried giraffe's bladders.

"I deliberately choose such graphic examples, because they are typical of the arguments promulgated by the proponents of modernity to denigrate tribal cultures and designed to minimize the tragedy of their disappearance.

"Let us stay above the fray and agree to recognize what is innovative, or, at the very least, perfectly honorable, in the Bushmen's culture. The Bushmen hunt together and share the products of their hunting equally.

"Does that make them idiots? Wasn't that the basis on which Communists theorists tried to build their ideal society? And isn't the principle of solidarity at the heart of the systems of redistribution and social welfare cherished by old Europe?

"The Bushmen wear nothing but loincloths, which leave their genitals exposed. Is that enough to disqualify them irrevocably? Obviously not. The notion of modesty in Western culture has evolved a great deal over the centuries. As fashions develop, men and women in our so-called developed societies think it perfectly normal to reveal a calf or a shoulder, whereas ten years earlier they took pains to conceal them. When Francesca says she's modest, do you think she means the same thing as Fernando or Youssef?"

"Definitely not," the three people named cried out almost in unison, to much laughter from the gathering. I was grateful to Djibo for lightening the mood and giving Youssef back his smile. Youssef saw that I was watching him and mouthed the word "Bravo."

"We have become accustomed," Djibo continued, "to regarding tribal peoples as being backward, as if history were an irreversible process, or as if, because some of their practices recall our own past, such populations were doomed to have no future different from ours. I reject that vision, the CFR rejects that vision. Tribal peoples are not backward; they simply live in another time, a time that is neither early nor late, neither better nor worse, than our own. Today, their time and ours have diverged, but who can say that one day they won't come together again?

"The Bushmen abandon their old people to certain death when they know they can no longer afford to feed them. Who in this room would like to wager that our societies will never reach that point, when healthcare spending devours an ever-increasing share of national budgets, and pension systems all around the world are virtually bankrupt.

"I ask you this: if the day ever comes when, for the sake of our children, we have to leave our parents to flicker and die like candles, won't we have a few lessons to learn from the Bushmen? Or will we continue to claim that they are the ones who ought to be putting their old people in iron lungs to prolong their lives by a few wretched months?"

Djibo took another sip of water.

"I'm well aware I may be offending your beliefs. I'm not doing so for my own pleasure or out of some nasty sense of provocation. I'm trying to convince you to transcend your ethnic and cultural prejudices, to embrace the diversity of the world in the literal sense of the term.

"Your career paths, your experiences, are preparing you to become citizens of the world. In a way, you already are. You know — your intellect knows — that we must respect the Bushmen and their traditions. But deep inside you, even if you struggle against that inner voice, you are convinced that the Bushmen will end up being like us, will end up succumbing to the temptations of an easier, longer life.

"That is why your education is still imperfect. It will be complete only when you come to envy the Bushmen their simplicity and serenity, when you aspire to be like them, to be one with them, to marry their women, and give birth to the first true citizens of the world."

Seeing the confusion into which his last words had plunged the men in the audience, Djibo saw fit to add:

"I'm speaking in metaphorical terms, of course. But, however noble these considerations may be, they are not sufficient to mobilize people, much less influence governments. We will gain the support of the general public only when we can demonstrate that it is in its own interests to preserve tribal populations.

"That in my view is the principal error of the non-governmental organizations that defend indigenous peoples: their cause seems to them so self-evidently just that they don't see the need to justify it. I think, on the contrary, that we have to play governments at their own game and demonstrate to them that the eradication of their indigenous tribes is quite simply the worst economic decision they could make, because it will cost them more than it will bring them.

"Let's take the case of Botswana. With a territory as large as France and a population of only one and a half million, couldn't it both extract diamonds and provide land for fifty thousand unfortunate Bushmen? Wouldn't its embryonic tourist industry benefit from that? Not to mention its enhanced image on the international scene, an image that would be automatically reflected in reduced interest rates on its foreign debt. Instead of which, the government of Botswana does nothing to counter the general impression that all its ministers are corrupt, or to shield the country from a ruinous boycott by both businesses and tourists.

"That's where we come in. If we want to save the Bushmen from almost certain extinction, we have to attack both sides of the equation simultaneously, reducing Botswana's continuing profits from persecuting its 'primitive peoples' and increasing the tangible benefits of behaving more humanely.

"That's exactly what Sliv has been at pains to do in his first dossier, and that is why he has opened up a path that we will be urging many agents to take.

"It's been less than two months, and the repercussions of *The Diamonds of the Kalahari* are already considerable. The French newspapers have given extensive coverage to Gaston Chemineau's posthumous book, *Le Monde* going so far as to write: 'The government of Monsieur Masire will have to justify its appalling exclusionary policies at the very moment when it is seeking financial support from the international community.'

"The President of Botswana, Ketumile Masire, chose at first to ignore the attack from *Le Monde*. But then it was taken up in the English-speaking press, and, last week, while attending the Lagos summit, the President declared that Botswana would scrupulously respect the rights of the Bushmen.

"Several NGOs have also seized on the dossier. The most active of these, Survival International, has already announced that it will feature the Bushmen at the heart of its latest appeal for donations. This prospect seems to worry De Beers considering that it has just hired a consulting firm specialized in crisis management.

"Last, and certainly not least, our contacts at the United Nations have informed us that Sliv's dossier has caused a certain excitement in the ranks of the General Assembly. We intend to do everything in our considerable power to ensure that such excitement grows and brings about concrete results.

As you can see, Sliv has succeeded in giving history a push, and a little bird tells me that this is just the beginning. So I ask you to applaud your comrade one more time. He really deserves it."

Youssef, Magawati, Francesca and Fernando stood up and applauded loud enough to raise the roof. Djibo's speech had already brought tears to my eyes, and I found it very hard to keep from weeping.

Fortunately, Djibo now resumed speaking.

"A final word of congratulation to Francesca Baldini and Youssef Khrafedine. If the competition hadn't been quite so formidable, they would certainly have been up here on the podium. Francesca, Youssef, your dossiers are excellent, and I'm confident that we'll be hearing a lot more about them. It only remains for me to thank you all for the contributions you've made. It's been a delight for me to meet you and to get to know each one of you personally. I'll probably see you all again at the Academy in a few years. Each one of you has the potential to go a long way within our organization and your time at the Academy will be the next important stage in your personal and professional development. And now, my friends, let's eat and drink!"

Angoua Djibo did enjoy cultivating his image as an African patriarch.

PART TWO

Córdoba

1

It was the shrill voice of the stewardess on the flight from Santiago to Córdoba that awakened me. She must easily have rattled off about two hundred words, of which I understood only three — *Aerolineas* (the name of the airline), *Córdoba* (our destination in Argentina) and *gracias* (thank you) — not much of a feat for someone who'd been listening to tapes four hours a day for the past three weeks in order to brush up his Spanish.

The stewardess put down her microphone and began walking through the central aisle. I gestured to her as she was about to pass, and asked her, in my halting Spanish, what language she had just been speaking.

"*Pero en español, como vos, señor,*" she replied, looking surprised. "But in Spanish, like you." Strange, I thought, stretching in my excessively narrow seat, her announcement hadn't sounded anything like my recorded lessons.

Anyone who has flown a lot can't help but conclude that the cabin staff doesn't like to see passengers sleeping. No sooner have they sunk into the arms of Morpheus than the captain or the chief steward wakes them in order to share, in a multiplicity of languages, observations that range from the trivial ("We have now reached our cruising height") to the basely commercial ("A selection of duty-free items is now available"). I'd like to meet the genius who first decreed that untimely and repeated awakenings were to be part of the routine of air travel.

Because if anyone had ever needed to sleep, that person was me. I had left Reykjavík some twenty-seven hours earlier, and had changed planes in New York, Miami and Santiago. I felt dirty and unshaven, and if the stewardess's almost imperceptible sniffing was anything to go by, I must have been giving off a vaguely nauseating smell.

Unfortunately, that didn't look likely to be resolved any time soon, a careful study of the statistics of Iceland Air, American Airlines and Aerolineas having revealed that a passenger changing planes among these three airlines had only two chances in a thousand of his baggage waiting for him when he arrived at his final destination.

I had already planned to do a bit of shopping in the vicinity of the hotel so that the next day I could present myself decently the next day to the Compañía Argentina del Reaseguro and to my new boss, Alonso Diaz.

In informing me a month earlier that I was going to leave Reykjavík, Gunnar Eriksson had preferred to dwell on the exceptionally short duration of my first posting rather than to expand on the next one. "Class 2 Agent in twenty-one months," he had said, shaking my hand warmly. "I'd have to check, but I don't think you're far off the record. That bodes very well for the rest of your career." He had added that my glory partially redounded to the credit of those who had trained me, which I interpreted, perhaps a little freely, as confirmation of the rumor that he himself had been promoted to the rank of Senior Agent after I had won the trophy for the best first dossier.

Gunnar had been somewhat more circumspect when I asked what the company did in Córdoba. "You'll mainly be concerned with falsification. The Hong Kong Center that deals with matters of falsification is supported by three secondary bureaus: Córdoba, Malmö, and Vancouver." I must have frowned, because Gunnar added, "I'm sure you'd have preferred San Francisco or Sydney, so I should tell you that I personally intervened to have you sent to Argentina. You'll learn a great deal from working alongside Alonso Diaz. He's a personal friend of mine and one of the best falsifiers in our organization."

I'd always known I wouldn't stay in Iceland forever, but the news of my imminent departure took me by surprise. I liked my life at Baldur, Furuset & Thorberg, my apartment in old Reykjavík, the alternation between CFR dossiers and environmental studies, my all-expenses-paid trips to the most remote areas, and above all the awareness that in Gunnar I had the benefit of an incomparable mentor.

I tried to negotiate a few extra weeks, but Gunnar told me that I was already enjoying favorable treatment, and that other, less fortunate agents had been required to wind up their local lives in the space of a weekend.

So I gave notice to my landlord, sold my furniture (Human Resources had calculated that it would be cheaper for me to replace it once I was in my new post), and went to Húsavík to say goodbye to my mother, telling her (as I had done three days earlier to my colleagues at Baldur, Furuset & Thorberg) that I was becoming deputy director of the unit for the assessment of natural risks in a South American reinsurance company.

At that point I had only a vague notion of what reinsurance was, but reading the annual report of the Compañía Argentina del Reaseguro confirmed what I had suspected: that traditional insurers protect themselves against certain risks whose occurrence could endanger their very existence. When an individual loses his house in a fire, he turns to his insurer, which compensates him (most often parsimoniously, and after much stalling). But when ten thousand people are made homeless by a single catastrophe, e.g. a cyclone or an earthquake, the insurers no longer have the means to compensate everyone. That is when they have recourse from a reinsurer, to which they have been prudently paying a small part of the annual premiums collected from their customers.

In many ways, the Compañía Argentina del Reaseguro was an insurance company like any other, but it had only a handful of customers and the smallest disaster could cost it tens of millions of dollars. All the more reason to make a thorough assessment of the risks it could incur by agreeing to reinsure such and such a contract.

The unit for the assessment of natural risks employed six people, all trained geographers or geologists. Its director, Señor Osvaldo Ramirez, with whom I had spoken by phone a week earlier, had told me that my work would consist of assessing the risk of, say, Buenos Aires being engulfed by a giant wave, or of the dormant volcano Llullaillaco reawakening. The main fact I had retained from his explanations was that there was a volcano in South America whose name contained six instances of the letter 'l'. That at least was fascinating.

The plane touched down softly — my fourth landing of the day — and I gleaned from the announcement that the outside temperature was 64 degrees. It was as warm as it had been in Reykjavík, the main difference being that in Córdoba July was the middle of winter.

After I had waited for an hour for my baggage, then filled in a form declaring that it was missing, I went through customs and emerged into the modest international terminal of Córdoba Airport. I immediately recognized my guide from the banner he was brandishing at the exit to the terminal: *Welcome, Mister Dartungover.* Only two spelling mistakes, almost a record. My docent, who sported a black mustache so thick that for a moment I thought it was fake, was named Manuel.

He insisted upon carrying my little backpack to the car, a limousine with smoked windows, the kind I had thought existed only in TV series about the Mafia, then took the wheel and glided smoothly into the traffic.

"Welcome to Córdoba, Señor Dartungover," he said in English, looking at me in the rearview mirror. "Is great pleasure for me to be driver of you."

I know Manuel's syntax may seem a bit rough, but it was a lot better than his vocabulary or his accent.

"Not too tired? With difference of time, you not sleep maybe?"

"Very tired, when soon night, sleep a lot," I replied, aping his style in spite of myself.

"Not sleep now, Señor Ramirez waiting Señor Dartungover at La Compañía." Manuel was interspersing his sentences with an increasing number of Spanish words the further they got from the critical threshold of ten words. Unfortunately, I fear I had understood only too well the meaning of his last sentence.

"*Ciertamente un error,*" I stammered, frantically summoning my rudiments of Spanish. "*Voy al hotel. Iré a la oficina mañana.*"

"Not *mañana*, now," Manuel stated categorically, as if he had been warned that I would try to resist. Then he switched on the radio and concentrated on the road, making it quite clear that our discussion was over.

It's a distressing thing for a traveler without baggage to have to face a day of work in a foreign language, knowing that he won't sleep for another ten hours. I gave a long sigh and shifted my attention to the view from the car window. A few rare monuments from the seventeenth and eighteenth centuries weren't enough to disguise the fact that Córdoba is the country's industrial hub. And industrial hubs are seldom noted for their charm.

The Compañía Argentina del Reaseguro—or La Compañía as its employees called it more simply—occupied an eight-story building in the business district. Manuel pointed out, in his peculiar mixture of English and Spanish, that the number 32 bus stopped at the corner of the street and that he couldn't advise me strongly enough to use that means of transportation. I realized from his insistence that he didn't think I was capable of driving a car in the heavy Córdoba traffic.

Well, I thought as I took my backpack from the trunk, if the company's driver had already formed such a poor opinion of me, what would my new colleagues think when they heard me spouting about reinsurance in Spanish?

Manuel left me in the hands of the receptionist, who had been polishing her nails and listening to the radio. Gunnar had given me instructions to present myself to Alonso Diaz, who ran the bureau, even though my immediate superior was to be Osvaldo Ramirez.

Unfortunately, Gunnar must have been behind with the news, because the receptionist informed me that Señor Diaz was sick and that Señor Ramirez had been tasked with welcoming me. Then, rather than offering me a drink or suggesting that I sit down, she applied herself to blowing in a regular, uniform manner on her fingernails.

"Mr. Dartunghuver! What a pleasure to see you!" A short, prematurely bald man approached me from the end of the corridor.

Having no idea of his level of accreditation, I introduced myself to Ramirez as any new employee would have done: by apologizing for my appearance.

"Never mind about that; we should never judge a book by its cover," he replied, giving me a long but flabby handshake. It should be said that he himself was indifferently dressed, sporting an orange-colored tie that emphasized his olive complexion.

He made no reference to my lack of baggage, as if he found it normal that I should be coming to settle on the other side of the globe equipped with nothing but a toilet bag and a copy of the *International Herald Tribune*. Having uttered a few words in which there was a vague mention of eating, he must have taken my startled look for acquiescence, because he took me straight to the elevator and down to the basement, where the company restaurant was situated. There, he insisted on my trying the specialty of the canteen: a half-kilo steak with Béarnaise sauce. As I listened to him boasting about the excellence of Argentine cooking, with jet lag catching up with me, I realized that I'd never be able to get through this day without sleeping, and that I would have to find a pretext in the middle of the afternoon to grab a quick half-hour nap in the bathroom.

It is the custom of the CFR that a new recruit should be unaware of the names of his contacts within the entity to which he is assigned. I found it hard to believe that Ramirez, my immediate superior, could not be among the select few who knew that I was not there just to lower the company's loss ratio. But since I wasn't completely certain, I spent the entire meal looking in his words for some allusion, some change of tone, that would allow me to push my food away without fearing suspicion. But nothing came, and so I ended up taking him for what he was: a terrible bore.

His sole merit that day was to clear up the mystery that had been troubling me since my arrival: why the hell did nobody understand what I was saying? He explained to me that the Argentine language is very different from pure Castilian, not so much in its grammar (although the Argentines use the pronoun *vos* instead of *tú* for the second person singular) as in pronunciation. Before a vowel, for example, the 'c', which in Castilian Spanish is pronounced like an English 'th', becomes an 's'. The same 's' at the end of a word is barely heard, and, even more disconcerting 'll' is pronounced "sh". Hardly surprising, then, that in our exchanges Manuel should have kept to his Anglo-Spanish mishmash. I decided there and then to abandon my cassettes and start watching *telenovelas*, those sentimental TV serials of which the South Americans are so fond.

I also learned that Alonso Diaz was indeed ill, much more seriously than I had thought. He had been diagnosed three months ago with prostate cancer so advanced as to require chemotherapy. He visited the office from time to time, having delegated most of his functions to his deputy.

As I listened to Ramirez and made an effort to apply his phonetic precepts, I wondered if Gunnar was unaware of Diaz's condition — after all, a month earlier, he had called him a personal friend. Could it be that Diaz hadn't told Gunnar? Or had he assured him that he would still be able to find time between chemotherapy sessions to train me?

Be that as it may, Ramirez seemed quite determined not to release me. He announced with a big smile that he had reserved his entire afternoon for me, and that my four colleagues were impatient to meet me. I had vaguely hoped that some of them would be European, even Icelandic, but all were formidably Argentine. That did not prevent them from giving me a warm welcome. What I particularly appreciated was that none of them pointed out the fact that the youngest was at least twenty years older than me. I also noted with satisfaction that I had been assigned a private office (I had feared for a moment that I might have to share one with Ramirez), and that my computer had a modem, which was not all that common in 1993.

I have only a vague memory of that endless afternoon: a passionate tirade from Ramirez on the fantastic possibilities offered by the application of Riemannian models to the study of seismology; the equations he kept scribbling on a blackboard, then wiping out with his sleeve before I had had time to copy them; the secretary's stupid laughter that greeted all of my attempts to break down the wall of non-communication between us; the determination of a short, shapeless man to teach me how to read the coefficients of the tides in a kind of permanent almanac that he kept chained to his desk lest it disappear ...

The only thing I remember more or less distinctly is an animation film that the Compañía Argentina del Reaseguro had produced for educational purposes. The film, which lasted less than ten minutes, showed an imaginary village, whose name escapes me, that was hit by every scourge known to man. A swarm of voracious locusts ruined the harvests, and an overflowing stream swept away the housing projects in the northern part of the village. By the time the narrator, in his monotone voice, announced that a devastating avalanche was approaching, I found myself, like the character in *A Clockwork Orange* who was forced to watch the most unspeakable acts, begging for mercy.

I finally managed to slip away about five o'clock, pretending that I intended to tour the various departments. I refused Ramirez's offer to escort me, arguing that I wanted to form a personal opinion of the general atmosphere of the company. What I in fact did was to go take a taxi straight to my hotel, where I collapsed on my bed.

The phone awakened me just after eight, when I had already embarked upon what I had hoped would be a very long sleep. The caller was a woman, and quite extraordinarily here in the middle of Argentina, she was speaking Icelandic.

"Is this Sliv Dartunghuver's room?"

"Who is calling, please?"

"Lena Thorsen."

By now, I was wide awake. I propped myself up on one elbow, hesitating for a few seconds as to how to react.

"Hello, can you hear me?"

"Very well."

"Do you know who I am?"

"Yes. You spent three years with Baldur, Furuset & Thorberg."

"Two and a half, but that's not why I'm calling."

"Are you in Córdoba? I thought you were in Stuttgart…"

"I'm here now," she cut in, as if considering that we had already wasted enough time on preliminaries. "I was expecting to see you today. Didn't Ramirez show you around the place?"

"Er, no," I stammered, "we mainly talked about mathematics."
"Mathematics?"

"He places great hope in Riemann equations."

"Oh, really? I didn't know that." It was obvious she didn't give a damn.

"Given the current state of knowledge, I don't think we can blame him for that," I said in a pathetic attempt to establish some kind of complicity.

"It's possible, I don't know anything about it. Now, tell me, do you have any plans for this evening?"

Obviously I had. In fact I'd been in the middle of carrying them out when the phone had rung. But I realized that Thorsen also had plans, and that I was part of them.

"No, not really."

"Perfect. I'll come by and meet you in the lobby in fifteen minutes."

And she hung up without waiting for my reply.

2

When Lena Thorsen walked up to me in the lobby of the hotel, I understood why the staff of Baldur, Furuset & Thorberg had retained such a clear memory of her stint in Reykjavík. Lena Thorsen was certainly a lot harder to forget than Sliv Dartunghuver.

Physically, she was perfect: tall, slim, athletic, with regular features, hazel eyes, wonderful lips, and an unusually dark complexion for a Scandinavian, set off by blonde hair drawn back in a bun.

Damn it, I thought, how could Human Resources have sent such a Nordic beauty to such a macho country? And was the Compañía Argentina del Reaseguro so successful that it could afford such a loss of productivity from its male employees?

"Dartunghuver?" she asked in surprise, staring at the pattern of the bedspread that had imprinted itself on my cheek. I had barely had time to take a shower and comb my hair.

"Hello," I replied in Icelandic, even though I knew that Thorsen, who was Danish, also spoke English and German.

We briefly shook hands, and for a moment neither of us was quite sure what to say. Finally, I broke the ice.

"It's nice of you to think of taking me out on my first evening," I said. Obviously I didn't mean a word of it. What would have been really nice would have been to let me sleep as much as I wanted.

"Diaz asked me to," she replied, not bothering to lie. "I'm snowed under with work. I'll have to go back to the office after dinner. Well, then, shall we go?"

"I'm all yours," I said, thinking how many men would have liked to be able to say the same thing.

The temperature had dropped a few degrees. Night had long since fallen, but the street was as crowded as if it were broad daylight. My hotel was situated on a major thoroughfare, Isabel la Católica, but Thorsen soon led me into a maze of dimly lit alleyways.

She walked quickly, as if fearing she would have to speak to me if I managed to catch up with her. I looked at her again as she crossed the road ahead of me. She was wearing faded jeans, and black pumps with flat heels. Two motorists braked abruptly to let her pass, staring at her with a nerve and an open lust characteristic of males in Latin countries.

Finally, she led me down a narrow spiral staircase into a small basement. She greeted the owner without warmth, which didn't prevent him from seating us at the best table.

"Welcome to Córdoba, Dartunghuver," Thorsen said at last, unfolding her napkin.

"It's nice here," I said looking around. The whitewashed walls were covered with black-and-white photographs of bullfighting scenes.

"Do you come here often?"

"I'd like to, but I don't have the time. I usually have dinner at the office."

"Too much work?"

"I didn't say that," she rejoined, throwing me an angry look, as though I had tried to trap her. "Let's just say my workload has increased because of Diaz's health problems."

I suddenly realized that Thorsen was the famous deputy who had temporarily taken over from Diaz. I couldn't help feeling a touch of jealousy. How old was she? Twenty-nine, thirty at most? Thorsen must have read my thoughts, because she added:

"Nothing had prepared me for so many responsibilities at the age of twenty-eight, but I guess the war makes the soldier." Was that a Danish proverb? Certainly not Icelandic, anyway.

"When did you become aware of Diaz's problems?" I asked.

"A week after I arrived. He was having difficulty passing water, so he consulted a urologist. Twenty-four hours later he began chemo." Either Diaz's secretary had been free with her confidences, or Thorsen had researched the subject. In either case, her story was quite convincing.

"Did he stop working straight away?"

"Oh, no, he tried to play the hero at first," Thorsen said, as if she judged Diaz's efforts to be irrevocably doomed to failure. "He began to come in only in the morning; then he spaced out his visits, and now we almost never see him. Or rather, the staff almost never sees him. I visit his home every day to update him on current business."

"Of course," I said, as if approving of this new arrangement.

"He retains all his faculties, I assure you. He's a true professional."

"Yes, that's what Gunnar says," I agreed, hoping that she would catch the allusion to our common mentor. But she didn't react.

"That's why I was so touched yesterday when he said I'd taken over the Napoleon dossier in masterly fashion," she continued, watching my reaction.

I decided to oblige her. "That's quite a tribute," I said, without pressing for details. Instead, I opened the menu. "Shall we order?"

"Good idea. I recommend the steak. The owner's nephew has a ranch in the pampas."

I was to spend two years in Córdoba. You can trust me when I say that an Argentine always has an anecdote to tell you about the best steak he has ever eaten. Everyone has a brother or a cousin who owns a ranch and supplies him directly. I should add that a kilo of beef constituted the basic unit of the menu. At least I managed to skip the Béarnaise sauce.

"Am I mistaken, or did you spend quite a brief time in Stuttgart? Barely a year and a half, wasn't it?"

"Seventeen months, to be precise, four less than you spent in Reykjavík." Thorsen seemed to have been following my progress as closely as I had been observing hers.

"What's Stuttgart's specialty?"

"Ancient civilizations. They sent me there supposedly because I can read Cicero in the original. I was bored stiff."

"Bored?" I echoed in surprise. "How can anyone be bored by such a rich subject?"

"Rich but uninteresting. It's much too easy. Nobody's interested in the ancient world anymore. You can create a Christian martyr in three months, a slave revolt in two weeks. Who's going to contradict you? As long as your sources are in order — and believe me, mine were — nobody casts doubt on what you say. Academics are so busy reconstructing the mosaics of Pompeii, tile by tile, that they never cause trouble for you."

"And what about your boss there? You were the assistant to the head of the bureau, weren't you?"

"That's right. A good man, an academic himself, as it happens. He found it difficult to develop his dossiers. Whenever we said 'tomorrow', he understood 'before the end of the year.'"

I knew the type. I was reminded of one of my political science professors who drove his doctoral students crazy. At their first interview, he would draw up a fifteen-year work plan.

"And are you enjoying it here?" I asked as the owner placed in front of me a block of steak as big as my liver.

Thorsen looked at me as if she was hearing the word for the first time in her life. "That's not the word I'd use, but, yes, I'm quite happy here. The work is interesting and Diaz's little health problems create opportunities."

"Such as?" I asked, thinking how delighted Diaz would probably have been to learn that the cancer that was confining him to his bed had come under the category of the little accidents of life.

"Oh, you know perfectly well what I mean," she replied, bestowing an angelic smile. "Getting the post of deputy to the head of a bureau at the age of twenty-eight is itself an achievement, but actually directing operations in his place is probably the best thing that could have happened to my career. Just think about it: I interact with the other bureau heads on an equal footing."

"And aren't you afraid of making a blunder? After all, you are a little lacking in operational experience, aren't you?"

"Thank you for your concern, Dartunghuver, but I'm managing quite well at the moment, and I intend to continue that way.

Another year or two at this rate and they'll be obliged to promote me to Class 3."

I realized from her angry tone that I wouldn't get anywhere if I persisted along that path.

"Sliv," I said softly.

"What do you mean?"

"You can call me Sliv. I don't think we need to be so formal with each other."

She appeared to give this some serious thought. "It's not that I mind first names," she said at last. "But I'd prefer to keep things formal. It's a matter of respect."

"How does your boyfriend feel about that?" I asked, half-jokingly. Unfortunately for me, Thorsen didn't appreciate the joke.

"I don't think we're here to talk about my boyfriend," she retorted dryly. "Assuming there is one, of course."

It was an unnecessarily long explanation, that didn't answer my question. Was she so formal with her boyfriends? And if she wasn't, did that mean she didn't respect them? I was aware that I was probing a sensitive area, and for a moment I concentrated on my steak while searching for something positive to say.

"I read your dossier, *Skitos, Capital of Thessaly*," I said finally. "A remarkable job of falsification."

Her face lit up and she presented me with a dazzling smile. God, was she beautiful! What a pity she had to be flattered before she could smile.

"I'd never have thought of creating an Association for Thessalian Culture," I proceeded. "What a brilliant idea!"

"Thank you," she replied. "It was important to find a source that could link Nebraska and Greece. The Association makes the other sources credible, and they render it credible in return."

I had never seen it from that angle, but, on reflection, I understood the cleverness of the ploy. By placing a plaque on a shepherd's hut in Actinonia, Thorsen had not only confirmed the story of Spyros but also demonstrated the vitality of the Association. Why did I never have ideas like that?

"It's a great honor for Córdoba to welcome the winner of the trophy for best first dossier," she said in her turn.

"Oh, to hell with that trophy!" I said, pushing my plate away. "Let's not talk about it."

"But it's worth dwelling on," she replied. "It's a remarkable dossier."

So she had read it. I won't deny that this revelation gave me a certain pleasure.

She poured herself a glass of water. "A topical theme, an imaginative but also plausible scenario, full of colorful characters, but all dead or impossible to find…"

"You're embarrassing me, Lena," I cut in, wondering where this was headed.

"No, really. How did you get the idea of working on the Bushmen?"

I told her how reading Chemineau's obituary had led me to take an interest in the tribes of southern Africa. I saw from her puzzled look that she would have been incapable of such a digression.

"Congratulations," she said, finally. "It took nerve. And I suppose you had to produce your sources urgently?"

"A little, yes," I replied. "Barely two weeks to rewrite Chemineau's entire manuscript, and two more months to coordinate all the facets."

"Oh, right," Lena said. "I'd have thought you had less time than that."

"It seemed short enough, believe me," I said, remembering my two hectic weeks with Brioncet. Was she implying that only extreme haste could excuse the weakness of my sources?

"No, I only said that because Gunnar didn't send us the dossier for validation."

The owner chose this moment to come and ask us if the dinner was to our liking. Thorsen cut short his fawning in a not very polite manner.

"Maybe he sent it to Hong Kong or Malmö?" I suggested, as he walked away.

"No, I checked, the records are centralized."

"And what do you make of that?" I asked, vaguely anxious.

"Oh nothing," she said. "Just that Gunnar hasn't changed. He still prefers to do his own thing rather than rely on the judgment of true professionals."

I really didn't like the way she was criticizing Gunnar, especially when I remembered how passionately he evoked her memory. I took a gulp of wine to gain the strength not to lay into her.

"Given the results in this case," I said, "it's hard to blame him."

"That," she said, sententiously, "is still a bit too early to say. The best dossiers are those that stand the test of time. We don't even know yet if the legend of Nigel Maertens will withstand an investigation by De Beers. I wouldn't bet my savings on it."

This time, I lingered my drink, quite determined not to lose my temper. What would I gain by crossing swords with Lena Thorsen at our first encounter?

"Are you working on a new dossier?" I asked, as gently as possible.

"No," she replied reluctantly, as if upset with me for evading a promising battle of wits. "And I fear that you, too, will have to put your imagination away for a while. We're snowed under with requests, and we're severely understaffed. Were you planning to do any sightseeing?"

"Oh, yes, maybe," I said as if considering the question for the first time. In fact, Youssef and Magawati had asked me to organize a trek to Patagonia, the following year and I was planning to take four weeks off for that purpose.

"Don't count on it," Lena said categorically. "Or rather, do what I do: set aside half a day when you want to visit a museum."

"Thanks for the advice," I replied, looking out of the corner of my eye at a young rose seller who was approaching our table, singing at the top of his voice.

Lena turned abruptly and told him to clear off, but the boy, who didn't look more than twelve, wouldn't let himself be dismissed as easily as the owner had.

"A flower for the pretty lady?" he asked me, forcing Thorsen to smell his basket.

"A flower, Lena?" I said. "It would give me pleasure."

"Tell him to scram, Dartunghuver," Thorsen snapped, hunkering down in her chair. "He'll only listen to you."

"Are you sure? They're magnificent flowers," I said, signaling to the boy to start singing again, which he did with gusto, much to the delight of the neighboring tables.

"For heaven's sake, make him go away or I'm the one who will leave the table," Thorsen cried, exasperated beyond measure.

"I think it's best if you go," I said to the boy, slipping a bill into his hand.

He chose the most beautiful of the roses and handed it to me gravely, making a formal bow. I snipped off the stalk with my steak knife and put the blossom in my button-hole while Thorsen, avoiding my gaze, asked for the check.

As I started to put my hand in my pocket, Thorsen stopped me with a gesture and took out a credit card.

"Obviously, this is on the company. This was a working dinner."

"I hadn't thought of it any other way, Lena," I replied, stroking my rose with the back of my hand.

3

Two days later, Ramirez stuck his head through the doorway of my office to inform me that Alonso Diaz was in the building and wished to meet me. As I had spent the previous two hours looking through tables of maritime loss ratios, I was quite pleased with the diversion. I had greatly underestimated the mathematical component of my new responsibilities, and I dreaded the moment when Ramirez would notice that I didn't understand the first thing about the equations that filled his memos.

In the elevator taking me to the eighth floor, I found myself daydreaming that Diaz would tell me that my cover as a reinsurer had been sufficiently established, and that I could now devote myself exclusively to CFR business. Unfortunately, I knew this was very unlikely. All Class 1 and 2 agents lead double lives. Only Class 3 agents and, of course, the leaders of the CFR, organize their timetables as they please.

I had expected Diaz to be in poor shape, but I hadn't expected to be meeting a zombie. His clothes hung loosely on his emaciated frame. He had lost his hair, but out of bravado or vanity was not wearing a wig. The blood seemed to have drained from his face, which had become set in a stonelike rigidity. He drew me to him in a clumsy embrace, but I unconsciously held back for fear of going right through him.

"Dear Sliv," he said in English, "Gunnar has told me so much about you, I feel as if I'm meeting an old friend."

"Likewise," I lied, making an effort to conceal my shock at his spectral appearance. Why on earth had Gunnar hidden Diaz's condition from me, if he knew about it? Had he suspected that I wouldn't have been overjoyed by the prospect of working for Lena Thorsen?

"I'm sorry I wasn't able to welcome you upon your arrival. You may know I'm experiencing some health problems at the moment," he said, observing my reaction.

"Yes, I heard that," I replied, as if placing this information on the same level as the opening hours of the works canteen.

Diaz scrutinized me for a long time, and I could see in his eyes, as he must have seen in mine, a reluctance to linger on the subject of his illness. He seemed relieved, and his voice assumed a more cheerful tone. "Would you like a drink? A soda? A fruit juice?"

"Just a glass of water, please." If I was going to ingest a thousand calories of steak a day, it was best to start cutting back elsewhere.

"I'll get one for you," Diaz said, picking up the phone to call his secretary. "Sit down, my boy."

I drew up a Spartan wooden chair, remembering Gunnar's leather armchairs. The two men claimed to be friends but their styles couldn't have been more different. Gunnar had furnished his office comfortably, even luxuriously, carefully choosing the lighting and the materials, whereas Diaz, concerned solely with functionality, seemed to have gone out of his way to make his working quarters look like an East German police station. A clear advantage to Gunnar on that point, I thought, attempting — in vain — to find a pleasant position on my chair.

Just then, Lena Thorsen entered the room carrying a tray. She blushed on realizing that the carafe of water was meant for me, and that nothing she could say could ever make me forget that I had once seen her in the position of a servant.

"Oh, thank you, Lena," Diaz said. "Put it there. You know Sliv, I think."

"Yes, we have met," Thorsen said, nodding in my direction.

"All for the best, then," Diaz said, pouring me a glass of water. "You'll be working a lot together. Lena, maybe you could show Sliv around the city this weekend. Would that be agreeable?"

"I'd be glad to," Thorsen said, pouring herself a glass in her turn to hide how much she was having to grin and bear it. "But maybe Sliv has more urgent things to do?"

"Absolutely," I said, coming to her rescue. "But thanks for the invitation," I added, looking Thorsen in the eyes.

"Sit down, Lena," Diaz resumed. "You've come at the right moment. So, Sliv, how have your first days been at the Compañía Argentina del Reaseguro?"

"Fine," I said. "Although to be honest, I hadn't expected my immediate superior to be a civilian."

"Yes, I know," said Diaz, "it isn't ideal. We made a series of unwise recruitments, and now we're chronically understaffed. But Ramirez is harmless enough. All he asks is to be left alone to put together his equations. He thinks he's discovered an infallible predictive model."

"Based on Riemannian functions," I said. "Yes, he told me."

"You'll manage," Diaz said, putting paid to my last hopes of escaping all that dull actuarial work. "More seriously, I assume Gunnar explained the role of the Córdoba bureau."

"To be candid, he wasn't very explicit. All I know is that Córdoba is one of the four bodies dealing with questions of falsification."

Diaz took a sip of water and nodded. He was so pale that I thought for a moment he was about to faint.

"Having produced a few dossiers yourself, you know that it's up to your case officer to check your sources and make sure you've sufficiently authenticated your scenario."

"Of course," I said. How could I forget the two daily meetings in which Gunnar had dissected the Bushmen dossier?

"If your case officer has the slightest doubt," Diaz went on, "he sends the dossier to Hong Kong, which either studies it there and then or passes it on to one of the three subsidiary centers: Córdoba, Malmö, or Vancouver. There, they go through the dossier with a fine-tooth comb, checking the sources, collating the data, and, in collaboration with our internal experts, validating the main hypotheses."

"Could you give me an example?" I asked. "I don't quite see how you can make changes without having previously been involved in the genesis of the scenario."

"All right," Diaz said mischievously. "Let's take your third dossier: *Der Bettlerkönig*."

"What?" I exclaimed. "You've read *Der Bettlerkönig*?"

"Read it? I devoured it. Gunnar sent it to me last February, insisting I deal with it personally. He knows I'm a film buff and —"

"Could one of you please explain?" Thorsen interjected. "*Bettlerkönig*, the king of beggars?"

"Yes, that's a good translation," Diaz said. "Sliv, tell her your scenario."

"Where to start? In 1937, a young German aristocrat named Von C. submits a film project, *Der Bettlerkönig*, to several producers. They all reject it, giving various reasons. For example, Klaus Hoffmann of UFA writes to Von C.: '*Der Bettlerkönig* lacks the moral qualities that the German people demand of a contemporary production.'"

"A polite way of saying that the subject wasn't politically correct," Diaz said. He was regaining his color. I decided to humor him by drawing out my story.

"*Der Bettlerkönig* tells the story of a small Bavarian duchy in the fourteenth century. Duke Friedrich is finding it hard to process the death of his wife, Duchess Hilde. Sensing that his own end is near, he decides to marry off his only daughter, Gudrun, who is in love with a knight named Harald, one of the most upright and respected men in the region. Harald, who has fought for Emperor Ludwig IV of the House of Wittelsbach, he is genuinely in love with Gudrun, and Duke Friedrich sees him as an ideal successor.

"But anonymous letters begin to arrive at the Castle. They reveal to the Duke an unsuspected aspect of the character of his future son-in-law. We learn that Harald is encouraging the serfs of the duchy to stop paying taxes in kind. 'The earth belongs to those who till it,' he assures them. 'Your parents cultivated it before you and, before them, your parents' parents. Why should you share the fruits of your labor with those who are too lazy to sew and plow?'

Friedrich is stunned. He summons Harald to the castle and confronts him. Harald remains loyal to his convictions, even when

Friedrich threatens him with exile. 'I love Gudrun more than my life,' Harald replies, 'but my place is with the poor.'"

"Very moving," Thorsen said sarcastically.

"Wait," said Diaz who was beginning to enjoy himself, "the best is yet to come."

"Friedrich sends for Gudrun, hoping she will be able to persuade Harald to be reasonable, but Gudrun takes her suitor's side. She tells her father that he is a relic a bygone age, and that landed property passé.

Suddenly, we hear the long, drawn-out call of a hunting horn. Friedrich rushes to the window and beholds a mob of beggars led by Harald massing at the gates of the castle. In an inflexible tone, Gudrun informs her father that his men are now taking their orders from her. She descends and raises the drawbridge herself. While her father watches, dumbfounded, as the beggars peacefully overrun the castle, she declares, 'We won't harm you.'"

"Is that all?" asked Thorsen.

"That's only the story of the film!" Diaz exclaimed. "Hardly surprising that UFA refused to invest in it!"

"After all," I explained to Thorsen, "collectivist doctrines weren't exactly in favor in Nazi Germany. Four years earlier, Hitler had blamed the Reichstag fire on the Communists, arrested four thousand militants, then simply banned the Communist Party outright."

"Leni Riefenstahl's *Olympia* was more in keeping with the epoch," Diaz observed.

"But Von C. isn't deterred. He's young, rich, idealistic, and reckless. If no one is willing to film his script, he'll finance the production himself. In June 1937, he hires Babelsberg Studios, using a front man, Günther Niemals. Two weeks later, the Gestapo raids Babelsberg. Von C. manages to escape, but not Niemals or several the actors, who are sentenced to five years' imprisonment."

"I assume all this is documented," Thorsen said, in a tone that left little doubt of her opinion to the contrary.

"We'll come to that," Diaz replied. "But yes, overall, Sliv did a good job. There really was a Günther Niemals, and he was sentenced to prison, but for a sordid sexual case. I doubt that his descendants will show up and challenge our version. As for the fortnight of filming at the studio, that appears in due form in the shooting schedule preserved in the Babelsberg records."

"It takes more than that to discourage Von C., who is hardly aware that his thoughtlessness has just cost several of his colleagues their freedom. He sets off in search of a suitable medieval castle in which to resume the shooting. Meanwhile he continues to pay the cast and crew.

A tout tells him about the castle of Unterweikertshofen, in the north of Bavaria, not far from the small town of Erdweg. He hastens there and misleads the owner, Count Von Hund, by showing him a script with fewer political implications. The filming begins, in a somewhat surreal atmosphere. The actors fear for their safety: some demand masks or heavily made up, and they all relinquish the right to appear in the credits.

"Von C. shoots a lot of pointless scenes just to keep Von Hund happy. He hires local peasants for crowd scenes. The actress playing the role of Gudrun is injured, and Von C. replaces her with his own sister, Maria. In seven weeks, the film is in the can. Von C. edits it himself, using second-hand equipment. He entrusts the only copy of the film to Maria for safekeeping, and then contacts several independent distributors.

One of those reports him to the Gestapo, two of whose agents arrive to arrest him that same day. Von C. is sentenced to ten years' imprisonment. He is deported to Dachau in 1940, just a few miles from Unterweikertshofen, where he dies during a typhus epidemic in January 1945."

"Is that all?" Thorsen asked, disconcerted by this accumulation of details.

"Just be patient, that's only the start!" I joked. "At the beginning of the 1960s, Maria, Von C.'s sister, impulsively decides to show *Der Bettlerkönig*. She has kept the reels of film all these years, without ever

155

revealing their existence to anyone. After reading an article about the Oberhausen Manifesto, in which twenty-six young German film-makers proclaim that what they call 'papa's cinema' is dead, she contacts each of them individually and tries to interest them in her story.

"One of these, Franz-Josef Spieker, reacts favorably. He agrees to view the film and immediately realizes that it is nothing less than a masterpiece. He tells Maria that, given the current German political context, he doesn't have much hope of finding a distributor, but he suggests showing the film to his French friend Georges Sadoul, a perceptive critic, the author of a monumental story of the cinema, and above all a dedicated communist.

Maria agrees. Sadoul is highly impressed by *Der Bettlerkönig*, and immediately organizes a special screening at the Cinémathèque in Paris."

"Our friend isn't afraid of anything," Diaz said. "*Der Bettlerkönig* does indeed appear on the Cinémathèque's program for 12 November 1963."

"The auditorium of the Cinémathèque, then located on Rue d'Ulm, seats about two hundred and fifty people, but for this showing the rows are almost empty. In his haste, Sadoul neglected to gather the intelligentsia. Truffaut is there, though, as well as Serge Daney and Jacques Doniol-Valcroze. Chris Marker arrives late. Sadoul introduces the film in a few sentences, and invites his friends to discover a "major expressionist work even more powerful than *M*."

"Oh, yes?" Thorsen said, mockingly. In all likelihood she had never seen *M*. and probably thought Fritz Lang was a German fashion designer.

"We have several eyewitness accounts of that memorable evening. Daney writes: 'A giant was born and died last night.' Truffaut writes in his diary that the expressive faces of the Bavarian serfs moved him to tears, and that he found Gudrun's uncompromising stand quite chilling. Marker is astonished to discover that as early as 1937 Von C. had mastered the technique of combining still images, with a voice-over, a technique that he himself had used so successfully in *La jetée* a year earlier.

In spite of all these accounts, a strange mystery surrounds some aspects of the screening. For some, the film is silent, and there are titles to connect the scenes. According to Doniol-Valcroze, the actors speak in German, so Sadoul hires two interpreters that evening to provide a simultaneous translation of Harald's and Gudrun's long monologues.

"But *Der Bettlerkönig* truly becomes a legend the following week, when the reels of film burn in a fire at Maria's apartment in Munich. Sadoul, the only person to have seen the film twice, is shattered by the news, and writes an outline of the script in the hope that some day a director as inspired as Von C. will restore his characters to cinematic life."

"And I assume that by a kind of curse," Thorsen said, "all the players in this fable disappear in the following years, leaving you free rein to talk and write in their stead."

"Yes, indeed," I said calmly. "And to construct the myth of *Der Bettlerkönig* which, less than a year after its creation, has already found its place in the canon of pre-war cinema."

"Last week," Diaz said, "Godard told a journalist from Swiss television that he would never forgive himself for having missed the screening at the Cinémathèque on 12 November 1963. Can you imagine?"

"Godard?" Thorsen said. "Who's he?"

"Come on, Lena," Diaz protested. "Jean-Luc Godard: *Breathless*, *Contempt*..."

"Never heard of him," Thorsen muttered, annoyed by Diaz's paternalistic tone.

"That doesn't matter," I said to calm her. "What is important is that he's a great director, and that his commendation places *Der Bettlerkönig* above suspicion."

Noting that Diaz wasn't satisfied, I added, "But not as much as another French director, Claude Chabrol, who recently compared the distress of Duke Friedrich to that of Claude Rains at the end of Hitchcock's *Notorious*."

"Did he really say that?" Diaz asked, incredulous. "But then —"

"Oh, yes," I said, not displeased with the effect I was having, "he claims to have attended the 1963 screening. I'm certainly not going to contradict him..."

I was watching Thorsen out of the corner of my eye. She hadn't been able to conceal her surprise at hearing such perfect corroboration.

"Incredible..." Diaz said. "But tell me, Sliv, how did you derive the idea for this scenario?"

"Well, I've long been interested in the theme of lost works. Did you know that eight of the forty paintings by Leonardo da Vinci known to be genuine have never been tracked down? That Van Gogh's *Painter on the Road to Tarascon* is out there somewhere, but nobody knows where?"

"Apparently," Thorsen cut in, having found her feet again since we had stopped talking about films, "the CFR produced a fake novel by Alexandre Dumas."

"That's right," Diaz said. "*Le chevalier de Saint-Hermine*. We hid it in plain sight, but the French still haven't found it. The same with classical music: one of our agents is composing a piece by Bach as we speak."

"I noticed that the CFR had dealt with all of the arts except the cinema," I said. "At the same time, I had to adapt the Von C. scenario to bring it within the Plan's directive on landed property."

The theme "The Earth Belongs to Those Who Till It" was one of the priorities of the three-year plan 1992-1994. Even though Toronto had advised me that they would have preferred something contemporary set in South America rather than my medieval Bavarian epic, they had approved the dossier because of its potential.

I returned to the beginning of the conversation. "So tell me, Alonso — do you mind if I call you Alonso? — what corrections did you make in my dossier?"

"Ah, now we're getting down to it," Diaz said. "A lot, as it happens. I should have sent you back my corrections, but, knowing that you were on your way here, I preferred to wait until I could tell you in person.

"First of all, you made a few factual errors. For example, at that time the Cinémathèque's screenings began at 8.30 P.M., not at 8... Next, Von C. would never have sent his script to UFA in 1937, the very year the Nazi State took a 72% stake in the company. I checked, it was headline news at the time. Von C. may have been daring, but he wasn't stupid."

"I agree," I said, playing the good loser.

"Rather more worrying," Diaz continued, "is that François Truffaut couldn't have been present at the showing on 12 November 1963. That day he was in Lisbon, finishing shooting *La peau douce*."

"Oh!" Thorsen cried, making an effort to appear dismayed.

"That's the kind of stupid mistake that can cost one very dear. We moved the date of the screening to December 3, when all the prominent people you mention were in Paris. But you also take risks, some deliberate, others not so. You didn't think it necessary, for example, to falsify the Gestapo records, even though they arrested Von C."

"I'm ashamed to admit I didn't even know they existed," I confessed.

"Oh!" Thorsen said again.

"The Allies recovered almost all of them in 1945. The most important are preserved at Arolsen-Waldeck, in Germany. We did what was necessary. I have to say that I'm more worried when you mention the castle of Unterweikertshofen and the highly respected Von Hund family that has owned it for two centuries. Do you really think that seven weeks of filming could have gone unnoticed by the local peasants or by the heirs of Count Von Hund, who were children at the time and probably lived in the castle?"

"I suppose that's unlikely," I conceded.

"At the very least," Diaz insisted. "Above all, you take a risk for nothing. We only know the story of the shooting of the film from what Sadoul wrote, and he heard it from Spieker, who himself got it from Maria. You only need to say that the film was shot in Bavaria, a region dotted with hundreds of castles, and that Von C. tricked the owners.

"Another risk, perhaps a more calculated one: you do know that Chris Marker is still alive, don't you?"

Yes, I did, but this time I thought I had a persuasive argument. "He's never seen in public and he hasn't given an interview for ten years. I can't envision him emerging from his shell to denounce a hoax."

"Neither can I," Diaz said. "All the same, not all the characters in your dossier can be dead. Let's say that if one of them has to have survived, it might as well be Marker.

"Now let us come to the improvements," Diaz continued. "First, I changed Hilde to Hildegard. It's commonly agreed that the diminutive Hilde does not appear until the nineteenth century. Then I worked on the film crew. You modified the biographies of several of the actors, but curiously you forgot the crew.

"In our revision, the sound technician mentions the shooting of *Der Bettlerkönig* in his memoirs and the cameraman has recounted in several interviews how Von C. made him use short lenses in the confrontation between Friedrich and Gudrun.

"I also developed the critical apparatus. Did you know, for example, that before joining the Communist Party in 1932, Sadoul had belonged to the Surrealist movement, André Breton and Louis Aragon among his friends? Through its disdain for authority, its formal boldness, and its elliptical construction, *Der Bettlerkönig* could not help but remind him of the Surrealists, and he described this in a letter to his friend, Aragon. I'll let you have a copy, if you're interested."

"Yes," I said, "I'd like to see it."

"But above all," Diaz went on, "we widened the repercussions of *Der Bettlerkönig* beyond the purely cinematic sphere. Your dossier demonstrates a compartmentalized version of creation, whereas nowadays — and this has probably always been the case — great works affect the other arts and give rise to a genuinely interdisciplinary heritage."

"That's obvious," Thorsen intoned solemnly. I almost asked her to elaborate. Fortunately for her Diaz continued:

"Expressionism, which you mentioned earlier, was a movement in painting before being adapted to the cinema. Think of Schiele, Munch, Kokoschka... Moreover, expressionism doesn't stop with the visual arts. It influenced Schönberg in music, Kafka in literature, Mendelsohn, at a pinch, in architecture."

"Art history is Alonso's pet subject," Thorsen said, in what constituted her first (and it turned out, only) useful contribution to the conversation.

"The same with minimalism or neo-realism, not to mention cubism, which transcended painting to encompass sculpture and the visual arts in general."

Diaz paused to take a sip of water. The conversation was proving therapeutic for him. If I had been his doctor, I would have prescribed falsification sessions morning, noon, and night.

"I understand that," I said, "but *Der Bettlerkönig* didn't really invent a new style..."

"Are you so sure of that, my boy?" asked Diaz, amused.

Obviously, I wasn't. I hadn't seen the film. No one had.

"You see where I'm headed, don't you?" Diaz said. "I'm telling you that in *Der Bettlerkönig* Von C. reinterprets Surrealism, that the visual force of his mob of beggars inspired the silent demonstrations against the Vietnam War, that Marker may be lying when he claims to have invented still images with voice-over that the German photographer Andreas Gursky derived the idea for his enriched textures from a comment by Sadoul on the "expressive graininess" of Von C.'s film! Don't be afraid of going beyond your subject: you'll reinforce it with a broader foundation."

"Thanks for the advice," I said. "I have the impression that *Der Bettlerkönig* no longer has much to do with the project I submitted to Gunnar."

"You're mistaken," Diaz replied, graciously. "All I did was slightly flesh out a dossier that was already excellent. Now, Sliv, between you and me, you're already thinking of a sequel, aren't you?"

"A sequel?" Thorsen asked. "How could there be a sequel?"
"Von C. filmed for two weeks at Babelsberg before the Gestapo raid," I said, smiling. "The reels of film have never been found."

"That must represent about thirty minutes of film, wouldn't you say, Sliv?" Diaz gave me a knowing wink. The crafty old fox had guessed my next move, whereas Gunnar had no idea what I was planning.

"Pretty much," I said, implicitly acknowledging that he had seen right through me. "But my skills are limited to writing. On the other hand, if we have a young director in our ranks who'd care to try his hand at a medieval political epic, I'll be happy to assist him."

"We'll find him," Diaz said, rubbing his hands, "we'll find him. Ah, my boy, it's a blessing to have you here! Brilliant scenario writers are so rare."

"You're flattering me, Alonso!" I simpered, glancing at Thorsen, who was seething with rage. "I still have so much to learn."

"And modest to boot!" Diaz cried. "It's true you have a lot to learn. I would love to have been your instructor, but I fear that fate has decreed otherwise. I will leave you in Lena's hands. Trust her judgment in all circumstances. Her talents as a falsifier are unequaled."

I was expecting Thorsen to display false modesty, too, but she held her tongue, instead throwing me a smug glance that betrayed how much she savored that description.

4

The following week, I signed a two-year lease for a light-filled, three-room apartment in the center of Córdoba. I had had enough of hotel living and I moved happily into a building located behind the Cabildo, the most famous colonial edifice in Córdoba, now a historical museum.

I was close to the Plaza San Martin, where students gathered in late afternoon, and even closer to the sixteenth-century cathedral, which is still the city's main tourist attraction.

I was gradually revising my opinion of Córdoba. Although a walk in the historic district did not arouse architectural emotion (heavy pompous buildings from the colonial period, frankly ugly ones of the contemporary era), it was hard not to surrender to the charm of the Argentine street, an indefinable mixture of casualness, pride, and sweetness. Added to that, for the first time in my life, was a pleasant feeling of material well-being. Gunnar had raised my salary twice in two years, and the realtor, when demanding three months' rent in advance, could not have imagined that the wad of pesos I handed him was barely equivalent to a month's rent in Reykjavík. In short, the elements of my new life were gradually falling into place and I could almost have forgotten the boring Ramirez.

Unfortunately, Ramirez hadn't forgotten me. At my request, Diaz had informed him of my total lack of familiarity with the insurance world, and had advised him to offer me a crash course. Officially, the Compañía Argentina del Reaseguro had hired me for my sound geographical and geological skills. My time at Baldur, Furuset & Thorberg was supposed to have taught me to evaluate the impact of new construction or development on the ecosystem. I also possessed a smattering of seismological knowledge, a legacy of my master's degree, but, collectively these minor accomplishments hardly qualified me to perform my functions.

For a week I seldom left Ramirez's office. He trained me to read loss ratio tables, brushed up my rudiments in statistics, and explained to me how certain natural disasters could turn into financial disasters for the company. I didn't need any instruction to grasp that a cyclone hitting the coast of Florida cost our clients, the insurers, considerably more than a comparable hurricane off the coast of Bangladesh, but Ramirez put terrifyingly precise figures and ratios to such events. Liability-wise, an American citizen was worth one European family, a South American village, and a mid-sized African town. As far as I know, these relationships have remained fairly constant.

Ramirez seemed pleased with my progress and, to be honest, I was starting to develop a genuine interest in the subject. Even though my previous training might suggest the opposite, I have always enjoyed working with figures, and I felt a certain dexterity in classifying, manipulating, and understanding them.

I also have no difficulty memorizing demographic and economic indicators, which are less turgid and paradoxically more evocative than the often pointless descriptions of anthropologists. My imagination is more likely to take flight upon learning that the population of the Chinese city of Shenzhen increased one hundred-fold to three million in twenty years than on reading in a magazine that "the streets are swarming with businessmen" or that "the management committee of the airport has authorized the construction of a new terminal." How, then, could I not have gotten along with Ramirez, who, in order to say "It's a nice day today," would declare, "The temperature is twenty-seven degrees centigrade and the atmospheric pressure has stabilized around 1,020 millibars"?

I didn't do much by way of falsification during this period. I was eager to undertake my new responsibilities, but Ramirez did not leave me a free moment.

I eventually realized that he was unwittingly doing me a service. By agreeing to work intensively for a few weeks, I was increasing the likelihood of mastering the subject and of soon being able to reallocate most of my time without anyone noticing.

About a month after my arrival, events took a more radical and favorable turn than I had dared hope. Ramirez had asked me to evaluate our seismological exposure — in layman's language, to calculate the probability of an earthquake and of its financial impact on the Compañía Argentina del Reaseguro in relation to its locality and gravity. After reviewing my study, the management committee would judge whether it was necessary to rebalance our commitments.

For a week, I absorbed all the available literature on the subject, which led me to revise several prejudgments. One might have thought, for example, that recent earthquakes were the deadliest, if only because of the higher urban concentration. On the contrary: the worst earthquake in history occurred in 1556 in the Chinese province of Shanxi, when more than eight hundred thousand people died. In fact, China could lay claim to dubious honor of most dangerous country in the world, with five of the ten deadliest earthquakes to date. And even then, the Chinese figures had to be taken with a pinch of salt: it was widely accepted that Beijing consistently underestimated the numbers of victims by at least thirty percent.

I also learned that the secondary effects of earthquakes — fires, tidal waves, mass panic — often caused more destruction than the tremors themselves. The earthquake that shook the region of Kanto in Japan in 1923 would probably have caused fewer than thirty thousand deaths, had the fire not subsequently ravaged Tokyo and killed one hundred twenty thousand residents. Or consider the example of Lisbon, which in 1755 had been devastated in less than twenty-four hours by a tremor estimated at nine on the Richter scale, a huge fire, and a tidal wave?

These precedents had not escaped the attention of the insurers, whose natural risk policies were always couched in the most restrictive terms.

A few days before my arrival in Córdoba, a tsunami triggered by a 7.8 earthquake had swept the small Japanese island of Okushiri, destroying half the houses and causing two hundred deaths. I wouldn't have cared to be the adjuster informing the widows of the fishermen lost at sea that the insurance company would double the deductible amount because the quake and the giant wave had to be considered as two distinct disasters.

Discouragement set in when I started reading the weekly reports of the seismic observation centers around the world. I had naively expected them to contain historic tables, even probability ratios, that I could collate in order to predict the location of the next tectonic shift. Unfortunately, each report was more cautious than the last, reminding me that seismology was still a relatively new discipline, and that several more centuries of data would be required before a statistically reliable prediction was possible.

Since my report was due by the end of the week, I decided to dispense with a strictly scientific approach and directly invent the conclusions that Ramirez was expecting to see me draw from a close study of his tables.

During my Savoy assignment eighteen months earlier, I had read a fascinating article by a British geologist, who believed that civil engineers systematically underestimated the hydrostatic pressure that the water behind a dam exerted on tectonic faults. "Let us hope," he had written, "that the builders of dams will add a measure of redundancy before a tragic incident reveals the excessive conservatism of their algorithms."

Like so many pious hopes, this admonition, to the best of my knowledge, had gone unheeded. I decided to draw a composite map of the known geological faults, indicating the locations of dams constructed during the past thirty years. I noticed several places where they intersected, and spent the following days studying them one by one.

When I reached the fourth, I emitted a cry of mingled joy and surprise: in 1962, the Indian state of Maharashtra had completed a dam at Koyna. The reservoir, with a capacity of 2.8 billion cubic meters, had been filled in 1963. No one at the time paid any attention to the fact that Koyna was close to two faults well-known to seismologists: the Holocene and the Donichiwada.

In the spring of 1967, seismographs recorded several tremors measuring between three and four on the Richter scale, but the authorities failed to order a general evacuation. Then, on December 10, a quake measuring seven ravaged the city of Koyna Nagar, leaving two thousand people dead and fifty thousand homeless.

Had the world's largest democracy shut down the dam? Evidently not. The factories were dependent upon the hydroelectricity and the farmers had become accustomed to the reliable irrigation provided by the reservoir.

But the study of geography had taught me that nature is stubborn, and that the same causes almost always lead to the same effects. The question was not whether there would be another earthquake in Maharashtra, but when. So I was not really surprised to discover, while analyzing the recent measurements from the seismic station in Bombay, that since the beginning of the year the region of Koyna had recorded several tremors measuring between two and three on the Richter scale.

I wrote my report in three days, just as easily as I had written the *Bettlerkönig* scenario. When I could not provide a reference, I cited "a range of corroborating sources" or to "a number of American laboratories on the cutting edge of seismic research." I also abundantly quoted a Japanese expert, Professor Yuichiro Nakasone, "whose work at the University of Waseda on the internal structure of the earth has revolutionized our understanding of the spread of surface waves."

I concluded with the prediction that over the next two years there was a thirty percent probability of an earthquake causing significant human and material losses (an expression that reinsurers prefer to "costly disasters"). That percentage may seem small, but it is in fact enormous in a profession where risks are generally measured in parts per thousand.

As for the period of two years, I hadn't chosen it entirely at random: it was more or less the time I expected to spend in Córdoba. If there were no earthquake within the next twenty-four months, at least I would no longer have to face my superiors' anger.

"In conclusion," I wrote, "I cannot emphasize enough the importance strongly of reviewing our commitments in the Indian subcontinent, since a single disaster of the magnitude of the Koyna earthquake could cost the equivalent of a century's worth of insurance premiums."

Ramirez was delighted to accept my report. I had taken care to solicit his assistance, and, as I had foreseen, the pleasure of finding his beloved Riemann equations in the center of my thesis was enough for him to swallow the whole. He transmitted my report — I was going to say my dossier — to the management committee of the Compañía Argentina del Reaseguro, adding a handwritten note: *Level of reliability: 4/5.*

With hindsight, it seems as if events unfolded in an almost miraculous way. Startled by the high level of probability in my prognosis, the management committee decided to take another look at all our contracts in India. It canceled the least lucrative (which, by coincidence, were falling due the following month) and imposed fifty percent premium increases on the others.

Such a move led to rumors. One that made the rounds of the office was that the company was about to announce its total withdrawal from the emerging markets. My colleagues began looking at me strangely, not sure how to behave toward me: was I a soothsayer able to read the earth's entrails, or a Cassandra predicting the imminent bankruptcy of La Compañía?

For six weeks, this question fed discussions around the copy machine. And then, on September 30, I tore a newly arrived dispatch off the Reuters teleprinter and placed it on Ramirez's desk. It wasn't very long — but sufficient to establish my reputation in the small world of reinsurance: "Major earthquake at Killari in the district of Latur (Maharashtra, India). Thousands feared dead. Large-scale damage."

"*Fantástico!*" my boss shouted, evincing little compassion for the thousands of Indians buried beneath the rubble as we spoke. "*Riemann justificado!*" Riemann justified—well, that was one way of looking at it.

"Absolutely," I said, "and quite a saving for La Compañía."

"Yes, yes, of course," Ramirez replied mechanically, already preoccupied with the best way to exploit the situation.

The dispatches that continued to arrive over the next few days merely added to the legend. At about three o'clock in the morning of

September 29 to 30, the dogs and the farmyard animals had begun to show signs of nervousness. But the villagers, who had celebrated the religious feast of Ganesh Chethurthee the previous evening, were fast asleep. Many died in their sleep when ceilings collapsed on their heads. Others, awakened by the first tremor, barely had time to rush into the street before the earth shook again and destroyed the last buildings.

The peasants said they had suspected something ever since the well at the temple of Nilkantheshwar had suddenly dried up two months earlier, in the middle of the monsoon season. The disaster was compared to the one at Koyna, although nobody pointed out the possibly deadly role played by the dam.

The Killari earthquake devastated seventeen villages, leaving ten thousand people dead in its wake — one fifth of the population in the forty square miles around the epicenter. One hundred and fifty thousand homes were damaged.

The Indian government initially reckoned the cost of reconstruction at two billion rupees, but the actual amount far exceeded that estimate.

Of course, the vast majority of the buildings had not been insured. An earthquake of that magnitude would have caused infinitely more damage in Mumbai, situated one hundred and fifty miles to the east. All the same, La Compañía calculated that my memo had saved it eight hundred thousand dollars. The management committee awarded me a generous bonus of ten thousand dollars, of which I gave ten percent to each of my six colleagues. As you can imagine, this gesture cemented my acceptance.

Not everyone, however, appreciated my exploit to the same degree. Alonso Diaz, whom I had not seen again since our initial discussion in his office, sent me a note warning me against mingling matters that should be kept separate.

Gunnar, with whom I spoke to on the telephone shortly afterward, was more measured: "Don't wear the wrong hat, my boy—the Compañía Argentina del Reaseguro recruited an analyst, not a scenario writer." Then he advised me to fall back into line.

But the one who was most furious was undoubtedly Lena Thorsen. On the very day of my triumph, as I was relaxing in my chair, looking for the umpteenth time at the images from CNN, she burst into my office, hair disheveled, clearly ready to do battle. If I had thought for a moment that my memo would make her smile, her first words quickly dispelled that illusion.

"Tell me it isn't true, Dartunghuver!" she screamed over the voice of the Texan-accented CNN presenter, who insisted on calling Maharashtra "Maharajah".

"Quite a coincidence, in fact," I said, realizing somewhat belatedly that my answer probably did little to mitigate her obvious wrath.

"A coincidence! You dare to call that a coincidence. My God, you're dangerous."

"Come on," I replied, determined to avoid a confrontation. "You have to admit that this coincidence has reinforced my cover as an expert in reinsurance."

She was on the verge of answering, but stopped suddenly and studied me for a long time as if she had come to doubt my mental health.

"Incredible," she muttered, "he really needs to have everything explained to him." Then, resuming her angry tone: "You aren't here to pose as an expert, Dartunghuver. All we ask of you is not to make waves. Surely, that isn't too difficult. Approve of everything that Ramirez says; suggest a tiny modification in La Compañía's cover in Africa; at a pinch let it be known that you aren't completely in agreement with the plan for the next twenty years, but that you need time to organize your thoughts. In two years, three at the most, you'll be posted somewhere else, and everyone here will forget all about Sliv Dartunghuver."

"All the same," I said, lowering the volume on the television set, "I seem to be a lot more credible at the moment."

"Credible?" she spluttered. "Did you say credible? Quite the opposite. No reinsurance expert would dare give a natural disaster a thirty percent probability; or, if he were so brash, he'd spread his prediction over fifty years, when he'd be safely retired."

"I don't understand what you're blaming me for, Lena. That I tried to polish my image? Or that I took a risk? All right, I won't do it again. But, in the meantime, you must acknowledge the advantages of the situation. I'll finally be able to get down to the real work that I crossed the Atlantic to do. Do you think I enjoy poring over the tables of rainfall in Costa Rica?"

"Well, to be quite clear, I do want you working for me as soon as possible. With Diaz confined to his bed, and two vacancies to fill, please believe me when I say I don't want you working on pointless tasks either. But I have no place on my team for a clown who invents Japanese experts to justify his wild fantasies. I'm not saying the Compañía Argentina del Reaseguro is the Mossad, but all the same it does employ three internal auditors. What if one of them rereads your memo with a red pen in his hand and decides to call the University of Waseda, just out of curiosity?"

"I understand, and it won't happen again," I conceded, meeting her gaze and noticing, once again, how lovely she looked when she was angry.

"I haven't finished. Let's suppose the management committee discovers your ruse and blames the person who hired you: Diaz. Don't you think the poor man has enough on his plate at the moment? And if it is established that Diaz recruited an idiot, they'll think he may have recruited several. Have you thought about all the agents you're putting in danger with your recklessness?"

"All right, Lena, you've made your point," I said, ill at ease now that she had invoked Diaz. "I apologize."

"I accept your apology," she said coldly, "but I won't be so generous next time."

If I'd known then what the future had in store for us, I'd have made better use of my get-out-of-jail card.

5

Whatever Lena Thorsen thought of it, the Maharashtra memo (as a member of the management committee dubbed it) facilitated my integration into the Compañía Argentina del Reaseguro. Osvaldo Ramirez broadcast from the rooftops that my prediction was based on a Riemannian model, and then requested a doubling of his research budget.

As for my colleagues, they offered spontaneously to relieve me of my daily tasks so that I could devote myself fully to forecasting. Their gesture was hardly altruistic: all of them remembered their thousand-dollar bonuses and urged me to turn my attention to hurricanes, which, as everyone knows, are the largest meal-ticket for reinsurers.

I was happy to accept their help, and I professed an interest in the correlation between the degree of jaggedness of a coastline and the decrease in the speed of cyclones. Demonstrating a relationship between these would confer a decisive competitive advantage upon those who discovered it, I explained one October morning at a service meeting, while Ramirez looked on approvingly. But I needed calm. Calm and time. My team gave me both by leaving me alone for more than a year.

This matter temporarily settled, I undertook two additional tasks: learning Spanish, and honing my skills as a falsifier.

During the first few months, I went out almost every night. I had become friendly with two lively characters from the sales department, Alex and Sergio, who didn't need to be asked twice to introduce me to the nightlife of Córdoba. We would meet up after work at the Cafe Atlantico on Calle San Jeronimo to have a beer (or two or three). Then Sergio, whose father was a restaurant critic, would take us out to dinner at a steak restaurant, a different one each night, before Alex, the only Argentine I've ever met who could recognize more than twenty varieties of Belgian beer, dragged us from bar to bar until one or two in the morning.

The fruits of such a lifestyle were soon evident: I began to speak like an authentic gaucho, and I learned a whole lot of gossip about Lena Thorsen. Partly offsetting these benefits, I gained five kilos in three months, and I saved less than I had in Iceland.

Overall, I think I emerged a winner, and I eventually learned to space out my nocturnal excursions. I could now express myself almost without an accent, and I knew Córdoba almost as well as Reykjavík.

Now it was time to buckle down to serious work. And there was certainly no lack of it. Every week, the bureau received between thirty and forty dossiers from all the entities of the CFR. It was Thorsen who allocated them, according, she said, to their intrinsic difficulty and our specific skills. I had the impression of being assigned worse cases each time. Indeed, whenever I talked to my colleagues, I was always surprised by the straightforwardness of their dossiers, and I would happily have swapped five of theirs for one of mine.

There are in fact two kinds of dossiers, simply because there are two kinds of case officers.

The first, of which Gunnar Eriksson is a good example, deal with most of the problems in-house. They only turn to Hong Kong or Córdoba only as a last resort, when they can't dispel a feeling of uncertainty, or if they sense, without being able to articulate it, that another approach would improve the effectiveness-to-risk ratio. Their dossiers are both stimulating and vaguely demoralizing. The very fact that a case officer has been agonizing over them implies that the answer won't come easily.

Case officers in the second category refer all their agents' dossiers without perusing them. At least they can't be blamed for wasting time; they're covered.

When new dossiers arrive, their quality is obviously unequal, but out of every four, three require only a thorough reading to check that everything is in order. This allows the reviewer to concentrate on the dossier that really needs scrutiny.

By now it should be obvious that the dossiers assigned to me belonged almost exclusively to the first group.

Examining a dossier involves two stages.

First, it needs to be ascertained as thoroughly as possible that the agent has carried out the falsifications he describes.

In the case of *Der Bettlerkönig* for example, I had indicated that the two weeks of filming at Babelsberg were in the studio's records. Diaz hadn't taken my word for it: he had contacted the agent in Berlin, who had personally ordered the false document and had inserted it into the contemporary registers.

Such systematic confirmation, while it may seem tedious, frequently uncovers omissions. The scenario writer sends his request to the local falsifier, who acknowledges receipt and promises to act on it within a week... and then forgets, caught up in a whirl of ever more urgent requests.

Theoretically, the scenario writer cannot complete his dossier (and his case officer cannot validate it) until all the falsifications have been confirmed. But some agents don't keep duplicates of the requests they send out over the network, and sometimes find it difficult, when rereading the dossiers, to distinguish what is true from what still needs a little help to become true.

My colleagues tended to disparage this part of the work, which they considered dull, uninteresting, and unworthy of their talents. But I rather liked it because it afforded the opportunity to phone all over the world and thereby to familiarize myself with the tentacular structure of the CFR.

I learned at what time to call, whom to ask for, and how to formulate my questions in such a way as to avoid vague answers that wouldn't prove useful. I didn't hesitate to chat for a few minutes, or to ask the other person's opinion on the general quality of a dossier. Whenever anyone provided a service, I would offer to reciprocate whenever an opportunity arose. In short, I was building my list of contacts.

The second part of the job — improving the effectiveness-to-risk ratio of a dossier, i.e., trying to achieve the same objectives while reducing the odds of being discovered — is less easy to describe.

Again taking *Der Bettlerkönig* as an example, did I really need to invent a special show at the Cinémathèque in order to give Von C.'s "work" an existence? Wouldn't Sadoul's private screening have sufficed? Then there wouldn't have been any need to invoke Daney, Marker, or Doniol-Valcroze, or any danger of erring about the program times or of claiming that Truffaut was in Paris when he was filming in Portugal.

In this particular case, though, Diaz had judged that the risk was justified, and that the scenario wouldn't work so well without the account of that single screening in the presence of the Parisian intelligentsia. But he could just as easily have rejected the dossier in its then-current form, in which case it would have been up to him to suggest other less controversial sources.

That, obviously, is where the difficulties in the profession of falsifier lie. The lazy — and I confess, to my regret, that I was sometimes one of them — simply eliminate sources or repeat *ad infinitum* those they're sure of. Of course, by doing so they reduce the risks, but they also diminish a dossier's intrinsic interest, to the point of ruining any chance it might have of finding an audience.

True falsifiers, on the other hand, would die rather than weaken a scenario. They see each dossier as a new challenge, as a motivated story that must be made credible by any possible means. They aren't afraid of work: on the contrary, they like nothing better than to spend a sleepless night pulling a badly put together dossier into shape. No source is sacred; all are negotiable; all can — no, must — be improved.

The author puts his story in the mouth of a journalist from *Business Week*: why not a winner of the Nobel Prize for economics instead? He wants to establish a new German art movement: inventing another movement in reaction to it, called the Berchtesgaden Collective or Down with Dada, would increase its credibility, and too bad if that entails renting an office, choosing a chairman from the catalog of legends in Berlin, and publishing an insipid and conformist newsletter for a year.

I comprehended all that. I had been trained by the best: first by Gunnar Eriksson, then by the great specialists of the CFR in Honolulu, now by Alonso Diaz and Lena Thorsen. And yet I always got bogged down in my dossiers, seemingly incapable of departing from the traditional sources (the university thesis, the expert report, posthumous notes, and the like) to construct a character or a situation that would drastically change the story's perspective. And on the rare occasions when I managed to strengthen the structure of a dossier, I would commit some blunder that negated all my efforts, such as the day I attributed a 1971 report on ethnic rivalries in Africa to an Angolan general, without realizing that Angola had not gained its independence until 1975. That *faux pas* still makes me blush.

Of course I was trying to overcome my weaknesses. After all, that was what I had been sent to Córdoba. But months were passing, and even though I had unquestionably made progress methodologically, I still felt uncertain when it came to passing judgment on the soundness of a dossier.

It must be said that Thorsen did nothing to flatter my ego. For starters, she was constantly checking up on me. The smallest report, the slightest marginal note in a dossier, would end up on her desk and would earn me reprimands in which her exasperation came to the surface: "Review the protocols for cross-checking sources". "Your retired judge isn't credible. Ask Berlin to provide you with a legend"; "The landlady's testimony was quite sufficient: why do you always have to overdo it?"

More than once, by procrastinating as long as possible, I tried to avoid her fearsome judgments, but Thorsen was always on the alert. She would generally call me just before a deadline to make sure I would meet it. "So, Sliv, you'd better get down to that Congo dossier if you want me to review it before you submit it." It was as if a camera above my door were keeping her informed of my slightest move…

I often wondered whether we were all in the same boat. To the best of my knowledge, there were about ten of us handling the flood of dossiers that arrived each week. Thorsen couldn't reasonably devote equal time to all of us — even for her, there were only twenty-four hours in a day. When I once confronted her, she was very surprised and replied, "It's only natural that I should spend more time on the weaker analysts, isn't it?" This implied, of course, that the ranking of the different agents was common knowledge.

I respected Thorsen's professional judgment, but not the way she stuck her nose in my business even though I wasn't officially her subordinate. She took a wicked pleasure in reprimanding me in public, especially on the days when Diaz came into the office. Her favorite subject for these recriminations was my supposed lack of diligence.

It's true, I'm no workaholic, and I've never concealed that fact. I would arrive on the dot of eight in the morning, and in the evening, when the offices started to empty at about 6.30, I saw no reason not to join the exodus. I hadn't traveled to the other side of the world to vegetate all day at a computer.

Thorsen was clearly different. She spent her whole life in the office. The cleaning women would tell all and sundry that Señorita Thorsen arrived before them every morning and often left after midnight. She went home only to shower and to change clothes. The rest of the time, she would leave messages in an exaggeratedly professional tone on my voice mail, e.g. "Sliv, this is Thorsen. It's 9.30 P.M. Call me when you're back from dinner." Or "Sliv, it's 7.15 A.M. I'm waiting to sign off on this week's dossiers. Are you stuck in a traffic jam, or what?"

I also know she didn't approve of the way I behaved toward the Argentines. She nursed a particular loathing for Alex, who had made advances to her when she had first arrived. "Stop treating them as if they're your friends," she kept saying.

"But they are friends," I would reply, quite sincerely. "Manolita's teaching me to dance the tango, and I play football with the accounting department every Tuesday."

She would shake her head in false commiseration: "My poor Sliv, you'll never earn their respect." There wasn't much I could reply, except that it wasn't part of my job description, nor was it my intention, to cause them to respect me.

But I was hardly in a position to lecture Thorsen. She knew how to make people respect and even fear her. Those who worked in her team regarded her as some kind of vestal virgin, demanding of herself and ruthless toward others. It would never have occurred to anyone to return a dossier late, or to neglect to call her back after she had left a message.

That certainly doesn't imply that she was loved by her troops. The men tried to get into her good graces but never stood a chance, and the women hated her, not only for her beauty, but also for the contempt she evinced for the Argentine women who submissively accepted subordinate tasks.

There was one recurring rumor I couldn't help but hear: that Lena Thorsen had dumped her German boyfriend the day she had received notice of her posting to Córdoba. The poor man had offered to ask for leave of absence from his employer in order to accompany her, but she had dashed his hopes with a single sentence, of which several versions existed. "I'll have better things to do with my time than give you Spanish lessons." "Given how hard it was for you to find your current job, it would be more sensible for you to hold onto it." "I'll soon find someone else when I get there.".

The last of these was naturally the favorite of the gossips, because it gave rise to the most speculation. Had Lena Thorsen found among the Argentines a specimen she deemed worthy of sharing her life, or at least her bed? Personally, I doubted it, but I've never been much of an expert on women.

I must admit, though, that I had paid extra attention to this matter ever since Alex had declared one day in front of Lena that she and I had a duty to perpetuate the purity of the Scandinavian race. We had both blushed (seeing the blood suddenly rush to Lena Thorsen's cheeks is a sight every man should have the chance to witness at least once in his life) and the flash of anger I had seen in Lena's eyes had sent a delightfully erotic quiver through my body. (I later explained to Alex that, contrary to the commonly held idea,

Iceland isn't a Scandinavian country. The son of a bitch replied that he was perfectly well aware of that.)

There was no doubt that part of the harshness Thorsen made such a point of displaying toward me was attributable to jealousy. That in any case was what I told myself the evening I left the office, still shaken by the terse judgments I'd received from her in Icelandic at the end of a long afternoon, with three dossiers to be reworked.

Thorsen still hadn't gotten over the fact that I'd won a prize for the best first dossier: she often brought up the subject, sometimes finding in it the first warning signs of my shortcomings as a falsifier, sometimes casting doubt on the qualifications of the jury, "a bunch of apparatchiks who've forgotten what it's like to work in the field."

As I've already had occasion to relate, winning a trophy for the best first dossier is an honor that remains with an agent throughout his career. Diaz had made a great deal of my accomplishment when introducing me to the other agents in the bureau.

It was the one distinction missing from Thorsen's otherwise irreproachable service record, and I knew she felt some bitterness over it.

One evening, after she had rebuked me a little more sharply than usual, I sent her a letter that I had just composed for the London center and asked her to read through it. She immediately called me on the internal line to ask me why I had seen fit to place a star next to my signature.

"Oh, that?" I said. "That's the asterisk we winners of the trophy for best first dossier use to recognize each other."

I distinctly heard Thorsen swallow at the other end of the line. "Never heard that before," she retorted, a tad too quickly.

"That's only natural," I said, driving home my triumph. "Djibo told me he didn't want it to get around, because too many people might be tempted to usurp a star they hadn't earned." And I hung up, both exultant and vaguely ashamed of my meanness.

But I'm convinced that Thorsen's acrimony had another motive. Without wanting to indulge in pop psychology, I think the fact of being a woman greatly increased her competitive spirit. Women form no more than one third of the CFR's workforce, without there being any real explanation for it.

"Fewer women are hired," the men note, "and their proportion doesn't vary significantly as we rise through the ranks."

"False," the women invariably reply. "If the same criteria for promotion were applied to us as to the men, there'd have long since been a majority of us on the Executive Committee."

I considered this dispute bit pointless, given that none of the agents or case officers with whom I've discussed the matter know who is on the Executive Committee. But Thorsen has always been convinced that it's a woman who rules over the fate of the CFR. I imagine this belief gives her an added motivation to trample on her male colleagues.

Thorsen didn't like me. So be it. Unfortunately for me, in the match between us, she had the home advantage. That she was a formidable falsifier, I'd never dream of denying. Of course, she couldn't touch me when it came to writing scenarios, but, within the structure of the CFR, Córdoba deals with sources, not with scenarios.

It had taken me a while to appreciate the extent to which my current posting had landed me in a situation of weakness. Nothing in my work brought out my best qualities; in fact, it seemed that my post had been conceived to emphasize my shortcomings. I found myself in the position of a tennis player with a poor backhand whose opponent ruthlessly exploits that weakness. At best, he puts up a decent show; at worst, he's ridiculous. Most of the time, I was ridiculous.

In the end, it may have been Lena who best summed up my situation when she declared one day, without a trace of malice, "It's funny, Sliv, you're making less progress than I'd expected."

6

A few months later, I had the opportunity to witness firsthand Lena Thorsen's exceptional qualities as a falsifier. One Monday morning, she placed a thick dossier on my desk. "It's by a friend of yours," she said by way of introduction. "Let's see if you can improve it."

The friend in question was Francesca Baldini, one of the finalists for the trophy for best first dossier. We had kept in touch. In her last card, she had told me she was still based in Bologna, but had high hopes of being transferred to the United States within a year. I had often reread her *Geometry in the Anthills*, as I considered it one of the best animal-themed dossiers ever produced by the CFR. Whatever the subject on which she had chosen to write this time, I was impatient to learn the results of her imaginings.

She indicated in her introduction that her dossier — written in English — fell within the framework of the fourth directive of the three-year Plan, which was entitled "Highlighting the Weaknesses of Hyper-Financialized Economies."

Ismaïl Habri, one of the lecturers in Honolulu, had spoken at length about this directive, which he considered one of the Plan's most important for 1992-1994, and, although I hadn't understood all the terms he had used, I vaguely remembered the broad outlines.

Since the beginning of the 1980s, he had asserted, we had been witnessing a growing financialization of the economy. Private equity firms were buying family businesses that came up for sale, restructuring them and quickly reselling them to the highest bidder. Companies trying to increase returns on shareholders' equity were taking on more and more debt, exposing themselves to grave disappointment should they hit a rough patch.

Above all, investors now seemed to prefer virtual transactions to the buying and selling of actual goods. I had been fascinated, for example, to learn that a barrel of oil changed hands from five to ten times between the moment it was extracted from the ground and the moment it reached a refinery. At one moment, it belonged to a

Japanese bank; three seconds later, it appeared on the other side of the world in the accounts of a British trader.

Even more surprisingly, the financial markets encouraged businesses to monetize (the technical term was "securitize") all their assets. If an insurance company owned a thousand buildings, it could realize their market value by issuing a simple piece of paper guaranteeing that the purchasers would receive all future rental income from those properties. If the real estate market collapsed, and the tenants began to default, the insurer was immunized: he had already "transferred the risk" (an expression often used by finance professionals, which basically meant they had left someone else holding the bag).

Observing how aghast we all looked (only Magawati, who had studied economics in the United States, seemed familiar with such practices), Habri had emphasized that the CFR's purpose was not to question the workings of capitalism. "What concerns us," he had said, "is that the players in the market economy sometimes seem blinded by their faith in the solidity of the system. They forget — or choose to ignore — that these new instruments, while they may enhance the market's liquidity, also increase its volatility. Some traders build such complex positions that they can no longer quantify their potential losses from a sudden rise or fall in the dollar or in the price of oil.

The fourth directive aims to help political leaders, market regulators, and investors become aware of all this in a timely manner."

Personally, I would never have ventured into such a perilous field, but Francesca had felt confident enough to accept the challenge.

Her dossier presented two researchers from the University of Chicago, Fiedler and Staransky, who had developed a new criterion for analyzing businesses. Where banks habitually evaluated companies by analyzing the growth in their turnover, their cash flow, or the strength of their portfolios, Fiedler and Staransky were attempting to understand their attitudes, their idiosyncrasies, in a word their personalities.

All individuals possess a certain number of physical and intellectual characteristics that derive from their heredity and mold their behavior. Fiedler (a biologist) thought that the same reasoning could, under certain conditions, be applied to businesses, and that what were commonly called the values of a company were merely the product of its heritage (the personality of its creator) and its environment (the conditions in which it had originally developed).

This sounded simple, but it was an incredibly powerful idea that, once stated, was striking in its very simplicity and found immediate and unexpected confirmation. It might be thought, for example, that Microsoft and Apple, both founded in the 1970s by two entrepreneurs born the same year, have a great deal in common. Fiedler (or rather Francesca through Fiedler) demonstrated that on the contrary that the radically different trajectories of their leaders belied any resemblance.

Bill Gates, the son of a prominent corporate lawyer, attended the best schools and was studying computer science at Harvard when he created Microsoft.

Steve Jobs was abandoned by his mother a week after birth and raised by an adoptive family of modest means. He briefly studied calligraphy at a second-rate university, then traveled to India, where he shaved his head and took to wearing a sari, before starting Apple with a friend.

In short, said Fiedler, Microsoft and Apple have founders so different there is no way they can be similar.
This was where Staransky, a financier and mathematician, came in — and where Francesca's dossier really took off. Rather than focusing upon the corporate culture of Sony of General Motors, Staransky had developed a method of analysis based on a fifty-page questionnaire and applicable to any business.

The largest number of questions concerned the founder: his parents, number of siblings, level of education, etc. Did he own a pet when he was a child? Had he had to deal with a death before the age of ten? Did he play a musical instrument? At what age had he married (if applicable)? At what age had he first become a parent? Did he profess any religious beliefs?

Almost as important, apparently, were the place where the company's original location and the early years of its existence. Was the head office in an urban or rural setting? In a trendy suburb or in the midst of a farming community? How many of the first hundred employees were women, black people, foreigners, engineers? How many years after its creation had the company sought outside financing, either from venture capitalists or via the public markets?

Surprisingly, other criteria, which were more difficult to gather, were also taken into account: the sexual preferences of the board of directors, the founder's IQ, the age at which he had amassed his first million dollars, and so on.

Staransky soon realized the remarkable competitive advantage an informed portfolio manager could gain from the concept of Corporate DNA (as Fiedler had dubbed it). Asset managers spend all their time establishing comparisons between companies in order to identify the new stars of the stock exchange: if for example a study of past stock exchange prices convinces them that diversified companies are more successful than any others, they will buy shares in the former. Staransky therefore set out to discover new and surprising correlations among the most successful companies.

The results turned out to be far more conclusive than even he had hoped. For example, Staransky proved that businesses created by white men who were Presbyterians and had played basketball when they were younger had grown on average twice as fast as the rest of the business world over the past twenty years.

Conversely, an examination of the statistics resulted in an unequivocal recommendation to steer clear of companies whose head offices were situated more than six miles from an airport, and whose founder had suffered the death of a family pet during his teenage years: such companies, his research demonstrated, tended to pay smaller dividends than the others.

In March 1991, Fiedler and Staransky went to Boston to present their theories to Edward "Ned" Johnson, CEO of his family's financial investment group, Fidelity, the largest in the world. Although enthusiastic about the notion of Corporate DNA ("the simplest idea since the invention of the price-earnings ratio," he is reported to have said), Johnson was reluctant to associate the name of Fidelity with what could be described only as a daring experiment.

Instead, he advised the two men to start their own investment fund, and referred them to three private investors who he thought would be prepared put up a few tens of millions of dollars "just to see what would happen."

Two years later, those titans were one hundred million dollars wealthier, the new company — named WinDNA — having substantially outperformed the Dow Jones Industrial Index the Dow Jones Index in 1992 and 1993.

The dossier ended strangely. Fiedler quarreled with his associates. He wished to reveal their Corporate DNA model to the world, and to enjoy the academic prestige that would accrue from its publication, whereas Staransky and the three private investors were content to remain anonymous and to continue to amass wealth.

In the end, Fiedler left and sent a detailed article to *Fortune* magazine, in which he presented his premise but claimed not to be aware of the details of the complex model constructed by his former associate. Francesca clearly hoped that the prospect of huge gains would lead investors to pour millions into reconstructing these famous algorithms. One day, the realization would dawn that they had been chasing rainbows, and that they would have done better to analyze the fundamentals of the companies in which they invested. It was an original and elegant way of showing investors how far they had strayed from the essentials.

In a separate letter, Francesca's case officer asked us explicitly if we were capable of inserting an article in *Fortune* and of placing WinDNA into the mutual funds rankings.

I reread the entire dossier, once then again very slowly, dissecting each sentence. As was often the case, I felt a mixture of joy and jealousy. Why hadn't I thought of it first? I felt I could have done even better. Then I sighed, because I knew deep down that Francesca had handled a difficult subject brilliantly, and that I was frustrated by not having produced a single scenario for eight months.

I dialed the number of the Bologna bureau. Francesca picked up at the first ring and as usual was very forthcoming. She seemed genuinely happy to hear from me, especially when she realized that I had called to congratulate her.

"Oh, Sliv, that's really sweet of you. I was secretly hoping my dossier would land on your desk, but I didn't dare believe it would happen."

"It was a real stroke of luck," I responded, wondering if Thorsen had had an ulterior motive in entrusting her dossier to me.

"Do you think you're going to be able to land that article, Sliv? And the ranking of the investment fund? It can't be easy to arrange something like that."

"Don't worry," I replied, a trifle hastily perhaps. "It's in the bag."

"Oh, *carissimo*, how kind you are! I've been asking for the past six months to be sent to the East Coast to join my boyfriend, but Human Resources are dragging their feet. If my dossier is a hit, they won't be able to keep stalling."

"Actually," I said, "I was wondering if you'd agree to my adding a few items to the scenario. I know it isn't really what's expected of me, but I have a few interesting ideas."

"Such as?"

"Well, I can see one limitation to the concept of Corporate DNA, which is that it can apply only to straightforward companies that have developed along the lines envisioned by their founders. But conglomerates are the result of the combination of smaller businesses, each of which had its own founder and therefore its own DNA. I'd like to find a way of resolving that contradiction."

"You see, I was sure you'd see things I'd missed," Francesca said, admiringly. "You really are the best, Sliv!"

"Let's not exaggerate," I said modestly, while hoping that Lena Thorsen was listening in on our conversation. "All right, then, I'll get down to it straight away and call you back within a week."

"Thanks, *carissimo*," Francesca said, clearly delighted.

I made myself a pot of coffee and started scribbling marginal annotations in Francesca's dossier. Let's suppose that I'm a portfolio manager, I thought. In what other ways could I use Corporate DNA? Within a few hours, I'd developed an Index of Genetic Compatibility, the purpose of which was to gauge the likelihood that two given companies could merge harmoniously.

For the reasons mentioned above, any attempt at a rapprochement between Microsoft and Apple was bound to fail, but what about an alliance between Mercedes and Ford, or a takeover of Évian by Coca-Cola?

If the Index of Genetic Compatibility — the IGC — proved useful (and I was going to do all I could to make it indispensable), the predators would use it to identify their prey, the prey would apply it to choose between two predators, and managers would use it to anticipate mergers and acquisitions. It would be a whole new method of analysis available to financial players, at least until yet another, even more outlandish formula replaced the IGC in their toolkit.

For three days, I really went to town, twisting Corporate DNA and the IGC in all directions, adding two hundred new criteria to Staransky's model, and fleshing out the character of Fiedler, whom I described as torn between a hunger for honors and the lure of gain. I devoted only a few hours to the falsification of the sources — everything seemed in order — and unreservedly approved the idea of an article in *Fortune*. It was almost midnight on Thursday when I placed the dossier on Thorsen's desk. For once, she had left before me.

The following morning, I arrived late to find a message from Lena asking me to join her in her office. I suppose she wants to be the first to congratulate me, I thought, as I waited for the elevator.

"For heaven's sake, Sliv," she cried, looking genuinely dismayed, "I read your dossier when I arrived this morning, and I still can't figure out what on earth you've been doing since Monday."

This opening was so unexpected that my self-confidence collapsed immediately. I sat down, making an effort to recover my composure.

"I'm sorry, Lena, but I did a great deal of work. The scenario starts off from a brilliant idea but runs out of steam: the characters are too crudely drawn, Francesca cites only one concrete application of Corporate DNA, and Staransky's criteria are all a bit random. Trust me, I haven't been idle for the last four days."

"The worst thing is, I do believe you," she sighed. "Just as a point of information, can you remind me of the function of the Córdoba bureau?"

"The falsification of sources?" I ventured, feeling ill at ease.

"And your work has focused almost exclusively on…?"

"Francesca's scenario," I said, bowing my head like a schoolboy caught doing something stupid.

Thorsen let me think about my answer for a few seconds, then sighed again, as if already wearied by the explanation that was about to follow. Her unusually gentle tone when she next spoke surprised me even more than the content of what she was saying.

"Sliv, I think we need to have a real conversation, you and I. I have the impression that you still haven't understood what I expect of you. I'm sure I'm partly to blame for this misunderstanding."

"Thank you for admitting it, Lena," I said, in as dignified a manner as possible. "It's true we haven't had much time to talk about my work."

"Let's get one thing clear first of all. You are not under any circumstances to change the scenarios that come to us. Quite simply, that's not our role. If you get an idea for an improvement, write a note to the agent, with a copy for his or her case officer. That's what you should have done with your Index of Genetic Compatibility, which, by the way, is a brilliant invention."

"Understood," I said humbly, pleased in spite of everything that Thorsen liked the IGC.

"That would have left you time to take a proper look at the falsification section of the dossier, which really needed improvement," Thorsen continued, clearly determined to distribute good and bad marks equally. "Instead, you proceeded with additions to the scenario, supposedly to enrich it, but all, without exception, distorting the effectiveness-to-risk ratio of the dossier."

"How so?"

"Well, for starters, your new criteria don't add anything to Staransky's model. They merely repeat those of Baldini and verge constantly on the ridiculous. Next, you develop the character of Fiedler, without even asking yourself the question of whether Fiedler and Staransky ought to exist."

"What do you mean?" I asked, taken aback.

"Baldini makes her two characters professors at the University of Chicago: do you really think it's so easy to invent researchers from one of the most prestigious institutions in the United States? Especially as, if they really have created an infallible financial formula, journalists and investors will want to meet them. You simply can't assign names and faces to the inventors of Corporate DNA."

"But the public needs to know who the inventors are if they're going to be enthusiastic about their inventions," I cut in. "Of a hundred people who've heard of Einstein, you won't find one who can explain the theory of relativity. I'm afraid that without actual creators, Corporate DNA would simply be a project in someone's drawer."

"Are you so sure of that?" Thorsen asked. "Go back to Baldini's scenario and replace Fiedler with 'an idealistic biologist who prefers to remain anonymous' and Staransky with 'an unscrupulous financial genius.' I don't think the story would suffer at all."

"On the contrary," I said after a few moments' thought. "The media will get hold of the story and issue descriptions, while the investors hire private detectives to hunt for the two men all over the country."

"Bear in mind," Lena said, "that I'm less concerned with spicing up Baldini's scenario than with reducing the risk that people will see through it. I know it's tempting to invent Japanese academics, Canadian explorers, or South African conglomerates, but the added value they provide very seldom justifies the related risks for the scenarios and for our organization. If you follow my advice, you may well find skeptics who reject the notion of Corporate DNA out of hand, but, even if they spend a lot of time and money trying, they'll find it difficult to prove it's a hoax."

"I see," I said, "but then, any mention of WinDNA..."

"... Has to be deleted," Thorsen said. "Do you have any idea what you have to go through to register an investment fund in the United States? The efforts you'd need to make to alter performance data? So far, all our attempts to infiltrate Micropal, the company that centralizes the data on the market prices of thousands of investment funds, have met a brick wall. There are too many interests in play to allow troublemakers to compromise the sacrosanct efficiency of the markets. Believe me: I'd find it easier to cut the gross national product of Senegal by thirty percent than to add one penny to the share price of IBM on 7 January 1972."

"So what do we do with Staransky's company?"

"We turn it into a limited partnership based in Bermuda that isn't under the control of U.S. market regulators. Obviously, it can't be called WinDNA. We'll let the investigators speculate on its identity, as they scour through the list of the hundred best investment funds for the period 1992-1993."

"They won't find anything that corresponds with what they're looking for," I observed.

"So what? The more time and trouble they devote to it, the more the legend will grow. It's the quest that creates the myth, not the other way around. Do you think we'd still be talking about the Holy Grail or the philosopher's stone if the finest minds hadn't wasted so many years searching for them?"

"That's one way of looking at it," I said, reluctantly admiring Thorsen's theoretical expertise.

"It's the only way," she replied in a tone that brooked no argument. "But you may be thinking that I'm getting off lightly: after all, if I remove the names of the main characters, all that remains is a story, perhaps an amusing one, certainly, but a bit shallow and with nothing in it to compel belief. That's where the falsifier's talent comes in, provided he has any. I won't reveal the name of the company, but I'm ready to talk about everything else: what colonial-style house overlooking a beach it operates from; the power of the supercomputer that processes millions of data each night in order to establish unexpected connections among them, the twenty-page contract dividing the profits between the passive investors and the managers. That's what it's all about, Sliv: drown your readers in so many details that they'll forget you're hiding the essentials part from them."

"The Minutes of the Association for Thessalian Culture," I murmured.

"Precisely. Did Gunnar tell you about that?" Lena asked with a smile, and for the first time I felt a brief flash of complicity between us. "Now let's come to the question of the article in *Fortune* magazine," she went on. "I think you're making a serious error in approving Baldini's suggestion."

"Why? Aren't we capable of getting an article into *Fortune*?"

"That's not the point. Are you familiar with the concept of reference source?"

"I think so, yes," I stammered, feeling unpleasantly like a pupil being called to the blackboard. "A reference source is one that sets out the scenario in its entirety. Since it needs to be taken up in a host of other forms, which we call secondary sources, it has to be totally unassailable."

"Good," Thorsen said, "At least you have the theoretical basis. Let me tell you a story. I'm sure you remember the episode of the mass graves at Timişoara. The discovery of those graves, attributed to the cruelty of Ceauşescu's security forces, had a powerful effect on international opinion, which immediately sided with the opponents of the regime. Without those mass graves, it's likely that both NATO and the UN, legitimist by their very natures, would have maintained support for the regime longer. Instead, they let the population arrest the Ceauşescus and execute them. A few weeks later, a western journalist revealed that the number of corpses had been greatly overestimated. The graves existed, to be sure, but they contained between ten and twenty percent as many bodies as was stated at the time. The discrepancy was too big to be put down to negligence. Now, Sliv, do you have any idea how our agent in Craiova achieved that?"

Obviously I had no idea at all. I had only just discovered that what I had taken for one of the best pieces of media manipulation of the century was the work of the CFR. It made me feel quite proud.

"Think about it, if you wanted to get a piece of false information broadcast within a few hours, which channel would you use?"

"CNN?" I ventured.

"CNN, of course. Paradoxically, that service whose total worldwide audience doesn't exceed that of RAI, is watched by all news editors. All that Ilie, our agent in Craiova, had to do was to persuade the CNN correspondent to visit the spot. He showed him a few skulls, and two or three mutilated corpses, and assured him that the mass graves extended over tens of thousands of square feet.

As most of the bodies were buried, Ilie suggested arranging the bodies he had in such a way as to give the impression of catacombs as far as the eye could see. The American got his footage, which he sent to Atlanta by satellite. Two hours later, all the other TV channels interrupted their programs to broadcast the CNN images. In the meantime, Ilie, who by the way was not much older than you at the time, had dropped out of circulation."

"What a coup," I murmured, genuinely astonished.

"Wasn't it, though? He acted with a presence of mind that's quite rare in our field agents. Between his conceiving the hoax and its being broadcast, less than six hours elapsed. But his plan worked because Ilie had identified the reference source, the one all the others would feed off. If you can falsify your reference source, you've generally done at least half the work. That doesn't mean you must stop there: it's often important to falsify two or three additional sources that may be less well known but will tip the balance in your favor.

"When it comes to financial news, for example, you won't get anywhere if you don't have Reuters. That said, I'd advise you for good measure also to falsify Bloomberg and Telerate. Put yourself in the shoes of a trader who sees on his Reuters screen a news item he finds surprising. If he doesn't also find it on Bloomberg, it's likely he'll doubt its veracity. But if Bloomberg and Telerate confirm it, it will be difficult to cause him to change his mind.

"The difficult part of our job is to identify these famous reference sources. The examples of CNN and Reuters may well seem obvious to you. That's because their names are the first to come to mind as soon as we give it a moment's thought. I can assure you, however, that the search isn't always so easy. For example, whom would you choose if you were writing about wine?"

I confess a certain ignorance when it comes to wine, but I didn't wish to spoil Lena's demonstration. "I assume there's some kind of reference book, a dictionary. Something French, maybe?"

"A classic mistake. It's an American magazine called *The Wine Spectator*. That would have to be your priority. It was created by an ex-lawyer who liked his drink, and it is now considered *the* authority, even on European vintages. Another example: you want to launch a new management concept, like ultra-quality or paid generosity, something like that. How would you go about it?"

"I'd write a book and try to get a Nobel Prize winner to write an introduction?"

"And with a bit of luck, you'd sell two thousand copies, and the rest would end up on the shelves of a discount bookshop in Minnesota. No, there's another tactic that's unbeatable: an article in the *Harvard Business Review*, followed a few weeks later by a special report in the *McKinsey Quarterly*. With those two journals, your ideas will reach about fifty countries."

"But who's to say they'd agree to publish my papers?"

"To start with, you wouldn't submit them under the name Sliv Dartunghuver. We'd attribute them to one of our house gurus. We have a dozen to choose from. They've only ever published rubbish, but we make sure they appear in every possible bibliography."

I was still skeptical. "That wouldn't be enough to convince those people. They're not so easily fooled as CNN."

"That's why we have contacts inside the editorial committees of the main periodicals. Believe me, they're quite a drain on our budgets, so they can hardly refuse us a little service from time to time."

"But then all these people know about the existence of CFR. That's a crazy risk to take!"

"Do you really think I'm stupid enough to go and tell some factotum on the *Harvard Business Review* that we're going to use his magazine to falsify reality?"

"Why does he do it, then? For the money?"

"Sometimes, yes. But more often, he simply thinks he's helping out some over-the-hill consultant by offering him a couple of pages to present his latest theory. They always need something to print. And besides, if you think about it, ultra quality is no more dangerous than downsizing or Just In Time.

"As far as Baldini's dossier is concerned," Thorsen went on, "I can see two equally plausible reference sources: the specialized review *Institutional Investor,* and the *Wall Street Journal*'s monthly supplement on investment funds. *Fortune* is too mass-market for a first step."

"I'll go over the dossier again with that in mind," I said. "Thank you for the talk. I really needed it."

"We should have had this conversation on your first day," Lena graciously replied. "Put that scenario writer inside you to sleep for the moment, and think only in terms of risks, always remembering that, however many precautions you take, you're bound to make mistakes. There's always an element of the irrational in our job, and there's always an element of luck too.

Let's say you claim that one of your creations was born in a small town deep in the Scottish Highlands. By pure chance, your story falls into the hands of the midwife who worked in the local hospital for thirty years and was in the habit of writing in a notebook the names of all the children she brought into the world. You try to offset this by suggesting in an article that there's still a mystery surrounding the circumstances of the great man's birth. But it's too late by then."

"So what do we do in a case like that?"

"We do nothing. The CFR will get over a legend that's been blown; there have been others. But we can't allow one of our agents to be caught in the act. He'd be interrogated, tortured maybe…"

"Come on now!"

Thorsen was imbuing her words with such a solemn tone that I couldn't help interrupting. She must have sensed that I regretted this outburst, because she drove home her advantage by shaking her head for what seemed forever, then looking at me with the air of a veteran explaining to a young recruit that the sufferings incurred in combat are unspeakable. The tactic worked: I suddenly felt completely wretched.

"I don't think you quite grasp the fear our activities would instill if they were revealed to certain governments. In many countries, the secret police regard the falsification of reality as the most complete and most dangerous form of subversion. We're in a war, Dartunghuver, a dormant war that will never break out into the open, but in which our enemies use real bullets. How long would you stay silent if your nails were torn out one by one? Would you keep maintaining it was all a hoax if you had an electric current going through your body? I hope you never fall into the hands of our opponents…"

"That's the first kind word you've said to me, I'm flattered," I thought it funny to reply.
Thorsen regarded me with pity. Her reply was biting:

"I wasn't thinking of you, I was thinking of the hundreds of agents whom you could bring down with you. Please don't make them run that risk. Never falsify anything yourself; delegate the work to professionals. But if you must dirty your hands, concentrate on electronic sources. At worst, you'll be taken for one of those hackers who bet their friends they can booby-trap the Pentagon's computers. Electronic sources present another advantage: they're fed from so many places that it's extremely challenging to isolate the causes of a dysfunction. A modified figure or an extra line in a report, will be ascribed to an error in data capture, and nobody will think of looking any further. From that point of view, history is on the CFR's side, even though it also forces us to deal with an increasing number of sources."

I remember thinking at that moment that Lena Thorsen had a deep love of her profession. She was genuinely excited by the possibilities offered by the new media. While I most enjoy the play element of the job, Thorsen wasn't playing a game. Or if she was, it was with the firm intention of winning it, and she clearly felt justified in using all the means at her disposal. The answer she gave to my next question confirmed how right I was.

"Have we already suffered losses?" I asked. "I mean, do you know if the police or the counter-intelligence services of a country have ever been able to trace things back to us?"

"Not to my knowledge, but given how widely the CFR is spread, I'd be surprised if it had never happened. I know that one of my predecessors, an Italian, was forced to resign in mysterious circumstances at the beginning of the 1980s. Diaz refuses to tell me the story but, as it coincided with a serious tightening of controls in the bureau, I assume that at some point that must have neglected to cover his tracks. This won't happen to me. As long as I'm in this post, I won't let anyone put me at that type of risk."

Thorsen really didn't sound as if she were joking, and I felt sorry for the poor wretch who might get in the way of her rise to the highest echelons of the CFR. How could I have imagined that I would be that person?

7

The weeks were zooming by. I had reworked Francesca Baldini's dossier. Soon afterward, Francesca was transferred to the Washington bureau (Health and Medicine). My relations with Lena Thorsen had taken a more peaceable turn, while remaining professional. I now had a better sense of what she could teach me, and she in turn seemed determined to give me a chance to prove myself. That was all I asked.

The workload was still heavy, but, as I mastered some tasks by rote, I was able to organize my time better, and I managed to reserve three evenings a week for myself.

I played football on Tuesday evenings, and on Thursdays I took tango lessons with Manolita, a clerk in the back office who had bewitched me with her big black eyes. During the winter of 1994, we even did a bit more than dance, but neither of us was ready to commit and by mutual consent we broke up in the spring. The following year, Manolita got engaged to an insurance agent — a real one, at that.

I hadn't lost all contact with Iceland. Every month, Gunnar called me at home. I enjoyed our half-private, half-professional conversations, especially when Gunnar would tell me about the latest assignment undertaken by Baldur, Furuset & Thorberg, the refurbishment of the Reykjavík ice rink, or the recruitment — successful of course — of my replacement.

I was quite alone in Córdoba, far from my friends, my mother, and my sister. I didn't yet know about e-mail, and a single minute's call from Argentina to Europe cost more than two dollars.

The loyal Gunnar gradually became, in spite of the difference in our ages and our ranks, my best friend and confidant. He remained particularly fond of Lena Thorsen, as I suppose he did of the eleven other agents whom he had trained, even though she hadn't been in touch with him since she had left Iceland. He also regularly asked after Diaz, being too discreet to call his friend directly.

But above all we talked about my dossiers, the ones I had written as well as the ones I would write once I was out of purgatory, aka Córdoba.

Gunnar called one evening in October 1994, as I was watching a Boca Juniors football match on television, a Quilmes beer in my hand. I could tell from his tone, which was more cheerful than usual, that he had good news for me.

"Greetings from snowbound Reykjavík," he began.

"Greetings from mosquito-infested Córdoba," I immediately replied.

"Good week, my boy?"

"Oh, the usual routine: last night Lena made her secretary cry by asking her to retype a thirty-page memo; a training course on this new thing, the internet; a lot of work connected with the referendum on Norway joining the European Union..."

"You, too? I supervised a report on the development of the Trøndelag region for Moscow last month. No idea what they're going to do with it. Anyway, let's forget about that for the moment. I have more important things to tell you."

"I'm listening."

"According to our contacts at the UN, Boutros-Ghali is about to invite John Hardbattle to address the General Assembly."

"That's incredible!" I exclaimed.

In 1992, Hardbattle, the son of a Bushman farmer, had created an association called First People of the Kalahari, taking advantage of the wave of international indignation caused by the publication of Gaston Chemineau's testimony concerning the abuses of the government of Botswana. In less than two years, with the support if the British organization, Survival International, he had succeeded, if not in stopping, at least in slowing the expropriation program.

Hardbattle's efforts had spurred the major Western countries to declare their sympathy for the weak and oppressed, and, in turn, in December 1993 the UN proclaimed 1995-2004 the International Decade of the World's Indigenous Peoples. That day, my friend

Youssef had called me from Cairo and reminded me of the conversation we had had eighteen months earlier in Honolulu: my dossier really was changing the world.

"Of course, Botswana is doing its possible to have the invitation withdrawn," Gunnar continued, "but old Boutros-Ghali is as stubborn as a mule, and I'm sure he'll prevail."

"It's... I don't know what to say..."

"Then don't say anything; just enjoy it. Your dossier came at exactly the right moment. It crystallized what everyone knew but no one had the courage to say aloud. You can be proud of yourself, my boy."

Even more than the media coverage of John Hardbattle, it was the feeling that my work was beyond my control, possessing a life of it own, that thrilled me. Very few people can say as much.

"But I'm not calling you just to sing your praises. A young agent from Hamburg, Jürgen Dorfmeister, contacted me last week to say that he wants to write a sequel to your dossier."

"A sequel?" I echoed, hardly able to contain my excitement. "But then the Bushmen would become..."

"A saga, yes. Not bad for a twenty-six-year-old."

In CFR jargon, a saga is a story that is maintained and expanded by subsequent dossiers. The circumstances surrounding the death of Pope John Paul I, or the extraterrestrials at Roswell, are examples of sagas that the scenario writers of the CFR periodically revive. Some stretch over such long periods that those who launched them train their own replacements. The inventor of Roswell, a Canadian now over seventy, is said to have outlined episodes for the next twenty years in a letter kept locked in a safe at the Plan in Toronto.

I don't know a single young agent who hasn't dreamed of creating a saga. Up until now, I had rather placed my hopes in *Der Bettlerkönig*. Now I could dream of surpassing the record set by the Hungarian Bebeth, who had created three sagas by the age of thirty-four.

"I know Jürgen's case officer well," resumed Gunnar, "and he insisted that Dorfmeister submit his projected scenario to me. I'd like to have your opinion."

"Go ahead. I'm curious to hear what he has in mind."

"He proposes to focus on Maraqo's treasure. I'm sure you'll recall that the Morafe tribe discovered a deposit of very large and very pure diamonds. Their chief Maraqo gave some to Nigel Maertens to sell, as a means of financing his international public relations campaign. After Maertens' disappearance, Maraqo became paranoid, but nonetheless he did show a few stones to Chemineau, who photographed them."

"I remember it as well as you do, Gunnar. We wrote that dossier together."

"Fine, but there's still room to wonder what became of the diamonds. Jürgen would like to fabricate a new source to corroborate Chemineau's story, and to excite the interest of treasure hunters and other adventurers. He says there are American firms that specialize in the recovery of treasures and wrecks. The government of Botswana obviously wouldn't be overjoyed to see such scavengers turn up in the Kalahari. Jürgen's dossier may even suggest involving the Bushmen in the mining of the diamonds, in the hope that the tribes will reveal to it the location of the secret deposits."

"We could even cooperate with Survival International," I said, pensively. "The anthropological angle isn't enough. I think it's in our interests to move the debate into the economic field."

"That's exactly what Jürgen is suggesting," said Gunnar. "The word 'treasure' is enough to remind the international community that the expulsion of the Bushmen is motivated by venality."

"Well, I think he has something. Tell him I regard his idea as excellent — if he needs my approval, that is."

"Are you sure you don't mind another agent meddling with your dossier?" asked Gunnar. "Some scenario writers are quite sensitive about that."

"On the contrary, I interpret his interest as a recognition of the value of my work. Please tell him that he shouldn't hesitate to call me if he's stumped," I added, hoping to be taken at my word.

"I'll make sure to tell him. Take care of yourself, my boy."

Toward the end of the year 1994, I began to prepare for my journey to Patagonia. Lena Thorsen had dashed my hope of taking a whole month off, regally granting me just two weeks "during the slack period" (I'm sure she was the only one who had noted the seasonal nature of the falsification business).

It had been agreed that Youssef and Maga would join me in Córdoba, and then we would fly to Ushuaia, where a guide would be waiting. I could have simply chosen a package tour, but instead I became engrossed in studying atlases and travel accounts in order to plan a made-to-measure itinerary, a copy of which I sent to my two friends.

Youssef phoned me soon afterward from the Ho Chi Minh City bureau (Raw Materials), where he had just taken up a new post for the World Bank. It took him a few minutes to get to the real reason for his call.

"I've received my travel papers. You've really been working hard, it seems."

"I hope you're in good shape," I replied. "It's going to be strenuous."

"If I understand correctly, we'll initially spend two days in Córdoba. Where will we stay?"

"Here, of course! You weren't thinking of going to a hotel, were you?"

"I thought you only had a studio apartment. We're not all going to sleep in the same room, are we?" Youssef sounded very embarrassed.

So that was it: he didn't want to sleep next to a woman, even though she was his best friend.

"No," I assured him, "I have two bedrooms. You can have mine, and Maga will take the guest room. I'll sleep on the couch in the living room."

I heard him relax at the other end of the line.

"You can keep your room, and I'll go in the living room. Yes, yes, I insist. You know, I was just asking. No point mentioning it to Maga."

"You know me," I said, smiling in spite of myself, "I'm as diplomatic as a spokesman for the World Bank. By the way, how are you getting along there?"

I sensed him tensing again.

"Fine, fine. My post at the Bank leaves me lots of free time and Ho Chi Minh City is… fascinating, for want of a better word."

"Are you working on a dossier right now?" I asked, sensing that his discomfort was connected with neither his official duties nor his domestic arrangements.

Youssef hesitated for a few seconds before replying. "No. Or rather, yes. Not a dossier strictly speaking. It's what they call an initiative."

An initiative? Gunnar had once mentioned those large-scale, collective dossiers, whose duration was measured in years, or even in decades. Youssef was the first person I knew to participate in an initiative. I felt a twinge of jealousy.

"Really?" I said. "And what's it about?"

"Petroleum. But keep this to yourself: we intend to try to cause the price of crude oil to rise on a secular basis."

"What?" I exclaimed. "But that's crazy! Have you any idea of the hundreds of billions of dollars the oil industry earns every year? You have about as much chance of succeeding as a flotilla of ducks has of diverting an ocean liner."

"Well, that's what I thought at first, but now I'm not so sure. Look at the evolution of the price of a barrel of oil over the past thirty years, and you'll realize that the price of crude doesn't react only to variations in economic activity."

"That is common knowledge," I said. "It also reflects the geopolitical situation."

"Among other factors. For example, when the OPEC cartel quadrupled the price of a barrel unilaterally in 1973, all it was doing was expressing the new balance of power between the oil-producing countries and the oil-consuming nations. Same thing in 1990, when Saddam Hussein annexed Kuwait: fearing a slowdown in production, the investors sent the prices of hydrocarbons rocketing again. That's precisely what I'm trying to tell you: psychological phenomena play an essential role in determining the price of oil, and I suppose the same could be said of the other raw materials."

"And who's better at manipulating the collective unconscious than the CFR?" I said. "You're right, it may be feasible, after all. But why on earth tackle oil? And why force the price to rise?"

"That's precisely my problem. I've asked the question, but the only answer I receive is that I don't need to know that in order to do my work."

"The same old need-to-know," I said, referring to the cardinal rule universally imposed by secret services on their agents, allegedly for their own protection. If one of them is arrested, even torture can't make him reveal what he doesn't know.

"They can call it whatever they like," Youssef said scathingly, "but I'm not going to devote two years of my life to a project whose purpose may not merit my approbation."

"Well," I said, "that's something you should have thought of before joining. Besides, where's the problem? Everyone knows that the earth's reserves of oil are not infinite. It's obvious that, if prices rise, the industrial countries will keep a closer watch on their consumption. That's a good thing, isn't it?"

"It isn't as simple as that," Youssef said. "Believe me, I've looked at the problem from all angles, and I'd hesitate to draw any conclusions. Take a country like India, which imports about two thirds of the energy it consumes. Every time the price of a barrel rises by one dollar, its chances of developing its industry are compromised. Is that what we want: to stop a billion Indians from achieving progress? And all for what? So that the Sultan of Brunei can refurbish the eighty bathrooms in his palace and buy the latest McDonnell Douglas fighter jet?

"You know me, Sliv," Youssef continued, "I don't claim to know everything. I met the coordinator of the initiative. He's a Russian, not much older than I, and certainly not a stupid man. I'm sure he has excellent reasons to favor an increase in the price of oil to. If only he were prepared to share them with me..."

I could have retorted that of all my friends he was the most assertive. But Youssef needed my support not my sarcasm.

"We'll talk about it again when we get to Patagonia," I said. "I'm going to have a word with Gunnar, as he may have heard something. Meanwhile, just hold on. I'll look into it at this end. If they've found a reason, we should be able to discover it, too. We are part of the same organization, aren't we?"

But, as Youssef might have said, things weren't as simple as that.

8

The flight from Santiago with Youssef and Magawati on board was more than three hours late. And to think I had hurried to get through my pile of urgent dossiers before leaving on my vacation!

All week, I'd tried to prove to Lena Thorsen that the bureau could spare for me for two weeks; all week, she had left new dossiers on my desk, pretending to forget that I wouldn't be here to handle them. She had whistled disdainfully when she saw me leave in the middle of the afternoon, and it wasn't hard to imagine her already preparing her revenge.

I sat down at a table in the only café in the arrivals hall at Córdoba Airport, a greasy spoon that calls itself a pub on the pretext that it serves Guinness at a price that only American tourists can afford.

Deep down, I wasn't upset to have a little time to read the local newspapers. I never had so many ideas for scenarios as when I was leafing through *Gente* ("the magazine of the stars and the beautiful people"), *Pescar* ("the magazine for people who love fishing") or *Grill* ("Special issue: 101 ways to cook steak"). And how could I not feel immense professional respect for journalists capable of finding something each week to fill the three newspapers exclusively devoted to Belgrano and Talleres, Córdoba's two football clubs, which, since the previous year and for the first time in decades, were now both in the *primera division*?

The loudspeaker finally announced that Aerolineas Flight 45 from Santiago had landed. Hundreds of people were squeezing up against the barriers, so I decided to keep my distance. After all, there was no danger that I would miss Youssef, who was over six foot six. And besides, I hadn't quite finished reading a long article about the right length of the studs for the boots Belgrano would wear the following Saturday during the team's risky away game with Rosario. Nine or ten millimeters — the author of the article was careful not to come down on one side or the other.

It was Magawati who saw me first. She hugged me and gave me a kiss on one cheek, American-style. As for Youssef, I understood why I hadn't spotted him: he was almost buried beneath the backpacks, tents, and sleeping bags that he was carrying across his shoulders.

"Don't you have any luggage, Maga?" I asked. "Or am I to understand that Kili is a perfect gentleman?"

"A stupid mug, you mean," Youssef grunted, dropping all his gear to give me a hug. I had the impression that I was embracing a standing stone.

"You must be exhausted," I said, noticing the rings under their eyes.

"You said it," Magawati said with a yawn. "I don't know why the airlines don't just offer direct flights from Djakarta to Córdoba."

"Or at least impose a maximum of three connections per flight," Youssef said, rather more reasonably, as he tried to peel off the countless labels with which his bag was festooned.

"At least they haven't lost your luggage," I said, picking up the sleeping bags and one of the tents. "Follow me. We'll catch a taxi. By the way, Maga, you'll never guess what I was working on this afternoon. A sequel to the gallowfish!"

"No kidding? I knew about it, but I never imagined it'd end up on your desk. So tell me, what's it like?"

"Actually, it's not bad. The gallowfish definitely seems to have disappeared from Europe. But all is not lost: a closely related species has been discovered in the South Pacific. The author is full of conjectures: what is a fish of the *Scombridae* family doing in such warm waters? And, above all, how did the gallowfish cover all that distance? Has the species mutated?"

"I like the idea of mutation," Magawati commented cheerfully. "It opens the door to all kinds of wild possibilities. I'd be happy to write the sequel to that one myself!"

I expected Youssef to scold Maga for her happy-go-lucky attitude, but he had already fallen asleep in the back of the taxi. He awakened only long enough to drag himself to my bed and collapse on it fully clothed. I was tempted to make him share Magawati's bed, just to see his face when he woke up.

I had planned to show my friends around Córdoba, as our flight wasn't leaving until Sunday morning. But Youssef and Maga didn't emerge until about midday, so we spent the afternoon scouring the shops for the rest of the equipment we needed for our expedition.

I realized as soon as we began our descent to Ushuaia that we were in for an exceptional experience. In fact, I think I can say with hindsight that I've never taken a better vacation than those two weeks in Patagonia.

The reason Patagonia and Tierra del Fuego have fascinated so many famous explorers (Magellan, Drake, Darwin, et al.) is that they're a geographer's dream, a kind of windswept laboratory where nature experiments with the most unexpected combinations (sea and mountains, fjords and forests, volcanoes and glaciers, pumas, penguins and pink flamingos).

There are few traces of man's presence in Patagonia. The Straits of Magellan, which link the Atlantic and the Pacific, and owe their name to the Portuguese navigator who first sailed through them in 1520, have seldom been navigated since the opening of the Panama Canal. Similarly, of the five years that Darwin spent on board the *Beagle*, the great man's observations on the tortoises of the Galápagos are better remembered than his stay in Tierra del Fuego in 1832.

I told my friends on the first day that Patagonia means "big feet," because according to legend Magellan encountered a tribe of giants. Pigafetta, one of Magellan's companions, describes in his travel diary "men so big that we reached only to their waists"!

As Hernán Cortés (the Spanish conquistador to whom my friend Fernando de la Peña had denied the grace of baptism) also reported having seen giants at the same period in the Andes, Europe lived for two hundred years under the illusion that Patagonia was populated by colossi. It was only in the eighteenth century that British explorers, more rational than their predecessors, actually measured these colossi and found that they were just under six feet. The "big feet" may have been size 46, but no larger. Nobody, however, suggested renaming Patagonia.

Today, there are fewer than two million people inhabitants in a territory the size of Scandinavia. The economy rests above all on the exploitation of natural resources: wood, ore, cattle farming, and oil.

Our guide, a rough but charming young man by the name of Felipe, told us that his uncle owned an oilfield, but that he was waiting for a rise in the world price to begin drilling. "At current prices," he said, "it wouldn't be profitable." The poor boy had probably not expected the flood of questions that followed. Youssef put his curiosity down to his job with the World Bank, but I could see that Felipe considered his interest a trifle excessive.

I'd made an effort to limit the number of journeys by bus, but they were unavoidable if we wanted to visit all the main sights in two weeks. We had landed at Ushuaia, crossed into Chile to view the Straits of Magellan, then back over the border into Argentina. We walked seven or eight hours each day, but without bags or camping equipment, which an employee from the travel agency brought to our camp in the evenings.

When night fell, as we put up the tents (I shared one with Youssef, while Felipe and Magawati each had their own), Felipe would light a fire and prepare dinner, invariably steak, although by a different recipe each night (maybe he had read the special issue of *Grill*).

The unearthly beauty of the landscapes was a constant invitation to meditate and yet the memory I have of that journey is one of an uninterrupted conversation, which began in the morning on the roads, continued around the fire, and persisted even in the tent with Youssef, or between the two tents with Magawati.

Maga never seemed tired of talking. She had that uncanny ability to change the subject unexpectedly in order to follow an association of ideas and somehow get closer to the crux of an issue. For example, she might be talking about the latest box office hit in Indonesia one moment and then ask me the next if I felt I was using the CFR more than it was using me.

She was also extraordinarily skillful at judging the reactions of the person she was talking to and moving the conversation in a particular direction, such as the time she asked me what I thought of Lena Thorsen, professionally, morally, and aesthetically (I thought for a moment she was going to add "physically"), and she watched me formulate a needlessly convoluted reply. When I had finished, she said cuttingly, "In other words, you don't yet have an opinion. Of course you've only known her for a year."

Maga neither forgot anything nor let anything pass, and although I don't consider myself especially dense, she regularly staggered me with her sharpness and ready wit.

Her twin cultures — Indonesian and American — allowed her to discuss almost any subject in a free and unbiased way, where someone like Youssef clearly showed the limitations of his upbringing. He was tolerant philosophically, while Maga was naturally so, as only those who have either traveled extensively or grown up with roots in several cultures can be.

The insistence with which Maga tried to coax me into revealing something of my personal life had staggered me at first. She questioned me endlessly about my father, who had died of a brain tumor when I was eleven. Had he known he was dying? Had he talked to me about his impending death? Could I say what it was I had learned from him?

Such curiosity — Youssef called it shamelessness — was part and parcel of the idea Maga had of friendship. She simply probed my soul, without exaggerated solemnity but never carelessly, as if to say, "If you want me to be your friend, you have to let me inside your heart and mind."

I found myself telling Maga things that I had never told anyone, or that I had taken several years to discover for myself. I had never imagined such a level of trust in someone with whom I had basically spent no more than a few dozen hours. Gunnar had the same gift, although the difference in our ages and our awareness of our respective positions within the CFR ruled out certain subjects.

209

I was less skillful at probing, but Maga did in fact confide somewhat in me. The CFR was urging her to resume her studies in the United States and obtain an MBA. Business and economics are obviously a fertile field for falsifiers, but there are few agents with sufficient knowledge of the methods and practices of the business world to really leave their mark on it.

The CFR, which primarily recruits young agents, has no choice but to train them, something to which it is prepared to devote considerable resources. Maga told me she wouldn't have minded spending two years at Harvard or Stanford, but her fear was that then she would be stuck with dossiers on economics, when she was more interested in social themes.

She also admitted that she suffered from not being able to discuss her secret activities with her civilian friends. Of course she understood why we were sworn to secrecy, but that didn't make the situation any less painful for her. "When Djibo encouraged us to share our experiences," she said to me one day, "he should have told us that all friendships outside the CFR would be forbidden to us from now on. That at least would have had the merit of honesty."

My conversations with Youssef were quite different. Youssef openly despised anything that could be called small talk. He preferred serious, even solemn subjects, and he was particularly fond of moral dilemmas, on which he could discourse *ad infinitum*.

Although his thoughts were clear, they were expressed slowly, each word carefully weighed and each argument accompanied by several examples. I could have listened to him for hours. His exhaustive, perfectly cogent presentations reassured me. It was good to know that people as wise as Youssef were reflecting on the great questions of this world, and even better to realize that they would never be satisfied with simplistic answers.

Maga wasn't always as patient as I. Whenever she felt Youssef was splitting hairs, she would urge him to get to the point, but this generally resulted in his becoming even more turgid.

"I don't see what can be more urgent than determining the correct debt level for emerging countries," he said to Maga one evening, a tad irritably, when we were discussing the World Bank's recent relief of third-world debt.

"Moving my tent," she replied, giving him a dazzling smile. "A colony of ants has invaded my sleeping bag."

The two of them were always squabbling, but I was beginning to sense that something deeper was occurring. Since the episode at the airport, I had noticed the way Youssef would cater to Magawati's every need: putting up her tent, carrying her kit, serving her morning coffee.

Maga didn't abuse Youssef's thoughtfulness, but neither did she discourage him. Although, as I've noted, she sometimes interrupted Youssef, she never did so when he talked about himself. At such times, she would listen to him with an intensity that clearly exceeded her interest in me.

Another revealing sign was that she had stopped teasing him about Islam, doubtless having perceived that she had nothing to gain by offending him on such a sensitive subject.

My suspicions were confirmed one evening, when, as we were making a list of the greatest wonders of the world, Magawati described how awestruck she had been upon seeing the huge stone statues at Abu Simbel.

"When did you go to Egypt?" I asked.

"Oh, last year," she replied, blushing.

Youssef stood up suddenly to check the fire, which didn't need checking.

"With Youssef?" I insisted, quite determined to press on.

"Yes, of course," Maga said. "Who else would have accompanied me?"

"I had to visit a farm on the shores of Lake Nasser for the bank, and from there it was only an hour by bus," Youssef said, as if I were interested in the route he had taken from Cairo. I was more curious about Magawati's itinerary from Djakarta.

"I see," I said, pretending to reflect on the implications of this information.

"You see nothing, nosy parker," Maga replied with an enigmatic smile that made me wonder if, after all, her slip of the tongue had not been deliberate.

I sensed that Youssef was less relaxed than he should have been.

His dossier about Karigasniemi, the Finnish forest believed to possess exceptional environmental properties, had met with deserved success. Two years earlier, 100,000 demonstrators had marched through the streets of Helsinki demanding the cancellation of the concession that had been granted to a paper company, and they had attained their goal.

Wreathed in glory from this achievement, Youssef had come up with two more personal scenarios, one on genetically modified organisms, a subject he knew well from his work at the World Bank, and the other on the Arabian Nights.

He was also rapidly climbing the ladder at the World Bank, and he admitted to me that he had not entirely ruled out the possibility of pursuing a career there. For now, he was keeping his options open, and at the appropriate juncture he would decide where he might be of greatest use.

I suspected that the cause of Youssef's torments was the famous Petroleum Initiative. He implicitly confirmed this conjecture by asking us our opinion one evening around the fire after Felipe had gone to bed.

"We have carte blanche to raise the price of oil over the next three to five years," he said, snug in his sleeping bag, a steaming cup of tea in his hand. "I estimate that there are several dozen agents working on this project, perhaps even a hundred, and that we've already spent several million dollars."

"Remind us of the basics," I said, more for Maga than myself.

"It's an extraordinarily complicated subject," Youssef sighed. "In less than a century, hydrocarbons have become the prime source of energy used in the world. They provide some 45% of the planet's needs. The main consuming countries are the United States, Japan, and the other large industrial countries. The main producers are the states of the Arabian Peninsula, led by Saudi Arabia, and Russia,

Norway, Great Britain, Mexico, and Venezuela. Historically, the great powers, notably the United States, have won concessions from the producing countries that gave them the right to prospect and to extract petroleum from their soil against the payment of token royalties. In the 1960s, the main oil-producing countries organized themselves into a cartel, in an effort to win more favorable terms. In 1973, the cartel succeeded in quadrupling the price of a barrel."

Typical Youssef, I thought. Not a word too many, and a properly professorial tone.

"Like all markets, the oil market obeys the laws of supply and demand. Demand is generally connected with economic activity: during periods of world growth, more oil is consumed, which pushes up prices. Supply, on the other hand, is a trickier proposition. The oil producing countries have vast reserves under the ground, but they extract only what they expect to be able to sell at a good price. That's OPEC's whole raison d'être: the producing countries collectively agree not to produce too much and to maintain an acceptable price level. Of course this last notion is highly subjective: Saudi Arabia, for example, could reduce its production and increase the price of a barrel, at least temporarily, but it would risk annoying its American friends, who guarantee it implicit military protection.

"OPEC' solidarity began to crumble when its members couldn't agree upon a suitable response to Iraq's invasion of Kuwait and the ensuing Gulf War. At the same time, other countries that weren't members of the organization greatly boosted their production. It took only a few mavericks to break up the cartel, and prices have fallen over the past several years by between ten and fifteen dollars a barrel."

"You speak of the balance between supply and demand at any given moment," I cut in, "but we can't ignore the fact that oil is a finite resource."

"I was coming to that," Youssef said, "because that is in fact what complicates matters. In 1971, an American geophysicist named Hubbert predicted that world oil production would peak in the year 2000, i.e., that from that date, on an annual basis, more oil would be extracted from the ground than would be discovered.

"Hubbert's theory seemed irrefutable, but as the oil companies continued to discover new deposits, the 2000 deadline began to seem too pessimistic, and at present most of the industry players seem unconcerned about the prospect of a world without oil."

"The fools!" Magawati cried, wrongly in my opinion. Petroleum executives may be many things, but they're not stupid.

"OK, now tell us what's troubling you," I said.

"It's quite simple: nobody seems able to explain to me why it's important to get prices to rise. The Russian who's leading the initiative says it's classified information, and we'd be wasting our time asking questions. Needless to say, I wasn't satisfied with that rejoinder. But I grinned and bore it, thinking that I could always influence the way the project was being managed. And that's where they tricked me."

"What happened?" asked Maga, who didn't like to think that her Youssef had been tricked.

"My first reflex, like that of most of my colleagues, was to say that we had to emphasize the scarcity angle: by making people believe that demand was greater than it really is, while at the same time suggesting that world reserves were being depleted, we would break the balance and increase the price of a barrel."

"That seems logical," Maga said. "Didn't they agree with you?"

"Far from it," replied Youssef. "Invoking a paradox that's apparently well known to economists, the Russian recommended precisely the opposite strategy. According to him, the fear of world reserves drying up would bring about a transfer of research budgets to alternative forms of energy. The industrialists who invest for a period of ten or twenty years would never risk having one day to convert their factories. They'd rather voluntarily move away from oil today than be forced to do so by events in twenty years. The prices of other fuels would shoot up, oil prices would decline along with consumption, and — here's the paradox — the reserves would last longer. So his solution is to let the world believe that reserves are inexhaustible, and to encourage car manufacturers to build ever-bigger gas guzzlers. Then demand will explode, as will prices."

"But that's criminal!" Maga cried. "You're going to encourage waste on a global scale."

"Unfortunately, it might well work," I said, pensively. "A lot of people will profit from it."

"That's what worries me," Youssef said. "I'm not even talking about the oil companies, which will be only too happy to dig more and more holes and to reap record profits. It's a well-known fact that the OPEC countries systematically overestimate their reserves. As they commit themselves jointly to producing a given number of barrels, each one tries to justify an increase in its own share of total production in proportion to the extent of its reserves. If we're plotting to help them to falsify their figures, I don't know where it will stop. As for consumers, I won't enumerate the effects on them. No one likes to lower his thermostat or to reduce his speed: when consumers find out that the threat of shortages has receded, they'll forget all the good habits that their governments have been trying so hard to instill in them."

"Has your team already begun work on this project?" I asked.

"Yes. We've looked through the various ways of reevaluating the reserves, and we have decided to focus on a particular kind of hydrocarbon: bituminous sands. Because they're difficult to extract, these bituminous sands aren't generally included in world reserves. If they were—and this will give you an idea of what's at stake—a country like Canada would suddenly find itself as rich as Saudi Arabia.

"We're going to try to convince the market that new techniques will eventually enable drastic reductions in the costs of extraction, thus justifying the exploitation of bituminous deposits. If we can do that, there's no reason why they can't be included in estimates of world reserves."

"Quite a challenge," I said, excited in spite of myself. "You're going to have fun."

"I doubt that," Youssef said. "I intend to resign."

"Youssef!" Maga cried. "You wouldn't, would you?"

"Why not?" Youssef asked. "Face facts: I'm not privy to the aim of the operation; then I'm asked to implement a strategy that will have a devastating effect on the environment. Even supposing the end justifies the means — which is far from being philosophically proved — I don't see how I could continue to participate in a project whose end I don't know and whose means disgust me."

Maga and I must have looked dismayed, because Youssef then smiled sadly and added, "Now, if either of you has other arguments to put forward, I'm listening."

We considered this for a few minutes. Maga was tempted to respond immediately, but she must have understood that Youssef wouldn't be content with sketchy arguments. In the end, I was the one who spoke first.

"I think you'd be making a mistake," I said. "Either their cause is just, and all you can blame them for is that they're keeping you in the dark; or it is unjust, and your staying a few more months won't make any difference."

"Not to them, perhaps, but to me," Youssef replied. "I'll have been complicit with something sinister, when I could have chosen not to be."

"Forgive me for being blunt, but if you look at it that way, you already are. I'm no moralist, but it seems to me that in a situation like this, it's your intentions that count. You can't really consider yourself complicit, so long as you don't know what the aim of the Petroleum Initiative."

"I understand your point," Youssef replied. "But you must realize how dangerous that argument is. I'd just have to claim that I was repressing my doubts while justifying the status quo. And even if my boss eventually explains to me the motives behind the initiative and I disapprove of them, I could always delude myself that he's concealing the truth from me in the higher interests of the CFR."

"You could do that," Maga said, "but you won't. We know you, Youssef Khrafedine: you'll continue to evaluate the situation on the basis of the information at your disposal, and you'll make the decision you deem appropriate when the time comes, without any kind of self-pity."

"But the more time I spend in the CFR," Youssef retorted, "the more difficult such decision would be. Anybody would find it hard to admit he's been wrong for such a long time."

"But you're not just anybody," Maga said simply.

Even from where I was, I could see a twinkle in Maga's eyes. She was shivering and glowing at the same time. I had just witnessed a declaration of love, although I wasn't certain that Youssef was fully aware of it.

"Mind you," I resumed, "our situation is not so different from yours. You don't know the aim of the Petroleum Initiative, but do you think I know the purpose of all the dossiers that cross my desk? The truth, Youssef, is that nothing has really changed since our conversation in Honolulu. We trust our superiors, because we have no other choice, and because, if we defy them, they'll drop us from the game. You mentioned earlier the millions of dollars you've already spent. Do you have the least idea where that money comes from? No, and neither do I. Yet, so far, that hasn't stopped us from spending it. As Maga says, all we can do is remain vigilant."

"I see," Youssef said, pensively. "Maga?"

"Sliv is right. Give yourself a bit more time. It's been only a few months. If events take a turn you don't like, you'll be more useful on the inside. Be careful, that's all I'm asking."

"Yes," Youssef said, without catching the implications of Maga's last words. "I suppose I could wait a little longer. But not forever. If in a year I still don't have the answers I need, I'll leave. My life is too short to risk devoting it to something unworthy."

"And you won't be alone," Maga said, putting her arm around Youssef's shoulders. "If you resign, I'll resign too."

In the tent that night, Youssef tossed and turned for a long time before falling asleep.

9

Once back in Córdoba, I resumed my routine: a lot of work, casual friendships, another fling, this time with a Spanish exchange student. My colleagues in La Compañía were starting to wonder more and more openly about the lack of concrete applications of my research into hurricanes.

Diaz was still alive, but his health continued to deteriorate. Lena was really hoping he would live: naively, she told me one day that if he did she could continue to run the bureau without being required to report to a new boss. She knew she was too young to be promoted to bureau head.

And then one day in June 1995, the 16th or 17th maybe, as we were discussing ways to infiltrate the CIA's computer records, Lena suddenly interjected, "Have you read that France is about to resume nuclear tests in Polynesia?"

"Yes, I did read that. How is that relevant to this dossier?"

"Not with this one, but you remember the dossier called *Save the Gallowfish* that we received at the beginning of the year. If my memory serves me well, part of that took place in Australia or New Zealand."

"You mean Rama Chandrapaj's dossier? Yes, a whole chunk of it was about the appearance of species similar to the gallowfish in the South Pacific."

"And did his argument hold up?"

"Er, I think so, yes," I said, not sure where Lena was going with this. "In so far as I recall, we didn't find anything to criticize. Why do you ask?"

"Oh, no reason. I just have the feeling that during the next few weeks people are going to be paying a lot more attention to the ecosystem of that part of the world."

Thorsen had succeeded in alarming me. As soon as our meeting had ended, I looked in my library for the dossier in question, which was called *The Gallowfish Reappears*. It was still where I had left it, months earlier, on the day I had left to pick up Youssef and Magawati from the airport.

I looked through the first few pages to remind myself of the broad outlines. Chandrapaj began by bringing the situation of the gallowfish up to date, three years after Magawati, in her first dossier, had drawn the attention of the international community to the fate of this bony fish of the *Scombridae* family.

Chances for the gallowfish's survival appeared bleak. Grants from the European Community had been insufficient to stem the creature's gradual extinction, which Maga had attributed to the collapse of an oil platform off the coast of Norway.

Futility dogged Brussels' ban on fishing for the species. Any specimen caught in the nets had to be thrown back immediately, on pain of a fine. Generous subventions were also promised to those fish farmers who undertook to raise gallowfish. Unfortunately, the number of eggs laid in each reproductive cycle was rapidly declining, making commercial farming impossible.

Nevertheless, a rather unusual type of gallowfish had been observed off the coast of New Zealand. The Pacific gallowfish differed from its European counterpart in a number of anatomical details, but the kinship of the two species had been positively established.

Chandrapaj did not attempt to explain how a new species could have appeared so suddenly in the ocean basin formed by Australia, Fiji, and New Zealand. He simply recounted how, from one year to the next, the gallowfish had been included in the annual statistics of New Zealand's Ministry of Agriculture and Fisheries. In his conclusion, he did hypothesize a mutation of the species, but I suspected him of holding back a more convincing explanation, which he would unveil to the scientific community in the third episode of the saga.

My opinion of *The Gallowfish Reappears* hadn't changed. It was a decent dossier, a bit lacking in humor, but one which had required only minor corrections. And yet, although I didn't quite know why,

Lena Thorsen's anxiety — rather a strong word perhaps for a casual comment — put me ill at ease.

I instinctively began to follow related developments more attentively. I couldn't pass the Associated Press wire that spat out dispatches from all over the world twenty-four hours a day without mechanically tearing off the printout and looking for the words "nuclear" or "New Zealand".

I may have been one of the first to notice the growing discomfort of the governments of the South Pacific, and the fierce determination of the environmental organizations, conscientiously fanned by the Asian industrial lobbies, which were only too pleased to see French products threatened with a boycott.

Poor old Chirac was clearly not prepared for the virulent anger aroused by the resumption of French nuclear tests. The more he explained, the less he was understood. However often he stated that the current round of tests was the last, and that from now on France would test its arsenal through computer simulations, public opinion was implacably opposed to his decision.

I wasn't the only one to be concerned. Lena Thorsen was also closely following the progress of anti-French sentiment in that part of the world. She added to my disquiet by summoning me at the beginning of July and bombarding me with questions. Was Chandrapaj's dossier foolproof? Had I noticed anything that could attract the attention of the local authorities? Last but not least, could I assure her that no agent of the CFR had left any traces behind him?

Thorsen must have sensed that I was somewhat less sure of myself, because she demanded that I compile a list of all of my contributions to the dossier. But she didn't give me time to comply. The very next day, she burst into my office, holding a copy of the *International Herald Tribune*. Without a word but in a state of nervousness akin to hysteria, she stuck the paper under my nose and pointed to a headline.

The Prime Minister of New Zealand had announced his intention to produce "an objective scientific study to assess the impact of

French nuclear tests on the ecosystem of the South Pacific." He said that he had taken this decision after consulting his Australian and Fijian neighbors, who were as anxious as he was to preserve their region's flora and fauna.

"Well?" I asked, a tad foolishly.

"*Well?*" Thorsen echoed. "Do you realize the flood of bad news that's about to fall on our heads?"

"It's just political grandstanding!"

"Political grandstanding, is it? I can see the scene now: the setting up of an independent commission, the formation of working groups, an official report to Parliament!"

"But that's absurd. Everyone knows that underground tests four thousand miles away can't affect on the ecosystem!"

"You know that, and probably Bolger, the Prime Minister of New Zealand, knows it too. But the average civilian lacks your expertise. He'll believe whatever he's told, especially if it panders to his nationalism. And with NGOs like Greenpeace, which will do everything in their power to support such charges, we can be sure that the report won't be impartial."

Obviously she was right.

"All the same, they won't find anything," I insisted.

"Are you really so sure?"

"I followed all the security rules," I said, conscious that I wasn't answering her question.

"I certainly hope so! Anyway, we'll soon know. Because now you can be certain they'll examine everything in great detail. There will be a full-scale audit: believe me, they'll look at everything. What about the list I asked you for: is it ready?"

"You said you needed it by Monday—"

"Change of plans. I want it on my desk first thing tomorrow morning. This is war, Dartunghuver, do you understand? War."

It took me a few minutes to recover my composure. The scene had left a nasty taste in my mouth. Oh, of course, I knew Lena Thorsen too well not to perceive that much of her anger was pure bombast. She was trying to frighten me, and she had succeeded. The situation was serious — fine, I'd gotten the message.

Nonetheless, I'd observed her closely during our conversation, expecting to see on her face a certain excitement at the thought of the battle to come. She was a fighter, accustomed to laying down the law, and the prospect of a good skirmish should have stimulated her. Yet the expression I had read in her eyes had nothing to do with the exhilaration of combat; it betrayed a quite different emotion: fear.

But what was Lena afraid of? Witnessing my first slip-up? Surely not. What, then? Having let a mistake get through in a dossier? Being held responsible for a failure and having to take the rap? Gunnar Eriksson liked to say that in order to make a career in the CFR, you had to be in the right place at the right time. It had never occurred to me to ask him what happened to young agents who found themselves in the wrong place at the wrong time.

I spent the evening and much of the night compiling the list Thorsen had demanded. The dossier wasn't a long one, but I reread every paragraph as if my life depended on it — and perhaps it did.

When I was finished reading the text, I still thought that Chandrapaj and I had done a commendable job. The description of the gallowfish's habits was highly convincing, but the dossier's main highlight was inarguably the European directive on the conservation of the species, the style of which was so pompous and technocratic that I suspected Chandrapaj had found a retired Brussels bureaucrat to write it.

To be candid, the European section of the dossier didn't greatly concern me. I knew that the commission's investigations would concentrate on the Pacific Basin. Fortunately, Chandrapaj hadn't devoted much space to that region. The New Zealand angle was clearly an ingenious means of reviving the dossier in preparation for a further installment of the saga.

The testimony of the fisherman who had been the first to bring up a specimen of gallowfish in his nets would withstand investigation: on Thorsen's advice, I'd used the services of a small community of fish merchants who, if need be, would corroborate their friend's claim.

And the photographs published in the *Pacific Rim Oceanographic Review* were worth all the speeches in the world. Two of them showed a Baltic gallowfish and a Pacific gallowfish side by side. Professor William N. Donnaught, an accredited professor of ichthyology at the University of Christchurch, listed the tiny differences between the two fish but had not the slightest hesitation in declaring that they were from the same species.

I was nearing the end of the dossier and had almost entirely dispelled my doubts, when I discovered the graph that was to seal my fate. Entitled *End of the Road for the Chondrichthyes?*, it showed the slow but inexorable rise of the Osteichthyes — fish with bony, as opposed to cartilaginous, skeletons — and demonstrated the most spectacular increases among such fish in the period 1988-1993: tarpons (+36 %), garfish (+51 %), triggerfish (+ 85 %), and gallowfish (+118 %). It wasn't so much the graph in itself, or where Chandrapaj had chosen to insert it (in Greenpeace's annual report on the oceanic fauna!) that worried me, as the attribution, *Data: Ministry of Agriculture and Fisheries,* Wellington, at the bottom of the page.

Nowhere in the dossier had Chandrapaj mentioned falsifying any sources inside the Ministry of Agriculture. And I couldn't recall having availed myself to the services of anyone in the New Zealand civil service.

At this late hour, it took me a while to grasp the extent of the problem. Chandrapaj had used a first source (statistics from the Ministry of Agriculture) to give credibility to another (the Greenpeace report), a classic, risk-free technique that any Class 1 agent can master. But in this case it was risk-free only if one remembered to falsify the first source. Otherwise, the entire structure might collapse.

How could I have overlooked such a stupid mistake? And then a second, equally disturbing question struck me: what would Lena Thorsen think?

I looked at my watch: one in the morning. That meant it was five in the afternoon in Wellington. I didn't have much time left. On impulse, I telephoned the New Zealand Ministry of Agriculture, telling the switchboard operator that I was a German journalist wishing to speak with the person in charge of fisheries. A moment later, she put me through to a man named John Harkleroad.

"John Harkleroad speaking."

"Hans Messerhalb from Munich. I'm a journalist with *Natur und Wissenschaft.*"

"I don't know your journal, but never mind. What can I do for you?"

Those two sentences and his tone of voice inspired confidence. All might not be lost.

"I believe you publish annual statistics on the different species of fish in the South Pacific."

"That's right. But this year's report isn't ready yet."

"When will it be released?" I forced myself to ask, even though I didn't care one jot.

"Oh, not until September, I'm afraid. What is this about?"

"Do you think I could obtain a copy of last year's report?"

"Of course, no problem. Do you have internet service?"

"Er, yes."

"Then just log onto the government's website and follow the guide. It will take you straight to the report for 1994."

"Thank you," I stammered.

"Don't mention it; pleased to be of help."

First I would have to check whether the official report contained the data on the gallowfish. If it did, it would mean that Chandrapaj had done his job, and had someone inside the ministry helping him. He would simply be reprimanded for not mentioning it in his dossier. But if he hadn't... No, I refused to even envisage the possibility. Chandrapaj had to have falsified the ministry's report. I switched on my computer.

My modem was excruciatingly slow. The home page of the New Zealand government site took nearly a minute to upload. Then I did something wrong that forced me to press the back button and consumed another thirty or forty seconds. At last I got to the Agriculture and Fisheries page. The report was there, two pages further on, ready to be downloaded as a PDF.

Within fifteen minutes, I had my answer. The gallowfish was nowhere to be seen. The chart that had appeared in the Greenpeace report did indeed exist. Tarpons, garfish and triggerfish were on it, but there was no mention of the gallowfish.

What was I going to tell Lena?

I decided to tell her the truth. For once, I arrived to the office before she did. But that day it would have taken much more to cheer her.

"Let's go over this, shall we?" She was very calm and fresh-looking (whereas I looked as if I'd slept in my clothes), her hair still wet and drawn back. "Chandrapaj is trying to convince people that the gallowfish has appeared in the South Pacific. In order to do that, he falsifies a number of sources, including a publication by Greenpeace. This publication refers directly to a report by the New Zealand Ministry of Agriculture and Fisheries. Chandrapaj didn't bother to falsify that report and you, who were supposed to be checking his work, didn't even notice. Is that accurate?"

"Absolutely," I replied. I could have added that Lena Thorsen, who herself was supposed to have checked my work, hadn't noticed the omission either, but, under the circumstances, I sensed that such a reply would be tactless. On that point at least, the remainder of the conversation proved me right.

"I don't think I need to tell you," Thorsen said, "how unspeakably stupid that first mistake was. A bloody stupid mistake. The kind freshmen laugh about because they can't believe there are agents so stupid as to be caught out like that. Congratulations, Dartunghuver, you've just earned your place in the manuals of the CFR. A word from me, and your career ends here in Córdoba."

"Let's not exaggerate—"

"You're right, the General Inspectorate might have forgiven you that blunder. After all, you're not the first idiot to rush through his dossiers in order to leave for a vacation. But what about the other matter?"

"What other matter?" I asked, surprised in spite of myself.

"*What other matter?*" Lena echoed theatrically. "Your ridiculous telephone call last night! 'Hello, my name's Hans, I wear lederhosen, and I'm interested in the little fishes in the Pacific...'"

"What? What did I do?"

"Don't you get it yet? My God, you really are dead from the neck up. All right, I'll phrase this another way. Let's take a ten-year-old boy. One day when his mother's back is turned, he steals a jar of jam from the pantry. He gets through the whole jar, then immediately regrets doing so, and hopes nobody will notice. In your opinion, what should he do, knowing it's impossible for him to confess?"

"Nothing," I replied, suddenly very demoralized. I could see where she was headed and there was nothing delightful about the prospect.

"Nothing, of course," Thorsen said, determined not to spare me any stage of her argument. "He keeps quiet and waits. But now let's suppose the boy in question is called Sliv and that he has an IQ not much above zero. What does he do? He telephones his mother, pretends to be someone else, and asks her if she's noticed anything suspicious on the jam shelf. Now do you understand?"

"Yes," I admitted, sheepishly. "I should have kept my mouth shut."

"You bet! Imagine what will happen if, in three months, Greenpeace notices the hoax. They inform the authorities. The ministry says that the gallowfish has never existed. To set her minds at rest, the Greenpeace representative asks to speak with the author of the report. She's patched through to John Harkleroad, who denies everything. But hold on, now that you mention it, there was that phone call, from a dubious character with a foreign accent..."

"Stop! That's as far as it will go. Greenpeace won't escalate the issue." I may have sounded confident, but there was a lot of wishful thinking involved.

"And what about the telephone records?" Lena exploded. "What if he remembers the date and checks the ministry's printouts? A call from Córdoba is hardly likely to go unnoticed, especially when it's one in the morning in Argentina!" She shook her head vehemently and muttered, more to herself than to me, "The whole thing's fucked up. There've been too many mistakes. We're never going to fix this mess."

For a split second, her pessimism made me fear the worst. "What do you mean, 'it's fucked up'? What are you going to do?"

"Talk to Diaz first. He'll start by giving me a dressing down; then he'll think of a way to cover himself. Poor Diaz: in his condition, this is all he needs."

She sounded almost sincere.

"And what about me? What can I do?"

"You, nothing."

"If I can help in any way..." I insisted, perhaps a tad heavy-handedly.

"If you wish to help, pray to whatever God you believe in, in any language you like. Pray for the CFR; pray for yourself. And if this fiasco does blow up in our faces, don't forget to ask Him to put a lot of distance between you and me on the day I hear the news. I never trusted you, and I was right. From now on, I won't have any qualms about burying you."

10

For several weeks, I lived in a kind of haze. On Diaz's orders — officially, at least, since I knew perfectly well who had really given them — I had been put in quarantine. Less than an hour after my conversation with Thorsen, my computer displayed the message *Access* denied, when I typed in my password. My CFR colleagues turned their eyes away when they passed me in the corridors. No new dossiers turned up to replace the ones I sent off.

But I didn't fully grasp the gravity of the situation until the day I received at home an encouraging note from Gunnar Eriksson ("I'm with you in this ordeal; don't give up."). If I hadn't gone back to work the following day, I don't think anybody would have noticed my absence.

But I hung on, less to please Gunnar Eriksson than because the idea that I could still be of use hadn't completely abandoned me. During the day, I devoted all my energies to my work in the unit for forecasting natural risks: I doubt that the Compañía Argentina del Reaseguro ever had an employee as zealous as me.

In the evening, I would go for a walk around the offices in search of a task that would ease my conscience, but the CFR people rejected my offers of help with a unanimity that spoke volumes. Only the accountant agreed from time to time to let me lend a hand. There followed a whole series of evenings during which he droned on in his lisping voice and I, with a pencil, marked entries on bank statements.

I read the newspapers, as I was still allowed to do, a right I exercised unreservedly. On July 6, the *Wellington Times* announced the composition of the commission set up by Prime Minister Bolger. I examined every name, hoping to recognize an ally, even a CFR agent. In vain: the list consisted entirely of honest government officials and a few lay people. Among the latter I was horrified to recognize the name of the deputy director of Greenpeace for New Zealand, who I was sure must already have formed his own conclusions on the subject. The mechanism was slowly falling into place.

Eight days later, on July 14, the chairman of the commission, a man named Abernathy, took advantage of a public meeting to announce that the members' initial work had brought to light a number of unexpected genetic mutations in a handful of animal species. "We will have a clearer understanding in a few weeks' time," he promised, "when our scientific experts have arrived at definite conclusions."

Mr. Abernathy had clearly not chosen the date of his speech at random, and it made for a charged atmosphere at the French ambassador's annual reception. I wasn't French, but that Bastille Day left me with a bitter taste, too. "They've been investigating for barely a week," I thought, "and they're already on the trail of the gallowfish."

I pestered Lena Thorsen with requests for meetings, but she refused to see me. Through her secretary, she kept sending me ominous press clippings or, more rarely, openly alarmist handwritten messages, like one dated July 22nd that warned: "The noose is tightening, Dartunghuver. It'll soon be time for payback." I pondered the meaning of that ellipsis for over an hour.

At last the inevitable transpired. One Friday morning (I had never gotten up so early as I did now that I had nothing to do), I found a note from Lena Thorsen on my desk, telling me that a team from Special Operations was arriving in Córdoba that very day. I was summoned to a meeting that would begin at 11 o'clock in the boardroom. I rushed to Thorsen's office and found her just about to leave.

"Ah, Dartunghuver!" she said curtly. "Did you get my note?"

"Yes," I stammered. "What exactly is going on? Are you leaving?"

"I'm going to meet them at the airport. Their plane lands at a quarter to ten."

"May I come with you? You can explain the situation to me in the car."

She considered this request for a few seconds, then said, "What the hell, they've come because of you. The least you can do is to carry their bags."

Thorsen drove a Chrysler LeBaron cabriolet. I sat beside her. I didn't beat about the bush. "Who are these men and what are they here for?"

"What do you think? To sort out your mess, obviously. I don't know them, I haven't even been told their names. All I know is that there are two of them, and that they're coming from Montreal. They're the ones who arranged the meeting. There won't be time to stop at their hotel."

"Did you book rooms for them?" I asked, trying to hold on to something concrete.

"At the Hilton. Two suites, the most expensive there are." Clearly, Thorsen shared my concerns.

"Good," I said. It was stupid, but, at that moment, I found the fact that my two executioners would sleep that night in silk sheets inexplicably reassuring. A thought occurred to me. "Who'll be at the meeting?"

"You, me and them."

"Is that all? Won't Diaz be there?"

"If you knew him better, you'd have learned that he hates to have blood on his hands. He said he had to undergo some tests at the hospital."

Blood on his hands? The conversation was taking a turn I didn't like at all. The car was now zooming down the highway and I had to shout to be heard.

"What's happening, Lena? I have a right to know."

"They've noticed. The man from Greenpeace swears to high heaven he got his data from the Ministry, but no one at the Ministry has ever heard of the gallowfish. To set their minds at rest, the commission has summoned Harkleroad for Monday morning."

So it had happened, and even sooner than I had feared. I looked at my hand, which was resting on my knee. It was shaking. I was terrified. "What are we going to do?"

"What are they going to do, you mean. They're the specialists. I hope they don't expect me to give them any ideas. I've looked at the problem from every angle. It's insoluble."

I wasn't especially pleased to see Córdoba Airport again. In the pub where I'd had a beer six months earlier, a traveler was turning the pages of a magazine. He looked perfectly calm, as I had been at that time. Would I ever regain such composure?

Above our heads, the loudspeakers announced that the flight from Montreal was delayed by half an hour.

I carefully studied all the travelers who were exiting the customs gate, without being sure what exactly I was seeking. I think I expected to see two hatchet-faced men wearing dark suits and carrying attaché cases.

Thorsen, who didn't know any more than I, held a ridiculous little sign reading *Compañía Argentina del Reaseguro* above the crowd. I had never seen her so nervous.

I was suddenly thumped in the back and almost fell. I turned quickly, ready to rise to my full six feet and look the lout in the eyes, instead of which I found myself confronted by a giant, whose face was beaming and who proffered a hand as big as an escalope.

"So you're the arsonist?" he asked me in decent English, although with a marked Slavic accent. "And you must be Thorsen," he went on, shamelessly undressing Lena with his eyes. "Khoyoulfaz, Special Operations. This is Jones," he said, gesturing with his chin at a man with a thinner but harder face, who fit my mental image of a Special Operations agent. I extended my hand out to Jones. His was as cold as a snake's skin.

"How did you manage to exit so quickly?" Thorsen asked. "The plane has only just touched down."

Khoyoulfaz burst into a loud laugh that made at least thirty people turn to look. "We weren't on the flight from Montreal, little miss!"

"An elementary precaution," Jones said. "We arrived an hour ago, long enough to take the temperature, so to speak."

"And it's bloody hot!" Khoyoulfaz added. Two big halos of sweat beneath his armpits testified to the truth of what he was saying.

"Would you like to go to your hotel to freshen up?" I suggested. From my point of view, anything that could delay the ordeal could only be good.

"No point," Jones replied.

"I booked two suites at the Hilton," Thorsen saw fit to add.

"We won't need them. We're leaving this evening."

"This evening?"

"A day should be long enough to settle this unfortunate business, shouldn't it, Yakoub?" Jones said, clearly accustomed to having his accomplice echo him.

"Oh yes, more than enough!" Khoyoulfaz chuckled. He initiated what seemed like a well-practiced exchange between the two men: "Reflection..."

"Action!" Jones cried, with a vague kind of smile, giving Khoyoulfaz a high-five.
They had brought no luggage. I led them to the car. Thorsen walked in front, without a word. She had manifestly envisaged all kinds of situations, but not this.

Jones sat down in front, next to Thorsen. I shared the back seat with Khoyoulfaz—although it would be more correct to say Khoyoulfaz shared it with me.

"So how do things look?" I asked, unable to wait until we got to the office to tackle the issue that had brought us together.

"Bad, obviously. What do you think, son? That we came to Córdoba to take tango lessons?"

"No, of course not," I said, taken aback. "But do you have a plan? Some way of reversing the situation?"

Khoyoulfaz turned to me, looking a tad upset. He put his big hand on my knee and I stiffened instinctively. "Listen, son, we'll have plenty of time to talk about this business of yours. So for now, shut your mouth and let me enjoy the view."

At that moment, I saw Thorsen's eyes in the rearview mirror. She looked every bit as panicky as I did. That was small comfort.

Khoyoulfaz turned back to Jones and said — we were traveling at more than 80 miles an hour on the highway, but he didn't need to shout to make himself heard — "That boy sitting next to you on the plane, Guillermo, didn't he remind you of someone?"

"Young Leonid?"

"Exactly," Khoyoulfaz guffawed.

"Is he a friend of yours?" I asked.

"He was," Khoyoulfaz replied. "He had an accident."

"A tragic accident," Jones said.
"We found him in Sydney Harbor with his feet in cement," Khoyoulfaz said, not bothering to stifle a laugh.

"Ultra-fast-setting cement," Jones elaborated.

"Poor Leonid," Khoyoulfaz said. "Such a gifted young man. Who'd have thought he'd end up a traitor?"

Everything was happening too quickly. I had only known these two characters for some fifteen minutes, and they were already talking about someone who'd been liquidated for high treason. But whom or what had he betrayed? The CFR?

I couldn't take them seriously. It was impossible to imagine that a highly structured and democratic organization like the CFR could entrust such dubious individuals with the task of eliminating some of its members. I suspected a deliberate performance. And yet...

Khoyoulfaz, whom I was watching out of the corner of my eye, certainly looked the type: about forty, as tall as a windsurfing board, built like an Ikea armoire — a single punch from him would have knocked out an ox.

His voice carried nearly a mile, and his laughter, which was even more stentorian, could have been mistaken for the initial rumblings of an earth tremor. He was wearing a heavily stained beige suit, which gave me an idea of his table manners. He wore no tie, and his unbuttoned shirt revealed a huge, pink, hairless chest, the skin as smooth as a baby's.

I understood from some of his remarks that he was an Azeri, and that he seemed to know a lot about the techniques of the KGB, although I couldn't figure out if he had practiced them, been victimized by them, or had learned to resist them.

He had been in Special Operations for ten years, a disclosure that led me to revise my judgment of that supposedly elite body. How could such an oaf, who was now making smutty jokes about Thorsen, have ever been selected for the Academy? And what contacts had he called on to join Special Operations, which was known to be among the most coveted positions?

Jones, who was Panamanian, seemed better qualified for Special Operations. Behind his half-shut eyes, one could sense a cold, calculating intelligence, more reasonable than that of Khoyoulfaz, but not necessarily less terrifying. He was clearly the brains of the team, Khoyoulfaz the brawn.

The division of roles between the two men wasn't very difficult to imagine. It was Jones's job to size up a situation, make a diagnosis, and deliver his verdict, and then Khoyoulfaz would implement it — discreetly, if possible but, to judge from some of the anecdotes spewing from the Azeri's loud mouth, that wasn't always the case.

We reached La Compañía. Far from enjoying the view, Khoyoulfaz had chattered away endlessly, with Jones feeding him the odd line from time to time.

As for Lena, she hadn't said a word, having fixed her eyes on the road, lest the car hit a pothole or some other unlikely obstacle. Our eyes met as we rode the elevator. She was terrified and what she read in my eyes did nothing to reassure her. For the first time, I felt there was a kind of bond between us.

But that wasn't fated to last long. Thorsen led us to the boardroom, and we took our places around a long burr walnut table. Jones and Khoyoulfaz sat down at one end, and indicated that I should sit across from them. Thorsen, who had left the room to order drinks, came back and took a chair between us, closer to the two visitors. The courtroom images that I had painstakingly dismissed from my mind now returned with a vengeance. My two judges were facing me, I could also see the prosecutor on my left, but what should have been my attorney's seat remained conspicuously empty. I would have to conduct my own defense.

"OK, Thorsen," Jones began, "give us the facts."

It was the signal Thorsen had awaited. "They're relatively straightforward," she said, and launched into a detailed account of the unfortunate story of the gallowfish.

The first dossier, she said, the one that had earned Magawati a certificate of merit in Honolulu, was a very good one.

She had initially found the second dossier less interesting, although she was well aware of the difficulty of continuing a saga. In quoting reams of reports from Brussels, Chandrapaj was simply mining the original vein. Then, clearly running out of inspiration, he had tried to prepare the third part of the saga by introducing a New Zealand connection.

The section devoted to the falsification of the sources, in the form in which it had been sent to the Córdoba bureau, was wanting in many ways. It was too vague, too sketchy. Thorsen claimed to have noticed this immediately. It was her responsibility to skim through all the dossiers before apportioning them to her agents and the one on the gallowfish had struck her as rather flimsy. In fact she had pointed this out to Agent Dartunghuver when she entrusted it to him.

That was completely false. I made a move to protest, but Khoyoulfaz signaled to me to let Thorsen continue. He didn't look as if he were joking, so I didn't insist.

When Dartunghuver had handed her back the corrected dossier, Lena continued, she had carefully reread it. Overall, Dartunghuver had done a good job. She had, however, pointed out to him a number of errors: a discrepancy in the date on which a European Commission official had taken up his post (perfectly correct); an implausible statement about the frequency of the gallowfish's reproductive cycle (also correct); and that infamous lack of falsification of the source from the New Zealand Ministry of Agriculture and Fisheries (an outright lie).

I was flabbergasted. Thorsen had never warned me on that score. In fact, she had implicitly admitted that she hadn't spotted Chandrapaj's error. Since I couldn't interrupt her, I tried to catch her eye, but to no avail. She was facing Jones and Khoyoulfaz, who hadn't taken their eyes off her.

Her mistake, Thorsen acknowledged, lay in not having checked that Dartunghuver had made the corrections she had requested. He had assured her that he had, and she had taken him at his word. She bitterly regretted the omission and apologized to the CFR.

"I can't take this anymore!" I exclaimed. "You never pointed out Chandrapaj's error. I'd remember that!"

"And I remember perfectly well drawing your attention to it," Thorsen replied coldly, looking me straight in the eyes. "But I admit I should have written to you."

"That's rich!" I exploded. "Why not admit you made a mistake, damn it? It can happen to anyone."

"I can admit my mistakes when I make them, Dartunghuver. In this particular case, I have nothing to confess."

"You're lying!"

"Calm down, you two!" Khoyoulfaz interposed. "We don't give a damn about who did what and when. We're not here to apportion blame. That will be up to the General Inspectorate."

"The General Inspectorate?" Thorsen wailed.

"Why, what was Miss World thinking? That they would send a Special Operations team to give it all a quick wipe, and that would be the end of it? Proceed with your soap opera. Jones and I find it fascinating."

Thorsen was dazed. I knew her well enough to read her thoughts: her hopes of promotion fading fast; the indelible stain that Córdoba would leave on her record; the happy days she had spent here before I had arrived to serve under her. She turned to me and muttered clenched jaws, just loud enough for me to hear: "You're dead, Dartunghuver."

Then she told the two men about my phone call in the middle of the night, taking advantage of every conceivable opportunity to condemn me even more harshly. I hadn't used a protected line, I'd given a false name, and I'd claimed to be from a journal that didn't exist. Worse, I'd expressly mentioned my interest in the report in question. At each of these points, Jones slowly shook his head as a sign of disapproval.

"Tut, tut, what a pity," he clucked.

"Yes, one almighty cock-up!" Khoyoulfaz added.

"That's my opinion, too," Thorsen said. "Without that unfortunate initiative, I think we might have been able to get away with it."

"Even so…" Jones said dubiously. "All they have to do now is to investigate a bit, and they'll trace it back to us."

"Why would they do that?" I interjected. "We're talking about a fish after all. They're hardly going to make it an affair of state!"

"Yakoub, sum up the situation for the young man," Jones said, pouring himself a glass of water.

"The net is tightening, son," Khoyoulfaz said. "The commission has asked all the environmental organizations to point out any anomalies they may have observed over the past few years. The idea is to blame everything on the nuclear tests in order to accuse France of ruining the planet."

"That doesn't make any sense," I protested.

"You're young, son. I don't know if you'll be permitted to continue much longer in this profession, but you still have a lot to learn. Greenpeace immediately raised the question of the gallowfish. According to them, no natural phenomenon can explain the sudden appearance of a new species. They are talking about genetic mutation…"

"A mutation caused by the previous nuclear tests," Jones elaborated.

"I was sure of it!" Thorsen exclaimed.

"We have a man inside the commission," Khoyoulfaz continued, imperturbably. "The members questioned the experts from Greenpeace yesterday morning. A representative of the Ministry of Agriculture pointed out that Greenpeace's data contradicted the report drawn up by his department. The commission has summoned Harkleroad to appear on Monday morning. That doesn't leave us much time."

"What could happen?" I asked, although I already knew the answer.

"Harkleroad will confirm his report. It may take a few days to check the data. It doesn't really matter. It will be proved that the figures in an official report were falsified by an outside agency."

"And that's very serious," Jones said solemnly.

"There are then two possibilities," Khoyoulfaz went on. "One, Harkleroad has forgotten your call, and the entire conundrum remains a complete mystery. The CFR has had a bit of a fright, but pulls through…"

"I wouldn't bet my pension on it," Jones said.

"Or, two, Harkleroad remembers you, and in less than fifteen minutes the commission has tracked you down."

"Are you sure?"

"Come on! You're as easy to spot as a powder trail in the snow!"

I had to admit that they were right. What on earth had possessed me to call a number on the other side of the world at one o'clock in the morning? It was a relief that Special Operations were taking matters in hand. They couldn't have come to Córdoba just to remind me of the mess I had created.

"What do we do now?"

"First we eat!" Khoyoulfaz exclaimed. "Thorsen, darling, order us some food. A nice rare steak for me, and a cold beer. It's stifling in here!"

"Nothing for me, Lena, I'm not hungry," I said.

"Listen to him!" Khoyoulfaz laughed. "Eat, son, you're going to need it."

Thorsen picked up the telephone and ordered four tray meals.

"To answer your question, son, I haven't the faintest idea."

"Don't you have an emergency plan?"

"What do you think? We are here to discuss it. Let's sum up: from which quarter does the threat arise?"

"One always has to put things in perspective," Jones said to Thorsen. "Every problem has a solution, provided it's well formulated."

Lena nodded vigorously, thinking perhaps she might avoid censure.

"Our problem is Harkleroad," I said. "Without him, the commission has no way of tracing the call back to us."

"Interesting, carry on."

"But since the commission is aware of the discrepancy, we can't get suppress the risk entirely. We simply have to contain it within acceptable limits. If Harkleroad appears before the commission on Monday, we're at the mercy of his memory."

"Is that a risk you'd describe as acceptable?" Jones asked.

"Obviously not," I replied. "At a rough guess, I'd say it's more than fifty percent. If, however, Harkleroad should fail to appear, the risk is considerably lessened."

"But is it acceptable?" Jones insisted.

I thought for a moment. "I think it is. I also think we don't have a choice. Given the circumstances, that's as far as we can reduce it."

"I agree with your analysis," Jones said in a good-natured tone.

Diaz's PA came in with our trays. For a few minutes, Jones and Khoyoulfaz ate with gusto—especially Khoyoulfaz, who really wolfed down his food. Thorsen pecked at hers: the latest developments had put a bit of color back in her cheeks. As for me, I couldn't make up my mind to even start on my tray. The knot in my stomach made the whole idea of food unbearable.

Tearing off the napkin he had knotted around his neck, Khoyoulfaz said in the most natural way possible, as if resuming the conversation where we had left off, "All right now, reflection... action. We have to get rid of this man Harkleroad." He turned to Jones. "No point in prolonging our visit, I noticed there's a flight at 4:50 P.M."

"Wait," I said. "What do you mean by getting rid of?"

Khoyoulfaz turned and looked at me in genuine surprise. "Why, the same thing as you, son. Neutralize, eliminate, remove from circulation!" He must have seen the alarm on my face, because he then added, "That *is* what you meant, isn't it?"

"Me? You're crazy! All I said was that it would be better for us if Harkleroad didn't appear before the commission on Monday morning."

"Practically speaking, son," Jones cut in, now also adopting his partner's familiar tone, "how else could you stop a man obeying an order from the government of his country?"

"I don't know," I stammered. "I'd kidnap him, I'd explain the situation to him, man to man..." Suddenly something that Gunnar Eriksson had said came back to me. "I'd give him a drug to make him lose his memory!"

"A what?" asked Khoyoulfaz.

"A drug to make him lose his memory," Jones said. "There is no such drug, son. You've seen too many movies."

"Hmm," Khoyoulfaz grunted. "What kind of thing do they teach these youngsters?"

Panic was gripping me. I'm dreaming, I thought. I'm going to awaken. This isn't possible. And yet, the images I had in front of me seemed all too real.

Jones didn't sound as if he were joking. When he had asked me if I knew any other way to silence a man, he had listened to my answer with interest, as if, after years spent in Special Operations, he still hoped to find a non-lethal method.

Khoyoulfaz had taken out his nail clippers. Annoyed at revealing his ignorance, he was refusing to comment, content to let us resolve the argument without interfering.

But the reaction that hurt me the most was Thorsen's. She was staring at a point on the ceiling, as if this discussion didn't in the least concern her, as if good manners required that she not intervene in men's affairs.

I turned to her. "Come on, Lena, say something. You've heard them: they're talking about killing a man, someone who hasn't done anything, and who may have a wife and children."

"He has two little girls," Khoyoulfaz said. "I checked before we left."

"Do you hear him, Lena? He's an animal who will do anything."

"Oh, shut up, Dartunghuver!" Thorsen had turned abruptly to look at me. "You really aren't making things any easier! What did you think? That Special Operations would turn up and wave a magic wand, and everything would be all right?"

"You screwed up, that's the problem, we can't change that. So what do we do now? Think about something else and wait for New Zealand's counter-intelligence to uncover our operations and arrest hundreds of CFR agents whose only crime is that they knew Sliv Dartunghuver?"

"They can question me, I won't talk," I retorted.

"I'm not talking about questioning," Lena irritably replied. "I'm talking about beatings, nails torn out, fingers broken..."

Khoyoulfaz finished the sentence for her. "Joints smashed with hammers, heads stuck in vises."

"Whether you like it or not, that's what we're looking at!" Thorsen continued. "So do we just fold our arms, or do we try to limit the damage?"

"I don't know what to say..." I stammered. "You're asking too much of me... Intimidate him, apply pressure, maybe, but don't kill him..."

"Come on, now, son," Jones cut in, "you knew this when you joined the firm."

"No!" I cried. All at once I had the impression that Jones had just proffered a lifeline. I grabbed it with all the energy of despair. "No, no one ever told me. I wouldn't have signed up if I'd known!"

"But you suspected, didn't you?" he insisted, surprised.

"Absolutely not, I swear."

Jones looked bewildered. Maybe he would give up his plan if I managed to convince him that my trust had been betrayed. But Thorsen dashed my last hopes.

"That's Dartunghuver all over," she said disdainfully. "He has a decent mind, but he only uses it when he finds it convenient to do so. One has to reflect for only a few moments to realize that an organization like the CFR must have the occasional misfire. One would have to be really dumb to imagine that such problems solve themselves."

"Did you know, Lena?" I counter-attacked. "Isn't this the first time this has happened to you?"

"Yes, it is the first time. But you won't hear me say I didn't know. Deep down, I knew. Deep down, all agents must suspect."

"Not me!"

"Then you're even stupider than I thought."

This exchange threw me into a mood of dejection that even Khoyoulfaz's odious words, of which I could still catch scraps, couldn't dispel.

Once again, Thorsen was right. Suddenly, random phrases came back to me and everything fell into place. Those retaliatory measures Gunnar Eriksson had mentioned, the reference to "collateral damage" by one of the lecturers in Honolulu, referring to the physical elimination of those who dared to stand in the way of the CFR.

But like all the other freshmen, like all my brilliant young colleagues, I'd pretended not to understand. While boasting how far I could take my ideas for scenarios, I'd been content with appearances, refusing to see what should have been obvious: that an organization with as many ramifications as the CFR must all too often have found itself confronted with the prospect of its own dissolution and in such circumstances it must have found no way to avoid eradicating the threat.

Behind those thoughts jostling in my brain, one question nagged at me insistently, one question I knew I would have to answer one day, but the implications of which I couldn't face at that juncture: would I have joined the CFR if I had known all that? I had heard myself assert vigorously to Thorsen that I wouldn't. Was I so sure? Even if blindness I had demonstrated was largely unconscious, that didn't excuse the fact that, deep down, by willfully refusing to acknowledge the rules of the game, I had tacitly accepted them.

I would have to reflect about all this later, I'd certainly have plenty of time. But for the moment a more urgent task commanded my full attention: to prevent the murder of the man I had myself identified to his executioners.

"I think I have an idea," I said. Thorsen, Jones, and Khoyoulfaz turned to look at me. Busy sorting out the practical details of their operation, they seemed to have forgotten my presence. "I'll assume full responsibility for the whole mess. I'll say I was deliberately committing a hoax. I'll pretend to be crazy, if necessary."

Thorsen shook her head. "That won't work."

"Why not? They need a culprit, I'll give them one."

"Naturally," Jones said, "the CFR has considered this possibility. But the rules of Special Operations expressly forbid us to abandon an agent."

"But you wouldn't be abandoning me!" I protested. "I'd be giving myself up. And I promise not to reveal anything. You have nothing to fear."

"I'm sorry," Jones said, "it's impossible."

"But —"

"Don't insist, son," Khoyoulfaz said.

I changed tactics, trying to convince Jones (it hadn't taken me long to realize that it was pointless to try to exchange what are commonly called ideas with Khoyoulfaz who, in any case, would end up doing whatever his superior decided) that we hadn't yet considered all the options. He seemed skeptical at first, then agreed to listen to my argument.

I approached the problem from another angle, without really knowing where I was headed, but hoping to discover a way out that all four of us might have missed. I spoke for nearly an hour. Every time inspiration deserted me, I imagined John Harkleroad with his wife and his two daughters — blonde, plump, and pretty was how I thought of them, and, of course, crazy about their father. Then a new idea would come to me immediately and I would begin again, although without making much progress.

I must acknowledge that Jones listened to me attentively, even striving to follow the obscure twists and turns of my argument.

Khoyoulfaz didn't even bother: as soon as I embarked upon my speech, he had taken a knife from his pocket, a knife that, when opened, was as long as my forearm. He kept sliding the blade of it under his nails, pulling out clotted strands of dirt that he scraped on the edge of the table.

As for Thorsen, she was clearly waiting to see which way the tide would turn so that she could rally to the winning side.

When it became obvious that I had exhausted all of my rhetorical resources, Jones finished me off with a single sentence. "Well," he said, "I think we can now agree that there's no other solution to this problem."

Thorsen nodded and turned toward me to seek my consent. Khoyoulfaz wiped the blade of his knife with his fingers, then shut it with a sinister click. Having refused to listen to a word of my speech, he was now eager to leave for the airport. The prospect of killing a man didn't disturb him in the least; in fact, I think it excited him.

As I hadn't replied, Jones took a sheet of paper and a pencil from his bag and handed them to Thorsen.

"These are the orders," he said. "The big boss has signed them, but I need countersignatures from both of you."

"Is this really necessary?" asked Thorsen. With hindsight, I think it was less the embarrassment at sending a man to his death that had provoked this question than the fear of leaving a trace of her complicity that might one day be turned against her.

"It's the rule," replied Jones.

"You wouldn't believe the paperwork," Khoyoulfaz grumbled.

A piece of paper condemned a man to death, and this monster dared to complain about bureaucracy!

Thorsen quickly read the orders, and signed. Then she rose and walked over to me.

"It's no use," I said, "I won't sign."

"Don't be a fool, Dartunghuver," she hissed. "You sign; they leave; and you won't hear any more about it."

"You can't force me," I retorted with a touch of bravado.

I've often pondered that reaction since. Why was I resisting, when doing so was so obviously pointless? Actually, I'm ashamed to admit that by that point I had already yielded. John Harkleroad was doomed, and I couldn't do anything about it. What I could do was to refuse to put my name next to those of Thorsen and the head of the CFR's butchers, and I was quite determined to avail myself of that right, the last that remained to me. How stupid I was!

"I'm sorry that it's come to this," Jones said, "but you really don't have a choice. By refusing to sign, you'd be excluding yourself from the CFR. And, given what you know, we wouldn't be able to let you live."

"You must understand that," Khoyoulfaz said in an indifferent tone.

The atmosphere had turned unusually chilly in the space of a few minutes. Not so long before, we had been searching together for a way to remove a New Zealand civil servant from the equation, and now a man with a gun (I could clearly make out the bump it made under his jacket) was urging me to sign a piece of paper, because, if I didn't he couldn't "let me live."

I read the orders. They were remarkably succinct: "Class 2 Agents Thorsen and Dartunghuver, having by their carelessness placed our organization at risk of discovery, I have asked Senior Agent Jones, of Special Operations, to take all possible measures, including the most extreme, to minimize the consequences of the acts of the aforementioned agents. Jones is authorized to enlist the assistance of a Special Operations agent of his choosing. I ask whoever reads this document to cooperate fully with Agent Jones and to place at his disposal all logistical and human means that he may require. Berlin, 5 August 1995."

I couldn't make out the name of the person who had signed, but he was referred to as the General Controller. I recognized Jones's signature above the handwritten words, "I accept this assignment." Thorsen had signed without further ado, leaving a place for my signature on the right-hand side of the paper.

I looked up. Three pairs of eyes were trained on me. Suddenly, I exploded. The anger that I had been suppressing all day came to a boil.

"Come on, Thorsen, tell me I'm dreaming. This isn't why we joined the CFR. You, I don't know... But all I ever wanted to do was to enjoy myself. It was so much fun to create imaginary characters, to invent stories, to falsify sources. We weren't harming anyone, and we had an illusion of power."

"Yes, you, Gunnar, and the others talked about war, captivity, torture, but I never took you seriously. For me, that was just part of the game, a way of spicing up the rules. Who could ever hate people like us, who spend our time depriving the Baltic of its marine life, at least on paper? You're surely not going to tell me we're threatening national security!"

"I did warn you, Dartunghuver," Thorsen rejoined, "but you wouldn't listen."

"Yes, that is true, I didn't listen. But then why talk in riddles? And, besides, you should have realized that I was never as involved as you were. You certainly reproached me often enough!"

"I don't know," she admitted truthfully. "You were always so casual…"

"Because I was playing, Lena. It's just a game to me."

"I assure you, it isn't a game," Khoyoulfaz said.

"Nothing is worth this," I continued. "OK, I fucked up. But surely we're not going to send a man to his death for that reason."

"It's too late, Sliv," Thorsen said, completely disoriented. I had never seen her like this. She had lost all her bearings in a single morning. "They're stronger than we are. There is nothing we can do."

"Don't say that; it's too easy. Just because Special Operations have sent these two heavies, we have to surrender? And the guilt: have you thought about the guilt? A death on one's conscience, is not so easy to forget. Do you think you'll still be able to look at yourself in the mirror after that?"

"Shut up," she entreated me. "Don't make matters even worse than they are. Sign the paper and let them leave."

"We have a lot to do," Khoyoulfaz said.

"Do you hear him, Lena? And it's to protect people like him that we have to eliminate a family man? So, Jones, Khoyoulfaz, I guess there must have been a day for the two of you when everything changed, when your boss summoned you and asked you to kill a man. What did you reply? 'Yes, chef.'? 'All right, boss.'?"

"Exactly," Khoyoulfaz replied. He must have decided that this farce had lasted long enough, because he put away his knife.

"Shall we go?" he asked Jones. He looked at me and laughed. "I'm not going to suggest you go with us to the airport."

"You're not going anywhere," I said.

"Oh, really?" Jones scoffed.

"You're not leaving this room." I walked over and stood in front of the door. Thorsen was watching me aghast. Khoyoulfaz was before me in two steps.

"Get away from there, my friend."

"No way!"

"You're being stupid," he said, landing me a knockout punch.

11

It was the following afternoon when I regained consciousness, feeling apathetic and nauseous. It took me a few minutes to recover my senses. Jones and Khoyoulfaz had drugged me and taken me to my apartment, to make sure I wouldn't thwart their plans. By now, they must have performed their sinister task. Just thinking about it made me retch, and I ran to the bathroom. Strangely, I couldn't vomit, which made me feel ashamed as well as guilty.

It was Saturday. I went to the office and placed a letter of resignation on Thorsen's desk. I didn't rehash my reasons; she knew them only too well.

In another letter intended for the chairman of the Compañía Argentina del Reaseguro, I resigned from my post, citing personal reasons for returning to Europe and requesting that the contractual period of notice be waived. I felt sorry for Osvaldo Ramirez, but I couldn't see myself spending one day longer within those walls.

I also left brief notes for Alex, Sergio and the members of my team. I had prepared everything in advance, in order to spend as little time as possible on the premises of La Compañía.

Then I went back home to pack. Too bad about the furniture, the appliances, my deposit — I knew in any case that the pesos would burn my fingers like Judas's thirty pieces of silver. My two suitcases and my trunk weren't spacious enough to pack everything in, so I sorted through my possessions and left some of my clothes and all of my books — a whole chunk of my life.

I initially intended not to keep the desert rose that Djibo had given me two years earlier, a trophy I proudly admired every night before going to bed. But after reflection I found space for it at the bottom of a suitcase. It was important evidence, the only object I could show the police to support my story. A trifle. It was enough to make me weep.

That evening, the phone rang. I sent the call to the answering machine, and soon Lena Thorsen's voice echoed through the living room: "We have to talk, Dartunghuver. Pick up if you're there."

Half an hour later, Lena knocked at the door, softly at first, then with increasing force.

"Open up, Dartunghuver," she said in Icelandic. "I know you're there, I saw you through the window. I dropped by the office and found your letter. You can't just leave like this. We have to talk."

I refrained from opening the door and telling her just what I thought of her and her friends. It wouldn't have accomplished anything. We had both faced the same crisis, a crisis in which John Harkleroad's life had been at stake. Thorsen had put her own interests before my demand for justice. She had buried me to save her skin. I had nothing more to say to her.

She continued knocking on my door for a while until my next-door neighbor threatened to call the police. "He doesn't want to talk to you," I heard him say with that typically Argentine familiarity. "Find someone else. It shouldn't be too difficult."

Hiding behind a curtain, I watched Lena leave the building and drive away in her convertible.

I left Córdoba on the following day without returning her call. This time, I understood every word uttered by the Aerolineas stewardess, but I didn't take any pleasure in the fact. So I could speak Spanish — big deal; so could millions of people. But I had also caused a man's death, and that club boasted far fewer members.

My mother was surprised and delighted to see me. I told her I'd been getting bored with my work and that I'd come back to settle in Europe. For the moment, I intended to spend a few weeks with her, while I contemplated my future. I could see in her eyes that she didn't fully believe me, but that she didn't care. She had been given back her son, and that was all that mattered. I moved back into the room I'd occupied as a teenager.

It is an understatement to say that life in Húsavík is nothing like that of a CFR agent. The time I spent there during the summer of 1995 opened my eyes to the sacrifices that I'd unwittingly been making for the past four years. More to the point, how could a peasant's son like me have agreed to be locked up in an office all day long, four hundred miles from the ocean?

I rediscovered the virtues of an outdoor life. At five o'clock in the morning (in Iceland in August, the sun practically never sets), when I was helping the local fishermen haul in the nets, I would lend a hand to my mother on the farm. She'd urge me to stay and have breakfast with her, but the prospect of having to answer her questions put me off and I preferred to eat with the lumberjacks of Húsavík. These tough men, some of them my childhood friends, had at first been suspicious of me, but I had won them over by talking about the Scandinavian forests, a subject I knew quite well since an assignment in Denmark during my time at Baldur, Furuset & Thorberg. I got them completely on my side the day I refused the pay offered by the foreman. If I was working for free, then…

What did I need money for? I would gladly have given everything I had for my conscience to be wiped clean. Fortunately, every stroke of the ax erased the memory of John Harkleroad for a few seconds. The intense physical effort and heavy breathing proved therapeutic. A firm grounding in reality replaced the mental gymnastics of the past four years. I sometimes remembered the Bushmen, *Der Bettlerkönig*, or the gallowfish, but never for very long. There was always something else to do: a sheep to tend, a tree to cut down…

Another problem soon presented itself: Gunnar was trying to contact me. He had sent me a telegram the day after my return (had he traced me through my credit card transactions, or had he guessed that I would return to familiar surroundings like a prisoner on the run?) consisting of three words: "I'm so sorry." Now he'd started phoning at all hours of the day. Each time he reached my mother, who thought my former boss was trying to persuade me to return to Baldur, Furuset & Thorberg. One evening, when she was singing the praises of environmental studies ("A good profession that seemed to suit you"), I took a sheet of paper and wrote to my former mentor. The words flowed with surprising ease.

Gunnar,

I would have liked to write "Dear Gunnar", but that's more than I can manage. I really liked you, Gunnar. For a while, I even thought of you a bit as a

251

father. But you betrayed me; you made me lose my self-esteem; and I can never forgive you for that.

Then why am I writing to you? To ease my conscience, I suppose. But also, and above all, because I want you to know what I've been feeling for the past twelve days. When I came to after being drugged by the hatchet men from Special Operations (but perhaps you didn't know about that episode, which is all too sadly revealing of the methods of the CFR), it was six in the morning in New Zealand, and I had become a murderer — by proxy, you may say, but a murderer all the same. Three people were already mourning the death of a man whose one mistake had been to cross the path of a stupid young agent.

The fact that you were twelve thousand miles from the scene of the crime won't prevent me from thinking of you as an accomplice. I'd compare your role to that of the crossing guard who welcomed the trains to the Nazi concentration camps. To date he has never been indicted, but there is no doubt about his responsibility. I don't know how you can live with that thought. Better than I, obviously.

I feel destroyed, Gunnar, and I do not wish to be told that time will heal my wounds. I doubt it will, and I rather hope that it doesn't. My crime was a serious one, and the punishment should be proportionate. For the moment it does, and I'm finding it hard to get back into the society of the living, even though rural Iceland provides a cross-section of the best of humankind. I constantly think about John Harkleroad, whose killers probably didn't even inform him why he was to be killed. I hope he didn't suffer. Unfortunately, I'm not even sure of that.

I loved the CFR and the game we played there. But must you despise your agents to the point of concealing the sinister aspects of the firm? I suppose it's because deep down you probably know that no one would accept them.

Please do not reply to this letter. I'd rather be spared your slimy excuses.

Sliv

P.S: Stop bothering my mother and me. I think I've at least earned the right to be left alone.

Some weeks passed. I was becoming hardened. My guilt hadn't eased, but the pain was gradually giving way to a kind of numbness. That I had developed a tougher skin was demonstrated by my reaction to the sudden sight of Gunnar Eriksson on the jetty as I was returning from a day's fishing.

A month earlier, I would probably have hidden in the hold, or asked the captain to land me along the coast. But now, the prospect of a conversation with Gunnar seemed to me less objectionable and even reasonable. I suppose I realized that I couldn't turn the page on the CFR without a final conversation with the man who had recruited me.

Gunnar hadn't changed much. "I'm so sorry," he had said in his telegram, so I had expected to find him looking haggard and distraught. Not a bit. Sorry he may have been, but he was in good form, his face a little bloated, his belly even rounder. Oh, of course, he had assumed a suitably solemn and formal expression, but it would have taken a lot more than that to seduce me.

"Hello, Sliv," he said when I had joined him on the dock.

"Hello, Gunnar," I replied as coldly as possible. He didn't hold out his hand. He knew I'd have refused to shake it.

"If you're prepared to give me a few minutes, I noticed a little café in the harbor."

"I know it, thanks," I retorted curtly. "Ten minutes only."

We walked side by side in silence until we reached the café, where we took seats at the back of the room. I ordered an Irish coffee, Gunnar his eternal tea. He waited to speak until the waitress had departed.

"I got your letter, I really am terribly sorry."

"How do you think I feel?" I said with a nervous laugh.

"You must have been through a really hard time," he said, pretending not to notice the hint of aggression in my words. "You should have called me. I might have been able to help."

"I doubt it. Listen, Gunnar, let's not beat about the bush. You wanted to see me. Here I am. If all you have to say is that you're sorry, you may as well return to Reykjavík."

The waitress arrived with our drinks. Gunnar tried to catch my eye while she served us, but in vain.

"Listen, Sliv, your letter made me very sad. But I don't hold it against you. I'm sure I would have reacted in the same way."

"Then why lie to me?" I retorted bitterly.

"I didn't really lie to you," he replied softly. "I simply finessed certain matters. Things aren't always as simple as we'd like."

"Yes, the world's a complicated place," I replied. "A bit hackneyed as an alibi, don't you think?"

"Let's swap roles for a moment. Try to see the situation from my point of view. My task is to recruit agents for the Reykjavík bureau. It's a difficult job, one that requires infinite subtlety and patience. In a good year, I may recruit one agent, very unusually two. In a bad year, I don't find anyone at all. I'm not complaining; my colleagues' success rates are no better. Now, do you think I'd improve my chances if I told every candidate that his mistakes might cost a man his life? Who'd try his luck under such conditions? And, besides, how would we regard a candidate who wasn't deterred by such a prospect?"

I couldn't believe what I was hearing. "Do you realize what you're saying, Gunnar? It isn't a matter of whether or not your recruitment score would be affected, but of respecting your candidates' freedom of choice."

"You're absolutely right, but you know deep down that it isn't possible. What would you have thought of me if I'd framed the discussion in those terms? I'll tell you: you would have considered me fit to be locked up, and you would have immediately reported me to the police."

"Which would have been the right thing to do!"

"No, I don't think so," he said, as if he had weighed the matter many times. "You see, life in a collective demands sacrifices. Your current crisis is one of them. Even in a democracy, a citizen must sometimes accept a measure or a judgment that he personally finds abhorrent. The CFR has thousands, perhaps tens of thousands of agents. It wouldn't have been fair for them to be arrested, even shot in some cases, all because of a mistake made by a young Class 2 agent in the Córdoba bureau."

Always the same argument: your mistakes can cost the lives of innocents. I had had time to mull over that.

"I understand your comparison, Gunnar, but I think it's a false one. The citizen who doesn't agree with his leaders can cling to two comforting thoughts. He can either tell himself that their decision, even if it offends his personal morality, is in the higher interests of the nation; or he can rationalize that it has been indirectly approved by a majority of his fellow citizens, who can choose another government at the next election."

"I don't see anything like that in the structure of the CFR. I, Class 2 Agent Dartunghuver, am unable to determine whether the elimination of John Harkleroad is or is not in the interests of the CFR, since I don't know my employer's objectives. For the past four years I've been working for an organization whose ultimate goals remain a mystery. Moreover, I have to tolerate my superiors, even if I regard them as incompetent. No, really, the democratic model doesn't strike me as very applicable to the CFR."

"There's much truth in what you say, Sliv," Gunnar replied after a moment's thought. "We don't choose our chiefs, and neither of us knows the aim of the CFR…"

"You don't either?" I exclaimed.

"No," he replied pensively, stirring his tea. "I don't know it and I don't think I ever will. The organization has many secrets, but its true purposes are the best-kept of all. You'll learn that eventually, I'd bet my life on it."

"Please, Gunnar, can you explain to me how it's possible to recruit agents without knowing what they're meant to be doing?" In spite of myself, I had recovered my curiosity.

"But I do know what they're meant to be doing: producing scenarios and falsifying reality. I know the how, but not the why. I don't claim that it hasn't been painful. Like you, I was a young agent who seemed to succeed in everything he undertook. But, unlike you, I nursed only one wish: to discover the aims of the CFR. Every action I took was directed toward that."

"And?" I asked impatiently. Gunnar Eriksson had never before revealed so much about himself.

"And it was a mistake. Our leaders don't like nosy parkers. For reasons it would take too long to explain, I stopped rising through the ranks, and I realized I would never know the secrets of the CFR. It was the worst time of my life."

"And subsequently?"

"Since then, I've never asked myself that question. For all I know, the CFR has only one aim: to survive. I base all my decisions on one criterion: will the candidate sitting on the other side of my desk prolong the life of the CFR or bring about its destruction?"

"In my case, you misjudged," I said bitterly.

"Only time will tell." He looked me straight in the eyes. "Sliv, I'd like you to believe me, even though, after what happened, I'd understand it if you dismissed what I'm about to say. This type of incident happens very, very rarely."

"How rarely?" I asked, immediately regretting the question, since asking it might imply I'd be satisfied with a very low number.

"I don't know; perhaps two or three times a year."

"That's a lot," I said.

"Not so much, given the CFR's international scope," Gunnar replied. "You were unlucky, that's all."

I could sense that Eriksson's dispassionate interpretation of events was beginning to convince me, so I guarded against that by evoking the memory of Khoyoulfaz.

"There's something else, Gunnar. Those goons from Special Operations weren't like you or me. They were cruel."

"What were their names?"

"The one in charge was Jones, a Panamanian. Not easy to describe. Very hard, terribly cold, yet consummately professional. He really tried to find a solution. But his partner! An Azeri named Khoyoulfaz, a bloodthirsty brute, who enjoys killing. He mentioned an agent who'd betrayed them, someone called Leonid, and you should have seen the gleam in his eyes. How can the CFR tolerate such agents in its ranks?"

"I don't know either of them. If what you say is true, it's very serious. I'll try to find out about this Khoyoulfaz. The General Inspectorate may have a file on him."

A long hiatus followed, during which I finished my coffee. We paid for our drinks, and the waitress cleared and wiped the table. In the end, it was Gunnar who resumed the conversation.

"What will you do now?"

I had been asking myself that question for two months, but I hadn't yet come to a decision.

"First, visit my sister in Germany. Fix the fence around my mother's farm. Travel a little."

"And then?"

"Then I'll look for a job on the continent, maybe in environmental studies. At least the CFR taught me a skill."

"You can't just hang up your gloves like that. They're still counting on you in high places."

"I resigned Gunnar, I'm a free man. I won't talk, if that's what's worrying them."

"It isn't about that. Didn't you know? They've rejected your resignation."

"So what? They'll just have to accept it. My life still belongs to me, as far as I know."

"Of course it does, Sliv. I just want you to know that they're not angry with you. The Disciplinary Committee will probably impose a sanction for form's sake, but —"

"The Disciplinary Committee?" I asked, taken aback.

"Oh, yes. You're really out of the loop, aren't you? They're meeting next week to examine your case as well as Thorsen's."

"Thorsen, too?"

"Of course. As your immediate superior, she's also responsible. In fact, in my opinion, she's going to incur a heavier penalty than you."

That didn't strike me as quite fair. So my name had not yet been deleted from the roster. I couldn't help asking, "What penalty is she likely to incur?"

"Six months' suspension. Perhaps a year. Knowing her, I'm sure she won't like being shunted aside. As for you…"

Had he sensed that I'd asked about Thorsen's fate because I didn't dare question him directly about mine?

"Oh, that doesn't matter," I said.

"You'll get six months, maximum."

"It doesn't matter," I repeated.

"One last thing," Gunnar added, rising. "Your friend Magawati is trying to reach you. She called Thorsen, who told her you'd resigned. I don't know how she found my number, but she left me a message yesterday, asking me to call her back as soon as possible. What should I tell her?"

Just what I'd been afraid of. I'd known this moment would come, but I still wasn't ready to face it.

"Just tell her I'm fine," I replied in a shaky voice. "Or, rather, no, tell her I'm alive, and that I'll explain one day."

12

Ten days later, I received a letter from Toronto. The Disciplinary Committee had decided to suspend me without pay for six months. I was given two weeks to appeal.

That same day, I flew to Bremen to visit my sister. Mathilde is six years my senior, an age gap that explains why we were never very close as children. But as the years passed, the difference became less significant and we increasingly shared common interests.

In 1989, Mathilde had married Horst Menschel, a German whom she had met while taking a course in Cologne, and with whom she had kept in touch for several years. Since 1990, they had resided in Bremen, where Horst held an important post (at least according to my mother) in a chemical company.

Mathilde had temporarily stopped working in order to look after little Uli, born in 1992, but now that he was attending kindergarten she had resumed her studies of drawing, which would eventually qualify her to teach.

Mathilde met me at the airport. It was the first time I'd seen her in two years, and only the third time I'd visited Germany. She seemed more radiant than ever. My sister is blessed with a naturally happy disposition. Nothing upsets her, and, even in the worst circumstances, as when our father died, she keeps calm, and that equanimity tends to affect those around her.

This time, as usual, she had nothing but good news to tell me. The little family had moved the previous winter to a large house it had built in Lilienthal, in the suburbs of Bremen. Horst had just won a long-pursued promotion, and his salary had risen accordingly. As for Uli, he would soon have a little brother or sister: Mathilde was two months pregnant and, knowing that I was coming, she had wished me to be the first to know. I congratulated her appropriately, then, I reflexively reached into my pocket for a letter that I'd received from Toronto in the morning. *Welcome to reality, Sliv*, I thought.

Horst arrived home earlier than I expected. I thought at first that he had made a special effort in my honor, but he told me that in Germany even managerial staff left work at five. Twice a week, he left after dinner to train with his company's football team. Knowing that I also played, he made me promise to join him one evening.

About six, we sat down to eat. Mathilde had deliberately prepared a traditional dinner: pork sausages and potato salad, with lager beer to drink. Over dessert, I solemnly gave little Uli a little wooden train typical of the crafts produced in Húsavík. Mathilde, recognizing the model she had played with as a child, laughed gaily and clapped her hands.

While Uli started playing with his new toy, Horst sank into what was clearly his armchair and switched on the television to watch the news.

This was my first exposure to world events since my return to Europe. In Córdoba, I had read a dozen newspapers every day, but for the past six weeks I had been content with the *Húsavík Messenger*, a pleasant little rag, entirely written by the local schoolmaster and printed on the school's photocopier, but not notable for its international coverage.

I would happily have caught up with the news, but Horst started to tell me all about his career prospects at Rheinberger. A month ago had been appointed head of exports for the polypropylene division. I soon grasped the fact that his territory wasn't quite as broad as he initially claimed, as it didn't extend much beyond Western Europe. But, as Horst observed smugly, the directors at Rheinberger would not have entrusted him with such responsibilities at a comparatively young age if they weren't grooming him for an even higher position.

For the moment, his mandate was to stimulate sales and restore margins. The polypropylene market had weathered some difficult years, but was now showing signs of recovery in Germany and France. He hoped the upturn would spread to Italy and Spain, two countries traditionally more resistant to the virtues of polypropylene.

Portugal was his next priority. He outlined the steps he was planning to take and asked me for my honest opinion. I replied that the measures he envisioned seemed pretty impressive and that I couldn't see Portuguese industrialists persist much longer in their anti-polypropylene obscurantism.

Once the Iberian Peninsula had been brought into line, he could lay claim on the position of sales director, occupied for the moment by a notorious incompetent named Hans-Harald Durchstetter. He uttered this name with a knowing look, implying that Durchstetter's infamy was firmly established.

I was about to contradict him when Mathilde, returning from the Uli's bedroom, interrupted her husband to suggest we look through her photograph albums. I agreed, although tiredness was starting to get the better of me.

While Mathilde was commenting about the pictures, I thought about Horst's self-absorbed monologue. He hadn't asked me a single question about my work. I didn't really care; in fact I was relieved, he had relieved me of the necessity of lying to my nearest and dearest. Then, too, how could my modest career as a reinsurer have borne a moment's comparison with my brother-in-law's epic rise in the chemical industry?

The CFR condemned its servants to concealment and solitude. I hadn't been especially aware of that during my two years spent in Córdoba, but, now that I had returned to Europe, I couldn't imagine a way to keep my mother and my sister consistently in the dark.

Horst nursed high ambitions. He was hoping, in the hackneyed phrase, "to make a career for himself." Did those words have any meaning in the case of the CFR? I later wondered, as I undressed in my room. It would have been foolish to ignore the fact that many young agents sought to rise through the ranks of the CFR in order to achieve better pay and the perks that went with it.

I had read several works on the theory of organizations, and, in the light of my experience, the CFR didn't differ all that much from more traditional employers, such as businesses or government agencies. The more ambitious, provided, of course, that they had the necessary skills, inevitably outperformed less career-minded agents, to the point of monopolizing the posts with greater responsibilities and higher pay.

What perhaps distinguished the CFR from classic organizations was its ability to motivate people who, indifferent to honors or rewards, were driven by a hunger for knowledge and a taste for game playing.

With hindsight, I recognized that I belonged to this latter category. The reason I'd been overjoyed by my rapid promotion to the rank of Class 2 agent wasn't so much because of the associated prestige, or a few thousand dollars of additional income. My success had aroused in me an excitement akin to that of a player of computer games who is told that he has completed one level and can now progress to the next one. A Class 1 agent has only a few tools at his disposal, hasn't mastered the game's complexities, and works within narrow boundaries set by his case officer. In contrast, a Class 2 agent has access to a much larger arsenal. Now familiar with the rules of the game, he can subvert them to his advantage, often bypassing his superiors. This doesn't mean, of course, that he is all-powerful: departments with such evocative names as the Plan, the General Inspectorate, or the Functional Divisions are there to keep his creativity in check, but let's say he enjoys relative autonomy.

Had I remained in the CFR, I thought as I slipped beneath the sheets, it wouldn't have taken me long to become a Class 3 agent. How many times had I dreamed of the day when, freed of the tyranny of Lena Thorsen, I would have been able to devote myself to developing the incredibly daring scenarios that I had been devising since my arrival in Córdoba! No more weekly briefings with the case officer; no more friendly advice from the old-timers who pat you on the shoulder in the corridors.

A Class 3 agent worked alone and wasn't accountable to anybody, except perhaps the General Inspectorate. He could live where he chose; had access to all the CFR's databases; and from time to time he could call on Class 1 agents for assistance. He was required to produce at least one dossier per year, in accordance with the general directions laid down by the Plan, but these were deliberately broad enough to leave him considerable room for maneuver.

Unlike Thorsen, who I thought was driven by the desire to lead teams and to exercise power, my ambition had been fed during those four years by the hope that one day I'd be able to practice my art without anyone telling me what to do. This insight threw such a harsh light on the individualistic motivations that had attracted me to the CFR that I concluded I was quite wrong for it.

If Gunnar Eriksson had been able to read my thoughts (although at the time he had recruited me, I would have been incapable of formulating them so clearly), I'm sure he would have crossed my name from his list of candidates.

At least, I told myself, my resignation will enable me to put things back in their rightful place: at heart, I wasn't cut out for that job.

That night I slept like a log for the first time in weeks. Mathilde had left a note for me on the kitchen table. She had classes all morning, but would be back with Uli for lunch. If I desired to sightsee in town, I would find a bus stop at the end of the street.

I decided to follow her advice and an hour later I was strolling on the streets of Bremen. It was a lovely day, already quite warm. I took refuge in Saint Peter's Cathedral, and sat down for a moment to read about its history in a guide book.

That was how I discovered that I was very near Sandstrasse, a street whose name was familiar to me because it was where the CFR bureau specializing in commercial law was located. I couldn't resist the temptation to walk along that street, seeking the fateful name plate on every façade. I eventually found it at No 42, a magnificently modern building that also housed the law firm of Claas & Rathenau.

Just then, a man came out of the building. With graying temples, toting a monogrammed attaché case, he seemed wonderfully at ease in his made-to-measure cream-colored linen suit. The perfect outfit for a business lawyer, I thought, then reconsidered: he could just as easily have been the head of the bureau posing as an attorney. He entered a large sedan car with smoked windows that awaited him at the curb, and left me to my thoughts.

That evening, Horst once again kept me from watching the TV news in order to ask my advice about a petty quarrel between him and the impostor Durchstetter (the more my brother-in-law denigrated his boss, the more I wanted to meet the man).

I soon realized that Horst wasn't really interested in my opinion: he was so sure he was right that he already had answers to all his questions. I noticed, with a pang in my heart, that Mathilde was literally drinking in his words. How narrow your horizons become in contact with mediocre people, I thought sadly. And poor Uli, whom his parents were raising in the worship of chemicals... I could already imagine Horst telling his son for the hundredth time how propylene had replaced olive oil in the front rank of domestic products in homes in the Mediterranean area...

There were many things you could hold against the CFR, but certainly not that it was inward-looking. In which other enterprise were personal curiosity and an international outlook so prized? I did a little calculation: in less than four years, I had been in contact with agents of thirty different nationalities. I could now speak five languages fluently. I had studied more than two hundred dossiers from all over the world, and I had been involved in some of the finest mystifications of the decade. Not bad for a twenty-seven-year-old!

It was hard for me to fall asleep that night. My hands folded under my head, I thought back over the best moments of those four years in the CFR: my trip to Greenland, the conversations with Bimard and his obsession with the Romantic poets, the thirteen days and thirteen nights I spent with Stéphane Brioncet on the Bushmen dossier, Angoua Djibo's electrifying speech in Honolulu, the intoxication I had felt upon hearing on the radio the secretary general of the UN announce the International Decade of The World's Indigenous People...

Córdoba also provided its fair share of memories: Ramirez's interminable lectures on the Riemann series, the evenings spent watching football at the San Feliz stadium, even the stormy discussions with Lena Thorsen. But then the voice of Harkleroad echoed in my head and dampened my nostalgia.

Other powerful if painful images came to the forefront, some of which I hadn't remarked at the time but that now came back to haunt me: Khoyoulfaz eating his steak with his fingers, Jones sadly shaking his head after listening to my monologue, Thorsen signing the orders that condemned Harkleroad without even reading them...

Gunnar liked to say that Lena Thorsen's dossiers were a mixture of the good and the bad. That formula applied even more to the CFR. But could one have the good without the bad? No, of course not. A man's death was the price to be paid periodically so that a group of practical jokers could continue to amuse themselves at the world's expense.

But that premise didn't excuse the behavior of someone like Khoyoulfaz. Even those countries that still impose the death penalty demand a modicum of dignity from their executioners. Khoyoulfaz's off-handed manner had traumatized me. The disgusting familiarity with which he had said: "I won't ask you to go with us to the airport," the greedy cruelty with which he had evoked the memory of young Leonid... What advantage was there for the CFR in employing such henchmen?

Sleep still eluded me. For the thousandth time, I wondered what to do about Youssef and Magawati. Should I get in touch with them? And how would I tell them my story? Six months earlier, in Patagonia, I would have sworn that I would never hide anything from them. Today, I was actually wondering if it was better to lie to them by commission or omission... I could imagine only too well what Youssef's reaction would be. He would make me promise to go to the police and tell them everything, while he himself would try to collect evidence inside the Ho Chi Minh City bureau, thus exposing himself to risks that I had no desire to make him take.

Above all, I dreaded his judgment. He would never understand how I had been able to leave Córdoba, flee my responsibilities, agree to see Gunnar Eriksson; how, by doing nothing, I had implicitly endorsed the existence and the conduct of Special Operations.

I couldn't understand that either, but I clung to the belief that the passing of time wouldn't make a significant difference, that my confession would be just as admissible and effective if I gave myself time to think.

Wrong, wrong, and wrong again, Youssef would argue. He would point out quite rightly that every day that passed allowed John Harkleroad's killers to destroy the evidence needed to confound them.

I had no answer to that, except that I wasn't ready. I wasn't prepared to have thousands of agents, including Gunnar Eriksson and Alonso Diaz, thrown into prison. I wasn't ready to cause the disbanding of a secret organization that had existed for decades, perhaps even centuries, one that had some unquestionable achievements to its credit (the Bushmen, Karigasniemi, the conquest of space, etc.), as I had been able to observe for myself.

And Magawati? She would certainly be less rigid, at least about my methods. Compassionate by nature, she more than Youssef would make an effort to understand the phases I had experienced.

Did that mean she would absolve me? I didn't think so. She would dissect my motives as delicately and methodically as she had questioned me in Patagonia about my father's death. She would recognize my contradictions, just as I did when I made the effort to delve into my conscience. Finally, she would pronounce her verdict, and that would be the end of the CFR. No, decidedly, I couldn't make up my mind to tell them the truth.

My dreams weren't very pleasant that night.

The next morning, I rode to Bremen's main station, where I bought a stack of newspapers: the *Frankfurter Allgemeine Zeitung*, the *Times*, *El País*, the *Corriere della Sera*, *Le Monde*, the *International Herald Tribune*, *USA Today* and even the English-language version of *Yomiuri Shimbun*. I had all day to catch up with current events. On the ride back to Lilienthal, I realized that this was the first pleasure I had granted myself since my return to Europe. It was a sobering thought.

I sat down at the kitchen table with a large cup of coffee and arranged the pile of newspapers in front of me. Honor to whom honor is due: I began with the national news in the *Frankfurter Allgemeine*. Nothing very startling at first glance. The opposition was blaming Chancellor Kohl for the cost of reunification. A political and financial scandal was shaking the Land of Baden-Wurtemberg. A neo-Nazi group had claimed responsibility for an attack on a Turkish hostel.

While none of that was of any great import, I plunged back with delight into the complexity of the world. An editorial claimed that a liberal party I'd never heard of would hold the balance of power at the next elections. The selector of the national handball team praised a young player currently competing in the Greek championship. So many facts to assimilate, so many pieces of information to collate, so much background material for a falsifier!

And no nation was left out. In Italy (where all the talk was of a young fashion designer named Venozzi), people were pretending to discover for the hundredth time that championship football matches were fixed. In England, the indiscretions of the Princess of Wales fueled the continuing saga of the misadventures of the royal family.

I particularly enjoyed an article in *El País*, entitled "The Price of Honor". In 1962, the famous matador Rodrigo Calmacho had stabbed to death his wife Manolita (the name of my tango partner!) for implying on live television that her husband was less impressive in bed than in the bullring. Calmacho had thrown the body down a well, then given himself up to the police, saying that he trusted his country's justice system.

The trial that followed had enthralled Franco's Spain and opened a national debate on the meaning of the word "honor". In the end, Calmacho had been sentenced to fifteen years' imprisonment by the court in Valencia, which had recognized that there were extenuating circumstances, since that Manolita's televised revelations could be construed as mental cruelty.

Thirty-three years later, this mental cruelty appeared so obvious to the Supreme Court that it had just pardoned Calmacho and awarded him seven million pesetas in damages for wrongful imprisonment.

What a story, almost too good to be true! I could just imagine Thorsen's face if I'd submitted a scenario like that! A number of ideas for bogus sources came to me, by reflex: an article by a psychoanalyst stressing the symbolism of the well; a press release during the Cannes Film Festival announcing that Almodóvar was planning to buy the rights to Calmacho's autobiography; an in-depth report in the journal of the Madrid Bar Association on the chances of having judicial decisions reversed…

I had only to open *Le Monde* to become serious again: I had unconsciously put France at the end of my tour of Europe, doubtless because I knew only too well what was in the news across the border. There was still a lot of talk about the nuclear tests. In spite of the pressure from international opinion, Jacques Chirac had not backtracked: the announced tests would indeed take place.

Diplomatic relations between France and New Zealand were again as frosty as they had been after the Rainbow Warrior incident ten years earlier. Fortunately, wrote *Le Monde*, the Bolger report had not been able to point to any impact of the French tests on the flora and fauna in that part of the world. I reread that phrase several times: "had not been able to point to…" So the gallowfish had gone unnoticed, thank God. I was already living with a man's death on my conscience; to have learned in addition that his murder had been in vain would have made my anguish unbearable.

What was happening in America? Once again, *USA Today* presented the image of an unshakable nation, sure of its rights and its destiny, fascinated by the spectacle of its own contradictions and obsessed with the stock market.

The list of candidates for the Republication nomination for the 1996 presidential elections had just been announced. One of the names caught my attention: a Texan millionaire named Randolph "Scottie" Marshall. I hadn't heard of him. Why should I have? you may ask. In both political parties, the primaries are traditionally an opportunity for a few wealthy eccentrics to express supposedly original views. These candidates usually lose by a wide margin in New Hampshire and then disappear as quickly as they appeared.

The problem was that at the beginning of the year I had worked on the Republican primaries. The Dundee bureau had planned to concoct a candidate and it had solicited our thoughts on the measures that would have to be taken. Our verdict was negative: the risks were far too great. Nevertheless, I had spent three weeks on that dossier and I thought I knew all the declared or potential candidates for the nomination. The name Marshall didn't ring a bell. Had the case officer in Dundee tried his luck anyway? It would have been interesting to find out...

I challenge anyone who has been involved with the CFR to be able to read a newspaper without immediately searching for signs of falsification: an interview with a university professor who is supposed to be a world authority on his subject; the review of a book by a major Polish novelist little known abroad; a description of a new sport, halfway between judo and Greco-Roman wrestling, to be demonstrated during the next Olympic Games.

That was what I experienced that day. Because I had been deprived of major newspapers for months, I made an effort to detect any trace of my former colleagues' work. Here a slightly absurd statistic, there an excessively weighty pronouncement by a new age guru: even though I knew it was highly unlikely that the papers spread in front of me contained the slightest misrepresentation, I searched for one like a hunting dog sniffing a trail, in order to reassure myself about my own talents and maybe also to show those who had brushed me aside that I was still, and would always be, superior to them.

Hearing Mathilde's key turning in the lock, I folded the *Herald Tribune*. Four hours had not been too much to catch up on what I had missed. Casting a surprised glance at the heap of newspapers, Mathilde invited me to accompany her to the kindergarten to fetch Uli.

Along the way, I began a conversation about the news by asking her what she thought of the SPD's economic program. Much to my surprise, she had no opinion about it. She didn't even know its broad outlines, although they weren't that different from that of any European socialist party.

She admitted she didn't follow the news very closely. "Anyway, Horst says that one is as bad as another," she said by way of excuse. That someone as intelligent and well-educated as Mathilde could be so indifferent to current affairs, I found quite bewildering.

In the CFR we had been taught that the critical spirit is like a muscle that atrophies when not exercised. The most insignificant freshman in the Rovaniemi bureau could have spoken for at least fifteen minutes on the internal debates raging inside the SPD. If he couldn't, his case officer would have sentenced him to read *Bild* from front to back for three months, a terrible punishment I wouldn't wish on anyone.

I had planned to spend two weeks with Horst and Mathilde. After five days, overwhelmed by their narrow-mindedness, I invented a job interview in Reykjavík and packed my bags. Horst wasn't only vain and conceited, he suffered from a simplistic attitude that made his company unbearable to any normal person.

I'm quite aware, in writing these lines, that I'm excluding my sister from that category, but I'd reached the conclusion that the poor woman had lost all common sense.

Dropping me at the airport, my brother-in-law gave me one last piece of advice: "You're right to go back. Never stray too far from the head office, or your bosses may forget your name." Quite apart from the fact that he was way off the mark (he probably hadn't been told that I was unemployed, and he certainly hadn't asked), his words made me think. Were my bosses forgetting my name? And, anyway, where was head office?

13

Reykjavík, February 25, 1996

Gunnar,

Six months have passed since the events that led me to resign from the CFR. I've often thought about the last time we met and my feelings toward you have been through many stages. I am now reconciled to the past. To put it simply, let's just say that I accept your motives, even if I don't understand them. I'm prepared to believe you when you say that it would be impossible to recruit young agents without lying to them, even if only by omission.

All the same, I have to say that you have never answered the one question worth asking: Should agents be recruited? Should the CFR continue to exist? I hope circumstances will allow us to have that discussion one day. I also hope that the heads of the CFR debate this regularly, and not only on the two or three occasions per year when the Controller-General signs orders like those I refused to sign in Córdoba.

I am not inclined to self-pity, but I must admit that I've lived through some painful moments. I began by hating the CFR, its lack of ethics, its compartmentalized structure that allows people not to look each other in the eyes; then guilt replaced anger on, the day I realized that the latter was precisely a comfortable way of shifting responsibility for my actions onto someone else, what's more, an anonymous entity.

For three months, H., his wife and daughters were uppermost in my thoughts. I traveled to Wellington, where I viewed H.'s grave; I sent money to his widow, so that she could raise her children with dignity. That pilgrimage didn't cure me, but it did calm me.

I have the impression that I narrowed the distance separating me from H.; paradoxically, I would have preferred to stab him through the heart rather than sign his death warrant by pressing a button in a conference room four thousand miles away. It would have been more... human.

I've been ruminating less about all this for a few weeks, but that doesn't make me any happier. On the contrary. What bothers me the most is no longer that I killed H., but that my feelings of remorse are fading. As you can see, my scruples are evolving but still haven't disappeared.

You will have realized by now that my resentment toward the CFR is not as strong as it was. The CFR has no life of its own; it's merely the sum of the individuals who comprise it. Had I continued to work on environmental studies, H. would still be alive. So there is no reason for my anger to be directed at the CFR: it is only toward myself.

I'm so angry with myself, Gunnar. I blame myself for not learning more about the CFR. I don't suppose anyone would have answered my questions, but I should still have asked them. How could an organization with several thousand members have remained secret for so long? Has it never been on the verge of being discovered, and, if it has, how did it react?

One needs to think for only five minutes to surmise that the CFR must have known several blunders in the past and yet I never took those five minutes. I can't believe I've been so careless.

I always took what my case officers said at face value. Worse still, I refused to see or discern in their words anything that might have contradicted the image I was forming of the CFR as a peaceful, game-playing, inoffensive organization. With hindsight, though, I remember your barely veiled threats when you recruited me, Lena Thorsen's outrageous remarks ("This is war, Dartunghuver!"), my instructors' quasi-military vocabulary ("Don't talk, even under torture," "We need a strategy for infiltrating governments," etc.).

I realize now that the CFR is a fearsome organization, prepared to do anything to avoid being uncovered. Having said that, I am forced to inquire further: Is the CFR hiding something else? Is its sole aim to produce scenarios? Is it a spy network or a criminal organization? I'm in the situation of the man who discovers he has been lied to once: he can't help thinking he may have been lied to several times, and so he starts to question everything.

Instinctively, I'd be tempted to seek answers to my questions from you, but can I really trust the man who recruited me into the CFR? You manipulated me, Gunnar, and, not content with taking me for a ride, your peers voted me the most brilliant scenario writer of my generation. What a farce!

But none of that really matters. What hurts me most is that, deep down, I didn't dismiss these anxieties for fear of what I might have found. How could a young man as intelligent and independent as I (now is not the time for false modesty) allow himself to be hoodwinked so thoroughly as never to have doubted or distrusted the CFR? Isn't that a sign that I unconsciously sensed that the CFR couldn't withstand such critical analysis? And let's go right to the end of that thought, for once: wasn't the reason I dismissed this uncomfortable introspection because I feared I might have to give up my cozy life as an agent? Or to put it another way, didn't I suppress my scruples for money? That's what makes me furious, Gunnar, and not furious with the CFR, but with myself.

On the surface, I behaved like an idiot; at a pinch I could forgive myself for that. But I'll never know what happened deep inside me, and that's unbearable.

I come now to the most painful part of my letter. Even though what I'm about to request won't surprise you, even though deep down you never doubted it, I beg you not to show it. I'd like to come back, Gunnar. I miss my life as a CFR agent too much. I've traveled a lot over the past six months, and I've had plenty of job interviews. I can't see myself resuming a "normal" life as an anonymous wage-earner. After what I experienced in the CFR, I'd feel like a walk-on, a puppet in the hands of a stage director.

You may remember that I once asked you what became of former agents. I realize now that there probably aren't very many of them. The CFR is like a drug; I don't see how I could do without it. I've had too many ideas for scenarios; I tried at first to dismiss them, but you know how it is, once you have a lead, you can't let go of it, you start by scribbling a few notes on a tablecloth and you end up filling entire notebooks.

Of course, all that is pointless. But what isn't? And besides, I haven't yet produced a dossier that deserves to go down to posterity. I don't repudiate my first attempts, but I take them for what they are, first drafts.

Will everything be the way it was before? No, of course not. I won't believe anything or anybody anymore. I'll weigh up the consequences of each of my decisions, in order to remain as free as possible. I will assume my responsibilities as an agent, without deceiving myself about my power, but without lying to myself either.

You can imagine how much this confession is costing me. Having slammed the door, here I am, back again, begging my judges for clemency. My self-esteem has taken a severe blow. That simple observation ought to convince you of my determination, and it may make the service I am going to ask of you a little easier.

Officially, the CFR never accepted my resignation. In fact, Thorsen didn't even acknowledge having received it. Later, the Disciplinary Committee suspended me for six months. I didn't appeal, nor did I say that I accepted the penalty. That's the situation as it stands. My suspension will end in a few days. I don't know the CFR's intentions toward me. Should I get back in touch? Should I wait to be informed of my next posting? Please relay my desire to be reinstated. If our leaders aren't afraid of having skeptics in their ranks, they should welcome me with open arms.

Thanking you in advance,

Sliv

14

Sir,

We are pleased to inform you that you have been promoted to the rank of Agent Class 3. You are posted to the Krasnoyarsk Center in Siberia, where you will attend classes at the Academy for three years. You will present yourself at 9 A.M. on March 10, 1996, to Senior Agent Quinteros, who will be in charge of your training.

PART THREE

Krasnoyarsk

1

Should I have seen it as an omen? My return to the ranks of the CFR began with a lie. When the fair-haired young immigration officer asked me the reason for my visit to Russia, I replied that I intended to study the language. I handed him the one-year renewable visa that I had found stapled to the well-read letter advising me of my posting. My visa had been issued by the Russian embassy in London on February 10, 1996. This could mean either that it had been issued before I informed Gunnar of my desire to rejoin the CFR, or that it was false. Of the two possibilities, I couldn't decide which was the more disturbing.

The officer studied me for a long time, then raised the visa to the light to examine its watermark. I panicked. Even from my vantage point, I could see that the paper had no special characteristics. Having survived a parliamentary commission of inquiry in New Zealand, was I about to be thwarted by a stupid blunder?

"*Khoroscho*," he said at last, vigorously stamping my passport. "Welcome to Moscow."

"*Spasibo*," I replied, hoping to render my pose as a language student a little more credible.

I was relieved, but it still didn't put my mind at rest. This was the first time I'd set foot behind the Iron Curtain, and even though it had officially fallen some years earlier, to me destinations like Moscow, Sofia, or Prague still exuded an aura of mystery that I found vaguely terrifying.

Who knew whether that man in the thin steel-rimmed glasses standing next to me at the carousel wasn't a plainclothes policeman assigned to tail me?

And I doubted that the KGB cameras, which, during the Cold War, had systematically recorded the faces of the tens of thousands of foreigners landing at Cheremetievo every day, had been magically disconnected on 26 December 1991, the day of the Supreme Soviet's dissolution.

But it was too late to turn back now, and I pushed my baggage cart to Aeroflot's domestic terminal, where the ground staff had probably already started checking in passengers for the Krasnoyarsk flight.

Even though the destinations were written in Cyrillic, I easily spotted the correct line: it was the one in which the passengers were the most warmly dressed. At the beginning of March in that part of Siberia, the temperature is usually -20°C, a level at which even vodka is no substitute for a fur coat.

In spite of being afforded very short notice, I'd had time to learn a little about my destination. In all the encyclopedias I had consulted, considerations of climate held pride of place, but I had also discovered that Krasnoyarsk is served by the legendary Trans-Siberian Railway, and that the city had been the center of the Soviet gulag system. This last point hadn't done anything to ease my anxiety.

Such doubts began to assail me again as soon as I learned of my next posting. My joy at being back in the CFR was supplanted by a wide range of emotions: a sadly familiar upsurge of guilt, a fear of not living up to what was expected of me, and an attack of nausea at the prospect of rejoining an organization that employed the repugnant Khoyoulfaz.

A year earlier, I had regarded the Academy as paradise; now I viewed it as a purgatory that I hoped wouldn't turn into hell, as it had for the millions of political dissidents deported by Stalin and Beria.

What business could possibly attract so many people to Krasnoyarsk? I asked myself as the plane began its descent. That a brave colonist might have pitched his tent there, dazzled by the River Yenisei glittering in the May sun, I could fathom. But that at a time when Russian citizens supposedly enjoyed freedom of movement, eight hundred thousand people should decide to raise their children in the very place in which the Bolshevik regime had exiled its enemies — that was beyond my comprehension. I chalked it up to either a fascination with wide open spaces, or some oddity of the famous Russian soul.

As was becoming a habit, a chauffeur was waiting for me at the airport, holding up a sign. This time, my name had been spelled correctly, suggesting that the amateurism so common in the provincial branches and bureaus had no place in Krasnoyarsk. Wearing white gloves and an earpiece, the driver spoke perfect English as he escorted me to our car, a black Zil limousine like those once used by members of the Politburo. Before climbing into the back seat, I heard him murmur into his buttonhole, "Package received. I repeat: Package received." Obviously I couldn't rule out the possibility that he had found a secret agent kit in a cereal box, but the mime was quite impressive nonetheless.

I had expected the Academy to be situated in the center of the city, but our leaders must have considered that isolation was better suited to our activities. We drove for almost an hour without passing another car, threading through a forest of huge fir trees and past immaculate frozen lakes. The Zil glided noiselessly in the semi-darkness, and I wasn't sure if that was due to the manufacturer's ingenuity or my driver's skill.

Eventually, on the side of a hill, we turned onto a narrow, unmarked path that could barely be seen from the road. Two kilometers further, we drove through the gate of the International Academy for Linguistic Cooperation, and the chauffeur parked the Zil by the front steps of a red-brick house that resembled a hunting lodge. As we negotiated the final bend, I had glimpsed, through a curtain of fir trees, two long single-story buildings bristling with antennas.

"Package delivered," my driver whispered into his buttonhole. This time, he didn't need to repeat himself; maybe the connection was better. Then, with choreographed precision, he took my cases from the trunk, placed them side by side at the top of the steps, and came around to open the car door for me. Last, but not least, he stroked the warm side of the Zil as if it were the head of a horse that had run well. Siberians depend on their vehicles, and show them a respect that would appear strange to the inhabitants of more temperate climes.

"Señor Dartunghuver, what a pleasure to welcome you to Krasnoyarsk," a small man as round as a billiard ball, who had materialized as if by magic at the top of the steps, exclaimed in Spanish. "I'm Alfredo Quinteros, director of the Academy."

"Pleased to meet you," I replied, extending my hand. He seized it warmly and held it in his a little too long for my taste, as if he were accustomed to prolonged sessions of official photographs.

"I hope I'm not too late," I said. "My flight was slightly delayed."

"Not at all," Quinteros replied, "The control tower kept us informed of your estimated time of arrival." He certainly wasn't either Spanish or Argentine; Colombian maybe.

"I'm Peruvian," he said, as if reading my thoughts. "You've been in Córdoba, I think. Congratulations on your Spanish. You worked with my friend, Alonso Diaz. A great professional, don't you agree?"

A great professional who hated having blood on his hands, as Lena Thorsen would have said.

"Yes, indeed," I responded, rather mechanically. "And a scholar."

"That's quite true." Quinteros sighed. "What a loss!"

"What? Is he dead?

"Oh, didn't you know?" Quinteros said, shaking his head. "Two months ago. A wretched end, so I've heard."

"I'm sorry," I said. "I wasn't told."

"Had you already left?"

"Yes, I took a few months' leave after the posting ended," I improvised: it sounded better than: "I brooded for a few months after taking off like a thief in the night." Was it possible that Quinteros didn't know about that unfortunate episode? He must surely have read my file.

"Let me walk you to your apartment," Quinteros offered. I made a motion to pick up my suitcases. "No, leave those. Someone will bring them to you later."

He stood aside to let me pass. What I had taken for a hunting lodge was in fact an ultramodern reception area, with a security guard, a telephone switchboard worthy of the Pentagon, and an entire wall of surveillance monitors. The nearest one, labeled "Smoking room", showed a chess game in progress between two Asians.

"I'll ask that you always come this way when entering and leaving the Academy. The rules oblige us to keep a register of arrivals and departures. If you need a car to go to Krasnoyarsk or anywhere else, advise reception, if possible an hour or two in advance."

"I'll make a note of that," I promised, admiring the hypocrisy of his wording: *The rules oblige us to keep a register of arrivals and departures.* Why not come out with it and say that he wished to know where we were at all hours of the day and night?

"We're officially a linguistic institute," Quinteros went on. "In fact, everybody here works for the CFR, even the ancillary staff. You can talk quite freely in front of the drivers and the chambermaids. It usually takes a few weeks for our students to become acclimated."

"I can imagine."

"In the summer, we open the back of the reception area. You see that trail?" Quinteros pointed to a path behind large French doors. "It leads to the residence and the study building. It's beautiful in July, but I wouldn't recommend trying it at this time of year."

He took my arm and led me to an opening barely concealed by a curtain.

"It's better to take the tunnel. The slope is quite gentle, to allow wheelchair access. Two hundred meters of well-heated corridors. Perhaps you feel a bit claustrophobic? You'll get used to it soon enough. We even have some students who go jogging here in the mornings."

It wasn't so much the narrowness of the passageway that I found oppressive as the cameras clearly visible every thirty meters. As for coughing up my lungs in the morning watched by guards talking into their buttonholes, that spooked me.

"How old is the building?" I asked.

"Oh, it's quite recent," Quinteros replied. "It was Andropov who ordered it to be built when he came to power in 1983. He missed the inauguration by one week. Poor fellow, they say the project was very dear to his heart."

"Hold on," I said, coming to a stop. "Yuri Andropov? The chairman of the Supreme Soviet?"

"Oh, yes," Quinteros chuckled, pulling me by the arm. "And the former head of the KGB. Believe me, the work was performed quite expeditiously."

"And what were the buildings intended for?" I asked, fearing the answer.

"It was a training center for KGB operatives. Andropov didn't spare any expense—he wanted the best for his men."

"I see," I said, thinking of Khoyoulfaz.

"It was in use for only eight years. We bought the building in 1992. The Yeltsin government needed ready cash, so it didn't need to be asked twice. A bit of refurbishment was done, and we took occupancy in 1993. Obviously, the conditions are a bit rougher than in Hamburg, where we were previously based, but in every other way we had the better of the bargain."

"Of course," I said, thinking that, in current circumstances, Hamburg would probably have suited me better.

"We're coming to the fork," Quinteros said, stopping. "On the left, the study building, where we're due to meet tomorrow. On the right, the residence, where the students and the teaching staff live. Follow me, and I'll take you to your apartment."

The tunnel opened into another reception area, which also had its security guard and its surveillance screens. The wall on the right was covered with approximately two hundred letterboxes.

"The mail arrives toward the end of the morning," Quinteros said. "The service is relatively fast, but I advise you to keep in mind that the Russian authorities may intercept your correspondence. We encode all of our confidential communications."

I would have suspected as much. What I would have liked to know was whether KGB were the only people to open letters.

"Here's the common room," Quinteros went on, moving into an adjoining room clearly designed to reproduce the atmosphere of an English pub, featuring paneled walls, thick carpets, and comfortable leather couches.

In front of a huge fireplace adorned with a stuffed stag's head, one of the students was reading a magazine that he had selected from a well-stocked display rack. He had his back to us, and didn't even seem to notice our presence.

At the foot of a large television screen was a row of infrared headphones that made it possible for one to follow the programs without disturbing one's neighbors.

"Given the somewhat compact size of the apartments," Quinteros said, "our boarders prefer to come here to read or to watch television. We receive programs from all over the world, perhaps even from Iceland," he added, trying to please me.

The residence was as singularly devoid of charm as the common room was welcoming. The long corridors, lit by fluorescent lights and interspersed at regular intervals with fire doors, all looked alike and seemed intended to drive any student already worn down by the long Siberian winter to suicide.

What Quinteros rather pompously called apartments were in fact studios, roughly thirty square meters in size, furnished in a Spartan fashion but each equipped with a bathroom, a television set, and a computer linked to the CFR's network.

Yuri Andropov must have judged that the KGB's operatives wouldn't need separate kitchens. Meals were taken in the cafeteria, located in the study building. Obviously I had to prepare to spend the next three years of my life in a setting about as inviting as an airport toilet.

Quinteros was just informing me that a chambermaid would come to clean my room twice a week when I heard someone knocking at my door.

"Sliv?" a familiar voice said. "Is that you?"

"Stéphane?" I cried, pushing Quinteros aside in order to open the door for Brioncet, who burst in laughing and fell into my arms.

"It's so unexpected to see you again," I said, quite moved. "Don't tell me you're working here!"

"Stéphane arrived this morning," Quinteros — whom I'd already forgotten — interposed. "He too will be studying here at the Academy."

"Going back to school at my age, can you imagine?" Stéphane joked — he was easily seven or eight years older than I.

"What have you been up to in the last four years?" I asked. "Did you stay in Paris?"

Quinteros cleared his throat to remind us of his presence. "I don't think you need me any longer tonight," he said. "I expect to see you tomorrow morning. We'll begin at nine sharp. Delighted to have made your acquaintance, Sliv."

I followed Stéphane into his room. He had had time to unpack, and he had already decorated a wall with a superb reproduction of the map of France in 1803, a period when Savoy and Upper Savoy were still Italian. He played a jazz record, made us both some herb tea, and told me what he had been doing since 1992.

His contribution to the Bushmen dossier had earned him a promotion to Class 3 agent. Now free to settle wherever he chose, he had moved to Montreal. "If I'd known I'd be going to Krasnoyarsk afterward, I'd have chosen Florida," he joked. He had produced five dossiers, assisted Jürgen Dorfmeister with his sequel to the Bushmen, and taken part in an initiative on the war in Yugoslavia.

He had also married a woman from Quebec, but had divorced her almost as quickly. I understood from the way his voice trembled that the wound was still fresh, and that he didn't wish to elaborate about it.

His selection for the Academy had taken him by surprise. He had assumed that at thirty-six, an age at which Class 3 agents generally no longer have any career prospects and start to worry about their complementary retirement plans, he was out of the running. But Human Resources had told him they were trying to gradually raise the average age of admission to the Academy, in order to enable young scenario writers to mingle with more experienced agents.

"They're counting on an old monkey like me to teach you lot a few grimaces," Stéphane joked.

Now I launched into an account of my own adventures. My description of Osvaldo Ramirez and his cry of joy at the news of the Killari earthquake (*"Fantastico! Riemann justificado!"*) made Stéphane roar with laughter, as did my planned scenario that involved replacing the sun of the Argentine flag with a side of beef.

He bombarded me with questions about Lena Thorsen, whose reputation had clearly crossed borders. I mentioned, in no particular order, her beauty, her professionalism, and her coldness, but said nothing about that day in August 1995 when she had disappointed me so deeply and so irreparably.

Nor, obviously, did I say a word about the circumstances under which I had left Córdoba. Instead, I trotted out the version I'd already recited to Quinteros.

I got back to my room about midnight. My baggage was stacked outside my door. I couldn't fall asleep immediately, my mind being too full of contradictory thoughts. In the space of a few hours, I had lied to three people, of whom at least one felt nothing but good toward me. I had already found it challenging enough to lead a double life; where was I going to find the strength to lead a triple one?

I had also rediscovered the CFR: its undeniable scope (a Peruvian as director of the Academy); its appalling defects (the pointlessly enigmatic driver, the ubiquitous cameras), its extraordinary ability to create an instant complicity between an Icelander and a Frenchman who hadn't seen each other for four years. As so often at night, my thoughts turned to Youssef and Magawati, who in my eyes embodied the best that the CFR had to offer. Would I ever be able to regain their respect?

2

"If everyone's here, I suggest we begin," Alfredo Quinteros said, raising his voice to be heard above the hubbub.

It was 9.15 and we were all still standing with tumblers of coffee, searching for words that would best describe the character of the study building. "Post-Hiroshima fantasy"; "Orwellian barracks"; or "Bijou residence designed by Kafka" were interesting suggestions, but Stéphane had gotten the most votes with his "Unfinished concerto for breeze blocks and metal girders."

It was beside Stéphane that I took a seat in the third row. The light of the Siberian morning flooded the room. Outside, the branches of the fir trees sagged under the weight of the snow.

"Good morning, everyone. My name is Alfredo Quinteros, and I've been the Director of the Academy since 1992. I myself received the same training you'll be given, in Hamburg in the 1970s. I subsequently occupied a number of posts in the Plan, first in North America then in Japan. And by the way, I'm Peruvian, but it's been a long time since I attached any importance to the color of my passport."

That sort of remark always made me uncomfortable: why did genuine citizens of the world — and Quinteros could legitimately claim that title — so often feel obliged to disavow their background? Personally, I had never felt more Icelandic than when living abroad.

"And now, I declare the fifty-second session of the Academy officially open," he said in a tone as self-important as if he were inaugurating the Olympic Games before a worldwide television audience. His grandiloquence was not entirely useless though, as it allowed the attentive listener to situate the establishment of the Academy around the year 1945. At a time when the world was licking its wounds, the CFR was busy training its elite.

Quinteros paused and looked around the audience, clearly expecting applause for such an eloquent preamble.

Getting none, he proceeded, unfazed:

"The Academy's mission is to prepare the best agents to fill the highest posts in our organization. All the members of the Executive Committee, the heads of the main divisions and the managing directors have, without exception, graduated from the Academy. But please don't assume that having studied at Krasnoyarsk is an automatic passport to success. Only the most gifted and industrious will rise through the ranks, eclipsing those who are less bright or who regard their stay here as three years of luxury tourism."

Apparently, I had underestimated Quinteros's sense of humor. Or perhaps he mistook our Siberian bunker for a five-star hotel, in which case I didn't dare imagine his conception of camping. However, beyond the witticism, his surprisingly incisive tone was thought-provoking.

A welcoming speech usually functions in two stages: the master of the house first establishes cohesion among the recipients ("you are the crème de la crème") and then paints an idyllic picture of their prospects. Generally, the audience is not taken in, but it is pleased to be promised glory and honors rather than sweat and tears. With his barely veiled threats, Quinteros appeared more like a Marine lieutenant than the unctuous apparatchik it was tempting to see in him. But then, as if to dispel this impression, he took a handkerchief from his sleeve and mopped his brow.

"Now for a few figures, which should prove more effective than a long speech in conveying the strategic nature of the Academy. The twenty of you represent seventeen countries and six continents. Collectively, you speak nineteen different languages. Your average age is thirty-three, and you've spent eight years in the field. During the course of your three years at Krasnoyarsk, you will receive fifteen hundred hours of theoretical instruction, and the CFR will spend more than one million dollars on your training."

This last figure was greeted with murmurs of incredulity.

"I did indeed say one million dollars, and that's not counting your salary," Quinteros continued proudly, as if the money came from his own pocket. "We make a considerable investment in each of you, commensurate with the level of responsibility we expect you to shoulder."

That put the operating budget of the Academy at more than twenty million dollars annually. What would have been interesting to know was the provenance of the money.

"The first year of teaching follows a standardized program. You will deepen your knowledge of the structure of the CFR, enlarge your range of narrative techniques with our best scenario writers, master the latest procedures for electronic falsification, and discover a number of episodes — some glorious, other tragic — of our organization.

"All of your work, whether individual or collective, will be graded. In addition, at the end of the first year, you'll undergo a series of tests that will allow us to rank you by order of excellence. Depending on where you stand in the rankings, you'll be able to choose the body in which you will spend the subsequent two years.

There are three of these bodies. The Plan, chaired by Angoua Djibo, whom some of you have already met, establishes the CFR's three-year objectives. The General Inspectorate, managed by Claas Verplanck, ensures that all codes and procedures are strictly adhered to, both at the central level and in the local branches and bureaus. Last, Special Operations, headed by Yakoub Khoyoulfaz, intervene whenever the existence of our organization is in danger of being discovered."

I shuddered. Khoyoulfaz, that bloodthirsty brute, was in charge of Special Operations? And there was I, thinking he took his orders from Jones. How could I have been so mistaken? And how could someone like him hold a position of equal importance to that of Angoua Djibo, the wisest, most discriminating person I had ever met?

"Last but not least," Quinteros continued, without noticing my astonishment, "those of you who are not lucky enough to be assigned to one of the major bodies will be transferred to the managerial sections: Finance, Human Resources, and Information Technology."

In other words, a high-class burial: no one joined the CFR to end up as IT manager of the Jackson, Mississippi bureau. Here too, our host wasn't mincing his words, but making it quite clear that the best places would be hard won.

"We're going to spend three years together," Quinteros continued, "and even though there'll be no lack of opportunities to get better acquainted, right now I'd like to ask each of you to present yourself in a few words. Perhaps we can start with the young lady in the front row?"

"Lena Thorsen, thirty years old, Danish," Lena said, turning around. "I began in the multi-purpose branch in Reykjavík. I was then moved to the Stuttgart Bureau, which specializes in ancient civilizations. Finally, I occupied the post of deputy director in Córdoba, which you all know. Oh, and I almost forgot: I won second prize in Honolulu in 1989."

Typical of Lena, I thought. She had emphasized her achievements, but not having been hauled before a disciplinary committee.

"Thank you, Lena," Quinteros said, apparently captivated. "A very impressive career indeed. A personal detail, perhaps?"

"I can't think of any right now," Lena said, in the same curt tone with which she had rebuked me in Córdoba when I'd inquired about a possible boyfriend.

"Matt Cox," said her neighbor, a fair-haired giant with a mouthful of teeth and an unmistakable American accent. "I'm from Lansing, Michigan. I played first base on the Georgia Tech baseball team. I've worked in the Chicago, Taiwan, and Nairobi bureaus. I also spent some time in Honolulu, but that was for my brother's stag party. We may have won a prize, but honestly I can't remember."

His joke made everybody laugh, except Lena, who turned bright red.

"This is the first time I've been in Europe," Matt added. I really liked him, although by now someone should have told him that Krasnoyarsk is in Asia.

We continued to introduce ourselves sequentially. The number of nationalities represented made me dizzy: two Italians, a Japanese, two Americans, a Brazilian woman, an Irish woman, a German, a

Russian, a Ukrainian, two Indians, a Chinese woman, a Nigerian, an Australian, a South African woman, a Danish woman, a Frenchman, an Icelander, and, of course, the inevitable Mexican. I didn't know anyone besides Stéphane and Lena, and I sensed that my former superior hadn't been exactly delighted to see me in the cafeteria that morning.

Her presence hadn't surprised me. Having been deposed together, it was only natural that we should be reinstated together. In any case, Lena had as much right to be in the Academy as I did.

While everyone gave their little speech, I had time to study her. She had cut her hair to shoulder-length, a style that emphasized the sternness of her face but also made her even more attractive. She was wearing a gray woolen roll-neck sweater. Hitherto I had only seen her in summer clothing. I sighed, thinking of all the agony I would undergo: Lena in the snow, Lena with a *shapka*, Lena warming herself by the fire…

After the last student, a young Irish woman named Aoifa with flaming red hair and a porcelain complexion, had introduced herself, Quinteros glanced at his watch and resumed speaking.

"Your first class will begin in fifteen minutes. In the meantime, I'd be happy to answer any questions."

"What are the aims of the CFR?" asked Amanda Postlethwaite, the South African woman sitting next to Matt Cox.

It was reassuring to realize that we all shared the same anxieties.

"That's a rather blunt question, don't you think?" Quinteros replied impassively.

"Not really," Amanda said, unfazed. "Put yourself in my shoes. I've been working for the CFR for ten years now, and, every time I've brought up this subject, my superiors have explained that my level of accreditation didn't give me access to that information. Today I'm told that I'm one of the select few, and that I'm going to spend the next thirty-six months of my life in a place where the outside temperature is only occasionally higher than my freezer's. I'm sure you'll agree that in such circumstances a clarification doesn't seem completely irrelevant."

It was well aimed, but it would have taken more than that to throw Quinteros.

"I understand your impatience," he said, "but I fear that once again we'll have to postpone that discussion."

"Will we at least receive an answer by the end of our stay here?" I insisted. Several of my fellow students nodded their support.

"It's possible," Quinteros said vaguely. "But certainly not today."

"Are you a member of the Executive Committee?" Stéphane asked.

"Why do you ask?" Quinteros retorted, suddenly on the defensive.

"Because I'd like to know if you're a member of the Executive Committee," Stéphane replied with disarming simplicity.

"The composition of the Executive Committee is confidential," Quinteros said, taking his handkerchief from his sleeve and turning it in his hand in search of a clean corner.

"Where does the money come from?" Matt Cox asked, with a broad smile that revealed dozens of impeccably straight teeth.

"The Academy's budget is voted on by the Executive Committee and financed equally by the main bodies, the managerial directorates, and the local units," Quinteros replied, recovering his self-assurance now that administrative questions were being tackled.

"Yes, but where does the money come from?" Cox insisted.

Quinteros mopped his brow, then consulted his watch again, making it obvious that he didn't like the turn the conversation had taken. "We'll discuss that later in the year. I can't disclose any more today."

He quickly gathered his notes, mentally measuring the distance to the door.

"Good, I'm now going to leave you in the hands of your instructor, Leopold... Yes, Vitaly?"

Vitaly, a half-bald Ukrainian, had raised his hand high enough to make it impossible for Quinteros to ignore him.

"What kind of relationship does the CFR maintain with the Russian authorities? We're in a building that used to belong to the KGB, isn't listed in the phone book, and doesn't appear on any map. I can only suppose that the CFR, or at least this establishment, enjoys protection at the highest levels of the Russian Federation. Am I correct?"

For an instant, I thought Quinteros was about to make a dash for the door, confident that no one would attempt to intercept him. But he finally replied, choosing his words carefully:

"We maintain very cordial relations with the regime, or rather with the Russian people. Yes, that's a more accurate way to express it: we're friends with the Russian people and... uh... in sympathy with the Russian soul. Now, if you'll excuse me."

And he rushed out, leaving us to ponder his last words. Vitaly yelled angrily at his neighbor in a language I didn't understand. Stéphane stood up to stretch his legs, and I followed suit. Our instructor hadn't yet arrived.

"Dartunghuver..."

I turned. Thorsen stood there, her features more closed than ever. In spite of myself I breathed in her scent, which I'd thought I had forgotten.

"Hello, Lena," I said, unable to give my words the biting tone I might have wished.

"Hello. Listen, we're going to spend three years in this bunker, and we'll have to meet from time to time, even work together."

"Yes, that's quite likely," I said, wondering if she was about to produce an olive branch from her sleeve.

"There's no way I can prevent you from crossing my path..." she went on.

"That's very kind of you," I said, mentally dismissing the olive branch theory.

"Let me finish. I'm just asking you never to speak to me for any reason other than a strictly professional one. You've caused me enough harm as it is."

And she turned on her heels, leaving Stéphane, who had heard our entire exchange, to comment admiringly.

"Professional, I don't know. But beautiful and cold, indisputably."

3

Gunnar often said that he stopped fearing the agents he had recruited would defect the day they entered the Academy. I wasn't yet ready to swear that I would end my days in the CFR, but I could understand Gunnar's remark. How could one not feel flattered by being included among the select few who would one day run one of the most secret organizations in the world? Was there any other employer capable of investing so much in the training of its future leaders? And what would the human resource managers of large multinationals have thought of a course that lasted three years, when they already balked at financing programs that lasted only a week? Perhaps only military academies could validly be compared with Krasnoyarsk.

The analogy didn't end there. The weekly timetable, distributed each Sunday evening, controlled our time with martial rigidity. Most of the courses — or modules, as Quinteros called them in his abominable business jargon — consisted of two half-day sessions a week for six or eight weeks. During these periods, the instructors, often former Academy students themselves, were quartered with us in the residence.

Some instructors, however, gave but a single lecture. They would arrive by Zil toward the end of the morning, have lunch with Quinteros in his private dining room on the upper floor of the hunting lodge, deliver their speech, and then return by plane to their units.

Occasionally, a visitor would land by helicopter on a prepared strip behind the study building. That revealed a great deal about the financial resources of the CFR, which bore such extravagant expenditures unflinchingly. Even after a great deal of thought, I would have been hard-pressed to name another location as inhospitable and expensive as Krasnoyarsk. Greenland and Tierra del Fuego come to mind.

The teaching program left nothing to chance. The first year began with a series of modules dealing with the workings of the CFR: its hierarchical structure, its financing, the roles of the bodies, recruitment techniques, etc. I'll come back later to the main lessons I gleaned from these classes, the basic purpose of which was to harmonize the agents' varying degrees of knowledge.

In my case, for example, my stay in Córdoba had given me a solid grounding in the links between branches, bureaus, and centers, but had taught me nothing about the challenges faced by the organization's recruiting agents, or about the strict budgeting discipline imposed by the financial division on the various entities.

By the end of the first semester, we all knew equally as much — or as little — about the CFR. Three months of intensive lectures had methodically leveled out eight years of individual experiences.

Then, during the remainder of the year, we alternated theoretical classes and sessions of practical work. I found that I preferred the latter, which took the form of case studies. Typically, our instructor would present us with a real situation, then raise a specific problem, to be solved by the next day. These hypothetical cases, conceived by actual agents, almost always awakened familiar echoes in me. I even recognized the influence of specific dossiers that had passed through my hands in Córdoba, like the one on Corporate DNA.

The theoretical classes dealt with the most eclectic and often the most unexpected subjects: literary techniques, information technology, geopolitics, military history, etc. We might discuss the Jewish Kabbalah in the morning, the strategic importance of the Suez Canal in the afternoon, and after dinner the role of vernacular languages in building independence movements.

The quality of the teaching was quite simply magnificent. I don't recall a single bad class in three years at the Academy. Some instructors left an indelible impression, like that Romanian professor of Russian literature at the University of Bucharest, who taught us how to characterize a protagonist without ever describing him; or the former colonel from Texas, who told us how the U.S. Army had lost domestic public support during the war in Vietnam.

They all dazzled me with their ability to rise above dogmas and prejudices. This held even for those who had grown up under a totalitarian ideology, such as the Armenian whose father had been deported under Stalin for economic crimes, and who was now lecturing on the flaws in capitalism.

It should also be said that on the most polemical subjects, e.g. the Inquisition, colonialism, or the rights of minorities, the CFR took care to present all sides of the argument.

I obviously appreciated the fact that our leaders recognized, even sometimes sanctified, the complexity of the world. Nothing is black or white, and, as several lecturers reminded us, history is always written by the victors.

But that didn't prevent our instructors from calling a spade a spade, even if it meant offending those who believed in being politically correct, of which there were some even in our ranks.

I remember one lecture with an apparently innocuous title, "The innate and the acquired", that sparked heated controversy when the lecturer, an Englishman named Wilkin, presented the results of a study purporting to demonstrate that black Americans had a slightly lower intelligence quotient than the national average, while their fellow countrymen of Asian origin scored higher than average in almost equal measures. Several students — including Stéphane and Buhari, the only black person among us that year — immediately protested and threatened to leave the room if Wilkin did not immediately condemn the study. The Englishman had clearly anticipated such an outcry. In wonderfully chosen words, he explained that, although he personally eschewed partisan political interpretations, he would never criticize the very principle of a study, especially if it was conducted in accordance with strict scientific protocol, as in the present case.

"Beware of reversing logical order. A scientist needs all the information available. If he abstains from collecting certain data because they might contradict or even disprove his interpretation of the world, he betrays his vocation as an objective scientist and becomes a censor. The results of the study I have described are indisputable, but the debate clearly does not stop there. Scientists now have to choose one of three possible explanations: that the protocol was defective (current IQ tests have a built-in bias that disadvantages blacks and, to a lesser extent, whites in favor of

Asians); or that intelligence, which is traditionally considered innate,, actually includes an acquired component (the social hypothesis), in which case the inferior results obtained by blacks could be explained by the fact that most grow up in comparatively less privileged environments; or that blacks are inherently less intelligent than the other races (the genetic hypothesis).

"Those who refuse to engage in discussion do a disservice to those whom they claim to defend. By abandoning science, they leave the field to charlatans and populists. They would do better to give up the notion that an individual is just a set of complex statistics and to devote their energies to educating the masses, who are really in need of intellectual stimulation and improvement."

At the conclusion of his formal lecture, all the students had returned to their seats, and a lively discussion began.

Stéphane subsequently admitted that Wilkin's speech had led him to revise his mindset. (I've always thought that after a certain age changing one's mind is evidence, not of inconsistency, but of courage.)

The brilliance of my fellow students impressed me at least as much as that of our instructors. Some projects were carried out in small groups, so that within a few weeks I came to know the nineteen other students, at least superficially. We got along well, which was doubtless as much a function of natural curiosity as of fear of being excluded from the cliques that would inevitably form.

In any case, camaraderie wasn't incompatible with the spirit of competition. The first sessions of practical work, in which participation was strongly encouraged, unequivocally established that every one of us deserved his or her place in Siberia. I had thought I could slack off and simply rely on my innate abilities, but I soon realized that I would need to work hard if I wanted to remain master of my own fate.

The first months were the most intense, as nobody had yet given up hope of ending up at the top of the rankings. All of us kept track of our neighbors' marks, while claiming to be concerned only with our own. Each of use managed stress differently. Stéphane would tell anyone who'd listen that he didn't do a stroke of work (which I strongly doubted, knowing his diligence); conversely, Amanda, the South African, who admitted to me several years later that she had sometimes gone to bed with her light on in an attempt of make us believe that she was cramming all night.

Not everyone was dissembling. Every midnight, the librarian had to evict the ten or so students who were still poring over encyclopedias under the green lamplight. At breakfast, one could recognize from their pale faces those — among whom I was often one — who had continued studying in the solitude of their rooms.

When I found a case intriguing, I was capable of working all night to track down the person or the source that would decisively improve a dossier's profit-to-risk ratio. My youth gave me an indisputable advantage over other, older agents, who found it hard to get back into the rhythm.

I had the impression I had never left school. For ten years now, I'd been handing in exercises: to my university teachers, to Gunnar Eriksson, to Lena Thorsen, and now to the Academy's instructors.

One aspect, though, had changed: the invention of the internet, which made research so accessible. I won't claim that as soon as I arrived in Krasnoyarsk I foresaw the central role that the World Wide Web would end up playing in our lives, but I soon intuited that it presented an extraordinary opportunity to the CFR and that in the long run this new technology would generate a phenomenal increase in productivity.

The scenario writers, much of whose work consisted of immersing themselves in texts, could effortlessly develop their ideas through, and could discover, through hypertext links, the unlikely connections from which enlightenment would come.

The falsifiers had perhaps even more to gain: launching rumors, creating reference sources, corrupting databases became child's play for those who mastered the internet's grammar and learned to cover their tracks.

Quinteros, who could more easily be imagined with a quill pen in his hand than a mouse, was quick to realize the extent of this revolution, and he accordingly introduced a number of optional seminars into the program, in which Russian specialists whom I suspected of being in the pay of the KGB, taught us the basic techniques of computer piracy. Lena and I never missed a session.

After two years in Córdoba, during which I'd often felt like a fish out of water, I was finally in my element. The course seemed to have been conceived expressly for me, playing to my strengths and mitigating my weaknesses. The polar cold, the workload, the intense competition: none of these things caused me to regret having returned to the fold.

Every day I rubbed up against the sharpest minds on the planet, men and women who, notwithstanding of their ethnic, cultural, or religious differences, spoke a common language and constantly tried to learn from each other. But, above all, I felt an almost permanent intellectual joy, a kind of pleasure that's superior to any other and very fortunately remains accessible to us all through our lives.

Anything could bring it about: the name of a legend, too good to be true and in fact false; Angoua Djibo's *Quarterly Reports on the Progress of the Plan*; the revelation that an idea for a dossier that had suddenly occurred to one of us had already been articulated by a Slovenian agent seven years earlier; the delightful sensation of manufacturing international news from the depths of Siberia.

And yet, even though I had chosen once again to link my destiny to that of the CFR, I remained constantly on my guard. I mistrusted my own instincts. The more spontaneous an impulse was, the more suspect it seemed. I gave no credit to our leaders' words unless I could verify them for myself.

For example, I was highly skeptical of the famous revelations that had been so carefully dispensed to us during the first classes. What had we learned? That only the members of the Executive Committee know the origins and aims of the CFR, and that we would be wasting our breaths asking any further questions. That its six members coopted one another and made their decisions collectively, without anyone having a casting vote. That the organization was funded by one or more founders, and that it had subsequently achieved massive profits. That the funds were managed by three of the best-known financial institutions in the world, who believed they were working for an American foundation.

All in all, I viewed this information positively. I wouldn't be learning the secrets of the CFR any time soon, but at least it was up to nobody but me to get there one day; I had six times more chances than I'd previously thought of getting to the top of the organization.

Moreover, the CFR seemed rich enough to withstand the temptation to use its expertise ill-advisedly. Nor had I found anything to criticize about the "three pairs of founding values," to use the expression Quinteros solemnly favored us with one day: tolerance and relativity, freedom of body and mind, science and progress. This motto seemed to sum up the main attributes that had attracted me in Gunnar Eriksson and Angoua Djibo.

These favorable impressions were partially offset by the cowardice of a Diaz or the cruelty of a Khoyoulfaz. I had learned the hard way that the essence of the CFR lay at least as much in what it kept quiet as in what it celebrated.

Unfortunately — or, for them, perhaps fortunately — my fellow students lacked my depth of experience. Their naiveté astonished me. They protested when our instructors didn't answer their questions, but it barely crossed their minds that they were being misled.

For example, when the financial director described the resources he had at his disposal, Stéphane Brioncet turned to me and whispered in my ear:

"At least we know now that the CFR isn't the sixth family of the Mafia."

I immediately replied: "Oh, really? Do you think he would have told us if it were?"

I didn't have the heart to upset Stéphane. I, too, had initially taken my case officer's words at face value. And if it had required a man's death for me to learn to read between the lines, could I decently wish the same insight on every student of the Academy?

Meanwhile, I conscientiously avoided the birthday parties and other celebrations that my fellow students organized at the slightest opportunity. Oh, of course, I was always urbane, ever a good comrade, but I didn't confide in anybody. In another life, I might well have become friends with Amanda or Ichiro, the Japanese, but I quite simply couldn't summon up the strength. Although they were six or seven years older than I, I felt too mature for them, wise beyond my ears. Their innocence touched me sometimes, but more often it dismayed me. And how ironic it was that the only person in the Academy with whom I could have talked on equal terms was the very one who refused to speak to me...

The first months were the hardest. Nobody wrote to me, nor did I initiate correspondence with anyone. Gunnar didn't put in an appearance; I assume he got his news directly from Quinteros. I missed Youssef and Magawati, but I anticipated rejection were I to approach them, and I didn't feel strong enough to be rejected.

I assuaged my solitude by exploring the surrounding area, which was transformed when the warmer weather arrived. According to popular belief, the word Siberia derives from a Turkish term which means "sleeping land." As in a fairy tale, the forest was just awakening from a night that had lasted eight months. Life was gradually reasserting itself. The snow had melted, revealing a boggy, spongy soil that the Mongols had once used as fuel. The trees—conifers and birches—rose under the pressure of the spring sap to face the assaults of the beavers emerging hungry from their lairs and planting their teeth in the fresh bark. Sturgeons, previously confined beneath a meter of ice, swam lazily with their bellies in the sun. Just a short distance from the Academy, one could see herds of reindeer on their way back to the tundra where they would spend the summer, as they had done annually for thousands of years.

The more alone I felt, the more I sought isolation. I would leave, without telling anyone, for two hours or two days, with a rucksack on my back and my binoculars around my neck. When I was tired of walking, I would close my eyes and fill my lungs with that indescribable aroma, a mixture of woody scents, methane and pollen, which reminded me of the Icelandic forest.

More than once, it occurred to me that I could easily become lost. I fantasized about who would be the first to notice my absence. My body would never be found.

The Academy and nature: I should have been happy, but I wasn't. I was doing well in my professional life, but I lacked a personal one. I was gradually become a machine — a machine for polishing scenarios and checking sources. Even in the depths of my distress, I remained aware of the beauty of the world; I was spared the ultimate punishment, but I felt socially inadequate.

Never before had my connection with humanity seemed so tenuous.

4

The first marks were awarded in June, and with them some students' hopes were dashed. The rankings, updated every week, were posted at the back of the classroom. I managed to remain in the top three, along with Lena Thorsen and Ichiro Harakawa. I had hoped it would be easier, but it would have been inappropriate to complain.

At the beginning of September, a series of good marks put me temporarily in the lead. It didn't make me particularly cheerful. Rather, I calculated that, absent an accident, I was already assured of being able to choose to which body to be assigned to at the end of the year. That meant I'd be able to relax enough to tackle a project that really interested me: writing a fourth dossier.

When I informed Quinteros of my intentions, he stared at me as if I had taken leave of my senses. Was I going to risk compromising my future for a dossier that could wait another year or two? As a special favor, he offered to submit a preliminary request on my behalf — an extremely rare procedure in which an agent reveals the broad outlines of his scenario in exchange for the assurance that London will block any similar projects for a limited period.

With all due modesty, I told Quinteros that I felt capable of fitting the writing of a dossier into my schedule, and that I wouldn't in any way permit my pet project to interfere with his treasure hunt. Actually, I felt an energy inside me that my walks in the forest were not enough to dissipate.

Quinteros reluctantly accepted my arguments and then, like a skilled gambler, offered his help. I was going to need it.

I had found the inspiration for this dossier one year earlier during my stay in Bremen, when the TV channel ARD had broadcast a program about the former East German police, the Ministärium für Staatsicherheit, better known as the Stasi. As former leaders of the Stasi confessed, the grip it had exercised on German society during the Cold War it was becoming ever clearer. For example, the Stasi's ranks included a special cell tasked with anonymously sending threatening letters to West German Jews announcing a resurgence of the far right. It had files, not only on all the major figures in West and East Germany, but also on hundreds of thousands of ordinary citizens, whose only crime might have been providing directions to a foreign tourist.

The report had become even more interesting when it broached the subject of the Stasi's records. In 1989, sensing that the end was near, the leaders of the Stasi ordered the destruction of all compromising documents, i.e., more or less everything stored in file cabinets in its headquarters on Normannenstrasse. Millions of pages were put through shredders that hadn't been designed to withstand such a heavy load and soon malfunctioned, forcing the employees to resort to tearing up manually as many sheets as possible.

After the Wall fell, the BND — the West German counter-intelligence service — seized more than seventeen thousand sacks containing a comprehensive record of the secret activities of the former East Germany, torn into thin printed strips.

The story didn't end there. Realizing the symbolic significance of these sacks, Chancellor Kohl had entrusted them to a team of experts in Zirndorf and assigned them the task of reconstructing the torn pages to the extent feasible. In their haste, the secretaries of the Stasi had shredded some documents width-wise rather than length-wise. Whole lines were distinctly legible, and with a bit of luck and much patience, the experts should be able to recover paragraphs, or even entire pages.

For those who might suspect a hoax, the report ended with some fascinating images, including one of a potbellied fellow — Karl Vollbrecht, a professor of modern history at the University of Heidelberg according to the caption — searching through a heap of confetti and extracting some promising strips, which he then attempted to piece together. If it hadn't been for a melodramatic description of "the German people's necessary effort of memory", one might easily have taken Professor Vollbrecht for a retire doing a jigsaw puzzle.

The same thought must have crossed my brother-in-law's narrow mind, because, switching off the TV, he had linked the Zirndorf experiment to recent tax increases. For my part, I had no idea if Kohl was right or wrong, but I knew that I had something. The sacks of shredded records could help me construct what I had always found the most difficult part in a dossier: a reference source.

But first, I had to invent a scenario. In the months after my stay in Bremen, I had researched about the Stasi extensively. As was my habit with any promising subject, I had bought a notebook in which to jot down my thoughts, notes on my characters, and bibliographical references.

Ever since Gunnar had had to explain to me what a legend was, I had read everything available about espionage, and I was eager to produce a dossier that would be set in the world of the Secret Service.

In consequence, I became interested in the Hauptverwaltung Aufklärung (HVA), the most mysterious body within the Stasi, and the East German equivalent of the American CIA or the First Directorate of the KGB.

Led with a rod of iron by Markus Wolf between 1957 and 1986, the HVA had embedded abroad thousands of agents, whose mandate was to deliver top-secret information.

One such agent, a German named Günter Guillaume, had led an extraordinary career. Sent to West Germany in the 1950s for the purpose of infiltrating the political inner sanctum, he had gradually climbed the rungs of the SPD, the Social Democratic party, and eventually become a personal assistant and friend to Chancellor Willy Brandt.

In 1973, however, anonymous sources drew the attention of the BND to Guillaume's activities. The West German secret police immediately informed Brandt, but asked him not to change his routine for the time being. Curiously, Guillaume was not arrested until April 1974.

The ensuing scandal was huge. It did not spare Brandt, who at first considered taking his own life (a suicide note that he had written was subsequently found), then changed his mind and simply resigned.

Fifteen years later, after the fall of the Berlin Wall, Markus Wolf declared that he had never intended to bring Brandt down, and that the unmasking of Guillaume was one of the Stasi's bitterest failures.

Two elements in the story of Günter Guillaume defied plausibility. First, the HVA, the secret branch of the Stasi, was an elite body, hardly less feared and respected than the Israeli Mossad. It was said that Guillaume's boss, Markus Wolf, had been John Le Carré's model for the spymaster Karla in *Tinker, Tailor, Soldier, Spy.* I found it hard to believe that such a professional, who actually "handled" Guillaume directly, could have allowed his agent to be compromised and trapped in the Federal Republic.

The behavior of the BND in this affair was no less puzzling. The West German Secret Service had taken almost nine months to make up its mind to arrest Guillaume, a span during which he had continued to betray state secrets and could even have made an attempt on the life of Brandt, whom he saw every day.

How could the BND have been so lacking in its duty? I could only speculate: had Brandt initially refused to believe his friend's guilt at first and forbidden the Secret Service to arrest him? That was quite possible: Brandt and Guillaume had even taken vacation together.

Or had the BND caught and "turned" Guillaume, forcing him to feed the Stasi false information? That also seemed possible.

Or had the BND mistrusted the motives of its informant and hesitated to accuse Guillaume without proof? Without being able to explain why, I sensed that this third hypothesis was the most plausible.

Pursuing my research, I unearthed another scandal. In May 1972, Chancellor Brandt had barely survived — by only two votes in a secret ballot — a motion of no confidence in Parliament.

Twenty-five years later, many historians believed that Brandt had owed his political longevity to the defection of a handful of Christian Democratic deputies whose votes had been purchased by the Stasi. This episode, provided it was authentic, provided support for Markus Wolf's assertion that the Stasi, which had been willing to bribe members of Parliament in order to keep Brandt in power, had certainly not been pleased to see him resign.

I tried to put myself in Wolf's place. It had taken him twenty years to place an informant at the summit of the West German state. At that point, it was clearly in his interest for Brandt to remain Chancellor for as long as possible.

But the Stasi's benevolence toward Brandt may have had another explanation. Upon taking office, Brandt had distinguished himself from his predecessors by developing a policy of openness toward the Eastern bloc. No one was yet talking about reuniting the two Germanies, but Brandt declared that he wasn't afraid of entering into a dialogue with the DDR, Poland, or even the Soviet Union.

Such pragmatism, which got under the skin of the Conservatives, made the Chancellor extremely popular with the younger voters and with the intelligentsia.

It had taken me several months to assemble all these elements, and above all to immerse myself in the extraordinarily complex climate of the period. Finally, one evening, I felt ready to fill in the blanks of history and set about writing the scenario. This was my hypothesis:

There existed within the HVA a small group of officers resolutely — but secretly — opposed to the West German Chancellor. They were led by one Andreas Stepanek, a highly politicized Czech immigrant with the rank of colonel in the Stasi. Stepanek was instinctively suspicious of Brandt, whom he considered a Machiavellian schemer. In his opinion, the Ostpolitik complacently described by the Western media was a trap laid by the Chancellor in order to soften up the East German population and make it swallow, when the time was ripe, a reunification that would irrevocably tear the Socialist bloc apart.

Stepanek had good reason to hate Germany. His parents, who had been involved in the creation of the Czech Communist Party in 1921, had been deported by the Nazis and died at Terezin in 1943. Upon liberation, young Andreas, now an orphan, had been placed with a foster family in Magdeburg. He had joined the Young

Communists, where he had been spotted by Erich Mielke, who would later become head of the Stasi. In 1962, Mielke had written to his "colleague and friend," Markus Wolf (actually his subordinate) asking him to find a place for Stepanek in the HVA.

Stepanek was a fanatic. He strongly favored German reunification, but one managed by the DDR, which would presage all of Western Europe falling into the Soviet fold. At the end of the 1960s, he recruited fifteen other Stasi officers, most of them his colleagues in the HVA. Not all were motivated by ideology. One had a handicapped child whom he couldn't afford to have treated in the West. Another bore a grudge against Brandt, who, while the mayor of Berlin, had had an affair with his wife (Brandt was a notorious lothario). A third had killed a policeman in Munich before the war and knew he would go to prison if reunification came.

But alliances of convenience are not necessarily transient, and as soon as Brandt became Chancellor, the conspirators — who resisted the temptation to form an organization or otherwise to identify themselves — did everything in their power to enlist the Christian Democrats in their cause. To them, an unequivocal enemy was preferable to a charismatic maverick with doubtful intentions.

In 1972, Stepanek thought the day of glory had arrived. The CDU was getting ready to propose a motion of no confidence which, in all probability, would bring about the fall of the Brandt government. The newspapers were already declaring the leader of the CDU, Rainer Barzel, to be the next Chancellor of the Federal Republic of Germany.

However, against all expectations, Brandt saved his skin. When Stepanek learned that the Stasi had bought the votes of two parliamentarians in the CDU (who ought to have voted against Brandt but had in fact supported him), he flew into a rage against Markus Wolf and realized that, if he wanted to bring about Brandt's rapid fall, he would have to take matters into his own hands.

Luck was on his side. In the spring of 1973, Stepanek had dinner with his mentor, Erich Mielke. Mielke wasn't accustomed to sharing a meal with someone he trusted totally. That evening he overdid the schnapps somewhat and he let slip precious confidences.

The HVA had a highly placed source within the Brandt administration. That bastard Wolf (the two men hated each other) refused to reveal the identity of his agent, even to him, the head of the Stasi, but he had come to the conclusion that the person in question could only be Guillaume.

Stepanek, who had so far skillfully oriented the conversation, took care not to insist. He was already plotting to hand Guillaume over to the BND.

He deliberately chose a traditional method. He recruited the services of a Czech call girl named Eva Brzyna, who lived in West Berlin and whom he had already used a few years earlier to compromise a Bavarian industrialist.

Obviously BND would never trust the word of a prostitute, so Stepanek had hatched a plan: the next time Brzyna took part in a "private party," he would anonymously inform the West German vice squad, which would mount a raid and haul everyone in. Brzyna would then offer the police a deal: if she were guaranteed impunity, she might be able to help the German state to unmask a crook, one of her clients, whom she had once surprised sending coded messages from a strange little machine, and whom she had recognized soon afterward in a "photograph of the government" (it was Stepanek who had provided her with this deliberately vague phrase).

Everything went as planned: the vice squad interrupted an orgy in which a number of major figures in Hamburg high society were taking part, nabbed half a dozen prostitutes, then turned an interested ear to the deal that Brzyna proposed as soon as she was threatened with prosecution.

That very night, an official from the BND came and showed some photographs to Eva, who formally identified Günter Guillaume. Once released, Brzyna waited for a few days, then resumed contact with Stepanek and collected her fee of one hundred fifty thousand Deutschmarks.

Weeks passed, and Stepanek became increasingly nervous. Guillaume was still accompanying Brandt everywhere, with a smile on his lips and dark glasses on his nose.

Brzyna's revelations had not passed unnoticed, however. The BND considered them credible, at least on the surface. Guillaume was known to enjoy the company of women, including professionals.

The BND had nothing on Brzyna. Of course, there was the matter of her Czech origin, but she had been a legal resident of Germany for nearly twenty years, and nothing indicated that she had ever worked for Moscow in any way, shape or form.

But Stepanek, his position notwithstanding, had formed only a meager knowledge of counter-intelligence techniques. Otherwise, he would have known that the head of the BND, Gerhard Wessel, always thought long and hard before doing anything. In fact, Wessel limited his actions to informing Willy Brandt and to ordering an investigation into Guillaume. By a chance that was less extraordinary than may appear (the Stasi had infiltrated the whole police apparatus of West Germany), one of the investigators worked for Wolf, who then realized that Guillaume's days were probably numbered.

As he was not one to see an agent compromised without intervening, he asked his contacts in the BND for the name of the person who had denounced Guillaume. Informed of the role played by Brzyna, and advised that she was not known to the West German police, he instinctively searched the Stasi's records and found a file on Eva Brzyna.

In it, he read that, in a minor operation managed by Colonel Stepanek, Brzyna had helped to compromise a Bavarian businessman. Stepanek? The Stepanek whom he had hired at Mielke's request? It took Wolf less than three minutes to reconstruct most of what had happened.

What he could not work out, he obtained by torture. The interrogation took place in a small soundproof chamber in the cellars of Normannenstrasse. Stepanek blustered at first, then confessed when Wolf set out to test his capacity for conducting electricity. He provided myriad details, including some that were not requested, notably the names of his fourteen coconspirators. Wolf took lots of notes.

What happened next was unfortunately predictable. Wolf called on the services of all his agents in the BND to impede the investigation as much as possible. He leaked the fact that Eva Brzyna had occasionally worked for the Stasi, hoping that the BND would then suspect an attempt at destabilization coming from East Germany and would therefore hesitate to accuse Guillaume.

Guillaume himself had already suspended his illicit activities. Having inferred from Brandt's silence that the Chancellor did not believe in his guilt, so he refused Wolf's offers to extricate him.

Wolf did not hold his counterparts in the BND in high esteem, but he never doubted that they would ultimately find a way to trap Guillaume. He was arrested on April 24, 1974. He did not conceal his surprise. That same day, a Stasi court martial found Stepanek and his collaborators guilty of high treason and sentenced them to death, which was administered immediately by bullets to the head.

5

"Let me guess: I assume your dossier falls within the sixth instruction of the three-year plan," Quinteros said, in Spanish.

Having handed in my scenario the previous evening, I was surprised to be summoned so quickly to discuss it.

"Absolutely," I replied, a touch apprehensively.

Angoua Djibo and his team had noted that after the brief period of euphoria that had followed the disappearance of the Iron Curtain, several Eastern European countries and former Soviet republics were being inundated by a wave of insidious nostalgia, which, in certain cases, even led them to re-elect former Communist leaders.

Consequently, the sixth instruction required the authors of all dossiers dealing with the Cold War to underline, even to emphasize the oppressive nature of these supposedly democratic states. The reason I was nervous was that I feared Quinteros might point out that, of all the former members of the Warsaw Pact, East Germany was the only one that seemed to have been unaffected by such nostalgia.

I looked out of the window while Quinteros weighed the pros and cons. Snowflakes were whirling in the morning light. After only a month, the autumn was already yielding to winter.

"It's unimpeachable," Quinteros said at last, taking the cap off his fountain pen. Holding the dossier, he meticulously retraced in ink the D6 he had penciled on the cover after a previous perusal, then added his initials. "I must say," he resumed in a slightly morose tone, "that I had been expecting something more original from you. The Brandt-Guillaume affair has already been written about extensively. What piqued your interest? The long-distance confrontation between Wolf and that paltry Czech Colonel blinded by ideology?"

"No," I replied, "I agree with you: the scenario in itself is of only minor interest. But I wouldn't say that of the treatment."

"I thought about that, of course," Quinteros conceded. "You will have to document it, fabricate the legend of Stepanek, write a police report on the arrest of Eva Brzyna, etc. I'm afraid the risks might turn out to be disproportionate to the significance of the dossier."

"I'm not so sure," I said with a smile.

And I told him about the seventeen thousand sacks of Stasi records, and about Helmut Kohl's recent decision to entrust their reconstruction to a team of specialists. As I detailed my plans, a rapid succession of disparate emotions passed over Quinteros's face: excitement, enthusiasm, incredulity.

"You mean that you intend to create the necessary sources, then shred them?" he asked, shaking his head.

"Precisely. Last week I had an intermediary purchase a second-hand shredder of the same model as the Stasi used. Nothing resembles a strip of paper more than another strip of paper. No one will realize that the reassembled documents are fakes. I know it may seem paradoxical, but never before will such sensitive sources have been so little suspected of having been doctored."

"Very clever," Quinteros murmured, visibly impressed by such audacity.

"Unfortunately there's a flaw," I sighed as if I had only just noticed it.

"A flaw? What flaw?" Quinteros asked in panic. It was amusing to see how quickly he had appropriated the dossier.

"We can't control the calendar," I explained. "According to my information, the people assembling the documents in Zirndorf typically process one sack every three months. Multiplied by seventeen thousand sacks — well, I'll let you do the math. In addition, we have to slip our fake documents into several different sacks, to take into account the fact that the files on Guillaume, Stepanek and Brzyna, among others, wouldn't have been kept in one place."

"But in that case," Quinteros protested, "the people doing the assembling won't find the sources simultaneously. How will they make the connection?"

That was a question with which I had wrestled repeatedly during my long walks in the forest. "I read that they started with the least damaged documents. I think I can work out the sizes of the strips and the direction in which the pages were fed into the shredder in order to estimate when the contents of a specific sack will be examined. And I don't care if the affair doesn't come to light right away. Guillaume and Brandt died a few years ago, but the other players are still alive, beginning with Markus Wolf and Erich Mielke…"

"Then why insist on writing your dossier now?" Quinteros cut in. "There's no urgency."

"You don't understand. The sacks won't be kept in Zirndorf indefinitely. In a few years, or perhaps less, the federal government will transfer them to the Ministry of Defense or to some other entity to which we won't have such easy access."

Quinteros's eyes lit up. "In other words, you're about to light the fuse now, but it will be a very long one."

"That's pretty much it, yes," I smiled, savoring the image. Beneath his facade of an affable bureaucrat, I could see the former agent and case officer. "I've thought a lot about the structure of the plot. It will function on several levels. At first, the people doing the assembly will come across Guillaume's file. Since I'm going to have to write it based on public documents, I obviously can't make it very long, but it will include several choice morsels: a few coded messages from Wolf in which he asks his agent to find out about certain very specific subjects; the story of Guillaume's recruitment; a psychological profile revealing his taste for high-class prostitutes; etc.

"A few years later, the people assembling the pieces will reconstruct two new sources, but won't think of linking them. The first, Eva Brzyna's file, will show how the Stasi, knowing Guillaume was under suspicion, tried to save him by discrediting the call girl's testimony. 'Stepanek' will appear for the first time, as the name of the Stasi colonel who had directed Brzyna's first operation several years earlier. The second new source will be the minutes of the top-secret trial for high treason of fifteen Stasi officers who will remain unnamed."

"I see what you're getting at," Quinteros said. "It's only some time later that they'll finally exhume the file on a certain Andreas Stepanek, who was tried, sentenced, and executed for high treason the very day that Guillaume was arrested. The BND will establish the link with the Stepanek who controlled Eva Brzyna, and will finally be able to put a name to the man who informed on Guillaume."

"Precisely," I said, impressed by Quinteros's mental agility. "Add to that the fact that the file on Stepanek will mention his special relationship with Erich Mielke, and the BND will have an insight into the internal struggles that tore the Stasi apart."

Quinteros was silent for a few moments. I could see that he was recapitulating the entire argument.

"I'm speechless," he resumed at last. "You're constructing a puzzle within a puzzle. That is brilliant."

"Thank you," I said, as modestly as possible. "I even see three puzzles: the putting together of the strips of paper, the spatial connection of the doctored sources, and the reconstruction of the story of Andreas Stepanek."

"Proceed expeditiously," Quinteros said, "so that I can put this dossier on the Academy's program for next year."

"Well," I said, "you did offer me your help..."

"You have it. What can I do for you?"

"First, I need information about the storehouse in Zirndorf: how is it guarded, whether the sacks are sealed, that kind of thing..."

"No sooner said than done. I'll call Munich immediately. What else?"

The functionary had metamorphosed into a man of action accustomed to making decisions quickly. I decided to take advantage of that.

"I also need examples of the secret codes used by the Stasi, plus a list of Guillaume's movements between 1969 and 1974."

"Mmm... I should be able to obtain those," Quinteros said, taking notes.

"And a German scholar, of course, preferably one with some experience of intelligence matters."

"You'll have all that, I guarantee."

The work on the sources took far longer than the writing of the scenario. I brought to it an almost Lena-like care. I made dozens of versions of the minutes of Stepanek's trial. I studied thousands of transmissions between Normannenstrasse and its agents in order to absorb Wolf's style and to identify his most characteristic abbreviations and turns of phrase. I forced myself to write fifteen pages on Stepanek's life, but actually used only two or three episodes from it.

I was progressing more slowly than usual, but feeling the genuine intoxication of the falsifier for the first time, even though the risks of being unmasked were minimal.

On December 5, 1996, I asked Quinteros, who was impatient to get on with it, to help me with the project's penultimate stage, which was also the most paradoxical, since it consisted of methodically destroying what I had constructed with such difficulty and of throwing a metaphorical bottle into the sea in the hope that a future generation would spot it.

One by one, the pieces of the dossier were shredded. On Quinteros' instructions, I changed the settings on the shredder between each document. When I close my eyes, I can still hear his quavering voice: "Space four millimeters. Insert lengthwise. When I give the command, go!" The machine would then spit out a few black and white strips, which I carefully collected in a pre-labeled plastic bag.

It would have been cruel to refuse Quinteros this little favor after all the help he had given me during the past few months. For example, he had unearthed a number of testimonies from former agents who had worked for Wolf and Mielke, which helped me to avoid a number of blunders that would probably have ruined the credibility of the dossier.

I had planned to sneak into the Zirndorf storehouse on the evening of December 24. The Munich bureau had secured the complicity of two of the three guards who were slated to be on duty that night. They were to call the security company at about five o'clock and claim that they had contracted an intestinal virus and were too ill to work that evening.

The dispatcher would first curse these shirkers, who had clearly taken time off to spend Christmas with their families, then realize that he no longer had time to find replacements. With only one guard and an alarm whose activation code I knew, it seemed worth a try.

Unfortunately, Quinteros didn't concur. He summoned me to his office the day before I was planning to leave for Munich.

"What's this I hear? That my best student is willing to risk ruining his career by impersonating a cat burglar? You know the house policy: we always subcontract the dirty work."

"It's a complex operation," I said in my defense. "I'm not sure I can gain access to all the sacks. I'll have to improvise. I may even have to abort the attempt."

"I don't buy that. You don't even know how to pick a lock. And what will you say if you're caught? I can see the headlines now: an Icelander doctors the records of the Stasi..."

How could I make him understand that since the gallowfish fiasco, I felt incapable of putting other people's lives at risk? It was my dossier, and I intended to take full responsibility for it.

"I've thought of all that," I said. "I'll say I'm nostalgic for the Warsaw Pact, and sought a souvenir of the Cold War."

Quinteros laughed. "That's funny. I gave exactly the same instructions to the two men I recruited. Except that they're East Germans, Berlin constructed a made-to-measure legend for them, and their neighbors will tell the BND they celebrate Erich Honecker's birthday every year. Oh, I almost forgot: they're also specialists in hand-to-hand combat, will wear night vision goggles, are trained to foil lie detectors, and won't incriminate the CFR for the very good reason that they don't even know it exists."

The son of a bitch had thought of everything. I sighed. "So I'm not going to Munich?"

"Yes, you are," Quinteros said. "You'll brief our men on the afternoon of the 24th and then wait for them at the Nuremberg airport, from where they'll leave once the mission's over."

Everything proceeded as planned. I gave my instructions to Quinteros's mercenaries in a hotel room on the outskirts of Munich. I also supplied a plan of the storehouse, which we had photographed one month earlier in the office of the architect who had designed the building. They didn't give a damn about our motives. When I tried to explain to one of them why he had to put the shredded documents into three different sacks, he stopped me and asked me to tell him the make and model of the alarm system instead.

They entered the storehouse at 8.52 P.M. and exited after exactly twenty-four minutes, just in time to catch the last flight to Berlin. They had disconnected the alarm and disabled the surveillance cameras, but the guard had noticed nothing, busy as he was watching a variety show on television. Professional to the end, the two men gave me back the plan of the warehouse and the plastic bags, then disappeared into the crowd. I realized that I didn't even know their names.

From Nuremberg, I flew to Iceland. I spent a week in Húsavík with my mother, who thought I was deputy chairman of a company commercially exploiting the Siberian forest. I arrived back to Krasnoyarsk on New Year's Eve, just in time to spend New Year in the TV room with only Charlie Chaplin for company.

During my time in Krasnoyarsk, I had developed a newfound passion for the cinema. The Academy, never miserly when it came to entertaining its boarders during the long winter evenings, owned several thousand videotapes in every imaginable combination of languages and subtitles. One just had to mention a film to the librarian and it would appear on the shelves a week later.

I watched all the Hitchcock movies, even those from his English period which are less well known than the ones he made in Hollywood; all of Fritz Lang; all of Mankiewicz. I endlessly replayed Kubrick's twelve films, with a particular fondness for the brilliant *Doctor Strangelove*.

Recently, Stéphane Brioncet had introduced me to the work of the French director Chris Marker. I had read a lot about him in connection with my *Bettlerkönig* dossier, but had never seen any of his films. According to Stéphane, Marker (the professional name of Christian François Bouche-Villeneuve) enjoyed a special aura in French intellectual circles, curiously because of his one work of fiction, a kind of photo-novel entitled *La Jetée*.

In that film, a group of scientists sends a man back into the past with the mission of collecting clues to help survivors of a devastating nuclear attack who live in the catacombs of Paris.

Whether it was the still images, the voices of the scientists whispering in German, the grainy black and white photography, or the beauty of the spoken text, the whole thing had a poetic charge that I've never found in any other film.

After that masterpiece, Marker had traveled a great deal, mostly making documentaries that might be viewed as politically committed, but which primarily conveyed his ever-renewed wonder at the beauty of the world. I would have liked to meet him.

When it came to entertainment, the Academy was no match for Adolf Hitler's bunker. During the first six months, I had spent most of my leisure time watching films and devouring the classics of South American literature — Borges, Cortázar, García Márquez, Bioy Casares. At night, when the memory of John Harkleroad kept me awake, I would drag myself to the language laboratory, don a pair of headphones, and brush up on my German and French. I learned a bit of Russian by talking with the chambermaids.

My fellow students preferred less cerebral distractions. Almost every Friday and Saturday evening, they visited the trendy nightclubs of Krasnoyarsk, where they mingled with crowds of agricultural engineers and soldiers on leave.

From my window, I would watch the girls, their faces caked with make-up, cautiously descend the icy steps of the hunting lodge and climb into the backs of the Zils. After a few hours' sleep, the most determined would even return to town on Sundays to support one of Krasnoyarsk's countless football and hockey teams. The ability of people to take up the cause of a club or a sport they'd never heard of a week earlier will never cease to amaze me. As for me, I was still loyal to the football team of my youth, Ungmennafélag Grindavíkur, which, in its sixty-one years of existence, had yet to win the national championship.

But you didn't need to be a genius to guess what most tormented the students of the Academy, eleven young men and nine young women, all unmarried, whose professional commitment seemed to condemn them to eternal celibacy. According to Stéphane, who had taken a fancy to the Irish girl, Aoifa (so far without reciprocation), the Academy represented our last chance of finding a soul mate.

In fact, he took it for granted that the members of the CFR, play the field as the might when they were young, would inevitably intermarry. He therefore concluded that we would never again have so wide a choice as during those three years in Krasnoyarsk. He urged me to get a move on: Amanda was already accounted for (she had been in a relationship with the Russian Valery since the summer); Lena avoided me as if I had the plague; and he advised me to stay away from Aoifa if I valued my life. That left me only six alternatives if I wished to graduate from the Academy with a ring on my finger.

Even had that been my aim, the misfortune that befell Matt Cox a few weeks later finally convinced me that such matters can't be rushed. We were all having dinner together in the cafeteria, when Lena arrived with her tray and stood in front of Matt, who offered to move over so that she could join us. We must have had a general premonition, because everyone abruptly stopped talking.

"Thank you, Matt," Lena said, "but I prefer to dine alone and reread my class notes. Oh, by the way, I owe you an answer." She turned toward us. "Matt proposed to me on Christmas Eve," she explained. "He showed me a diamond so big that I suspect it was stolen from the Bushmen. I asked him for a little time to think about it."

Without even glancing Matt in the eyes she proceeded:

"Obviously, the answer is 'no'. Come on, Matt, let's be serious: can you imagine me with an apron around my waist in a kitchen in Lansing, Michigan?"

Cox sat opposite me. He had been unable to avoid turning pale, but he made an effort to bounce back, summoning a courage that I've always admired in Americans. "Who said we'd live in the United States? We could live anywhere."

He should have remained silent, because Lena, who had rehearsed her answer, now delivered the knockout blow. "That's what you think. Given your current ranking, I very much doubt you'll be in a position to choose your next destination."

She turned on her heel and went and took a seat at the far end of the cafeteria, while I wondered yet again when fate would finally agree to deliver me from the company of Lena Thorsen, bitch extraordinaire.

6

The hundreds of hours I had spent on the Stasi dossier had had little effect on my performance. I was still in third place in the rankings at the beginning of the last week of exams.

The atmosphere in the residence had become noticeably more tense. People were going out less, the TV room was often empty, and it was not uncommon to encounter a fellow student with his nose in the CIA Atlas, sitting by the fire in the common room at two o'clock in the morning.

Quinteros, a real virtuoso of grades and rankings, had left nothing to chance: there were just enough marks left to be apportioned for the less well placed to still believe in their chances and for those in higher positions not to become complacent.

While I no longer doubted that I would get into one of the major bodies, only a place in the top three would guarantee that I could choose the Plan, on which I had set my heart ever since Angoua Djibo had visited us during the winter.

I had formed a better understanding of how the Plan worked. Young agents are generally familiar only with the bureaucratically turgid prose of its instructions, to which their case officers oblige them to conform scrupulously.

Over the years, I had come to consider the directives from Toronto as an intellectual barrier that could generally be bypassed with a little ingeniousness. I always put together my dossiers without referring to the Plan, confident that I would find a way to relate them to one of the directives at the appropriate juncture.

That was how *Der Bettlerkönig* had become a reflection on the theme of private property, and how the Stasi dossier turned into a fierce condemnation of the police state — two causes to which I was basically indifferent, but which I had pretended to espouse in order to obtain a rubber stamp.

Youssef worked in the opposite way. He would read the Plan thoroughly until he knew it practically by heart, then choose the directive that corresponded most closely to his personal convictions, and finally write a somewhat unimaginative scenario which he was surprised to hear described as academic.

Reflecting on his experience, I had somewhat hastily concluded that I would never find fulfillment in the Plan, which seemed better suited to more serious, less whimsical candidates than I.

The six lectures given by Djibo in January and February of 1997 caused me to reconsider my position. Listening to him, I realized that the directives logically derived from, rather than preceded, the CFR's vision on the meaning of history.

If the most recent three-year plan, for example, underlined the dangers of totalitarianism, it was because a handful of men and women, whose ranks I might soon join, had estimated that a few judiciously conceived dossiers might surreptitiously — but in a very real sense — tip the balance of the world and prevent it from falling back into the darkness from which it had only just emerged.

I already found it admirable that people from different backgrounds and cultures could form a consensus about subjects that were tearing the planet apart. The management committee of the Plan, in which all the major ethnic and religious groups were represented, had no equivalent in the world, not even at the United Nations, whose delegates never represent anything but the country that has appointed them.

The sages of Toronto, as they were nicknamed within the CFR, took an oath on the day of their appointment to serve the human race and to ignore the prejudices and dogmas that had divided nations throughout history. They relied on the work of the best historians, without judging their relative merits, but attempting instead to assimilate their collective wisdom, convinced that mankind progresses by acceptance and never by rejection.

Like all of us, they had noted the rise of the neo-conservatives in Washington, the laborious construction of the European Union, the emergence of a form of radical Islamism in Afghanistan, or the repression of human rights in China. But, unlike most of us, they resisted the temptation to award good and bad marks. They sought to understand rather than to judge, and started from the principle that, all men being equal, one part of mankind could never totally be right or wrong.

If China was taking its time liberalizing itself, that was no doubt because — at least now, at the end of the twentieth century — a country of more than a billion people could not be governed like Denmark or Singapore.

If American neoconservatives were gaining influence, that was probably because they weren't completely wrong to assert that the United States was now the sole guarantor of global security, a role that seemed to have been gradually abandoned by Europe, whose social programs absorbed an ever-growing percentage of its wealth. Toronto, Djibo asserted, was like a conference room in which an American, an Iranian, a Chinese, and a Frenchman had vowed to come to a consensus on the largest possible number of subjects, without regard to the posturing of their political or religious leaders.

"We are extremely confident about the future of mankind," Djibo had declared at the end of his last lecture. "All the indicators we use — some of which we have reconstructed over several centuries — are positive: child mortality, life expectancy, literacy, the number of victims of religious wars or epidemics all point in the right direction. The world economy experiencing an unprecedented expansion, nourished by the development of international trade and technological innovation.

"That obviously doesn't mean that everyone is profiting equally from globalization. Japan and some European nations that have lost both an appetite for work and a taste for making children are no longer thriving. The French, who are constantly talking about redistribution, can't resign themselves to sharing their wealth with the Indians or the Chinese. And yet, for every job that disappears in the West, there are ten families rising out of poverty in China and India.

What a pity that so many thinkers and journalists remain impervious to the figures that really give us an idea of the revolution that is underway. They'll tell you that AIDS is the curse of our age, pretending to forget — if they ever actually knew it — that in the year 1348 alone, the plague claimed more victims in Europe than

AIDS has in the world during the past twenty years. Or that it then took more than five centuries to eradicate the plague, whereas nobody would dare predict that AIDS will still be a killer in fifty years' time.

"If you join the Plan, we'll teach you to shed such blinders, and to consider the human race as an indivisible species that every day grows more confident in its ability to fashion its own destiny."

I'd be hard put to explain why this speech impressed me so profoundly. No doubt it articulated my vague sense of witnessing the birth of a world civilization, one still searching for a mode of governance, but more united than ever around a few key values like freedom, science, and material abundance.

For a long time, men had been able to ignore each other. Egyptians and Chinese had thought they could dominate the world without ever meeting; Catholics and Muslims had been sticking to their positions since the Crusades; the north had forgotten the south.

None of this was any longer possible. The mass media, air travel, and education had abolished distances and familiarized us with foreign lifestyles, arousing envy, rancor, or indignation in the process. Willy-nilly, the citizens of Eastern Europe had begun dreaming about cars and washing powder. Nations with a Christian heritage had discovered the iniquitous fate reserved for women in several societies; and many Muslims had felt insulted by the depravity of Western morals.

In some cases, the shock had been too sudden and had brought about unexpected consequences: nations had overthrown their tyrants, imams had decreed one fatwa after another.

But, at the same time, the instances of dialogue had multiplied — the United Nations, G8, OPEC, the Paris Club — and the discussions were proceeding apace. Virtually no one doubted any longer the necessity or learning to live together. As Chris Marker put it, "In the nineteenth century, mankind settled its account with space; the great issue of the twentieth century is the cohabitation of times."

Even though I felt I was more aware than most of my fellow students of the melody hidden in the cacophony of history, I had never imagined that I would be able to contribute toward writing the score. But that was what Djibo was offering us with his concept of historical tipping point. Every now and again, an ideology would move so far from its original mission that it would start to resemble those cartoon characters who run off a cliff but don't fall until they realize they're defying gravity.

The analysts of the Plan tried to predict several years in advance the moment when those regimes that seemed indestructible would suddenly collapse beneath the weight of their own inconsistencies. The directives they then drew up aimed at nothing less than hurrying history along, in the same way that a chemical agent forces suspended particles to form at the bottom of a glass.

Djibo responded to our incredulity by reminding us of the story of Ilie, the agent from Craiova who, with the unwitting help of CNN, had accelerated the downfall of Ceauşescu. The Romanians had known for a long time that Communism had failed, but they had never found the strength to throw out its representative. And yet the moment they were shown the images of the mass graves at Timişoara, they emerged from their lethargy and rose up *en masse*. Three days later, Ceauşescu was dead.

As Djibo said, "The Romanian regime was a wounded bull, all it took was a well-placed banderilla to finish it off." What his modesty prevented him from saying was that the three-year plan for 1989-1991 had encouraged the agents of the CFR to "expose the injustices and acts of cruelty perpetrated in the name of Communism."

Djibo's words had put me at ease. When Amanda Postlethwaite had asked him if we should interpret his historical humanism as an indication of the aims of the CFR, he had given a slight smile and replied enigmatically, "Partly, but not exclusively." The mere fact that Djibo hadn't completely evaded the question had electrified the audience. For the first time, a member of the Executive Committee had consented to lift, even if just a little, the veil concealing of our organization's *raison d'être*. It would be a long time before I was granted the supreme revelation — if I ever was — but I now felt that I could live more comfortably with my own ignorance.

The presentations by the two other bodies had seemed to me quite dull by comparison. In spite of all the efforts of Claas Verplanck, the Dutchman who ran the General Inspectorate, I couldn't imagine myself as some kind of super-controller arriving unexpectedly at a branch to evaluate the security of its transmission protocols, or to assess how well it was implementing the latest directive from Human Resources on sexual harassment. I'm obviously not unaware that every organization needs auditors, and I've always admired the devotion of those who ensure that things work smoothly, but frankly I couldn't see myself in that role.

There remained Special Operations. The ghastly Khoyoulfaz hadn't deigned to appear (he was apparently on assignment) but had sent instead his Japanese deputy, a man named Ito, who had merely reiterated in his horrible accent what we already knew: Special Operations intervened whenever the CFR was threatened; it had less than a hundred members whose knowledge of the organization's shameful secrets obliged them to maintain the strictest secrecy.

But Ito didn't need to be a brilliant speaker: Special Operations already had all the prestige it needed, and all of my fellow students dreamed of joining it. The night we celebrated the end of exams, Stéphane Brioncet even compared the "S.O. boys" to those MI6 agents with a 00 number, meaning they were licensed to kill.

I refrained from pointing out that Khoyoulfaz had an even itchier trigger finger than James Bond. Stéphane wouldn't have believed me.

The great day arrived. That morning there was a strange atmosphere in the residence; excitement at the prospect of leaving for vacation (we were generously entitled to two months' leave), mingled with fear of ending up in the bottom half of the rankings.

Unusually, we all had breakfast together, in a kind of naïve attempt to assert our solidarity just as the administration was getting ready to divide us. Anyone seeing us with our various dishes — herring fillets and rice for Ichiro, a bowl of cereal for Matt, an omelet for Amanda — would never have believed that we were a single team. Yet that morning, the camaraderie was palpable. Even Lena, who had put on an almost imperceptible touch of make-up in anticipation of the honors awaiting her, seemed cheerful and laughed at Stéphane's jokes.

Suddenly, Luis Carildo, the Mexican, commanded attention by tapping his glass with his knife. He wanted to wish us a pleasant vacation and thank us for "a magnificent year." It wasn't until I heard my neighbors burst out laughing that I realized he was imitating Alfredo Quinteros: the same pompous tone, the same meaningless adjectives, the same bombastic bureaucratic style, as he told us that, given the current geopolitical situation, he had advised the management committee of the Academy to install surveillance cameras in every toilet and shower in the residence.

Giggles turned into howls of laughter when Luis started dabbing his forehead with a table napkin, which he then stuffed into his right sleeve and pushed all the way up to the biceps (Quinteros boasted of doing two hundred push-ups every morning — one would never have believed it, seeing his tubby figure).

Then Luis took a list from his pocket and read out a "special list of prize winners" in which he awarded each student a unique prize reflecting his or her contribution to the life of the community.

The titles were lacking neither in humor nor in accuracy. Stéphane and Lena were distinguished in the category "Most Unchangeable Mood", subcategory "Good" for Stéphane and "Bad" for Lena. Vitaly was given the title of "Best Male Performer" (for singing Boris Godunov in costume in the common room) and the Chinese Ling Yi that of "Best Reference Source" (she could effortlessly reel off hundreds of economic or demographic statistics about any country in the world).

When my turn came, Luis assigned me the title of "Lonesome Cowboy" in reference to my interminable walks in the forest. I opened my mouth to protest, but perceived from everyone's laughter that the Mexican had scored a bullseye.

And I realized in a flash that I had failed my year. Oh, of course, I would come out near the top of the heap, and my Stasi dossier would remain in the annals of the CFR. But I had failed in the most basic way: by not understanding what the Academy had to offer. There I was, surrounded by nineteen of the most remarkable minds on the planet, and I had spent my year shut up in my room, cutting strips of paper and endlessly watching shorts by a French documentary filmmaker. I had been incapable of getting back in touch with Youssef and Magawati. And, last but not least, I had only once left Krasnoyarsk to play at being a secret agent in an industrial zone on the outskirts of Nuremberg. It was pathetic, and tears welled in my eyes.

Luis was applauded; then everyone stood up. It was time. I felt Stéphane touch my shoulder, but I could hardly hear his voice. It was as if I had stuffed cotton balls into my ears. The implications of my sudden insight were tormenting me. The year had slipped through my fingers like water... I would never get a chance like this again... A million dollars gone up in smoke... I had stolen the place from someone else who might have deserved it more... That morbid fascination with the Siberian *taiga*... And those words of Djibo's in Honolulu: "You have so much to learn from each other... A diversity unequaled in the world... Each of you is unique... Don't let your richness die out with you..."

I followed Stéphane like an automaton. I couldn't continue like this, deceiving everyone including myself. I had to choose between the present and the past, between the world of the living and the realm of ghosts.

I have only a vague recollection of the rest of the morning. Quinteros was wearing a freshly ironed white suit. I seem to remember that in his speech he compared the CFR to an army, of which it now fell to him to appoint the commanding officers. In any case, I was too dazed to follow his military metaphors. And anyway I might be mixing it up with another day, he held forth so often. Someone must have turned the radiators full on, for everyone was sweating profusely. Or was I the only one? For once, Lena had sat down in the back row. She would savor her triumph more fully if she could see us turn to look at her. The heat didn't seem to bother her.

At last, Quinteros took an envelope from his pocket and explained to us for the umpteenth time the protocol of the ceremony that was about to take place. Each of us, on hearing his name, was to indicate the body he wished to join, provided there were places available. Those less well ranked would be assigned to the central directorates. Surprisingly, he had forgotten to polish his shoes. He was also sweating, although less profusely than some. He dabbed his forehead with his handkerchief, the famous cloth stored in his sleeve.

Lena's was the first name to be called. Hardly surprising. Of all of us, she was the best, the most ambitious, and the hardest working. She smiled when we all turned to look at her, and I knew I'd been right. She chose Special Operations without a trace of hesitation. Only I knew what it must have cost her to place herself under the command of Yakoub Khoyoulfaz, but the potential prestige had proved irresistible. If all the best students in the Academy joined Special Operations, Lena Thorsen simply couldn't go anywhere else. A strange way to live your life, even though I hardly felt justified in teaching her lessons right now.

All things considered, the option taken by Lena increased my chances of joining the Plan. I laughed nervously at the thought that she had just rendered me a service.

"Are you feeling all right, old buddy?" Stéphane murmured. "You're sweating like a pig."

"I now call Sliv Dartunghuver," Quinteros announced, giving me no time to answer Stéphane.

I rose from my seat mechanically. That was a gaffe. We weren't supposed to stand up. Lena hadn't done so. Quinteros was erect, but that wasn't the same. Lena had chosen Special Operations. She was looking at me. Everyone was looking at me. My God, how hot it was. A wasted year. Now that I was on my feet, I couldn't sit down again. What did these people want from me? Why did people always expect so much of me?

"I choose Special Operations," I said, in a voice that didn't belong to me.

7

The temptation had been too strong.

The temptation to join the most mysterious body of the CFR, the one which, if it couldn't reveal the aims of the organization, would at least unveil some of its best-kept secrets.

The temptation to see Khoyoulfaz again, to rub shoulders with him for two years in order to answer the question that had been haunting me ever since my arrival at the Academy: how could such a coarse brute be in charge of the most sensitive unit in the CFR? I must have missed something.

The temptation to take the most difficult path once again, the one that might well cause me the most suffering, but which would one day bring me the most pride.

And last but not least — why deny it? — the temptation to follow for a while longer in the footsteps of Lena Thorsen, with whom, since my first day at Baldur, Furuset & Thorberg, I seemed to have been engaged in a fight without mercy.

I had started dreaming about the trophy for the best first dossier on the day Gunnar had told me that Lena had stumbled on the second step of the podium in Honolulu. And I was fairly certain that Lena, having been unable to bear the fact that I had been outperforming her for much of the year, had made a Herculean effort in the final weeks to pull ahead of me. Whatever our feelings toward each other, this emulation played an essential role in our mutual success. There couldn't have been more than three or four bends in the road left to the summit, but I doubt I would have mustered the courage to carry on hadn't I known that Lena was walking beside me.

As soon as I had announced my decision, I sat down again in a state of shock, regaining my composure only a few hours later, when Stéphane came to say goodbye before he left for the airport.

I hadn't expected to see him so happy, given that his seventeenth place doomed him to one of the central directorates. But Aoifa, only two positions above him in fifteenth place, was taking him to Ireland to meet her parents. They were planning to get married before the new school year began. "Under these circumstances, old man," he laughed, "I'm sure you'll understand if I abandon you to your Homeric struggle with the Valkyrie and the samurai." (Ichiro Harakawa had come third, and had also chosen Special Operations.)

The final series of exams had had little effect on the rankings. Only Matt Cox had surprised everyone by making a spectacular comeback to secure a place in the General Inspectorate. Over a beer that night, he told me that Lena's public putdown of him had been so humiliating that it had spurred him to prove his potential.

"What she did was despicable," he said soberly, "but the fact remains that I owe my ranking to her."

Decidedly, I thought, Lena had a knack for pushing men to surpass themselves.

Amanda Postlethwaite, Ling Yi (the "reference source") and Francesco Cinotti were joining the Plan. Buhari Obawan, Vitaly Orazov, Ana Gomes and Matt Cox were assigned to the General Inspectorate. Luis, our resident comedian, had placed eleventh.

That didn't deter him from proposing a karaoke session in the common room after dinner. Once again, I was startled by the size and range of the Academy's collection of discs. Luis went through the whole repertoire of the Rolling Stones. Vitaly turned out to be a big fan of the Sex Pistols and the Cure. For the first time in eighteen months, I forgot Khoyoulfaz, as Amanda and I sang John Travolta and Olivia Newton-John's duets from *Grease*.

Lena hummed along in her corner, then retired early. She, Ichiro, and I were due to meet an instructor from Special Operations on the following morning for what Quinteros billed a simple getting-to-know-you session. I didn't see any reason not to unwind, and that night I drank a great many of the tequila-vodka-grenadine cocktails that Matt kept mixing.

After a couple of hours of sleep, I opened the door of the little conference room to find Thorsen and Harakawa already seated. Lena threw a disapproving glance at my hair. Ichiro, who had drunk quite a bit too, was staring stoically at a point on the ceiling. We

335

waited for a few minutes in silence. Ichiro and I were unable to speak. And Lena usually reserved her words for her superiors.

Suddenly, the door opened, and Khoyoulfaz entered. I had been preparing myself for this eventuality since the previous day. I'll never forget that Lena's first reflex was to turn toward me, as if I had the power to make huge Azeri men disappear at will. I shrugged my shoulders in a gesture of helplessness. After all, if Khoyoulfaz was in charge of Special Operations, it was only natural that he should want to meet us as soon as possible.

"Good morning," he began, sitting down opposite us. "My name is Yakoub Khoyoulfaz, and I run Special Operations."

The mere sound of his voice was enough to sober me. But nothing in his introduction suggested that he had already met Lena and me.

"First, I'd like to congratulate you on your brilliant achievements. I've studied your files in detail and followed your rankings throughout the year, and I have little doubt that I shall have the honor of working with the three best students in the Academy.

"Special Operations is a separate unit within the CFR. Unlike the Plan or the General Inspectorate, which hire at all levels of the organization, we recruit only three new agents annually. This mode of selection has several consequences: each of us has proved his worth and his determination; there are only one hundred of us, and we all know each other; and, last but not least — and I stress this point — we're more closely knit than the five fingers of one hand.

"Our unit being so tight, and its cohesion so essential to its success, I will personally be intensely involved in your training. The lectures and the written questions are over: you'll be spending the next few years in the field, wherever the CFR needs you, always in a team with a more experienced agent. You will only return to Krasnoyarsk between assignments, and never for more than a few days…"

Something was amiss. The Khoyoulfaz who was in front of me was not the one who had knocked me senseless eighteen months earlier in Córdoba. Of course, it was the same man — the same bull-like neck, the same boxer's chest — but he seemed to have a completely different personality.

This Khoyoulfaz was impeccably dressed: navy blue cashmere suit and monogrammed tie. He expressed himself in a calm, less sonorous voice. And his tone, respectful and warm, no longer betrayed any trace of the vulgarity that had so profoundly shocked me. I couldn't imagine him calling Lena "darling" or cleaning his nails with a knife. On the contrary, he exuded a charisma to which it was difficult to remain insensitive.

"It remains only for me to wish you a happy vacation. Come back fresh and ready, because we're going to hit the ground running."

The meeting was over. But as we stood up, Khoyoulfaz grabbed my arm. I instinctively jumped and freed my arm. Lena had noticed, and her eyes were as terrified as those of a rabbit caught in headlights.

"Calm down," Khoyoulfaz whispered. Then, out loud: "Thank you, Harakawa. Dartunghuver, Thorsen, you stay with me."

Ichiro made no comment and left us. A few seconds later, the door opened once again, this time to reveal an old acquaintance.

"Gunnar!" I exclaimed. "What are you doing here?"

"It's good to see you," Lena said, clearly relieved by the sight of a familiar face. After all, I'd proved in the past that I was incapable of defending her against Khoyoulfaz. Gunnar gave me a hug and merely nodded at Lena. Then he sat down between us, on the chair previously occupied by Ichiro.

"Oh, I wouldn't have missed this moment for the world: two of my former protégés admitted on the same day to Special Operations.

"It's a first," Khoyoulfaz said, in a mocking tone. "Do you think we should put up a plaque?"

"Don't make fun of me," Gunnar replied. "This is the best day of my career."

I met Lena's eyes. Her brain was working overtime — as was mine, without any result for the moment.

"Yes, I can see I owe you an explanation," Gunnar said. "You may not like it at first, but I'm sure that in time you'll understand."

"Let us be the judges of that, Gunnar," Lena hissed. She was no longer afraid. She was just angry, hating nothing so much as being surprised.

"Of course," Gunnar said, in a conciliatory tone. He turned to me. "My story concerns you more particularly, Sliv. It begins with your arrival at Baldur, Furuset & Thorberg five years ago. I immediately recognized that I was dealing with someone exceptional. Your imagination, your intellectual curiosity, your understanding of the world placed you a notch above all my previous recruits. No offense, Lena: you know what I think of your qualities as a falsifier."

"None taken," Lena said curtly. "Proceed with your story."

"I tried to keep a cool head. Yakoub here will tell you that our most brilliant members have sometimes caused this organization its most crushing defeats. The greatest weaknesses of gifted scenario writers are carelessness and a misplaced confidence that they can wriggle out of any problem or crisis through the sheer force of their imagination. Without realizing it, they take more and more risks, thereby increasing the workloads of those charged to control them."

"I can testify to that," Lena grunted.

"It was obvious from reading your first dossier that this was the fault that threatened you," Gunnar continued, ignoring Lena's pique. "Your scenario on the Bushmen had an irresistible force and momentum, but you lacked patience and rigor. Nothing too serious yet; had you not won first prize in Honolulu, I'm convinced that you would have improved.

"Unfortunately, being awarded that trophy did you the disservice or reinforcing your bad habits. You decided, consciously or not, that the quality of your scenarios would always compensate for the mediocrity of your falsifications.

"I knew that for certain when I read your third dossier, *Der Bettlerkönig*, a wonderful project, but filled with errors that made it completely unacceptable. I realized that you had derived all that was possible from your first post, and that you would learn nothing further in Reykjavík. So I requested your transfer.

"Human Resources proposed sending you to the Hong Kong Center, which is in overall charge of falsification, so that you could learn to detect in other people's dossiers what was lacking in yours.

"I preferred to call my friend Alonso Diaz, who agreed to take you in Córdoba, where I hoped you would benefit from more personalized treatment. I couldn't predict that Alonso would fall ill before you arrived, or that Lena would be too overworked to give you the attention you required."

"I wasn't overworked," Lena said. "I was prioritizing."

"Nobody cares about that, Lena," I said, deeply annoyed. "Let Gunnar finish."

"To say that your transfer did not produce the expected results would be an understatement," Gunnar continued undeterred. "Left to your own devices, in a country and a profession about which you knew nothing, you reacted by taking ever more risks, ending up with that harebrained memo on the risks of an earthquake in Maharashtra and causing an outcry at the highest levels of the organization."

"I did warn him," Lena muttered.

I glared at her.

"A member of the Executive Committee even called me in the middle of the night to ask if you'd gone off your rocker. Who was this clown who had allowed his secret activities to affect what was meant to be his cover?

"Human Resources, which still resented my having bypassed them by calling Diaz directly, placed you under surveillance. From that day on, all the dossiers you handed over to Lena were sent in duplicate to the General Inspectorate, which carefully reviewed them to monitor your progress.

You appeared to reform for a few months. But one day, Claas Verplanck, the head of the GI, called me, incensed by your treatment of the dossier on Corporate DNA. He didn't find your embellishments amusing. Above all, he couldn't forgive you for not changing the names of Fiedler and Staransky. I'd never heard him so irritated. 'What on earth does he imagine? That Berlin has shelves full of ready-made legends? This young man must be neutralized before he drags us all down.'

"He called an emergency meeting in London to rule on your case. There were five of us around the table: Verplank's right-hand man, a representative from Human Resources, two members of the Executive Committee, and yours truly. We studied every possibility: sending you back to civilian life, putting you through an intensive course in Hong Kong, appointing you to a post in the Plan where you wouldn't have any contact with the field...

"I pleaded that you be given another chance. In my opinion, you weren't aware of the risks your actions entailed, because you assumed — wrongly, of course — that these actions concerned only you. Having been favorably impressed by your moral rectitude, I argued that you wouldn't learn your lesson until you realized that your actions had consequences on other people's lives. The representatives of the Executive Committee authorized me to set up an experiment, while making it quite clear to me that if it failed, I'd fall into disfavor with you.

"The General Inspectorate then sent me all the dossiers you'd worked on in Córdoba. I immediately chose the one on the gallowfish. People were starting to talk about the French nuclear tests in the South Pacific, and the political implications were already becoming clear. If you want my opinion, Chandrapaj didn't exactly strain himself as far as that scenario was concerned. But his sources held up. Among other things, he'd inserted in the Greenpeace report that famous graph showing the spectacular progress of the gallowfish in the region's waters, although without claiming that it came from the Ministry of Agriculture and Fisheries in New Zealand. I was the one who had that added to the two copies of the dossier kept in Córdoba.

"I then called Alonso Diaz and asked him to increase the pressure on Lena. Poor fellow, I wish I could have spared him that. What happened next, you know. Lena asked you to reopen the dossier, and you discovered the problem. I feared that you might overreact, but you surpassed yourself. When you called Wellington in the middle of the night and passed yourself off as a German journalist, you both supplied me with a dramatic motive I'd never hoped for and proved how dangerous you had become."

"I had no idea..." I murmured, feeling crushed. "I should have been told..."

"You wouldn't listen to me," Lena retorted implacably.

"This is where I entered the picture," Khoyoulfaz said — I had almost forgotten his presence during Gunnar's account. "Eriksson called me in the spring of 1995. I'd heard of you, Sliv, but when he related the whole story, I could hardly believe my ears.

"It was my idea to get rid of Harkleroad. Gunnar didn't think it was necessary to go that far, but I persuaded him you'd only learn your lesson only if a death were involved. The John Harkleroad who answered the phone that summer of '95 really does exist. But the John Harkleroad over whose grave you meditated is a legend supplied by Berlin. We cashed the checks you sent his widow in order not to alert you, but we'll refund the money. The real John Harkleroad is alive and well, as are his wife and their two little girls."

"My God," I said, unable to hold back my tears. "I'm sorry," I stammered, "it's so sudden..."
Gunnar handed me a paper handkerchief. "You don't need to apologize," he said. "We're the ones who owe you an apology."

"Especially me," Khoyoulfaz said. "I messed you up pretty badly."

"But then," I said, still skeptical, "you were playacting from beginning to end?"
"Gunnar asked me to make the scene a bit dramatic," Khoyoulfaz explained. "He didn't need to ask twice. I'd done a bit of acting in my youth, and apparently I have a tendency to ham it up. Didn't you suspect anything?"
"No," I said, searching in my memory. "Or, rather, yes, at the beginning, when you talked about young Leonid who was found with his feet encased in cement in Sydney Harbor. That was like a bad Mafia movie. And then later too, when you started eating your steak with your fingers..."

"You didn't tell me about that," Gunnar laughed. "I can see you're a stickler for detail."

"Yes, we may have overdone it a little," Khoyoulfaz admitted. "But you seemed so terrified. I think we could have made you swallow anything."

Thoughts were swirling in my head. "What about Jones?" I asked, abruptly. "I was sure he was your boss."

"That was my idea," Khoyoulfaz replied. "Guillermo works for me. A charming young man; you'll get a chance to meet him."

"And where did I fit in?"

All three of us turned toward Lena. These were the first words she had uttered since hearing Khoyoulfaz's revelations.

"Yes, me," she persisted in a high-pitched voice fully expressing her indignation. "You're telling this whole story as if only Dartunghuver were involved. But I was suspended for six months, I was humiliated in front of my team even though I hadn't done anything wrong. And all for what? So that Sliv should finally understand what I'd repeatedly been trying to tell him for two years?"

"I'm sorry, Lena," Gunnar said humbly. "You were collateral damage. Rest assured that Human Resources and the Executive Committee appreciated your unwitting cooperation. In fact they've asked me to tell you that all references to your suspension will be expunged from your file."

"And my pay?"

"Will be refunded to you in full, with interest."

"Thank you, Gunnar," Lena replied, a little calmer. "That means a lot to me."

"I can see that," Gunnar said. "More, apparently, than your relief at no longer having John Harkleroad's death on your conscience."

8

"All the same," I said, "was it really necessary?"
Gunnar and I were comfortably seated in the Zil on the way to the airport at Krasnoyarsk. Knowing that I was flying back to Reykjavík that day, Gunnar had booked a seat on the same flight. "In case you have any questions to ask me," he had explained.

"What do you mean?"

"That whole performance: Khoyoulfaz's vulgarity, young Leonid... They only had to tell me they were getting rid of John Harkleroad because of my blunder. I'd have learned the lesson just as well."

"In your head, perhaps," Gunnar said, "but not in your body. We can tell our mind stories, but we can't control our guts. I needed you to feel your guilt physically, to the point of retching at the mention of the gallowfish dossier."

"It worked," I admitted ruefully. "I throw up every time I hear the words New Zealand."

"You had to see the other side of the picture once and for all," Gunnar went on. "You had to understand that when scenario writers do something stupid, it isn't other scenario writers who get them out of trouble, but professionals who are paid to clean up other people's mistakes and whose methods it would be wrong to criticize. Special Operations come in at the end of the process. If their agents seem so brutal, it's because they have only a short space of time to sort out situations that have been degenerating for months, sometimes years. They're like a surgeon who's forced to perform an emergency operation because the physician who preceded him made an incorrect diagnosis."

"Something else bothers me: why were we asked to sign the order? I thought Special Operations dispensed with that type of formality."

"You're right," Gunnar said. "Let's just say that I wanted to see how Lena and you would react. Yakoub made no bones about his intention of getting rid of Harkleroad, but I asked him to extend the charade. I predicted that in adversity you'd both reveal your true natures."

"And...?" I asked anxiously.

"And I'm proud of you," Gunnar said. "You fought like a lion."

"A lion with blunt claws," I said with sad irony. "Khoyoulfaz knocked me out with a single blow."

"But at least you chose to fight," Gunnar replied, making no attempt to hide his bitterness. He didn't say so, but it was obvious that Lena's behavior had disappointed him.

"She was under incredible pressure," I found myself saying. "Her boss dying, dozens of dossiers piling up on her desk, and to crown it all, a subordinate who might have cost her career by doing exactly as he pleased."

"Even so," Gunnar said, lost in thought, "she behaved badly. Like the way she asked about the money we owed her. That was indecent."

His mind was made up and I wouldn't change it. We sat there for a while in silence. From time to time, our driver clicked his tongue. I was going to miss the Siberian forest, I thought, watching the snow-covered fir trees speeding past the window.

Suddenly, Gunnar asked in a strange vibrato, "You're upset with me, aren't you? I can understand that. If I'd been in your shoes, I don't know how I would have reacted."

I'd had time to prepare my response while packing my bags in the residence, and I was glad he'd asked me the question.

"No, Gunnar," I said. "I'm not upset with you. I need to think about it further, but I believe you acted out of altruism. The way I was heading, I'd have been thrown out of the CFR before long, and you thought that would have been regrettable. Perhaps you also were somewhat concerned for yourself, but I'm sure you were mainly thinking of me. You made the only decision that allowed you to turn things around. But I want you to know that I lived through eighteen terrible months. Nothing will ever erase that memory."

"All the same, I'm pleased you're taking it constructively," Gunnar said with a sigh of relief. "I think constantly about the letter you wrote me after you left Córdoba. You know, the one in which you — "

"I remember the letter," I cut in, embarrassed.

Gunnar, I would have liked to write "Dear Gunnar", but that's more than I can manage. I really liked you, Gunnar. For a while I even thought of you a bit as a father. But you betrayed me; you made me lose my self-esteem, and I can never forgive you for that.

"Please, let's just forget it," I said, looking deep into his eyes.

Gunnar's face lit up. "Oh, my boy, you don't know how happy you've made me. For a while, there..."

He looked so moved that I said, "Good Lord, Gunnar, you're not about to weep, too? Let's not mention it anymore."

"You're right," he said with a smile. "Let's talk about something else. I'm sure you have other questions to ask me."

"Yes, I do. In fact, there's one I've been dying to ask since this morning: does the CFR kill in self-defense?"

"To the best of my knowledge, that has never happened," Gunnar replied. "But it's one of the best kept secrets in the organization. You should ask Yakoub. Given his position, he must know more about the subject than I do. But I think you understand now why, in certain very unusual circumstances, Special Operations might be forced to take drastic measures."

I did understand. The question remained as to whether I could live with it.

"Please note that I'm certain of one thing," Gunnar continued. "If it has ever happened, nobody took it lightly. Such a decision can be taken only by the Executive Committee and, believe me, its members are very scrupulous and principled."

"Is Angoua Djibo on the Executive Committee?" I asked.

Gunnar nodded. His answer satisfied me, at least for the moment. I trusted Djibo.

"Do you think I was right to choose Special Operations?"

"Yes," Gunnar said. "It was the choice I hoped you'd make. Yakoub is a peerless instructor, worshipped by his troops. You'll learn an enormous amount from him. As for the General Inspectorate, I've never believed in it. You'd have been bored after a week…"

"And the Plan?"

"I'm prepared to bet that you'll end up in the Plan. You have the ideal profile: boundless curiosity, infinite tolerance, and a deep comprehension of history. By the way, I read your Stasi dossier. I wanted to congratulate you: it's far and away the best work you've accomplished to date, both the scenario and the sources."

"Thank you," I said, blushing with pleasure. Gunnar was the first to notice the care I'd taken over the falsification aspect of the dossier. "But if you think I'm best suited for the Plan, why not join it now?"

"In order not to end up like those executives in Toronto who live in a fantasy world. Oh, if only you could see them! They take their own directives as a kind of infallible guide. They think overthrowing Communism or sending a man into space is hardly more complicated than inventing an Amazonian tribe: apply a good dose of the fourth directive, add a dose of seventh instruction, put in the oven, and remove after an hour. A few years in Special Operations will teach you that matters aren't so simple."

The driver clicked his tongue again and steered the Zil onto the ramp that led to the airport. I decided to ask the question that had been nagging at me since the morning.

"Quinteros told us that only the members of the Executive Committee know the aims of the CFR."

"If Quinteros said so, I suppose it must be true," Gunnar cautiously replied.

"Do you think I still have a chance to become a member of the Executive Committee some day? Until this morning, I tended to think I did, but now, I'm not so sure. All these highly placed people who've formed a bad opinion of me can't be good for my career prospects."

Gunnar hesitated.

"Level with me," I implored him. "I have a right to know if I'm finished."

"I'm weighing my words because I don't want to give you false hopes," Gunnar replied. "But yes, I think you still have plenty of chances. If Human Resources and the General Inspectorate had wanted to dismiss you, they would have done so after the Maharashtra memo, and dispensed with that personalized test that involved dozens of people and cost a small fortune. I can't help thinking that the big wigs on the Executive Committee wouldn't be following your progress so closely if they didn't have a career path in mind for you. And you haven't made a single misstep in the past year. Your reaction to the Harkleroad affair, your ranking, the Stasi dossier: you've scored points. Quinteros just told me you hardly ever ventured out of your room…"

"That's about to change," I said. "I'm determined."

The Zil stopped outside the Aeroflot terminal. Gunnar hailed a porter and told me he'd had me upgraded.

"Academy students don't travel economy class. Didn't they tell you that in Krasnoyarsk?"

"No," I admitted. "Or else I didn't pay attention."

Gunnar shook his head. "Serious mistake, my boy. You should never turn up your nose at perks."

My mentor's attraction to status symbols remained an enigma to me. I knew his theory: since the CFR was unable to match the salaries offered by the multinationals, it didn't quibble with its agents over expenses. What bothered me was that this airport epicureanism didn't fit with the image I had formed of Gunnar as a young man: a gifted agent rapidly climbing the ladder, apparently destined for the highest offices, but whose career mysteriously stalled after he left the Academy in the mid-1970s.

What had happened at that point, and why had he been held back? Gunnar had always refused to answer that question. He liked to say that he hadn't been willing to leave Iceland, an argument that I discounted, having observed this unfettered curiosity, his fluency in

347

several languages, and his ability to acclimate effortlessly in Greenland, France and Russia. I regarded him as one of those people who take their lives with them and are happy anywhere.

I had also noted that Khoyoulfaz and Quinteros showed him a lot more respect than his position within the organization would seem to warrant: after all he wasn't even the head of a branch, a post to which any of my fellow students could already have laid claim. What did such deference imply? That they were showing respect to the man who had discovered the two best students in the Academy? Or did it mean that they were treating a keeper of shameful secrets with kid gloves? I hoped to find out one day.

Our flight — or rather our flights since we changed planes in Moscow and London — was uneventful. Sprawling in his wide leather armchair, Gunnar devoured caviar and guzzled vodka, while sharing the latest gossip from Baldur, Furuset & Thorberg.

My replacement was giving him grief. In three years, he had produced only two dossiers, both mediocre. "Either I'm losing my touch," Gunnar said, turning his glass, "or I've exhausted my quota of champions. In either case, it might be better for me to retire." He had already drunk quite a bit by this stage, and I didn't know if he was serious.

We landed in Reykjavík about midnight. I had expected to spend the night in a hotel in the center of town, and to take the first bus for Húsavík the following morning. As we were parting, Gunnar casually said, "Oh, I almost forgot: your Indonesian friend keeps calling me."

"Magawati?" I asked, a sudden lump in my throat. "And what do you tell her?"

"Oh, the usual story: that you're alive, but that I'm not authorized to give her your contact details. Unless, of course, you allow me," he added with a wink that made an Iceland Air hostess turn around.

"I've already told you, Gunnar, Maga's a friend. And there's no point in giving her my contact details, I'll call her. She didn't leave you her number, by any chance?"

"Actually, she did," Gunnar said. "I remember writing it down somewhere, but where?" He assumed a puzzled air, pretended to search in his attaché case, then struck his forehead with his palm and, as if by magic took a card from his jacket pocket. "Here it is, I knew I'd kept it. 34 93 284 3835."

I tore the card from Gunnar's hand. *Call day or night*, I read beside the number. "Is it in Spain?" I said. The last time I'd talked to Maga, she was still living in Djakarta.

"Barcelona, to be precise," Gunnar said, savoring his childishness. "Right, I'm off. Try to drop by the office one of these days. Everyone will be really pleased to see you."

I watched as the doors of the elevator closed. What time was it in Barcelona? Two in the morning? *Call day or night*, she had said. I pushed my cart to a phone booth and inserted my credit card. It took me so long to get through that I thought Gunnar had played a trick on me. At last, the tone echoed in my eardrum. I realized I was squeezing the receiver so tightly that my knuckles were white.

"Hello," a hazy voice said suddenly.

"Maga. It's me," were the only words that came into my mind.

"Sliv?" the voice cried. "Sliv, is that you? Are you all right?"

"I'm fine," I replied, futilely attempting to contain my emotions. "I'm calling from Reykjavík airport. I know it's late, but Gunnar Eriksson just gave me your number, and I couldn't resist."

"You did the right thing. What's happened, Sliv?"
"It's a long story, and my credit card wouldn't be sufficient. I don't want to discuss it over the phone anyway, I'll tell you everything in person. Are you in Barcelona?"

"Yes, I've been here for a year."

"Are you happy?" I asked without thinking.

I heard her laughing at the other end. "You're not wasting time on preliminaries tonight..."

"I've already wasted too much time. Answer me."

"Yes, Sliv, I'm happy. Very happy even. But I'll be even happier when I can give you a hug."

I imagined her sitting against a wall, gradually awakening. I had missed her so much. "I'll be there soon," I said. "First I'm going to see my mother in Húsavík. I'll call you again to tell you when I'm coming."

"And I'm going to tell Youssef. He's never understood why you didn't keep in touch."

"I'd prefer you not do that just yet," I said. "I dread his reaction. If it doesn't bother you, I'd like to see you alone first."

She didn't seem shocked by my request. "As you wish," she replied. "Good night, Sliv."

I replaced the receiver, exhausted but proud in spite of everything of the way I had dealt with that day's events. In the space of a few hours, I had regained mastery of my fate, hadn't yielded to rancor, and renewed contact with Maga. Youssef would follow soon.

The next day, I visited my mother and her sheep. She had fallen ill in January — her neighbor had cared for her animals — but was now fully recovered. After lecturing me on the way I looked (bad, obviously), she attacked my pointlessly sophisticated lifestyle (if only she had known!), and tried to persuade me to stay in Iceland and to find a wife. She wanted more grandchildren, citing my sister Mathilde's happiness as an example. She couldn't have chosen a worse model.

We almost came to blows when she suggested visiting me in Krasnoyarsk. To discourage her, I painted such a grim picture of Siberia that she wondered aloud what was keeping me in that godforsaken place. We finally agreed to meet in St Petersburg the following summer and to embark on a cruise of the Baltic.

I treated myself to a rest cure, rediscovering the delicious pleasure of dreamless nights. I also visited Baldur, Furuset & Thorberg, where — Gunnar hadn't lied — I was feted like the prodigal son. Eventually, unable to wait any longer, I bought an open ticket for Barcelona. I called Maga to tell her I was coming, and she gave me her address on the Ramblas. I dissuaded her from meeting me at the airport.

I arrived in Barcelona in early March. The weather was already as mild as at the height of summer in Iceland. This was my first trip to Spain. The taxi driver immediately spotted my Argentine accent. One week earlier, I might have tried to tone it down, but right now I was happy to assume my Córdoban heritage.

The taxi dropped me at the edge of the Plaza de Catalunya, in front of a two-story building with rough-cast ocher walls. From her window, Maga had a view of the entire street as far as the monument of Christopher Columbus.

I slowly climbed the stairs, my bag over my shoulder. My heart was pounding, but not because of the steps. I stopped outside the door. The only sounds I could hear were the cries of children playing football in the backyard. I took a deep breath and rang the bell.

It was Youssef who opened the door. We fell into each other's arms.

9

"It's a long story," I said.

"We have plenty of time," Maga replied.

We all recognized that our outpourings of emotion wouldn't be entirely genuine until they had heard my story. Once past the spontaneous impulse that had thrown him into my arms, Youssef had recovered his customary stiffness. Sitting cross-legged on the couch, and holding Maga's hand a little closer to his knee than the Koran probably prescribed, he was clearly waiting for an explanation.

And that was what he received. I went back more than three years, to the genesis of the Maharashtra memo. Without sparing myself, I recounted how I'd rushed through the work of verifying the sources for the gallowfish dossier so that I could leave for Patagonia.

When I reached the deplorable episode of my night call to John Harkleroad, I saw Youssef frown. He said nothing, but I knew what he was thinking: he would not have panicked like me. He would have worked out several strategies, then evaluated them on the basis of objective criteria. The Thorsen method, in other words.

Maga and Youssef paid even closer attention when I described the visit of Khoyoulfaz and Jones. I saw on their faces a succession of the same emotions through which I had passed: the childish fear of being reprimanded, then the hope that Special Operations would devise a solution I'd missed, and finally the horror when the two men had recommended the physical elimination of John Harkleroad.

"The bastards!" Youssef roared. "Deep down, I always knew. They've been deceiving us since Day One."

"Let him speak, Youssef," Maga said. "He hasn't finished."

I painted the scene in detail, enabling them to relive it with me: my fruitless discussions with Jones, Khoyoulfaz's revolting comments, Lena's almost immediate surrender, and the orders that we had been asked to sign, "so that the file should be complete."

"Lena signed it without even reading it," I said. "I refused, for honor's sake, because I couldn't see what else to do. But my resistance was useless. They knocked me out, then drugged me. When I came to, it was already too late, Harkleroad had been eliminated."

"Unbelievable," Youssef muttered, as dazed as a boxer on the ropes. "Poor man. Obviously, you resigned?"

"The same day," I said. "I packed my bags and flew back to Europe..."

"Did you tell the police?"

"No," I admitted, embarrassed.

"We wouldn't be here if he had," Maga commented judiciously, quite determined, as usual, to gather all the facts before reaching a verdict.

"But why?" Youssef asked. I could sense that he was making an effort not to shout.

"I don't know. I needed time to think, to decide on a strategy. And besides, I couldn't reconcile myself to the idea that you would all be arrested, you and hundreds of other agents who had nothing to blame themselves for. I know it's hard to understand. Listen to the rest of the story before you judge me."

I told them about the weeks I'd spent cutting down trees in the forest in Húsavík, Gunnar's repeated phone calls, and finally my meeting with him in the harbor café. I related our conversation as faithfully as possible.

"What repulsive logic!" Youssef exploded. "He hadn't told you anything when he hired you, because he was afraid of putting you off? Well, I understand him! Who would choose to join a band of murderers?"

"At least now we know the way their minds work," Maga said, with impressive self-control.

I had just told her that the organization employing her systematically eliminated those who stood in its way, and she was remaining calm while she analyzed its motivations.

Now I was arriving to the most delicate part of my story, the letter in which I had begged Gunnar to have me reinstated. I knew all too well what Youssef's reaction would be, so I took the initiative.

"I know this will seem incredible to you. But two factors came together. I visited my sister in Germany, and that glimpse of ordinary life convinced me that I could never return to it. I realized that falsification had become an essential part of my existence, that it was the prism through which I saw the world, a drug I was ashamed to consume but which I couldn't do without. Although I hated myself for my weakness, I plunged back into my addiction like any other junkie."

"I've already felt that," said Maga, whom I suspected of trying to support me. "That impression that life would be desperately boring without the CFR."

"And the second factor?" Youssef asked, abruptly.

"I went over and over Gunnar's arguments and came to the conclusion that he wasn't completely wrong. My error hadn't been to forget to check that wretched source. It had been not to ask several years earlier how the CFR would react if it was threatened. When I realized that Gunnar had lied to me by omission, I understood that he had preferred to let me draw my own inferences."

"What blindness..." Youssef commented laconically, making no attempt to hide his exasperation. He rose and opened a window, as if the pile of nonsense I'd been spouting had made the air in the room unbreathable.

"You must have been through some difficult moments," Maga said, in yet another conciliatory effort. "How did they greet your request? Did they take you back?"

"They not only took me back, but they even promoted me and sent me to the Academy."

I described my year in Krasnoyarsk, without concealing my failings, especially my inability to relate to those around me. Finally, the revelation of Gunnar's maneuver left them totally dumbfounded—and silent.

Now I, too, stepped to the window. The bustle of the street reminded me a little of Córdoba. The sun had almost entirely disappeared behind the massive neighboring University. People were starting to fill the café terraces, where they would soon be sipping cocktails and indulging in the hardest task of the day: choosing somewhere to eat.

"Why didn't you tell us anything, Sliv?" Maga asked from behind me.

"Because I was too ashamed, obviously," I replied, without turning around.

On one corner of the square, a little old lady wearing a cap adorned with the Olympic logo was selling lottery tickets. That reminded me that I had never asked Stéphane to describe his role in the selection of Atlanta for the 1996 Games.

"When I think back, I realize that I made one mistake after another. I didn't ask Gunnar any of the important questions during my recruitment. I invented earthquakes when I was asked to check sources. I was taken in by an amateur actor who ate with his fingers. I handed in my resignation then retracted it, and last but not least I took a year to understand that Yakoub Khoyoulfaz couldn't both run Special Operations and clean his nails with a knife. Do you remember our conversation in Patagonia, when Youssef said he would resign if he learned that he'd been misled? I agreed with him at the time, but when the hour of truth came, I behaved like a coward."

"I don't see it like that," Maga said, as I stood there still engrossed in the spectacle of the street.

"I can't really see it any other way," Youssef rebutted her. By now, he must have regretted feeling sorry for me a little earlier.

"You should have called us," Maga went on, ignoring Youssef's remark. "Friends help; they don't judge."

"Friendship presupposes respect," Youssef grumbled, just loud enough for me to hear him.

I turned and held his gaze.

"What do you take from this story?" Youssef asked, rising to his full height.

"What do you mean?" Maga said.

"It's quite simple!" stormed Youssef. "He thought he'd killed a man, but preferred to take refuge in Siberia surrounded by his accomplices rather than denounce them to the police, only to discover in the end that his future boss had enjoyed a good laugh at his expense. I hope that even though he's not particularly inclined to remorse, Sliv must still have garnered one or two lessons from his adventures. Isn't that so, Sliv?"

His aggressiveness was painful. For me but also, surely, for him.

"I've decided that my fate and that of the CFR are inextricably linked," I said. "I'm going to continue to climb the ladder that leads to the Executive Committee, in the hope that once there I'll find that the aims of the CFR live up to my expectations."

Youssef openly sneered. "I'm sorry, but that's the stupidest conclusion you could have drawn!"

"Youssef!" Maga cried.

"It's true," Youssef went on. "Frankly, why was that charade necessary? Weren't you following Lena Thorsen's instructions? What was the big deal? Your dear Gunnar should have dropped by unexpectedly to warn you of the risks of your carelessness. You're quite bright; you would have understood the message."

"It wouldn't have been the same," I said. "I'm a better agent today."

"You were already a very good agent," Youssef replied. It was the first kind word that had come out of his mouth.

"I don't know," I said.

It was true: I didn't know. A good agent would never have put his own pleasure before the safety of his friends and colleagues.

"Mind control has always been the first step toward totalitarianism," Youssef resumed – he could never resist the temptation to turn his fits of anger into theories. "Trust us, we're going to make you happy in spite of yourselves... Complete bullshit, if you want my opinion!"

"Djibo devoted twenty hours of classes to the future of mankind," I replied, quick as a flash. "I don't claim to equal your ease with concepts, but I didn't have the impression that making everyone think the same way was high on the list of the CFR's priorities."

Youssef advanced toward me with his hundred and twenty kilos of muscle. I instinctively recoiled, sensing that he was about to pounce.

"They've deprived you of your free will, Sliv, don't you see that? Nothing can justify that."

"Perhaps I was no longer able to exercise it," I said, immediately recognizing the absurdity of my answer.

Youssef retreated and stared at me in horror. Then he turned abruptly and in three strides reached the door of the apartment.

"Where are you going?" Maga asked.

"I've heard enough for today," Youssef answered and left, slamming the door behind him.

I sat down again facing Maga. That heated exchange had made my head spin. "Now you understand why I asked to see you alone first," I sighed.

"Forgive me," Maga replied. "When you told me you were coming to Barcelona, I couldn't help calling him. He found it difficult to understand silence, you know."

Not as much as I did, I thought.

"That's possible," I muttered.

"And without indulging in pseudo-psychology, I told myself as I listened to you that you'd already lost your father. Deep down, you may not have been ready to lose Gunnar."

When I didn't respond, she added, "He might even have played on that a little."

"Oh, my God, Maga, you're not going to start either? It's easy for you: you still have your parents, and you love Youssef!"

357

I immediately regretted those words. Maga's goodwill toward me wasn't in any doubt.

"We met again only two hours ago," she said sadly, "and we're already arguing…"

"I know," I moaned. "That's precisely what I had hoped to avoid…"

"But who knows? That may be part of the process of recovery."

We were silent for a few moments. The last rays of the sun filled the room with a magical light.

"What about you?" I asked. "What do you take away from all that?"

"You mean, apart from the fact that Lena Thorsen is a bitch?"

"Oh, yes, apart from that, please. I don't feel I'm strong enough to conduct a conversation on that subject, especially with you."

"What I take from it foremost is that the CFR has plans for you. All those maneuvers, your being selected for the Academy… I even wonder if Youssef isn't a bit jealous. He feels that he's vegetating in his current post. I hope he'll talk to you about that."

"I hope so too. I'll tell him to hang on. One sees problems in a different light at the Academy. And if he does succeed in being appointed to the Plan, he'll finally meet people on his own level."

"I hope you're right," she said pensively. She stood up abruptly. "Well, let's not wait for Youssef. I know him, he'll return after you're in bed. Can you lay the table for me while I make us some dinner?"

We entered the kitchen.

"Do you like it?" Maga asked, noticing me staring at a wall of *azulejos*.

"It's magnificent."

"A legacy from the Arabs, like so many things in Spanish culture."

"You haven't told me what brought you to Spain."

"I asked to come here. The Barcelona bureau deals with the position of women in the world, a subject that's always been close to my heart. I asked for the transfer at the beginning of 1996, when the Afghan Taliban began to close girls' schools in the areas under their control. It can't be said that the situation has improved much since then, but at least I have the impression of helping a little."

"I find it hard to see how the CFR can help the cause of women. Are you going to falsify the constitution of Saudi Arabia in order to give them the right to vote?"

Maga burst out laughing. "So that Special Operations will come for us and administer us electric shocks? No, thanks. No, we're mainly working on the representation of women in religious imagery."

"Take the example of public office. A majority of Sunnis claim that women can't exercise political functions, because Muhammad is supposed to have said that a nation led by a woman is doomed. For decades, feminist organizations around the world have been vainly trying to persuade Arab countries that women are just as capable as men. The CFR prefers to encourage the belief that the prophet regularly sought advice from his wife Aisha in the conduct of political affairs."

"All the same," I said, "I think victory would have a sweeter taste if it were achieved through reason."

"A typically male comment, if you don't mind me saying. At the present juncture many women want change regardless of how it is attained."

"One point to you," I said, with a smile. "And what does Youssef think?"

"More or less the same as you. Besides he hates our tinkering with the accepted biography of Muhammad. As if the Taliban had any qualms about interpreting the Koran in a way that suits their purposes."

"I saw you holding hands on the couch just now. Have you been together long?"

"Nearly six months."

"I'm not going to ask you if it's serious..."

"Do you know of anything that's not serious where Youssef's concerned?" she replied, amused.

We ate dinner together in the kitchen. Maga bombarded me with questions about the Academy. I told her about that strange sensation I had felt of being cut off from the human race. She listened to me attentively, then presented her analysis.

"It's funny," she said. "When you talk about it, it's as though you are the one refusing to mix with your fellow students, on the pretext that you find them naïve and immature. Whereas deep down I'm convinced you considered yourself unworthy of them."

Maga retired after dinner. I was lying on the sofa-bed in the living room, reflecting on what she had said, when I heard the key turn in the lock. It was Youssef, trying hard not to make noise. I switched on the light and threw off the sheets.

Youssef's huge silhouette was framed in the door. "I was hoping you'd be asleep by now," he said, taking a seat on the edge of the bed.

"I've been waiting for you."

"I want to apologize," he said in a contrite and manifestly sincere tone.

"You don't need to apologize, Youssef," I said.

"Let's say I don't need to, but I'm going to do it all the same," he replied with a smile.

We didn't know what to say to each other.

"I was afraid for you, you know?" he resumed at last. "Afraid that something terrible had happened to you."

"I did ask Gunnar to tell you I was fine, even if it was a lie."

"You really should have talked to us."

"I know," I admitted for the first time. "I should have called on that crucial day. Afterward, it was too late. The longer I waited, the more disgusted I was with myself. In Patagonia, you were ready to quit because of that petroleum business, and I didn't have the courage to resign over a man's death."

"You must have suffered terribly," he said. "I can't even imagine what you endured."

He opened his arms to me. His embrace was so vigorous that for a moment I thought he hadn't believed a word of what I'd just said, and was trying to smother me.

"You understand," he said, releasing his grip, "free will is sacred. You can starve me, throw me in prison, or torture me, but you can never stop me from thinking. That's what I reproach them for: having distorted your judgment."

"You're right. And at the same time, I think Gunnar knew what he was doing. He would never have chosen the same procedure with you, for example. I suppose he knew I was more flexible, more malleable..."

"You mean less committed to your principles?"

"That, too," I conceded with a smile. "The fact remains that he expected me to survive the ordeal more or less intact. And events have proved him right."

He was about to say something but changed his mind. "Will you come to the kitchen with me? I need to eat."

I accompanied him. He set about whipping up an omelet, while I sipped a beer.

"You mentioned Djibo earlier," he said, suddenly. "Have you seen him again?"

"At the Academy. He came and gave a series of lectures."

"Tell me about them. I want to know everything."

It wasn't difficult to comply. Djibo's last class was permanently engraved on my memory.

"I absolutely must join the Plan," Youssef said pensively when I had finished. "Maga and I have conveyed the message that we wouldn't consider attending the Academy without each other. That obviously penalizes one of us, most likely her, I'm afraid."

I refrained from contradicting him. He was right. I chugged some beer, then changed the subject.

"There's something else I didn't tell you. Only the six members of the Executive Committee know the aims of the CFR."

This revelation didn't produce the expected effect on Youssef. "So there is a meaning to all this," he said. "I've had my doubts about that sometimes. Take this Petroleum Initiative, for example: I'm surrounded by professionals, each more brilliant than the next. We're beginning to have an impact, but I still can't discern an overall plan."

"There must be one," I said, toying absentmindedly with my empty bottle. "I can't imagine it any other way."

10

"Three dangers threaten the CFR: carelessness, betrayal, and error. Remember these words well: you will meet them again in connection with all the dossiers processed by Special Operations, most often singly, sometimes in pairs. In a while I'll tell you a story that, unusually, combined all three."

Listening to Yakoub Khoyoulfaz speak with such fluency, I wondered yet again how I could have mistaken him for a killer. The previous evening, arriving at the residence, I'd found a basket of fruit in my room, with a card pinned to it, saying: *I hope you had a good vacation*; and this morning, he had insisted on serving us tea himself in china cups. Either he was naturally attentive, or he could play the part of a gentleman with as much flair as he had impersonated a thug.

Actually, it didn't really matter. I was beginning my second year with all the eagerness of a patient who, believing that that he's been stricken with an incurable illness, has just learned that his doctor had misdiagnosed his ailment. It had taken me a few weeks to come to terms with Gunnar's revelations, and to shed my anxiety. The support of my friends during this transition phase had proved crucial. Maga had cheered me up in the tapas bars of Barcelona, while Youssef, with whom I had subsequently crisscrossed Vietnam toting a rucksack for two weeks, had helped me to see my adventures as a kind of initiation.

Relieved of the burden of guilt, I was now free, according to him, to devote myself to the search for the Grail — the purpose of the CFR — and to find my place in the world. In my simpler words, I was finally going to be able to make friends again and to show the Executive Committee what I was capable of.

"Let's begin with carelessness," Khoyoulfaz continued. "The Executive Committee has long understood that it's not possible to give a precise definition of such a notion in an organization whose members are paid to take calculated risks. That's why we prefer to rely on a classification that has proved its worth, one that divides agents into three groups: the gamblers, the idealists, and the guardians of the temple.

"The gamblers function on adrenaline. They take more risks than the others, because they're always looking for a major coup that will enshrine them in the pantheon of the CFR. They're generally better scenario writers than falsifiers; they find it hard to tolerate the authority of their superiors; and they scorn the directives of the Plan, which they accuse of curbing their imagination. Indifferent to the possibility of improving the lot of mankind, they evaluate dossiers according to purely aesthetic criteria, and they'd kill their own parents to see one of their creations make the front page of *Le Monde* or the *New York Times*. Few of them pass through the Academy, and they generally end up as Class 2 or 3 agents."

Lena threw me a sidelong glance. Clearly, apart from the last point, Khoyoulfaz' description of the gamblers could have been written about me.

"The second group consists of the idealists. They've joined the CFR in order to change the world. For them, the purpose of a dossier is either to correct an injustice or to highlight a dysfunction in society. They prize a scenario's moral value over and above its ingenuity. They get along well with their superiors, so long as they profess the same concerns. Almost all of them wind up in the Plan."

Youssef, I thought immediately.

"Last, but not least, the guardians of the temple are the most devoted to the CFR. They feel they've been invested with the responsibility to protect our organization not only against the outside world but also against its own demons. They're better falsifiers than scenario writers, and tend to produce solid but unimaginative dossiers. You'll rarely find them on the podium in Honolulu, but they provide battalions of Academy students. The best of them join the General Inspectorate, where they can unreservedly indulge in their passion for rules and procedures."

I found some characteristics of Lena in this description. But she was too ambitious for the General Inspectorate. Her aim was nothing less than the Executive Committee.

"Every agent exhibit each of those archetypes in varying degrees. We all entered the CFR because of a love of games; we're all afraid of being unmasked; and we all prefer — whenever possible — to rectify inequities rather than to encourage them. It is the distribution of these three basic attributes that makes each of us unique. So far, I've never met a monolithic agent."

I would have to introduce him to Youssef. My Sudanese friend was a monolith in every sense of the word.

"As you'll doubtless have realized, the gamblers are the ones most likely to endanger the CFR. Even the best gamblers sometimes lose, but, in our case, each defeat threatens the safety of thousands of individuals. It's the Gordian knot of our organization: we need the gamblers, but at any moment they can cost us our lives. That's why we try so hard to minimize the risk they embody by placing them under the command of experienced case officers, or even under the surveillance of the General Inspectorate."

Sometimes, I thought, we make them think that they have a death on their conscience. Immediate effect guaranteed.

"Then again, if we only had to deal with careless people, Special Operations would be a sinecure. Unfortunately, we regularly have to deal with cases of betrayal, which are a lot more serious. I'm not thinking of the wretched blackmailers who, seeking early retirement, fantasize that the CFR will be prepared to buy their silence for a princely sum. I'm talking about agents who, most often out of self-interest, place their talents as falsifiers at the service of a cause that hasn't previously been approved by our organization."

"Consider, for example, the case of an agent in Stuttgart who commissioned the forger Konrad Kujau to produce diaries, purporting to be Hitler's, which he then sold for ten million Deutschmarks to the magazine *Stern*."

"Or take the case of an American who reported us to the FBI, but whom we managed at the last moment to have committed to a mental hospital…"

Seeing me shudder, Khoyoulfaz smiled. I could imagine him only too well in a white coat, brandishing a CT scan of the informer's skull, and explaining that his patient's schizophrenia had its origins in a fall from a horse during his adolescence.

"But I shan't elaborate further on this topic," Khoyoulfaz remarked. "You won't be authorized to investigate cases of betrayal until you leave the Academy."

A pity, I thought, they were probably the most interesting. Probably also those where Special Operations used the least acceptable methods, which would explain Khoyoulfaz's reticence.

"Errors," he continued, "are by far the main cause of our interventions. I'm sure you can guess the most frequent: unmasking of the reference source, contradictory alterations, excessive detail..."

"Historical inconsistencies, material impossibilities, clumsy forgeries..." Lena completed the list, all the while glaring at me as if to remind me that I had committed each of these blunders in Córdoba at least a dozen times.

"Everyone makes mistakes," Khoyoulfaz said, coming unwittingly to my rescue. "Mistrust agents who think they are infallible. Being too proud to ask for help, they try to repair their missteps themselves, and generally only manage to exacerbate the situation. That's all the more foolish since we manage to resolve 99% of the problems that are immediately reported to us."

Besides, what we call an error is often a case of bad luck: for example, a historian discovers a new source that an agent hadn't been able to falsify — and with good reason, because at the time he was unaware of its existence."

"Faced with an error, we really have only three options: correction, abandonment, or creating a new scenario. Correction is obviously the preferable solution, but it isn't always possible.

"Let's take a textbook case: a young agent calls us because he just realized that he forgot to inscribe the date of birth of one of his creations in the municipal register."

Lena emitted a scornful "Pah!" as if Khoyoulfaz had just insulted her intelligence.

"Yet that's the kind of thing we deal with every day," Khoyoulfaz continued. "Your first reflex would be to call Berlin, which secretly pays thousands of registry officers around the world. They'll be able to get you out of trouble most of the time, but not always."

"What could prevent them?" Ichiro asked.

"The register is kept in a safe, or the pages are numbered and the entries are too close together for a new one to be inserted. You should then ask yourself if it mightn't be best to leave well enough alone."

"Give up?" Lena asked in an incredulous tone.

"Sometimes that's the best decision," Khoyoulfaz replied. "After all, what's the risk? Even if anyone checks — and frankly, who ever checks registers of births — historians will note the discrepancy and construct all kinds of hypotheses: maybe our character was of unknown parentage? Maybe he changed his name to escape conscription or a demanding wife? With a little luck, such vagueness will even serve the dossier."

"Luck..." Lena echoed, scornfully.

"Absolutely," Khoyoulfaz retorted, barely able to conceal his irritation. "All we do here is to evaluate probabilities. Accept that once and for all. If it's less risky to do nothing than to mount a night-time expedition and break into the national archives, you should do nothing, trust me."

"You mentioned a third option," I said to ease the tension.

"Yes, thank you, Sliv. If you can't correct a mistake, and if you can't trust in luck, you can always rewrite a scenario, i.e. invent a new one that explains the error instead of concealing it. In the previous example, you could insert the birth date in the register of a nearby spa town, explaining that the mother went there for a rest cure after giving birth."

"However, I draw your attention to the fact that, like all scenarios, a new one will require a rigorous effort of falsification, conceivably even greater than for the original dossier. But that shouldn't pose any problem, should it, Lena?"

She blushed, but didn't unclench her jaw. Ichiro smiled politely. As for me, I savored the conclusion of Khoyoulfaz's presentation. He hadn't mentioned physical elimination as a possible last resort in our interventions. He'd merely passed a little quickly for my taste over the question of betrayal, maybe because it was the only case where the CFR allowed itself to eliminate its enemies. Was I willing to accept that? I would have to think about it.

"Any questions?" Khoyoulfaz asked. "Now for the story: I have it from one of its protagonists, the Turk Memet Okür, who was my teacher in Hamburg twenty-five years ago. In his eighties, this former director of Special Operations liked nothing better than to share his experiences with the students of the Academy. He himself had completed his training in the 1920s, at a time when the CFR, which was then a more close-knit and less bureaucratic organization, had no hesitation in entrusting its young agents with major responsibilities. Okür had only just been co-opted into Special Operations — the Academy didn't yet exist — when his chief sent him to London for the purpose, he told him, of clarifying the affair of the Zinoviev letter.

"Okür was taken aback. The Zinoviev letter had already been front-page news for several weeks, and he had never suspected that the CFR might be involved. Just out of curiosity, does any of you know the broad outlines of that affair?"

It was the first time I'd heard of it. A glance at Lena and Ichiro confirmed that they shared my ignorance.

"I wonder what they teach you at the Academy," Khoyoulfaz muttered. "In 1924, just four days before the general election, the British newspaper *The Daily Mail* published a letter supposedly written by Grigori Zinoviev, then head of the Soviet Komintern, addressed to the central committee of the British Communist Party. In it, he urged his British comrades to foment social unrest in order to prepare the revolution that would one day crush the dominant bourgeois class."

"The publication of this letter couldn't have occurred at a more inopportune moment for the Labour government of Ramsay MacDonald. For several months, it had been negotiating a peace treaty with Russia, notwithstanding fierce opposition from the Conservative members of Parliament, who rejected the very principle of an alliance with a Bolshevik state."

368

"The Zinoviev letter, which described the motives of the Soviet Union in most unpleasant terms, discredited the policy of the government in the most alarming way, all the more so when Zinoviev waited for several weeks before denying that he had written the letter. MacDonald made every effort to publicly question the authenticity of the letter, but he was unable to reverse things, and the Labour Party was heavily defeated in the elections."

"One month later, the new conservative government came out strongly against the ratification of the Anglo-Russian treaty."

"As you're probably doing at this very moment, Memet Okür considered several possibilities. The letter might, of course, be genuine, the Komintern already having the reputation at the time of supporting European Communist parties both logistically and financially."

"But Okür soon came to regard the letter as a fake. In it, Zinoviev had presented himself as the chairman of the Presidium of the Executive Committee of the Komintern, whereas he was in fact chairman of the Executive Committee itself. In addition, in another part of the missive, he had referred to the Third Bolshevik International, an expression used only by Westerners at that time. If Zinoviev wasn't the author of the letter, who do you think could have written it?"

"The British Conservatives, in order to compromise MacDonald?" Lena suggested.

"The NKVD, the Soviet secret police, to spread confusion in Great Britain?" Ichiro proposed.

"The CFR?" I ventured.

Khoyoulfaz looked at us. "Apparently I haven't been wrong about you," he said with a self-satisfied smile. "Okür presented these three hypotheses to his chief, who listened to him attentively then replied that he knew the culprit: Philip Murray, a CFR agent from the Birmingham branch."

"Murray, a Class 2 agent specializing in revolutionary movements, had bet a colleague one hundred pounds that the Conservatives would win the next general election. Since, one month from the poll, the Labour Party still had some hope of winning, he came up with the idea of the Zinoviev letter. Being very knowledgeable about Communism, he easily struck the right tone, although he committed those two technical errors that later drew the attention of the experts given the task of evaluating the authenticity of the document."

"Murray still had to find a way of putting the letter into circulation. So he teamed up with a special agent from the Manchester bureau, who agreed for ideological reasons — he despised the Labour Party — to transmit a copy of the letter to the British Secret Service, one of whose agents arranged to leak it to the *Daily Mail.*"

"Notice that Murray would probably never have been unmasked if he hadn't insinuated that he had given fate a push in order to win his bet. His colleague, suspecting a trick, alerted Special Operations, which opened an investigation."

"Okür loved to tell this story, because it displayed all the varieties of behavior that justify the existence of Special Operations."

"Carelessness first of all, as exhibited by Murray, who was ready to derail history just in order to win a bet. The investigation showed that he wagered on horse races, and that the General Inspectorate had placed him under surveillance one year earlier.

"Next, betrayal, committed by the agent from Manchester, who took the risk of blowing the cover of the CFR because he didn't like Ramsey MacDonald.

"And finally, errors, which inevitably slip into a dossier when it isn't properly vetted.

"And the irony is that Murray succeeded in getting the Labour Party defeated. We'll never know if MacDonald would have been reelected, but all historians acknowledge that the Zinoviev letter was a major factor in the last days of the campaign."

"But what role did Okür play, if his chief already knew the culprit?" I asked.

Ichiro nodded. He had been wondering the same thing as me.

"He was assigned the responsibility of rewriting the scenario," Khoyoulfaz replied — it was obvious he never tired of telling this story. "Just think about it. Correction was no longer an option: the letter had already been published. Giving up? Out of the question: the British and Russian secret services had already launched their investigations. There was only one solution left: to point the finger at a plausible culprit, but one who would turn out to be impossible to apprehend."

"The White Russians?" Ichiro suggested.

Khoyoulfaz was mute with admiration for a few seconds. "Bullseye. In Okür's version, those Russian monarchists who had fled the Soviet regime had been outraged to learn that Britain was negotiating a peace treaty with the Bolsheviks, and they had hired Baltic forgers to compose the Zinoviev letter. He scattered a few clues here and there: telegrams between various groups of White Russians based in various European capitals; traces of a payment to a Lithuanian intermediary; a half-erased note tracing the itinerary of the letter within MI5."

"This latter document, whose sole objective was to dissuade the British secret services from pursuing their investigation too far, fulfilled its function admirably. The scandal of the Zinoviev letter gradually faded and the CFR was never impacted."

"And what about Murray?" I asked.

"Oh, yes, Murray," Khoyoulfaz echoed, as if the name had only just recurred to him. "It was Okür who negotiated with him the terms of his departure. It was agreed that he would resign. I think he might have kept his right to a pension, but he ended up giving it up when Okür showed him another letter: the one he had written to comrade Zinoviev revealing the name of the man who had scuppered the Anglo-Russian treaty by usurping his identity."

"The Soviets, you see, were sticklers for discipline. I even wonder if Murray returned the hundred pounds," he added pensively.

11

Yakoub Khoyoulfaz didn't believe in theoretical classes. "They're OK for the grinds of the General Inspectorate," he would say with a laugh. He was a firm believer in learning on the job. After five days of commando training in Krasnoyarsk, I was parachuted into Sweden for my first assignment. Niklas Sundström, the director of the Stockholm Bureau, needed help in tidying up a dossier dealing with the adolescence of August Strindberg. Many of the great man's biographers had begun to point out the contradictions in it, so Sundström had followed the rules and alerted the Executive Committee, the only organ authorized to deploy Special Operations.

I presented myself one Monday morning to Sundström, who greeted me with open arms. To my great surprise, he described me to his team as "the messiah from Krasnoyarsk." I realized from his colleagues' relieved expressions that the other bodies had an idea of Special Operations that was quite different from what I expected. The agents in the field didn't see us as judges or censors, but as infallible magicians capable of vaporizing problems that they had created through their own clumsiness. That was why they rolled out the red carpet, boarding us in the best hotels, and granting our every wish.

I loved these short assignments — they rarely lasted more than a few days — in which I would land in a foreign country, have the situation explained to me, and immediately begin to devise a solution. The problems were incredibly varied, both in the subjects and in the approach to be adopted.

I remember for example my stay in Minneapolis (whose winters have little to envy Siberia's) where, with the help of two young agents, I rewrote the entire public health policy of Lesotho in a weekend.

I was making rapid progress, as if all my previous experiences had had only one purpose: to prepare me for this job. I had a better sense now of what I had learned in Córdoba: I could immediately spot the faults in a dossier unhesitatingly evaluate the chances of their being detected. A few phone calls were usually enough to determine the scope of the necessary repairs.

Even though I was by nature more inclined to write a new scenario rather than to correct an existing one, I no longer let my predilections dictate my decisions. I was rewarded with a sense of accomplishment every time I closed a dossier. Having once endangered this organization, I was now its most conscientious defender, and not its least skillful.

The post also included a social dimension that was far from negligible. My network was quickly expanding. My reputation preceded me everywhere I went. I could see that that those I consulted invariably sought my approval. As the heads of units traditionally invited visiting agents from Special Operations to their tables, I found myself conversing as an equal with managers who were twenty or thirty years my senior.

Obviously, I didn't work alone. I usually collaborated with a more experienced agent with me, generally a special agent, who supervised my work closely, but who was happy to abandon his part of the task to me if it meant he could spend time with old friends.

I didn't object: I was young, and I still had much to learn. Besides, I expected something else from these veterans: that they would share their experiences with me. Some had several hundred assignments under their belts, and could regale me with anecdotes for hours. I made them talk about the CFR itself, the evolution of the role of Special Operations, and the strict separation of powers that existed between the bodies and the Executive Committee. I learned more from them during my first six months in Special Operations than I had in the course of my first five years combined.

On two occasions, I had the immense privilege of forming a team with Khoyoulfaz, who overwhelmed me with kindness. For him, the CFR was only a concept; what mattered were the men and women who comprised it. "Our organization," he explained, "has only a few thousand members. With patience and a good memory, it's possible to know almost all of them."

That attitude explained why he didn't seem out of place anywhere. I saw him eating monkey in the Congo and dining on grasshoppers in Bangkok. He had chosen our joint assignments carefully. The first, an especially difficult one, was beyond my skills and provided a valuable insight into his expertise. The second was trivial, and left us time to return to the subject of his acting performance in Córdoba. I realized the full extent of his delicacy when he told me what I did not dare admit to myself: that it would take me several years to fully exorcise the memory of that day. "Lena has buried it deep in her memory, but I can see that you don't want to forget. It's good that we know each other. I'll arrange it so that you can renew with acquaintance with Jones when you're next in Krasnoyarsk."

The problem was that I was no longer spending a lot of time in Siberia. The world had become my garden. Thanks to spending so much time on planes, it seemed to me quite natural to finish an assignment in Karachi on Thursday and to start a new one in Brisbane on the following Monday.

I managed to fit in a few days' sightseeing whenever possible, even if it meant not returning to the Academy. Unfortunately, this meant that I would never make up for the time I had not spent with my fellow students during the first year. Luis Carildo would continue to see me as a lonesome cowboy, and I had to admit that his accurate characterization saddened me. From time to time, I called Stéphane Brioncet, whose marital bliss helped him bear the dullness of his position in Human Resources.

I crossed paths with Lena only once that year. I succeeded her in Milan, where she had tracked down a joker who'd been amusing himself by putting the Italian police on the trails of imaginary Mafiosi. She had turned the whole bureau against her in less than a week.

At the beginning of December, Khoyoulfaz entrusted me with my first solo assignment. Unlike most dossiers, which required immediate intervention, this one was of no particular urgency and could be handled from Krasnoyarsk. The CFR wasn't yet in danger of being unmasked, but one of its scenarios, produced at the beginning of the 1950s, was being widely criticized and on the verge of disintegrating.

I spent several days reading the dossier, which was more than a thousand pages long. Shortly after World War II, the Norwegian Class 3 agent Ole Gabriel Hagen had resolved to prove that the Vikings had discovered the American continent several centuries before Christopher Columbus.

That was perfectly plausible: the Vikings had discovered Iceland in 870 and colonized Greenland in the 10th century. It required only a small step to imagine that they might have sailed as far as America. In fact, a number of Scandinavian legends mentioned such an odyssey. But, in 1950, no historian took them seriously.

Hagen's notes, religiously preserved in the CFR's archives, shed little light on his intentions. Hagen clearly sought to remind the United States of its debt to Europe (at a time when the Marshall Plan might have made them think they were free of it), underlining in passing the advantage that the CFR would derive from being able to use the great figures of Nordic mythology as a means of deciphering American idiosyncrasies.

I suspected his real motive to be more prosaic: an inveterate gambler (several citations from the General Inspectorate peppered his personal file), he had become fascinated with the Vikings after he had discovered that he was an almost direct descendant of the famous warlord Harald Bluetooth.

Hagen's plan was of Biblical simplicity: to have America appear on a pre-1492 *mappa mundi*, a map of the world. It was his life's work, and he didn't intend to neglect any of its aspects. He first attempted to acquire — outside official channels — a very old virgin parchment, but all those offered to him were either already used or too recent.

But in 1951, after three years of searching, he purchased the entire collection of the library of an Andalusian monastery, solely because it contained several rolls of sheepskin parchment dating from the first half of the fifteenth century.

Producing the mappa mundi was a collective effort, in which Hagen coordinated the work of five cartographers who specialized in the Middle Ages. He never told them why he was utilizing their talents. He made two controversial decisions: the depictions of Europe, Africa, and Asia had to resemble as closely as possible the documents of the time so as to render credible the inclusion of America; and the map had to derive certain elements from sources in Scandinavian legend (what Lena in her pedantry would have called a "corroborating factor").

The best forger in the CFR — a Greek named Kandalis, whose son I had used three years earlier in Córdoba — took on the task of actually realizing the map. He spoiled three parchments before Hagen declared himself satisfied with the result.

The Norwegian had clearly refrained from representing America in its contemporary configuration. He had drawn instead an oblong island stretching from north to south, about half the area of Europe, on which he had added a Latin text meaning more or less: "By the will of God, after a long voyage from the island of Greenland to the furthest remaining parts of the Western Ocean, sailing south surrounded by ice, the companions Bjarni and Leif Eriksson discovered a new land, extremely fertile, and even having vines, which they accordingly named Vinland." I smiled upon reading these lines, which borrowed elements from a story well known to Icelandic schoolchildren, the Saga of Erik the Red.

Hagen, aware that his work would be scrupulously examined, figured that it would be more credible if it appeared alongside other, authentic pieces. By luck, the CFR had in its collection — this was the first time I learned of its existence, and I vowed to ask Khoyoulfaz about it — a priceless manuscript, a Codex entitled *Historia Tartorum* (History of the Tartars), in which a Franciscan monk, Giovanni da Pian del Carpine, tells of his journey to the Khan of Karakoram in about 1245. The file included an impassioned letter dated January 12, 1953, in which Hagen begged the Executive Committee to let him combine the story of the Tartars and the Vinland map into a single, unified work.

His petition was approved in the spring of 1953, the signature at the bottom of the letter of acceptance being unsurprisingly illegible. Four years later, the Vinland map turned up in a second-hand bookshop in Geneva, passed through several hands, including those of art merchant Laurence C. Whitten and philanthropist Paul Mellon, who offered it to Yale University in 1965 amid a storm of publicity.

Yale immediately enlisted the services of Dr. Raleigh Ashlin Skelton, a highly regarded British cartographer, whose report concluded that the document was authentic. This had two unexpected consequences: Yale insured the Vinland map for 25 million dollars and Ole Gabriel Hagen was promoted to special agent.

But Hagen was not to enjoy his triumph for very long. In 1972, another scholar, Walter McCrone, analyzed the ink used in the map, and discovered traces of anatase, a crystalline form of titanium dioxide unknown before the 20th century. As though expecting for such a revelation for years, several historians crawled out of the woodwork and enumerated the document's inconsistencies.

It was generally believed that the first circumnavigation of Greenland dated back no further than 1900: how, then, could the Vinland map portray the exact shape and size of Greenland so accurately?

Linguists also got in on the act. The Latin text contained several occurrences of the diphthong "æ", whereas the copyists of the fifteenth century used a simple "e"; furthermore, the name "Eriksson" would never have been Latinized as "Erissonius," since this custom did not appear until the seventeenth century.

Faced with this avalanche of corroborating evidence, the curators at Yale beat a cautious retreat by announcing that they sided with the dominant opinion: the Vinland map was a fake.

Hagen saw the reversal as a betrayal. In his diary (which was attached to the dossier), he lambasted the cowardice of "those scholars who always agree with whoever has been the last to speak." In the 1980s, he began to lose his marbles. A medical report produced at the request of the General Inspectorate discloses that, in the final years of his life, Hagen identified so strongly with his cause that he sometimes forgot it had never existed except in his imagination. He committed suicide in 1990, after learning that Yale had loaned the Vinland map to the British Museum for an exhibition entitled *Fake?* The map was assigned pride of place in it, next to the Shroud of Turin.

Yale may have capitulated, but the CFR remained loyal to its own. Stunned by Hagen's death, Svein Jacobsen, his friend and colleague at the Oslo Bureau, set himself the insane objective of having the Vinland map re-authenticated. He asked Special Operations for help, and Khoyoulfaz did not have the courage to refuse him.

The CFR expended considerable sums to mount an unprecedented diversionary operation. Its strategy was partially effective: in 1992, an American historian named Thomas Cahill claimed to have found anatase in several other medieval manuscripts whose authenticity was beyond dispute; but he also stipulated that the anatase in the Vinland map was of a different, and probably synthetic, origin. Nevertheless, some historians regained faith in Leif Eriksson's odyssey. The reputation of Ole Gabriel Hagen had been momentarily rescued.

But Khoyoulfaz was well aware that the Vinland map would continue to haunt the CFR. In 1995, Yale had been unable to resist the temptation to publish a new work that reaffirmed the authenticity of its *mappa mundi*. Many scientists, stung to the quick by such intellectual arrogance, were already proposing to subject the document and its ink to further analysis. Khoyoulfaz had been very clear on the point: the CFR could no longer merely react; it must become proactive.

Of course, I thought as I closed the dossier. But how? One of these days, it would be indisputably established that the map was a fake. A hundred years ago, experts examined doubtful works under a microscope. Fifty years later, they had rushed to use a newly invented technique, carbon dating, which made it possible to determine, to within a few years, when a picture had even painted.

Today, new molecular technologies made life even more difficult for forgers. In fact, almost all of the great fakes in the history of the CFR had been ultimately discovered. They had fooled people for five years or two centuries before being submitted to new tests that their creator, however skillful, could not have anticipated.

Svein Jacobsen had paid a final tribute to his friend Hagen, but he had merely postponed the inevitable. I clearly wouldn't be able to save the Vinland map, that was obvious, but I could at least offer it an honorable exit. I decided to broaden the field of my research.

On the first day, I made a remarkable discovery. In 1960, a pair of Norwegian explorers, Helge and Anne Stine Ingstad had discovered the remains of a Viking village at L'Anse aux Meadows, on the Canadian island of Newfoundland. Carbon dating had established beyond doubt that the ruins — several buildings, including a forge and a sawmill — dated back to the end of the tenth century. That erased any further doubt: the Vikings had indeed landed in North America five hundred years before Christopher Columbus, even though, according to historians, they had settled there more than a few years.

The CFR sometimes merely anticipates history, Gunnar liked to say. This dossier was the best example of such prescience: in what may be viewed as a flash of intuition, Ole Gabriel Hagen had imagined history, and the facts had corroborated it.

The most surprising aspect was that he wasn't satisfied with that *tour de force*. He might have considered, upon learning the news of the discovery of L'Anse-aux-Meadows, that his assignment had been fulfilled. Nobody would have begrudged him his success. And yet he didn't stop there. Not content to have demonstrated that the Vikings had indeed crossed the Atlantic, he still hoped to prove that they had done so by following his map. The CFR had an expression for such perseverance, typical of gamblers: the demigod syndrome.

I knew that I was nearing my goal when I came across an article about another colorful character: Father Joseph Fischer, an Austrian Jesuit, and an aficionado of medieval cartography, who had suggested back in 1902 that the Vikings had set foot in America long before Christopher Columbus. Fischer wasn't averse to scoops: he was responsible for the discovery of the first map containing the word America.

At this point, I asked the Vienna bureau to provide me with further information about him. I held my breath as I read a short biography prepared by a young Class I agent: Fischer's father, it showed, was a painter, and it might be supposed that he had taught his son the elementary techniques of mixing pigments. The remainder of the biography described a subtle man, sure of his own ideas, who would no doubt have gotten along well with Ole Gabriel Hagen.

This was all I needed: I had a few letters fabricated, signed by Father Fischer in a script that imitated the writing on the Vinland map. Then I launched the rumor that the priest was the author of the false *mappa mundi*. I added that he had produced the document solely for his personal use, and that it had been confiscated when the Nazis had seized the collection of the Jesuit school where he officiated. This ploy explained why the map had not reappeared until some years later. I never imagined that my version would win broad acceptance so quickly. Today, almost nobody doubts the Austrian origins of the Vinland map. Father Fischer had gained a richly deserved place in history.

So all was well that ended well. The Vikings really had discovered America. Ole Gabriel Hagen could rest in peace. We had lost the battle of the Vinland map, but no one would ever suspect our role in the affair. One thing bothered me though: the propensity of the CFR to produce false documents that risked backfiring on it one day. I shared my anxiety with Yakoub, who advised me to put my thoughts in writing. I readily complied, expounding why, in my opinion, physical falsification had had its day.

"The production of convincing forgeries, capable of withstanding thorough scientific examination, will become increasingly difficult, if not downright impossible," I wrote at the conclusion of my memo. "Dossiers like the Vinland map no longer have a place in our organization. They jeopardize it for the sake of victories that will prove increasingly ephemeral. Why take this risk when the advent of the digital era opens up so many fabulous opportunities for us? I think it is time the CFR changed paradigm and concentrated its efforts on what it does best: the manipulation of words and ideas."

12

Every year at Christmas time I made a little donation to Survival International, which supports indigenous tribes scattered throughout the world. In return, I received regular news of the Bushmen. It wasn't very good. If the representatives of Survival International were to be believed, Botswana had recently doubled its efforts to expel the Bushmen from their ancestral home, the Kalahari. The international community, which had once supported their cause, had gradually lost interest, leaving President Masire free to displace the tribes thwarting his plans for the diamond industry.

In January 1998, I read in the organization's newsletter that the government of Botswana had agreed to open discussions with the Bushmen. In my opinion, this wasn't a good omen. The government's lawyers, trained in the best American universities, were going to make short work of the Bushmen representatives, who were probably illiterate.

While Masire was confirming his reputation as a skillful tactician by bringing the Bushmen to the negotiating table, he was simultaneously undermining those who attacked his unilateral handling of the issue. I remained convinced that deep down he was quite determined to yield nothing essential. In short, the unfortunate tribes of the Kalahari were about to fall into a trap.

Unless...

I called Survival International that very day and offered my services within the framework of the forthcoming negotiations. I introduced myself as a specialist in environmental studies (only half a lie) ready to work voluntarily for a few weeks in the spring (the school year ended in mid-February and only resumed at the beginning of April).

My offer was warmly accepted. "We never refuse offers of help," the head of the southern Africa program said, before adding, "especially when they're free." After all the Bushmen had done for me, I thought, this was the least I could do for them.

I had already traveled widely by this time, including to poor countries such as India or Vietnam, but I had only once been to Africa, and that was on a lightning assignment in the Congo.

My initial impression was favorable. Gaborone, the capital of Botswana where I rested for forty-eight hours, from my exhausting flight, is a city that's both picturesque and modern. Lyle Owen, the Survival International representative — himself Botswanan — was kind enough to show me around, but he didn't hide from me the fact that I was likely to be disturbed by my stay in the desert. Here was yet another person who, because I was Icelandic, assumed that I had never looked poverty in the face, I thought, as I climbed into the back of his Jeep.

And yet Lyle was right: nothing could have prepared me for what I witnessed when he stopped at the end of the afternoon on the edge of a tribal camp in the region of Ghanzi. It wasn't primarily the Bushmen's poverty that struck me, but rather a sense of being taken back millennia into the past, to the dawn of mankind.

The beggars of Calcutta lived on the street, surrounded by cars and advertising posters, immersed in spite of everything in the modern world; the Bushmen, in contrast, live in small groups in huts made of branches, with no neighboring tribes for hundreds of kilometers. Poor Indians lack phones; the Bushmen don't even know they exist.

I spent much of the night conversing with Lyle, who spoke a little Khoisan, around a fire maintained with great difficulty by our hosts (when the sun went down, it wasn't much warmer than Krasnoyarsk).

I was taken aback. I had imagined a fine-looking, proud, spiritual people: I found eyes that expressed only submission and total exhaustion. The Bushmen, once known for their rock frescoes, hadn't painted for decades. They no longer had the time, occupied as they were with sucking the morning dew through straws and then pouring the precious liquid into the ostrich eggs they used as jars. As far as spirituality was concerned, they smoked hemp to escape the boredom of everyday life. Sometimes — rarely — they decorated their faces and danced.

In the weeks that followed, which I spent among different tribes, my initial impression was confirmed: the Bushmen had no chance of surviving. If the Huguenots hadn't chased them from the game-rich lands in which they had hunted three centuries earlier, they might have developed harmoniously, multiplied, and enriched an already respectable culture and folklore, while gradually assimilating the advances in health and education that civilization could offer them. Instead, they seemed doomed.

I had estimated there were a hundred thousand of them, but only a few thousand were left. In the space of a few generations, they had forgotten how to work with stone. They now only possessed two tools: their bows and the *kwé*, a kind of pole ending in an animal's horn, which had as many uses as a Swiss Army knife. They imitated the cries of birds perfectly, but were reduced to following the trajectories of vultures across the sky in the hope that it would indicate the location of some hyena or monkey carcass.

I would never have admitted this to Lyle, but I was almost starting to understand the government's position. At a time when Botswana was finally clawing its way out of poverty and boasted of possessing the most dynamic economy on the African continent, the Bushmen stood out like a sore thumb, not because they were developing less rapidly or because they had chosen another path, but rather because they were regressing and decaying before everyone's eyes.

When I heard Lyle lambaste the official policy of resettling the inhabitants of the Kalahari for their own welfare, I found it increasingly difficult to nod in assent.

When one faced the facts, wouldn't the Bushmen be better suited to a less arid land? And even should they one day aspire to join the rest of society, did their current status as a tourist attraction and an object of study for white-bearded ethnologists give them the slightest chance of survival?

Lyle underlined the inalienable right of all peoples to remain on their lands, but forgot that it was first the Bantu, then the European colonizers, who had driven the Bushmen into the Kalahari. Such hunter gatherers, would never themselves have chosen to settle in an inhospitable place where there was so little to hunt and almost nothing to gather. Then why persist, except on principle?

I kept my doubts to myself. In many ways, Survival International's mission was admirable. The representatives of First People of the Kalahari — the only movement that the government of Botswana accepted as a valid negotiating partner — freely acknowledged their debt toward the British organization and could hardly contain their excitement over the forthcoming negotiations.

The organization's executives understood my position — Masire would hear them out but grant them nothing concrete — but they couldn't entirely abandon their optimism. There might be a miracle, they steadfastly believed.

The last days before the opening of negotiations did a great deal to temper their hopes. The parties would be meeting in Gaborone, not in the Kalahari. This reversal (we'd lose the advantage of being on home ground) was compounded when Ketumile Masire stood down in favor of his vice-president, Festus Mogae. That Masire, who had governed the country for eighteen years, should choose this week of all weeks to retire spoke volumes about the importance that the government attached to our summit. Then the retiring president dealt us the final blow by announcing that he would still chair the negotiations, thus granting his successor every latitude subsequently to disown their outcome. The discussions hadn't begun yet, but they were *de facto* closed.

When the appointed day arrived, Masire cleverly strung us along. The subject was complicated, he asserted. It was because he cared about the fate of the Basarwa (the official name for the Bushmen, although they rejected it) that he had been trying for several years to help them. The Kalahari was not an environment adapted to their way of life, and it afforded them no chance to develop (on this point, he was correct). The fact that the subsoil of the Kalahari might contain diamonds (that "might" was charming, when one recalled that Orapa had recently become the first mine in the world to produce more than ten million karats annually) did not influence his judgment in any way.

Why, then, not look together for a site more appropriate to the culture of the Basarwa?

Our delegation explained why in detail. Masire listened to all our arguments, as if hearing them for the first time, his eyes penetrating, his chest thrust forward, and the tips of his fingers joined. I tried to divine his thoughts: "Above all don't interrupt them. Shake their hands for a long time on the steps of the presidential palace, smiling at the Botswanan television cameras. Arrange to meet them again in six months, once my successor has had time to settle into the job." He met my gaze and seemed to wonder what I was doing there. I hadn't opened my mouth during the meeting, because I didn't know what to say.

I returned to Krasnoyarsk filled with a muted anger, confounded by my experience, torn between so many unforgettable memories (the dance of blood, the famous Mokama, the pregnant woman who had slipped alone into the brush in order to give birth and had returned without a baby, because she didn't have the means to raise another child), and the sense that by sanctifying the Bushmen I was conspiring in their decline.

Arriving at the residence on the day before the school year commenced, I was startled to see some familiar faces. Youssef and Magawati were awaiting me in the common room. I hadn't seen them for a year, and I hugged them, realizing suddenly how much I had missed them.

"Don't tell me you're moving in," I blurted, incredulously.

"Yes, of course," Youssef replied gaily. "You see before you the Academy students Donogurai and Khrafedine."

"Both of you?" I exclaimed. My third year was suddenly taking quite a different turn.

"It wasn't easy," Maga said, leading me to imagine all kinds of complicated negotiations.

"You could at least have warned me."

"Believe me, we tried," Youssef said.

"When did you last turn on your cell phone?" Maga asked.

"Let's just say I've been a bit hard to reach lately," I conceded.

They knew that full well, anyway. I had called them before I left for Botswana.

"Shall we go to your room?" Maga suggested. "I'm sure agents from Special Operations have infinitely better accommodation than freshmen..."

"Not really."

I could have added that I had spent less time in my room during the previous year than in the lounges of some airlines.

"And besides," Maga went on, "we have something to tell you."

At these words, a Chinese girl who was sitting nearby and had overheard our entire conversation quickly plunged her nose in her magazine.

"You're right. Follow me."

Once I'd offered them tea, and Maga had finished going into ecstasies over the decor of my room ("Admit you were inspired by *Cold Chamber*, the magazine of refrigeration professionals"), Youssef cleared his throat and said, "We wanted you to be the first to know. We became engaged in Khartoum last week."

"That's great news!" I exclaimed. "Although I can't say it's a complete surprise. When are you planning to get married?"

"In three years," Maga replied. "When we finish at the Academy."

"We'll live separately until then," Youssef said in a perfectly pointless attempt at clarification.

"We'd like you to be our best man," Maga said.

"We said we'd ask him later," Youssef muttered.

"I didn't hear a thing," I said, in a conciliatory tone. "But I accept, obviously."

"Why, did you think you had a choice?" Maga joked. "I'm sure you won't mind a journey to Indonesia. By the way, please tell us about your vacation in Africa."

I sighed. "It wasn't a vacation."

I described in detail the living conditions of the Bushmen, the inflexible attitude of the Botswanan government, and the growing unease I had felt. I had thought that distance would provide perspective, but, even ten thousand kilometers distant, my voice shook with contained rage.

"Don't you think you're taking it too personally?" Youssef asked.

"But you don't understand," I replied, annoyed with myself rather than with him. "I devoted my first dossier to the Bushmen. Since then, a marketing genius in London decreed that the subject was worthy of expansion into a saga, but no one has yet considered what the Bushmen are enduring every day!"

"But you've helped them, Sliv," Magawati cut in. "Your dossier did more for them than any organization."

"No," I said. "That's exactly the problem. Trust me, I had the opportunity to think about it in my hut. The articles in the international press, the decade of indigenous peoples, that's all just show. I won't say that the publicity didn't flatter my ego for a while, but when you get down to it, what did it do for the Bushmen? Nothing. So I made the great powers sensitive to the fate of the oldest people in the world? Big deal! And that way of always using superlatives: what arrogance! As if the kids I saw over there were concerned with their thousand-year history…"

"You can't say that," Youssef retorted. "The Bushmen are a symbol."

"For you or me, yes. At a pinch, for the CFR. But they themselves don't see it that way. All they want is a land with game and water in abundance, and they're not moving any closer to their objective. Before I left, I asked myself: has their lot improved in the last five years? Well, I can give you the answer: it has not. On the contrary, it hasn't stopped deteriorating since I first wrote about them, to the point where one might wonder if they can still be saved."

"Is that really what you think?" Magawati asked.

"I don't know, I replied, honestly. "But I hate thinking that the Bushmen have done much more for me than I have for them."

"You can surely restore the balance," Youssef said.

"How?" Maga asked. "By offering to help them directly?"

"I thought about it," I said, "but it would be pointless. What could I do? Dig wells? Teach the children to read? I'm not even sure I'd be doing the Bushmen a service."

"But that seems to me beyond question," Youssef replied.

"You say that because you've never met them," I said. "I refuse to presume that they aspire to be like us. If they had wished to emulate us, they would have begun long ago. If we really want to respect their identity, we need to help them to realize the essential nature, or what it would have become had history not tossed them around for centuries like wisps of straw."

"And what is their essence, in your opinion?" Youssef asked.

"I hate speaking on their behalf, but I'd say basically, they're a peaceful people of hunter-gatherers with talents for painting and dancing."

"Maybe this will shock you," Maga said, "but do you think that in the year 2000 there is still a place on this planet for a people answering that description?"

"You don't shock me," I replied, pensively. "Obviously that's the central question. If we adopt a Darwinian reading of history, we must acknowledge that the Bushmen haven't carved a place for themselves in the food chain..."

"I'm not so sure I can agree with you," Youssef interrupted. "Since when do peoples have to prove that they can ensure their own survival?"

Magawati answered her fiancé. "Since the dawn of time, my dear. History mercilessly sweeps away ethnic or religious groups who are incapable of demonstrating that they can contribute anything, commercially, politically or artistically. When we say of two peoples that they live on good terms, it simply means they'd have more to lose by fighting than by coexisting."

"Precisely," I said. "The Bushmen have never wished to compete with others, and to be honest, I doubt that they could. But they do have one trump card at this juncture: the land on which they live is bursting with diamonds. Provided they play that card skillfully, they may have a chance to pull through."

"Do you intend to assist them in their negotiations with the government?" Youssef asked.

"Not in their actual form," I replied, "because they won't lead to anything. The two parties seek the same outcome, but for different reasons: Botswana covets access to the subsoil of the Kalahari, while the organizations assert the right of the Bushmen to remain on the lands that they've inhabited for three centuries. Under such circumstances, there's no possible compromise."

"What do you suggest?" Maga asked.

"To reframe the issue. The organizations are fighting the wrong battle. The Bushmen don't need the Kalahari and its diamonds; they need land with more game and a milder climate, and an environment capable of feeding them and of sustaining their population growth. I suspect that Masire or his successor might agree to surrender a few thousand square kilometers in exchange for unfettered exploitation of the Kalahari. Their country is as spacious as Thailand and fifty times less populated. The sacrifice shouldn't be too onerous for the government."

"An exchange of land?" Youssef said. "That's clever. But in twenty years, bauxite or palladium will be discovered beneath the Bushmen's feet, and they'll be forced to move again."

"Not if they're a sovereign state," I said.

"You're implying they would have obtained their independence," Maga said.

"It's not as absurd as it sounds. Who would object? Surely not Botswana, if their support for the new state is part of the conditions of an agreement. Certainly not the United Nations, which would view it as the crowning achievement of their famous 'Decade of Indigenous Peoples.'"

"The Bushmen themselves?" Youssef ventured.

"I'm sure they'll be the hardest to convince, but I'm ready to take that risk. Everything would become so much simpler: they'd finally be free to organize themselves as they wish, to accept or to refuse the aid they'd be bound to be offered by the various agencies of the United Nations…"

"Do you realize what you're suggesting?" Maga interjected. "Given their stage of development, I doubt the Bushmen would be capable of writing a constitution or requesting agricultural subsidies."

"Of course not," I said. "But there won't be any shortage of people willing to help them. And, besides, it's their only chance. If we do nothing, the Bushmen will have disappeared within twenty years."

"Sliv's right," Youssef said. "But you're underestimating the extent of the task. Obtaining the independence of the Bushmen nation all on your own from Krasnoyarsk? Do you have any notion of the constitutional criteria for a state?"

"No," I said, with a big smile, pleased to see that my friends weren't taking me totally for an utter lunatic. "But I can't wait to get down to work."

I did not begin my research as quickly as I would have wished, however. Two long assignments, one in Beijing, the other in Seattle, consumed all my energy for a full semester. It wasn't until July of 1998 that I found time to explore the mysteries of international law.

First I studied the concepts of country, state, and nation, which up until then I had tended to consider interchangeable.

A nation is a human community united by a common language, religion, or culture. It generally has its roots in a founding myth (Romulus and Remus, Moses leading the people of Israel) or in historical events (both the colonists of the Mayflower, and, later, the revolt against the English had contributed toward the establishment of the American nation). The Bushmen could beyond any question lay claim to the title of nation.

A state is a nation (or group of nations) organized within a specific territory, subjected to a government and to common laws. Most states comprise a single nation (Japan, France, etc.), and we therefore speak of nation states. Belgium, however, is an example of a state that comprises two nations: one Flemish, the other Walloon.

The word "country", which is often confused with the word "state", is less restrictive in meaning. A country is not necessarily sovereign. Greenland and Denmark are both countries, but only Denmark is a state. The Kalahari wasn't a country, let alone a state.

I then learned that there exist two large categories of states: those that are recognized by the United Nations, and those that are not. Size doesn't matter: Switzerland with its seven million inhabitants was still not in the UN in 1998, whereas the Marshall Islands, with only one hundredth of the population of Switzerland, had joined it in 1991.

There are several reasons why a state may not belong to the UN: it elects not to be (as was then the case with Switzerland); it doesn't have the financial and diplomatic means to join; or it knows that its candidacy won't be taken seriously (every year crazy billionaires buy islands in the Pacific, proclaim themselves monarchs, and pick a flag and a national anthem). Even so, there's nothing to prevent a state not recognized by the UN from maintaining bilateral diplomatic relations with other states.

In the case at hand, it seemed obvious to me that a Bushman state would seek international recognition. The sympathy aroused by the CFR and others for the Bushmen would be a precious asset during their negotiations with Botswana, conferring them the aura of credibility they lacked today.

Last but not least, I researched the criteria commonly used to evaluate the legitimacy of a country claiming the status of a state. There turned out to be eight of them.

1. Its borders must be recognized by the international community.

2. It must be absolutely sovereign over its own territory.

3. It must be recognized by other sovereign states.

4. It must issue currency and be a locus of significant economic activity.

5. It must have permanent residents.

6. It must possess a network of communication and transport.

7. It must guarantee basic public services, such as a justice system and the maintenance of order.

8. It must guarantee the civil rights of its residents, including access to healthcare and education.

These requirements plunged me into a state of profound dejection. The Bushmen seemed so far off the mark that it was almost comical. For the moment, they met only the fifth criterion (having permanent residents). As concepts such as "sovereign" or "transport network" probably didn't even exist in the Khoisan language.

But I couldn't give up. On closer inspection, I saw that the seven other criteria could be classified into two categories.

Fulfilling those in the first category would depend almost exclusively on the outcome of the negotiations with Botswana.

If the latter agreed to exchange the Kalahari for a new territory, it would contractually be recognizing the borders of the Bushman state (criterion number one) and yielding its sovereignty over such territory (criterion number two).

And once Botswana had recognized the new state, it was quite likely that other African countries would follow (criterion number three). In other words, three of the seven unfulfilled criteria rested on Botswana. I had been able to observe Masire in action, and I was fairly certain that I could obtain his agreement.

The criteria in the second category — having a police force, a currency, a health system, and so on — at first appeared to depend on the Bushmen themselves.

I was clearheaded enough to realize that a people unable either to read or to count didn't have the ghost of a chance of attaining those objectives.

In addition, any attempt to conceal the structural weaknesses of their situation would merely expose the Bushmen to international ridicule.

It therefore seemed preferable to put our cards on the table by seeking the immediate support of the UN, whose specialized agencies, such as the World Health Organization or the Development Program, were specifically designed to help poor or insufficiently organized countries.

If the United Nations were to support the creation of a Bushman state — a hypothesis that required validation — it would place lawyers, engineers, and economists at that government's disposal and thus ensure that the criteria were met. This analysis confirmed me in my belief that the UN had to be associated with the negotiations as soon as possible.

Overall, the task looked daunting. The Bushmen and the organizations that gravitated around them would first have to be convinced; then the government of Botswana would have to agree to an exchange of territories; and, finally, the blessing of the international community would need to be obtained. I could never hope to achieve all that by myself.

As always, when I didn't know where to turn, I called Gunnar with details of my project.

He listened attentively, then issued his verdict. "I understand why you feel a need to help the Bushmen," he said, "but we aren't a humanitarian organization. I won't be able to transmit your dossier to the Executive Committee, if it appears to be an attempt at personal redemption. Do us both a favor: avoid waxing lyrical, but instead demonstrate how a Bushman state would serve the interests of the CFR. In the long run, that's the only argument that would convince them."

I set to work that very evening.

13

A few months later, Khoyoulfaz dispatched me to Toronto, where the famous Petroleum Initiative was collapsing. I must admit that when Youssef had first told me about it, the plan put together by Vassili Podorenko, the special agent in charge of the project, deeply counter-intuitive as it was, had struck me as quite ingenious.

The objective of the initiative was to raise the price of crude oil. Instead of heightening public awareness of the diminution of world reserves, Podorenko claimed on the contrary that the planet had almost unlimited resources in its strata.

To support his theory, he cited the existence of huge deposits of bituminous sands (a degraded form of petroleum). Although the current costs of mining were quite prohibitive, rapid technological advances seemed likely to spawn efficiencies of scale before long. With the threat of shortages receding, governments would lower their guard, and consumers would stop rationing their consumption. Demand for petroleum products would increase, and prices would rise steadily.

The theory was seductive, but, so far, it hadn't been validated by facts. Rather than increasing, the price of crude had been declining for the past eighteen months. Another agent might have admitted his error. But, throwing caution to the proverbial winds, Vassili Podorenko had committed himself to a suicidal gamble. Inevitably, his attempts at manipulation, which were becoming less and less subtle, had finally drawn the attention of the energy industry.

"If there's anything I dread, it's finding myself under the microscope of the oil companies," Khoyoulfaz confided. I had never seen him so concerned. "They have more resources than we do, and far fewer scruples. Right now, I'm sure they're trying to find out who is so interested in bituminous sands. We can't permit them to trace the chain back to Podorenko."

"Why Toronto?" I asked. "Is there a connection with the Plan?"

"That's one of the questions you'll need to answer. Like any other dossier, Podorenko's initiative was approved by London. But the English claim that they would have rejected the project had it not been endorsed in an accompanying letter from the Plan explaining how it contributed in an essential way to one of the three-year directives. The problem is that nobody in Toronto remembers having written, much less signed, such a letter."

"An accomplice on the inside?" I suggested.

"That can't be ruled out," Khoyoulfaz replied evasively.

"Isn't this the kind of case usually investigated by the General Inspectorate?"

"They'll be there too," Khoyoulfaz somberly replied. "It's a special."

In CFR jargon, "a special" was a joint intervention by Special Operations and the General Inspectorate. It was never good news for the person targeted.

"You and Guillermo Jones will work as a team. He'll give you a copy of the dossier. In the meantime, not a word to the members of the Initiative, and above all not to your friend, Khrafedine."

Jones and I arrived in Toronto late in the afternoon of the last Thursday in November. Our taxi entered the business district, and dropped us outside a building of breathtaking luxury, a veritable cathedral of glass and steel: the headquarters of the Plan.

My colleague was amused by my open-eyed wonder. "Admit you're staggered! They finished building it last year. Officially, it is the headquarters of a finance company."

"Incredible," I murmured. The Academy's premises bore witness to the CFR's influence, but the building before me evoked a sense of supreme power.

We were expected. Angoua Djibo's deputy, a Canadian named Walter Vinokur, personally greeted us. Dispensing with bowing and scraping, he escorted us to the floor and led us to a conference room with padded walls. There, he introduced the team from the General Inspectorate, among whom I recognized my fellow student from the Academy, the Nigerian Buhari Obawan. We nodded to each other.

"Thank you all for coming so quickly," Vinokur said. A tall, thin man, he was an expert on the history of religions. "We are in danger of losing control of the Petroleum Initiative," he began. "For the past few weeks, our specialists in the commodities markets have been reporting some worrying rumors. Apparently, representatives of the major oil companies met in Geneva last Tuesday to pool their knowledge of bituminous sands. Everyone is pointing to Canada and Venezuela, the two countries with the largest deposits and consequently the most interest in developing new techniques of exploration and production. It's a welcome diversion, but unlikely to persist.

"I'm sure you all realize the gravity of the situation. Special Agent Podorenko, who was managing the Initiative, is refusing to cooperate. We officially suspended him yesterday. He claims to have respected all the security protocols, but we stopped believing him after we discovered that he forged a letter from the Plan in order to get his Initiative approved. Reading his file should enlighten you further about his character."

He handed each of us a thick cardboard folder.

"I need those files back fully intact before you leave. I suggest we divide up the task as follows. Hanoune and Obawan, you'll interrogate Podorenko, starting tonight. Try to find out if he worked alone, or if he was following orders. Tanaka, you'll form a team with my head of security. He's collected the files of several agents from the Plan, and I'd like you to examine them. It's clear that we have a traitor in our midst. Jones and Dartunghuver, you'll review all the sources produced under Podorenko's orders. I want to know if the man is simply reckless, or if we've been missing something. We'll meet twice a day to assess the situation. Any questions? Then let's get down to work."

Vinokur knew his job, and the investigation made rapid progress. Podorenko was a brilliant young man. The fact that he had declined an offer to join the Academy hadn't prevented him from being promoted to special agent at the age of thirty-six. He had produced several extremely spectacular dossiers, of which one, concerning continental drift, had caused such a stir that the head of the Committee for the Approval of Dossiers had subsequently apologized for accepting it.

Podorenko personally chose his collaborators. He liked them young and malleable. He never worked twice with the same agents. He owned several sports cars, which wasn't totally implausible given his salary but nevertheless indicated a sense of priorities that was unusual in our organization.

By the second day, we knew what we were dealing with: Podorenko was a gambler, one of those desperadoes who get their kicks from tackling supposedly impossible challenges, like raising the price of petroleum, or launching a false candidacy for the Nobel Peace Prize.

Suspecting that London would turn down his project, he had sought support from the Plan, where an accomplice, all too happy to serve such an ambitious cause, had forged a letter and slipped it into a pile of documents awaiting an official signature.

On the third day, Podorenko disclosed the name of his confederate in the Plan: Piotr Barowski, a young Polish agent, who had already had brushes with the General Inspectorate. Terrified at finding himself at the center of an internal inquiry of such magnitude, Barowski soon confessed and tendered his resignation. Vinokur refused it, but seized his passport and informed him that a disciplinary committee would soon determine his fate.

On the fourth day, Jones recommended on behalf of Special Operations that the affair should be dropped. Even if the oil companies had noted that an unidentified player was trying to destabilize the market, it seemed extremely unlikely that they would trace the attempt to Podorenko. It was better to let them mull over the meager evidence in their possession than to risk drawing their attention by launching an alternative scenario.

It was too early to judge whether Podorenko's campaigns would ultimately prove effective, but anyway, that was no longer our concern. The General Inspectorate endorsed our analysis. Vinokur thanked us for our cooperation and closed the assignment.

It was six o'clock that Monday evening. Our plane wouldn't leave until the next morning. I ventured to the end of the corridor, where Angoua Djibo's office was located. I hadn't seen him since my arrival, and I was hoping to pay my respects. The door was open. I tapped on it to signal my presence.

"Sliv," Djibo exclaimed, raising his head from the report he had been studying. "Come in. I was expecting you."

The man was a marvel. He seemed able to predict the slightest actions of his fellow men, as if everything they did was completely logical. Or, I thought, perhaps he was bluffing by way of apology for not having come to see me first.

"I've booked a table in the dining room," he said with a smile as if he had read my thoughts once again. "You're having dinner with me."

He slipped a few documents in a briefcase and rose. The decor of his office reflected his eclecticism. African masks had been hung next to abstract paintings, several ancient maps adorned the walls. On a shelf, I recognized a desert rose similar to the one I had been given by Djibo four and a half years earlier in Honolulu.

The dining room could seat ten people. That evening, however, the table had been set for two. The head waiter recited the menu and added that he had taken the liberty of serving Vouvray with the entrée, a spinach consommé.

"Excellent choice," Djibo commented, as particular about his wine as ever.

"I'm delighted to see you again," he resumed, after the head waiter had withdrawn. "I was the one who asked Yakoub to assign you to this. When did I last see you? A year ago?"

"Nine months ago. When you came to Krasnoyarsk to give a series of lectures about the Plan."

"Clearly I was a big hit, since Lena and you have opted for Special Operations."

"I didn't mean…"

"No need to explain," Djibo cut in. "I was teasing you. I'm confident that you made the right choice. Yakoub never stops singing your praises."

"I'm pleased to hear that. He's an exceptional instructor."

"He sometimes uses unconventional methods, but I think I can say that Special Operations has never been so effective as it is under his direction."

I could have elaborated on the theme of Khoyoulfaz's unorthodox methods, but that was a topic I chose not to raise with Djibo. He surely hadn't sent for me in Toronto to dwell on the past.

"I'd like to inform you of the outcome of your memo about the Vinland map," he said.

"Actually I was wondering what had happened to that."

"The Executive Committee read it. Indeed, it was even on the agenda at one of our meetings. That's quite rare for a document from a Class 3 agent. We all approved your decision to drop the Vinland project, and I say that even though it's painful to me personally. I knew Ole Gabriel Hagen well. Our friendly feelings toward him, his colleagues' and mine, clouded our judgment for a long time. We should have closed the matter much earlier, when that American scholar analyzed the ink on the map and found traces of anatase, which was unknown in the Middle Ages."

"I think so too," I said.

"Your recommendation to discontinue all forms of physical falsification gave rise to a heated debate," Djibo continued. "The subject is undeniably topical. Yakoub Khoyoulfaz regularly complains that his teams spend their time patching leaky vessels. He reopens some dossiers every year, knowing full well that they have no future, that eventually they'll have to be torpedoed, as you torpedoed the Vinland map. Like you, I think it's pointless to fight scientific progress — the very thing, ironically, that the Plan exalts in all its directives."

"It's more than pointless," I said. "It's dangerous."

"And yet some members of the Executive Committee strongly defended physical falsification," Djibo continued, ignoring my comment. "They point out that our organization owes it some of its greatest successes and that by giving it up, we would be repudiating part of our heritage. Of course, they're right."

"Of course," I said, "but we must think of our survival first. If we aren't careful, physical falsification will end up being the death of us."

Once again, Djibo didn't respond to my remark. He seemed engrossed in his own thoughts. I sensed that the discussions, which touched on the CFR's core values, had been stormy.

"We put the question to a vote," he said. "Three votes on each side. Things seemed blocked. But then, in the second round of voting, one of us reversed his position. Those in favor of your memo carried it by four votes to two. The GI is currently formulating a directive that will proscribe recourse to physical falsification."

"It's a wise decision," I said, taking care not to appear too triumphant. I suspected from the tone of his voice that he himself was the member of the Executive Committee who had changed sides.

"I expect fierce opposition from the old-timers," Djibo went on. "The directive will profoundly change their manner of working. Actually, I may ask you to do the rounds of the main units to explain the factors behind this reform."

"I'll be glad to," I said.

The head waiter removed my plate, replacing it with one containing a turbot and baked potatoes. Djibo inspected the label on the accompanying bottle of wine, a 1990 Meursault.

"I also wish to discuss the document that you sent to Gunnar Eriksson," he said, casually, as he filled my glass.

"The Bushmen memo?" I asked, all my senses suddenly alert.

"It's a truly remarkable project."

"Thank you," I said, "I put a lot of effort into it."

"I realize that," Djibo said. "That's why I wanted to be the person to ask you to give it up."

The sky fell on my head. "Give it up? Why?"

"Because it doesn't fall within the CFR's priorities," Djibo said simply.

I thought I could see in his eyes that he lamented the fact, so I felt encouraged to plead my case. "Then it may be time to reevaluate our priorities. Have you thought of the immense advantages that a Bushman state would bring us: countless legends, the ability to print our own passports, not to mention diplomatic immunity or representation at the UN? Wouldn't you like to know what's being said in the corridors of the United Nations?"

"We don't need an ambassador at the UN to know what's going on there," Djibo replied.

"Of course. But you must admit that a state would strengthen our organization. It would protect it from national police forces, and give it a voice on the great international questions. In a word, it would institutionalize it. Of course, I'm not completely naïve, I know it will take time. The negotiations could take years, maybe even decades, but I'm convinced they're worth it."

Djibo leaned forward and looked me straight in the eyes. "I'm not unaware of all that, Sliv. I've read your dossier. All your arguments are spot on, even though, presumably on Eriksson's advice, you've omitted the most important of them: the need to repair the historical injustice of which the Bushmen have been victims. Believe me, no one is more sensitive than I to their fate. But we can't get involved in this struggle now. We're already engaged in many other, more important battles, that we have a better chance of winning."

"What, for example?" I asked impudently.

"You know I won't answer that," Djibo said without taking offense at my insolence. "I can only ask you to believe me when I invoke the higher interests of the CFR."

"Oh no!" I said angrily, pushing away my plate. "Don't give me the old clichés! Don't you think I've already paid my dues to the higher interests?"

"We're all aware of the courage and loyalty you've shown at certain difficult moments," Djibo conceded tactfully.

"Difficult moments?" I was getting carried away. "I almost threw myself out of the window! Angoua, you know who I am: you'll never find a soldier more hard-working or more devoted than me. I'll probably never marry, my friends can be counted on the fingers of one hand; I visit my mother once a year. I'm climbing the ladder faster than anyone, but it seems as if my opinion still isn't worth a damn. Those two memos are the proof of that: the Executive Committee accepts one and refuses the other, without even giving me a chance to defend them."

"You're defending them now, quite eloquently," Djibo said.

"And yet at the end of the day, the decisions are taken over my head. I demand a say. I no longer want to be the young agent who throws ideas up in the air and has one of them accepted from time to time."

"Your hour will come…"

"But when, Angoua? When? Surely I've earned my spurs, have I not? I've published four dossiers, of which two are studied at the Academy; I resisted the temptation to denounce the CFR even when my case officer was holding my head underwater; and I have a flawless record in Special Operations. What more do you need? Tell me, and I'll do it."

Djibo took a sip of his Meursault to consider his response. I could feel the adrenaline physically ebb inside my body.

"There is nothing more to be done," he said at last. "Continue the way you are, maintaining your standards, demonstrating the same level of commitment. I'm not authorized to make any promises, but I'm sure that you'll eventually exercise the power to which you aspire."

"I don't care about power," I said. "I just want to have all the elements at my disposal, to state my opinions, and to debate with my peers."

"Your hour will come," Djibo said again. "But you must be patient."

"I'll turn thirty in three months," I said, not too sure what I was trying to prove by that remark.

"That's precisely what I'm saying. You're still a young man. Trust me, Sliv."

"Why should I trust you?" I asked, having exhausted my arguments.

"I can't answer that question for you," Djibo said.

As if he had been crouching behind the door, listening to us, the head waiter now entered and cleared our plates. We watched him officiate in silence, Djibo swirling the wine in his glass, me cogitating his last words.

The phone rang. The head waiter answered, then held the receiver out to Djibo, who let the person at the other end do all the speaking.

"That was Vinokur," he said when he had hung up. "He'd asked the Moscow Bureau to take a look at Podorenko's bank accounts. We've just received the results. Podorenko has received several substantial deposits during the past few months. Everything seems to indicate that he was working secretly for a Kremlin-connected businessman, who, in 1994, purchased two huge deposits of bituminous sands in Alberta."

"1994?" I said. "That was before the launch of the Initiative."

"Precisely. Had the initiative succeeded, he would have netted several hundred million dollars."

"So Podorenko's a crook... And I took him for a gambler."

"That was what he hoped we would believe. The flashy scenarios, the sports cars: it was all part of his cover."

"And Barowski?" I asked, still in shock.

"The investigation will tell us that, but he was probably being manipulated by Podorenko."

We discussed the implications of this revelation as we drank our coffee.

"In any case," Djibo said, "you're staying here for a few more days."

As a matter of fact it took us a whole week to untangle the whole affair. For years, Podorenko had been performing small services for his oligarch, but his plan to raise the value of Canadian bituminous deposits surpassed all his previous operations in boldness and complexity. I now understood why he had refused to answer Youssef's questions about the purpose of the project.

Podorenko and Barowski were expelled from the CFR, and returned to civilian life. Before dismissing the Russian, we warned him that we knew a number of embarrassing secrets about him and his mentor. In the shady circles in which the two men moved, public exposure of those secrets would have been tantamount to a death sentence.

14

I returned to Krasnoyarsk with mixed feelings.

The Executive Committee had approved one of my proposals. Better still, it associated me with the promulgation of an epoch-making directive. For the first time, I had the impression that I was influencing the history of the CFR.

It would have taken a lot more, though, to make me happy. Angoua Djibo also had effectively crushed my pet project, to which I had devoted six months of my life. By evoking "other more important battles," Djibo had reminded me that the CFR neither belonged to its agents nor felt obliged to embrace their causes, however noble. The Bushmen would have to find another champion — it wouldn't be easy.

Once again, I thought in the plane taking me back to Siberia, Djibo had given me as many reasons to hate the CFR as to love it. He had demonstrated his trust by assigning me to visit far-flung offices so that I could promote a controversial reform to the veterans of the organization. He had aroused my curiosity with a few carefully chosen words: what could these other battles be, and how could they be more important than helping an oppressed people obtain its independence? And he had painted an image of the CFR as an organization more concerned about its cohesion than its actions, more preoccupied with its survival than its achievements.

This bitter-sweet observation shouldn't have surprised me. And yet it was the first time in three years that I had felt capable of passing an objective judgment on the CFR. For eighteen months — from the episode with Jones and Khoyoulfaz in Córdoba to my decision to join Special Operations — I hadn't been able to judge the CFR without judging myself. Our destinies were inextricably linked.

Depression had suddenly given way to euphoria when Gunnar had freed me of the burden of my guilt. For the next eighteen months, I had fallen under the spell of Yakoub Khoyoulfaz, and started again to attribute a host of virtues and powers to the CFR, including the ability to redraw borders.

This phase was ending today and, just like my depression after Cordoba, which was already nothing but a bad memory, it would probably soon seem anachronistic, if not totally inappropriate.

But I suppose it was necessary for me to pass through these two phases in order to recognize that hitherto the CFR had served as a mirror that reflected whatever I projected. An ideal when I had been an idealist, it had become contemptible when I despised myself.

So long as I didn't know its aims, it would continue to ricochet my questions back to me. It couldn't reveal my identity to me. At best, it might help me to discover it.

One cycle was ending, another about to begin, but I couldn't yet discern its outlines. Deep down I doubted that it would cause me less frustration than the first. I just hoped to find a measure of happiness, a spark of joy that would stop me from being filled with bitterness or jealousy on Youssef's and Maga's wedding day.

The rest of the year sped by: more assignments, ever more varied, ever more wide-ranging (Delhi, Panama City, Venice, etc.), kept me away from Krasnoyarsk, where Youssef and Maga were completing their first year. As the final series of examinations began, both had maintained their chances of being able to land their dream job: the Plan for Youssef, who had been reassured when the resolution of the Petroleum Initiative had demonstrated the CFR's determination to track down its black sheep; and Special Operations for Maga, who liked nothing better than to hear me recount my investigations.

As for me, I was free, like any other Class 3 agent, to settle in the country and city of my choice as soon as I graduated from the Academy. After considering several South American destinations, I decided to return to Reykjavík. I missed Gunnar; my mother longed to see her son; and I found amusing the prospect of serving a worldwide organization from one of the smallest capitals in the world.

Once again, Lena Thorsen's reasoning was precisely the opposite of mine: she announced her intention to move to Los Angeles.

407

As the farewell parties succeeded one another in the corridors of the residence, my friends used my thirtieth birthday as an excuse to organize a surprise excursion to Krasnoyarsk the night before I left. Not suspecting anything, I was busy finishing my packing when Stéphane burst into my room and, refusing to answer my questions, dragged me outside to a Zil in which Youssef, Maga, and the five-month pregnant Aoifa were awaiting me.

The driver took us to the Nikolai, the best restaurant in the city, where the menu features no fewer than seven dishes, including blinis, caviar, pelmeni (dumplings filled with spiced meat, a Siberian specialty), and piroshki (a kind of pie stuffed with fish or meat). Youssef, who as usual was drinking mineral water, nonetheless consented to raise his glass with us for a series of toasts that seemed intended to make me blush.

"To the best scenario writer I've ever met," Stéphane said, clinking his glass of vodka against mine.

"To an idealist who doesn't know he is one," Youssef said, after Stéphane had refilled our glasses.

"To my friend, Sliv," Maga said, looking me straight in the eyes.

"To the future godfather of our child," Aoifa said, squeezing Stéphane's free hand in hers.

"Really?" I said, taken aback. "But are you really counting on me to teach him his catechism? I might be inclined to take a few liberties with the Scriptures..."

Aoifa assumed a horrified air. "You don't think I'm going to entrust my child's religious education to a Lutheran? And a falsifier to boot!"

"You'll teach him other things," Stéphane said.

"How to cut wood, how to predict an earthquake, how to find your way in the Siberian *taiga*..." Maga said, as I refilled the glasses with a trembling hand.

"It's my turn to propose a toast," I said, lifting my glass. "I drink to true friends: to you, Stéphane, who held the pen in my first dossier, with the brilliance and success we all know; to you, Youssef, for helping me to ask the questions I don't always have the courage

to answer; to you, Maga, who forgives without judging; to you, Aoifa, who's bearing a child I will cherish as my own."

"To all of us!" Stéphane cried, before our eyes totally misted up.

"To all of us!" we all cried in unison.

Chris Marker has one of his characters say, "Having been around the world several times, the only thing that still interests me is ordinariness." I think I know what he means. No image of my many trips around the world has been imprinted on my brain so strongly as the images of that night. I remember Stéphane, who just had to click his fingers for food and drink to appear as if by magic; Youssef, who agreed, "just to please me," to dance with us to the frenzied tempo of Cossack violins; Maga, who never took her eyes off me all evening, and finally asked me, as if she were worried to wean me from her bosom, "if I was ready."

"I've never been readier," I replied, with a smile.

At precisely two o'clock in the morning, the manager of the restaurant threw us out. The driver sprang out of the Zil like a jack-in-the-box and rushed to open the doors for us, without the slightest remark about our pitiful appearances. Yielding the back seat to the two couples, I climbed in front. Aoifa and Maga chatted for a few minutes; then silence fell, that same sylvan silence that had penetrated me three years earlier when I had arrived at the Academy.

Thirty years old, I reflected, closing my eyes. At an age by which Picasso had already painted *Les Demoiselles d'Avignon*, and Mozart had written most of his works, I was still afraid that I was devoting my life to an idea that wasn't worth it.

Could it have been otherwise? Now that I thought about it, I had taken only one risk in rejoining the CFR, but it had been a considerable one: I had put my fate in the hands of other men (mainly Gunnar Eriksson and Angoua Djibo) assuming that their values reflected those of our employer.

With hindsight, this reasoning appeared extraordinarily shaky. Unfortunately, I didn't have a better one. Sometimes, climbing a staircase is the only way to discover where it leads.

I glanced in the back. Maga had fallen asleep with her head on Youssef's shoulder. Stéphane was snoring slightly. We really are trusting, I thought. Here we are, five fine minds, our senses blunted by alcohol, piled up in a car speeding through the night driven by a chauffeur whose name we don't even know.

Since I was sitting in front, I kept my eyes on the road in a futile attempt to stay awake.

To be continued in The Pathfinders…

From the same author

The Pathfinders (novel)

In this second installment of the *Falsifiers* trilogy, the stakes have gotten higher. Sliv is tasked with daunting missions: to help a small Asian country gain its independence, to chase a rogue CFR agent, and to convince the Bush Administration that Saddam Hussein no longer possesses weapons of mass destruction. Yet, in a post 9/11 world, Sliv and his colleagues are not the only ones tampering with reality.

The Pathfinders was awarded the prestigious Prix France Culture Telerama in 2009. It is preceded by *The Falsifiers* and followed by *The Showrunners* but can be read independently.

The Showrunners (novel)

In this third and last installment of the *Falsifiers* trilogy, Sliv and Lena find a way to cooperate on a groundbreaking falsification that will glue TV viewers around the world to their screens. Along the way, the CFR has Barack Obama elected president and Sliv finds the truth about global warming suprisingly hard to sort out.

An American Novel

Vlad Eisinger, a journalist at *The Wall Street Tribune*, is publishing a series of articles about life settlement, a little-known practice that allows senior or terminally ill people to sell their life insurance policies to private investors. The buyer keeps paying the annual premiums and collects the death benefit when the seller eventually dies. Vlad draws most of his anecdotes from Destin Terrace, a close-knit community in Destin, Florida. Each of the articles, which come out every Tuesday for seven consecutive weeks, brings its share of disturbing revelations: Bruce, the flight attendant, sold his policy in the '80s when he was diagnosed with AIDS; Steve, the dentist who purchased Bruce's policy, is furious with him for not dying; Brian, an ex-doctor, writes up life expectancy reports from his basement; his wife Sharon, a nurse, earns a finder's fee for each elderly client whom she convinces to sell his or her policy.

Dan Siver used to be Vlad's roommate, back when they were studying comparative literature at Columbia University. Vlad has become a successful journalist, Dan a struggling novelist who lives in Destin Terrace, in the small house he inherited from his mother.

The story oscillates between Vlad's articles and Dan's observations, as his neighbors react to the ever-bigger stories unfolding week after week. The two men also revive a long-running spat about the respective merits of journalism and literature, before a final twist.

The Missing Piece (novel)

Between March and September of the year 1995, five murders shook the professional Speed Puzzle Tour. The modus operandi was always the same: the murderer would amputate a limb of the victim, then leave on the body a piece of a Polaroid photograph depicting the corresponding limb of another man. Evidently, speed puzzle, a sport by then as popular as football and basketball, had become the hunting ground of a serious killer.

Suspects are in no short supply: from the tyrannical president of the erudite Society of Puzzlology to the reigning champion who has mysteriously vanished to the billionaire who started the Tour.

Can you solve the puzzle?

The Missing Piece has been translated into a dozen languages.

The Disappearance of Emilie Brunet (novel)

Detective Achille Dunot suffers from a strange form of amnesia. Since a recent accident, his brain has lost the ability to form new memories. Every morning he wakes up with no recollection of the events of the previous day. When the chief of police asks him to investigate the disappearance of a wealthy heiress named Emily Brunet, Achille decides to keep a journal in which he logs his findings before going to bed. This diehard fan of Agatha Christie thus becomes both the hero and the reader of a strange detective novel, of which he also happens to be the author.

412

Before long, all clues point to Claude Brunet, Emily's husband. Brunet had many reasons to kill his wife, offers no alibi, and not-so-subtly boasts of having committed the perfect crime. As a world-class neuroscientist, he's also one of the very few people who can grasp Achille's ailment.

Legends (short story)

A civil servant of the British intelligence agency is tasked with animating a stock of legends - those disposable identities assumed by spies during their missions.

Mr. Luigi's Binoculars (short story)

A young card player from Missouri is hired to help the world champion retain his title against a rising Russian master.

Printed in Great Britain
by Amazon

12942761R00243